TROUBLE

MADE & BROKEN III

NORA ASH

ABOUT THE AUTHOR

Nora Ash writes thrilling romance and sexy paranormal fantasy.

Visit her website to learn more about her upcoming books.

WWW.NORA-ASH.COM

ONE

AUDREY

I've generally always seen myself as on the right path, job-wise, but if there was ever a time I'd regretted my choice of career, it was today.

"Sonuva*bitch!*"

My screech echoed across Potters Fields Park, making a cluster of pigeons take flight. I windmilled desperately to avoid face-planting into the deep puddle on the pavement that I'd attempted—and failed—to jump across in my three-inch heels.

My feet skidded out, but I managed to right myself at the last second—and heard the distinct *snap* of my right heel breaking underneath me, followed by a splash as I stepped heavily into the water, soaking my foot to the ankle.

Yup, today I would have traded my years of university and corporate ladder-climbing for a nice, trainer-wearing shop floor job. Bet I could have made the jump if I hadn't been forced to climb into these ridiculous stilts!

I limped out of the puddle, aware that my broken heel and defeated disposition made me resemble the hunchback of Notre Dame. The fifty-page report from my briefcase had gone flying across the path. A couple of pages were *in* the damn puddle, and the rest seemed busy soaking up the wet London grime covering the pavement.

I gave them a miserable look. Apparently I wouldn't just be late for my morning meeting now—I'd also be presenting the clients with waterlogged paperwork.

Smashing.

"You all right there, love?"

I jolted at the amused, masculine voice that sounded right behind me.

"Yes, I'm fucking *fantastic*," I hissed at whoever thought it was a great idea to do a drive-by mocking. Instead of giving the perpetrator any more of my attention, I tried to limp a step to the side to grab at my fleeing report and managed to stumble on my broken heel and re-soak my foot in the puddle once again.

"Jesus fuck!"

"Hang on, I've got you," the same voice said, this time with a full laugh. A male figure bent from behind me, easily snatching up several pages. When he took a couple more steps down the path to gather the rest of my flighty report, I saw he was wearing jog pants, trainers and a tight vest that showed off wide shoulders and strong arms.

Clearly a health nut. *Great.*

"Here you go," he said as he turned around, holding out the smudged pages to me. "Not sure they're all salvageable, though."

I opened my mouth to thank him, but as my fingertips grazed over his warm hand, I looked up into his face —and promptly lost all ability to control my tongue.

"Huh... ank... s." I was vaguely aware that the noise I'd produced didn't much resemble human speech, but most of my focus was pulled toward his eyes.

They were a startling, silvery gray, but what captured my attention so completely wasn't the color—it was the warm mirth dancing in them, pulling at me like a magnet. His gaze was so completely filled with *life,* it made the rest of the world seem dull and mute by comparison.

He had a chiseled jaw and the kind of facial features a runway model would kill for, crowned by a shock of red hair, but mainly I just couldn't stop staring at those amazing eyes.

"Happy to help." The slight sardonic note to his voice made it clear he was fully aware of my open-mouthed staring. It was enough to finally break the spell, and I flushed beet-red when I realized what I'd been doing.

"S-sorry, I should get going," I muttered, pulling away from him. The distance gave me a new view of his broad shoulders and—holy hell, he was definitely in good shape, the way those pecs and abs practically strained against his vest. *Wow,* men hadn't looked like *that* when I'd last dated, that's for sure...

"See something you like, love?"

I took a step further back, mortified at the wry grin on his full lips. He'd clearly caught my gaze sweeping up and down his body.

I squeaked out a weird little sound that was supposed to be 'thanks for the help' but sounded more like a trapped mouse, and spun around to flee.

Only I'd forgotten about my broken heel, and the next second, I was flailing wildly in a desperate attempt at not face-planting on the pavement.

"Whoa, steady there." Large hands gripped my shoulders, pulling me safely upright and turning me back around.

The redhead sank down in a crouch in front of me and pulled out what looked distinctly like a zip-tie from his pocket. "Give me your foot, darling."

Too mortified to do anything but obey, I did what he asked while attempting to keep my balance on one leg.

"You can lean on me," he said without taking his eyes off my shoe, probably because I was wobbling unsteadily above him on my high heel.

I didn't want to, but I also didn't want to fall on my

arse, so I awkwardly placed my fingertips against his ginger mane to steady myself while I tried to pretend I didn't see the amused looks from passersby.

Nothing to see here, people, just a woman in a business suit, making a complete twat out of herself.

I glanced down at the young man kneeling in front of me. He seemed fully focused on my foot, and I briefly wondered what kind of obsessed handyman had zip-ties in his jog pants.

Handyman, complete Adonis, kind helper of strangers. If he'd been a decade older, he'd have been my dream guy.

But he's not, you absolute pervert, I mentally scolded myself. He looked to be several years my junior, and I wasn't exactly some hot blooded cougar.

The only thing that got close to my lady parts these days was my trusty Magic Wand.

Just as the words *Magic Wand* flashed through my head, the young man looked up with that wicked smile curving his lips, as if the knew what sort of thoughts were running rampant through my head.

"There you go, that should hold you through the day."

I blinked and looked down at my shoe. He'd looped the zip-tie around the heel and secured it around the sole, managing to stabilize it completely.

"Wow," I muttered, momentarily shaken out of my embarrassment by complete awe of his MacGyver skills. "Thank you so, so much. You're an absolute life-saver."

"Happy to help a pretty lady," he said, giving me a friendly wink.

Only, he was still crouched down in front of me, and that wink made me realize his face was right in front of my crotch.

Oh, God!

"I, um, h-have to get to work. Thanks again!"

This time, my shoe supported me perfectly when I spun around to flee.

TWO

AUDREY

"You're late," Eileen said the second I stormed into our office like a panicked goat, arms full of the still-sopping report. "What were you thinking, being late the one day you have a morning meeting scheduled with Perkinson, of all people? He's already been waiting ten minutes, and you know how he gets."

"I know, I know!" I threw my handbag on my desk and pulled my emergency supply of Kleenex out of a drawer. "I had an accident. Now just help me dab!"

"I'M TERRIBLY SORRY, Mr. Perkinson. I had a bit of a disastrous morning," I hurled out the second I stepped into the meeting room, a stiff smile plastered across my lips. "I trust Nadine's been keeping you with coffee?"

"Tell me, Miss Waits, is it normal procedure for Caslik Consulting to assume their clients have nothing better to do than wait all morning for a young woman to waltz into work long after business hours have commenced?"

I gritted my teeth, somehow managing not to lose the fake smile despite my sudden urge to throw the damp-despite-my-best-efforts report in his face. I'd only been assigned to Perkinson the previous Thursday, but he'd already become my least favorite client of all time. "I can only apologize and assure you it won't happen again."

"It better not," he rumbled, irritation clear on his pudgy face as he swiveled around in his cushioned seat to face the table. "I don't want to have to remind your boss how much money I'm prepared to walk away with if he can't get me a halfway competent consultant."

I did my best ignore the dig, despite my temper flaring up like a hot burst of acid in my gut. I'd worked hard for my position at Caslik, and before that, I'd busted my arse at university so I could prove to my parents I was good enough, smart enough. My career was everything to me, and to have this arrogant pig insult and threaten it gave me rage-induced acid reflux. But I swallowed my anger and, despite the urge to slap the haughty bastard, smiled until my cheeks hurt. If he actually followed through on his threat and went to my boss with a complaint about me, I'd be having a rather unpleasant chat with HR before I could blink.

Perkinson brought in the kind of money that had everyone rolling over like over-excited puppies. He was my first major client, and up until last Thursday, I'd been absolutely thrilled. His company was my first major account, and I knew that if I did well with him, I was that much closer to the senior position my manager had been dangling in front of me like a carrot for the past three years.

"Have you had an opportunity to consider the branding options for your new vodka we went over on Thursday?" I said as I sat down in front of him, doing my best to ignore the throbbing vein in my temple. I wasn't about to let a man like Perkinson snatch away what I'd been working so hard for for so long. Mel, my older sister, was made managing director of the snazzy little design company she'd been working for for the past ten years just last Christmas, and I'd not heard the end of it from Mum and Dad. *Perfect Mel, with her perfect life, and her perfect promotion.* No, I was getting this client wrangled, whatever it took. I could live with my anger for a few weeks.

"Yes, we'll be going with the upscale Playboy demographic. I want every man to get hard when he sees a bottle of our booze. He needs to think that buying Perk Vodka turns him into literal James-fucking-Bond. You got it, sweet cheeks?"

Okay, so apparently I'd also be swallowing my pride too.

"Sure." If I smiled any harder, my face would be in danger of cracking. "Sounds good. I've put together a launch strategy—if you care to have a look?" I slid the still-damp report across the table to my client. "I apologize for the state of it. I had a bit of a fall while on my way to work."

Perkinson took the offered papers with a look of mild contempt, making sure only to turn the pages with the very tips of his fingers. He made small grunts along the way, and I took the lack of berating to mean he didn't find any flaws with my work. Finally, at the end of the 30-something pages, he placed his index finger against the slightly smudged text. "This. The launch party. I want that to take center stage. I want you to blow my socks off—invite everyone who's anyone, a casino night, strippers, you know, the classy kind. Girls serving my vodka with their titties. You get my drift?"

"I believe I do. I'll get that coordinated with the event planner. We just need to decide on a dat—"

"No!" I jumped in my seat when Perkinson slapped his hairy knuckles against the table. "You're my account manager, right? I want *you* in charge of this event. I pay your company an awful lot of money, so I expect you to do the heavy lifting, got it? I want you to have your hands in every aspect of that launch party—and no excuses about your monthly or whatever else you pampered business girls come up with to get out of hard work."

I tried to contain the grimace on my face at the prospect of planning an event where I'd have to hire girls to serve vodka with their *'titties'*. "I understand where you're coming from, Mr. Perkinson, but I believe you'd be much better served with someone whose entire focus is on event planning. I will oversee everything, of course, but as the account manager, I have to keep track of everything with this launch, not just the part—"

"Girl, do I need to go to your boss and tell him you can't do the job I'm asking? And paying for, I might add." Perkinson's cool blue eyes narrowed as he leaned back in his seat, and I knew with uncompromising clarity that I hated that man. I hated him, because I knew I was going to bend over backwards to please him, even though he was the biggest prick I'd ever met. And I'd met my fair share in London's business world.

"No, of course not, Mr. Perkinson," I managed through my teeth. "I'll do your party myself. And it'll be spectacular, I promise."

THREE
LIAM

"I hope you two realize how serious the situation is."

I suppressed a grimace as I took a swig of my beer. "Pretty hard not to, when we have to play whack-a-mole a couple of times a week with whichever patriarch thinks his Family is strong enough to steal the throne while we're still bloody on it."

"Or the men you've had stationed around our flat for the past few months," my twin said, a carefree note to his voice I knew he didn't feel. We both knew why those men were there, and it wasn't to protect us. "We're not Blaine. We don't do the whole entourage thing."

"I have three sons left, Liam. I'm not risking your security," our father said as he looked at Louis with that trademark *William Steel* gleam in his eyes.

Neither of us bothered pointing out that he'd gotten our names mixed up.

"It's been two months. If anyone was going to try to get at us, it would have happened by now. And you know we can defend ourselves," Louis said. But despite his words, we all knew what he truly meant—what we couldn't just come out and say: *It's been two months. We've proven we're loyal. Call your watchdogs off.*

Our father sighed, flattening the napkin under his beer bottle with a couple of fingers. "Perhaps I have been over-protective. You'll forgive a father for wanting to ensure his youngest sons are safe. Maybe one day, when you have children of your own, you will know. But you do have a point—and I could use the extra manpower to strengthen the watch we keep on the Bellucci Family, now they've openly sworn fealty to Mort."

This time I didn't bother holding back my grimace. Our Family's supporters were deserting us at a faster pace than we could keep up with. It would have been a lot easier to keep under control if we'd still had all our brothers in town, but I didn't say that out loud.

Our father rapped his knuckles against the table and got up. Wesley, who'd been standing by the near wall, straightened up the second Dad moved. Like a faithful dog, waiting for his master's command.

No one'd thought he'd pull through the two bullets he took to the chest just a few months ago, but unfortunately he had. And Dad had kept him even closer since.

Lucky for me, none of his loyal men saw who pulled

the trigger.

"I have business to attend. I trust I can see you two at the meeting tomorrow night?" our father said, giving each of us a firm stare.

Louis grinned. "You're never going to let that go, are you? We said we were sorry. And we paid you back."

"As you should have. One hundred grand down the drain because my horndog sons were too busy with a pair of floozies to get to a drop off on time." He shook his head, eyes narrowed. "Perhaps it's time I arrange a marriage for both of you. Blaine settled down well, after the initial drama."

"No thanks, Dad." Louis shuddered for emphasis. "We'll be on time. Promise. No need to threaten capital punishment."

"Just see to it." Despite our father's stern tone, a glimmer of amusement shone in his eyes as he turned to nod at Wesley before walking out of the pub.

I knew he had a softer spot for me and Louis than he did our brothers. Not that William Steel's *soft spot* was actually all that cushy, and I was under no illusion that it'd save our hides if he ever found out what we were planning behind his back.

"Sometimes I still can't believe he had Jeremy killed," Louis said softly as we watched our father and his bodyguard cross the street through the pub window. "But then I remember what he tried to do to Marcus."

"It's pretty impressive that things could get any

more fucked up than they were while we were growing up," I agreed. Then, through sheer force of will, I pushed away the gloom threatening to settle into my chest and gave my twin a cheerful smile as I stole his last chip and shoved it in my mouth before he could stop me. "But all we have to do to fix that is to stage a coup, somehow not get killed in the process, and then gain control over twenty Families on the brink of rebellion. Who says we don't have a solid plan?"

Louis grimaced. "Blaine, for starters. Something about covering our arses."

"Blaine." I rolled my eyes. "Blaine's such a scaredy-cat. Mira's lovely, but getting married really took the edge off our dear brother. She's tough enough to deal with our family bullshit. He doesn't need to fucking coddle her."

"Indeed." Louis stretched lazily and pushed away from the table. "But try telling him that. He nearly took my head off when I gave their kid that gun for his birthday. Get him prepped at an early age, you know?"

"Overprotective fucker," I agreed with a smirk. "Who wouldn't want their toddler playing with a handgun?"

"*You* suggested it, you prick," Louis growled, but his eyes twinkled with amusement at the memory of our older brother's reaction to his kid's birthday present. "And it wasn't like it was loaded."

"As a joke!" I held my hands up in mock-defense.

"How was I to know you'd be stupid enough to actually follow through?"

"I'm getting you back, you wanker. Whenever Marcus resurfaces, I'm telling him you've been smack-talking his girl."

Some of my amusement faded. Marcus, our other brother, had high-tailed it out of the country only a couple of months ago, after attempting to take down our dad to save his fiancée. He was protective to the extreme of the girl, and also nuts as fuck—and likely wouldn't wait to hear me out before bashing my skull in.

"That's not even funny." I arched an eyebrow at Louis. "He'd murder me on the spot, and then what would you do?"

"Turn your bedroom into a cigar club and drown my sorrows in whiskey and pussy," he said with an easy smile.

"Twat," I shot back. I leaned back in my seat and spread my arms out in an all-encompassing gesture. "As if you'd ever pull any pussy without me. I'm the good-looking brother, after a—huh."

"We're identical," my twin's dry voice sounded, but I wasn't paying him any attention, because my gaze had been caught by a vaguely familiar length of brown hair tied back in a tight braid. The woman it was attached to was standing at the bar to the pub with a couple of notes in her hand, dressed in a loose shirt and a fitted pencil skirt that emphasized her full ass and round thighs.

I leaned back a bit further to catch a glimpse of her shoes and smirked in recognition. Well, what were the odds...

"Speaking of pussy, huh?" Louis said. "Who're you eying up?"

"Brunette chick with the arse," I said with a happy smile, pushing my chair back so I could stand. "Saved her from a shoe-incident on my jog this morning—and a few hours later here she is, ready to fall all over my dick in gratitude. It's gotta be Fate, right?"

"Not sure Fate's in the business of setting up your one-night stands for you, mate." He arched an eyebrow as he gave her a once-over. "She looks like the definition of a prude. In the mood for a challenge, I take it?"

"Always." I gave him a wink. "Does this mean you don't want a go once I've broken her in?"

He snorted. "We'll see if she's worth the trouble."

Ha, he was so full of shit. I quirked my eyebrow at him before I shifted my focus to the brunette. At this point, doing a swap on our lady friends was practically tradition, and I was pretty damn sure it'd be a cold day in hell before he'd pass up on an arse like the one I currently had my sights set on.

It was funny, really—almost like Fate really *did* want me to fuck this particular girl. I'd not bothered this morning, since she was obviously late for work and I had plans with Louis and Dad anyway, but running into her twice in a couple of hours? Well, I wasn't about to look a gift horse in the mouth. Not when I'd already pulled the knight in shining armor gig on her.

I walked up behind her, smirking at her complete obliviousness as she tapped the bar with an irritated finger, clearly annoyed with the staff not getting to her yet.

"I trust my craftsmanship is still holding up?"

She squeaked at the sound of my voice right next to her ear and spun around, nearly knocking her head into my face as she did. I pulled back a little and gave her a smile. "Hello again."

"Oh, uh... hi. I didn't know you worked in this area." Her pretty face flushed. "I mean, of course I didn't—we didn't exactly exchange business cards. I mean... um..."

I took mercy on her awkward stuttering and tilted my head back in direction of my table that was half-hidden from the bar. "I'm here on lunch with my brother. And you? You work around here?"

"Yeah, just up the street. I'm here on a business lunch." She hesitated for a moment, and then indicated the bar with a nod. "Look, I'm actually glad I ran into you. You really saved my morning meeting. Can I buy you a beer or something? As a thank-you?"

"Hmm." I pursed my lips to hide my smirk. Bird walked right into that one, bless her. "I'm just about to head back to the office, but what about tonight? After work?"

"Oh." She looked surprised. "Yeah, okay, I guess we

can do that. I won't be off until some time after five, though."

"That's fine."

She dove a hand into her purse and pulled out a business card, handing it to me. "Give me a call after four, I should know when I'm off then."

"Will do," I said, and then eyed the waiter who'd finally gotten around to my brunette companion. She turned her attention to him as well and paid her bill before she looked back at me.

"Sorry, I really need to get back to my client. I'll speak with you later."

"Looking forward to it," I said, and then she was off with a smile and a nod that I could only describe as *professional*. I glanced down at the business card in my hand, unable to hold back my grin. She'd been plenty into me this morning, I knew from her lingering looks and profuse blushing, but it was pretty obvious from how completely non-flirty she'd been while being asked out on a date that she probably didn't realize my ulterior motives.

Which didn't exactly promise an easy conquest— but I always loved a challenge.

Cheerfully whistling, I shoved the card into my pocket and strolled back to my table where Louis was waiting.

FOUR

AUDREY

I'd forgotten all about my lunch encounter with the redheaded guy by the time four o'clock rolled around. I was neck-deep in reports and business calls, and so when my private line rang, I assumed it was just another client remembering that *oops,* they needed me to finish a report today, or their entire damn company would go up in smoke.

"Caslik Consulting, Audrey Waits speaking," I said as I picked up, without taking my focus off the Excel sheet I'd spent the past thirty minutes plowing through.

"Audrey. It's Liam. Liam Steel."

I frowned, trying to allocate the name, but with no luck. "What can I do for you, Mr. Steel?"

A small chuckle. *"It's past four—you asked me to call you."*

I did? Internally cussing, I grabbed for my diary and desperately flicked through the crammed pages, but no appointments were noted in for past four. *Shit!* The damn thing was my lifeline, but I'd obviously completely spaced on noting down this guy's call.

"I'm terribly sorry, Mr. Steel, but could you just remind me which report this is concerning?" I asked, doing my best to keep my tone as calm and *don't-you-worry-your-company-is-in-excellent-hands* as I could while I frantically rummaged around my desk for any hint of which company he might be working for.

"*Well, Miss Waits,*" he drawled, and I got the distinct impression he was both aware of and enjoying my squirming, "*it was about the very important meeting we set up earlier today. You wouldn't have forgotten about it, would you now?*"

"No, of course not, I'm just pulling your file up now, Mr. Steel," I lied, sending my co-worker Eileen a desperate look as she stared at me with an amused grin from her desk next to me, being not the least bit helpful.

"*I'm glad to hear it, Miss Waits,*" my nightmare client said, and I frowned at the way he intoned my surname. Hadn't he called me Audrey when I picked up? "*When can I expect to pick up the package, then?*"

Package? I stared in bewilderment at Eileen, who still didn't offer me so much as the shakiest lifeline.

"Package, Mr. Steel?"

"The beer, love." He sounded like he was smiling widely now, his timbre changing from stern business to something much warmer that made me blink in confusion. *"It's Liam, from the park this morning. You gave me your card at lunch."*

"The... beer? *Oh!* The beer!" I mentally facepalmed when my brain finally connected the dots. "Of course, I'm so sorry! I didn't catch your name before."

"That's quite all right," he said, and this time I was certain there was a laugh in his voice. *"But what do you say,* Miss Waits? *Are you still up for it?"*

"Yes, let me just check my schedule..." I flipped back to the right page in my diary. "I should be done about six. Is that all right?"

"That's fine. Meet you at the pub?"

"Yes, I'll meet you there."

"That's a date, then. Bye for now, love."

"Bye, Liam," I said, hanging up the phone.

It was only when I saw Eileen's teasing smirk that I realized my lips were quirked up in an involuntary smile. There was something about that cheerful voice that made it impossible not to smile—as if he was overflowing with so much zest for life, it was impossible not to be infected.

"Audrey Waits... was that... a *date* I heard you arrange just now? And on company time, no less!"

I quickly pulled my mouth into a straight line and

tried to ignore the faint blush on my cheeks. "No, of course not."

"Really, though? Are you sure about that? Because from where I was sitting—"

"It's just one beer," I interrupted her, shooting an annoyed glare at her across my piled-up reports. "As a thank-you. He saved me from having to limp back home with a broken shoe and be an hour late for the meeting with Perkinson this morning."

"I'm sorry, he *saved* you?" Eileen lit up like a damn Christmas tree and rolled her office chair out from behind her desk in classic *gossip pose.* "Do tell me more."

I rolled my eyes, but nevertheless told her the story of my disastrous morning. Only when I was done, her face was still stuck in a wide grin.

"Sounds like you gave it as quite the damsel in distress," she mused, flicking a pen between her well-manicured fingernails.

"I did not!"

"Tell me, was he handsome, this *savior* of yours?"

I paused, the image of Liam's silver eyes and fiery hair—and the way all his rows of muscle had been so clearly visible through his clothes—flickering before my mind's eye. "That's neither here nor there. He can't be more than early twenties, and I'm not exactly a cougar here. Nothing's going to happen—it's just a thank-you beer."

"Mmhm," Eileen hummed. She swiveled around on her chair to rummage through her purse, but before I could get back to work, she pulled out a string of foil packs and turned back around to me with a smirk, hand outstretched.

"You should probably take these, though. You know, just in case you slip on your way to the bar and land on his dick. It can be tricky for old maids like yourself to navigate around a hot young stud without stumbling."

"Eileen, put those away!" I hissed, glancing out the open door of our shared office out of fear of one of our superiors seeing her lewd offering. "It's not a date, and I'm certainly not going to need *condoms!* Are you crazy?"

"Just looking out for you and your cobweb-infested vagina," she said, shaking the row of condoms at me. "Come on, Audrey. When did you even get laid last? You'll let that young man take you home—and then you'll ride him like a pony."

"I most certainly will not." I turned my attention back to my screen. "And I'm not taking those from you, either. Now, if you'll excuse me, I have work to do."

———

WHEN I WALKED into the same pub I'd run into Liam at earlier, it was with an obscene amount of condoms stashed away in the depths of my purse and a nagging fear that every other patron in the place had suddenly developed X-ray vision. Despite Eileen's commentary throughout the afternoon, I wasn't exactly a blushing virgin, but there was just something about walking into a pub to meet a guy with a purse full of condoms that made me feel like a perverted predator.

I had zero interest in the kind of things a guy like Liam had to offer, and besides—Eileen was just full of it. There was nothing sexual in an after-work beer with the guy who'd saved you from getting chewed out by your boss. It was just a friendly thank-you. The end.

My train of thought halted when I spotted Liam's red hair up by the bar. He was lounging on a bar stool, a pint of beer next to him.

He lit up in a smile the moment our eyes met, and my breath got stuck in my chest by the sheer force of his expression. I'd never met anyone who could do that— who could light up the entire room, pushing every hint of dark thoughts aside in an easy sweep as if they never existed, just with a smile.

"Miss Waits," he rumbled, quirking a teasing eyebrow at me when I walked up next to him.

I flushed at the reminder of my blunder earlier and gave him a stern look. *"Mr. Steel.* I'm glad my panic was amusing to you."

"Oh, it was, love," he said. "I take it you thought I was some fancy client ready to throw a tantrum?"

"Yeah," I said with a small sigh at the reminder of

my current high-maintenance client, Perkinson. "We get some pretty highly strung managers on the line. The one I was on my way to meeting this morning is one of the worst, so I really can't thank you enough for the rescue."

Liam glanced down at my shoes. "It's still holding up?"

"Yeah." I wiggled my foot for emphasis. "Which is more than can be said for my feet."

The smile that was never far away from his handsome face returned, bathing me in its warmth. "I never understood why women put themselves through such torture."

"After this morning, neither do I," I grumbled, earning me a low laugh.

"We should probably find a seat then, love, so you can give your feet a break, eh?" He winked. "Listen, would you mind if we grabbed dinner before we get down to the business-end of that beer you owe me? I'm absolutely starving."

"Oh. Yeah, sure, I guess that would be nice," I said, checking the time on my phone. It was close to dinner time, of course, and the idea of a nice pub meal made my stomach rumble in agreement. It would be a welcome change from all my takeaway, anyway.

Liam slid off the bar stool with an easy movement that displayed perfect control of his body and held out his arm to guide me toward one of the empty tables by the window.

"So what do you do, Liam?" I asked as we sat down, grabbing the menus. "I presume something business-related, since you were in the area this morning and around lunch?"

"Nah, I live close by," he said distractedly as he looked at first page. "You in the mood for a starter? Nachos sound good?"

"Uh, sure." I blinked at him, taking in his casual shirt-and-jeans outfit. *"The area"* was mainly big corporation HQs and a few high-class pubs like the one we were at. The residential buildings I knew of lay right down by the river, and... the kind of people who lived there generally pulled home seven-figure salaries and weren't seen without their Louis Moinet watches and Roberto Cavalli ties. What the hell did a twenty-something guy do for a living that had him shacked up with a view over the Thames?

"You in IT then?"

"Nope. I think I'll do the ribeye for mains. Have you got something selected?"

"The soup of the day."

"Dessert?"

"No thanks."

He shot me a decidedly wicked smirk. "Guess we'll just see what we're in the mood for at the time. Stay put, I'll order."

I fought to control my blush as he sauntered up to the bar to put in our order. He was clearly a tease, judging by the prank he'd put me through when he called my office earlier.

And what was about not telling me what he did for a living?

Liam returned shortly after with a bottle of white wine and two glasses.

"Oh, I wasn't going to drink," I said when he put them down on our table and slid back into his seat.

"Oh come now, love. You weren't going to let me drink that beer on my own, were you?" he said, easily pouring a healthy measure first in my glass and then his own.

I paused, quirking an eyebrow at him. "Are you really peer pressuring me into drinking on a work night, Mr. Steel?"

He let out that rumbly laugh of his that seemed to warm my chest in the most pleasant way, as if his amusement was as infectious as his easy smile. "Of course."

I sighed and eyed the full wine glass in front of me. It looked more inviting than it had any right doing—I hadn't really enjoyed a cold glass of wine in good company in way too long.

For some reason, the bloody condoms in my purse flashed in front of my mind's eye again, and I scrunched up my nose in annoyance. Damn Eileen for putting those sorts of thoughts in my head!

I glanced from the glass to Liam, then reached out,

quickly swapping our glasses before I raised his to my lips and took a sip. It tasted heavenly.

"Clever girl," he said, raising my swapped glass to drink long and deep without breaking eye contact. Demonstrating that my safety measure wasn't needed.

"Sorry, I—"

He waved me off with a hand. "Don't apologize for being smart, love. A single girl has to look out for herself, I get it. In fact..." Liam reached into his pocket and pulled out a small, sealed plastic bag. He put it on the table, shoving it over to me. "Use these, if you don't have your own. I won't be offended."

I stared down at the small, factory-sealed kit of CYD test-strips. Who the fuck carried a set of drinks-testers around to hand out to random women?

"Wow, that's... a bit intense," I said, arching an eyebrow at the offering.

He smiled that disarming smile, shrugging as if there wasn't a date rape drug-kit on the table between us. "You seem the type who likes to know she's in control. I own a couple of nightclubs—we hand them out to all our patrons. Don't worry, they're leftovers from last night. It's not that I carry them around as a pulling technique."

Right, then. At least that answered the *"what do you do for a living"* question.

"I don't know, *'Hey honey, wanna see if I've slipped you a roofie'* might be a great ice breaker with the kids

these days. Would go well with the zip-ties you have
handy in your jog pants."

Liam barked a loud laugh, his eyes twinkling as he
looked at me over his wine glass. "That's quite a bit of
sass from a bird who's still running around with said zip-
tie holding her shoe together."

I glanced down at my shoe. The tie was thankfully
discreet enough no one would notice unless they stared
at my heel. "Hey, I'm not knocking it. I'm just saying it's
not every twenty-something who feels the need to stock
his pockets with zip-ties and drug test kits."

He shrugged with a nonchalant move that seemed to
emphasize the width of his shoulders. "What can I say?
In my business, it's best to be prepared." His tone was
light, but the small twitch of his soft lips almost looked
like regret.

Then he smiled at me, and I was too busy ignoring
the responding buzz low in my stomach to pay that
flicker of emotion any further mind.

Damn, but that man was bursting with an almost
tangible energy. It seemed to radiate off him, nearly
overwhelming me when he so much as quirked his lips.
His smirk brought to the forefront of my mind the
condoms in my purse, and I hid my hefty blush behind
my glass of wine as I gulped down a couple of mouthfuls
to settle my embarrassment.

Eileen may have had a point about it being too long
since I was intimate with a man, if all it took to wind me

up was a couple of smiles from a handsome guy. Especially one almost a decade my junior.

The arrival of our starters saved me from that particular train of thought.

"So, your nightclub business... did you start it on your own?" I asked, opting to steer the conversation toward topics that hopefully wouldn't have my mind running wild with inappropriate scenarios.

"No, it's a family business," Liam said, shoving a cheese-covered tortilla chip into his mouth. "We run several different places. I mainly work with my brothers, but my father's the head honcho."

"That must be nice, working with family," I said, nibbling at my own nacho even though I kind of wanted to follow Liam's example and just shovel them in. I hadn't eaten since lunch, and my stomach was twisting angrily. Still... even though this wasn't a date, there was no need to shock the poor guy.

"What made you follow that path? Money, or...?"

"Or a deep interest in watching over drunk people bumping and grinding?" He grinned. "It was never really a choice. All of us just kind of grew up knowing we were going into the family business. It's all right, though. Dunno what else I'd do—I never had the patience for school."

"Oh." I didn't quite know what to say to that. Since I went to university, it seemed like I'd only ever met people who strove after grades and promotions as single-mindedly as I did.

Judging from Liam's playful smile as he watched me trying to find a response, he knew what I was thinking.

"I'm more of a spur-of-the moment kind of guy. I don't do well with suits and reports. The family business allows me a lot of freedom. But what about you, *Miss Waits?* Your card said *Business Consultant.* That sounds several shades of serious."

"Yes, well... I guess it is." That warm, teasing tone of his made me feel so completely out of my element. I hid my once-again warm face by taking another sip of my wine. "I've always been interested in the business world. I was recruited to Caslik Consulting right after my Masters."

"Always?" He arched his eyebrows at me. "How about when you were a girl? What did you dream about then? 'Cause I'm almost certain it wasn't being a business consultant."

I couldn't hold back my own wry smile at his teasing. "Well, what do you know? I'm sure there are many little girls out there who dream of business suits and spreadsheets."

He chuckled, and for some reason my chest heated up. I drank another gulp of wine.

"No, I wanted to be a famous equestrian. Or a ballerina. Which, perhaps, is a bit on the silly side, since I never took any dance lessons."

"But you rode horses?"

I sighed, not realizing how wistful it sounded before I saw it register on Liam's face. I shrugged, trying to play it off.

"When I was younger. But I never did find the time to pick it back up after I went off to uni."

"If that's the case, then you work too much, love," he said, not taking his gaze off me. "Tell me, what was it about riding that you miss?"

"I don't miss it, as such. Sure, it was fun, but—" I tried, but Liam's snort interrupted me.

"Bullshit. I saw that look on your face just before. That was pure longing. You gave it up to focus on work, sure, I get it, but there's something you're missing about it even to this day."

I honestly hadn't thought about it, not until tonight, but as I looked at him and at the earnest glow of pure *life* in his eyes, I found myself nodding.

"The freedom," I admitted. "Being utterly and completely *free,* just me and the horse and the wind in my face." I laughed, a little embarrassed when I realized how open I'd been. "I know that probably sounds really silly—"

"Nah, love. It doesn't sound silly at all. What it *does* sound like is that maybe somewhere along the line, you forgot that there are other things in life than work."

He was right, I realized. Maybe it was the wine, or the way my entire body felt warm and relaxed in Liam's company, but for the first time since I'd started working toward my career, I let myself think the thought that maybe there *was* something missing in my life. Though what exactly that something was, I wasn't entirely sure.

THE REST of the meal went by in a blur of cozy chatter. Liam steered the conversation toward lighter subjects, and by the end of it, my cheeks and stomach hurt from too much laughter.

He was excellent dinner company, apart from nearly making me choke on my chocolate tart with his rendition of the stuffy businessmen he usually saw on his morning jog in the park we'd met in. I hadn't had this much fun in... well, my head was too foggy from the laughter and wine to remember a time I'd ever enjoyed myself quite this much.

Only when Liam asked for the bill did it dawn on me that I still hadn't fulfilled my end of the bargain for our dinner.

"Wait! I haven't bought you that beer yet," I protested when the waitress walked off, leaving behind a tray with the bill and two complimentary mints.

"I thought maybe we could find a bar for that. If you don't mind?" Liam fished up his wallet from his back pocket and threw a couple of bills on the tray. It more than covered both our meals, plus a very generous tip.

"No, don't be silly," he said, waving my hands away when I tried to put down money for my half. "This one was on me."

I opened my mouth to protest, but he just quirked an eyebrow at me. "Let go of the reins, Audrey. You might just enjoy it."

I stared at him. "I'm not... I just want to pay for my part."

"Guess you're out of luck then, huh?" he teased, snatching the tray—with his money still on it—before I could make another attempt at tossing any notes at him. "Let me know what you think of that beer when I get back, love."

I pinched my lips at his retreating back. It was starting to dawn on me that perhaps Eileen hadn't been *entirely* wrong when she'd dubbed my meeting with Liam a date.

But maybe that was just what he was like—he seemed like a nice person, underneath all the swagger. I mean, who asked a woman out on a date without even letting her know?

When Liam returned, smile still in place, I'd convinced myself I was being ridiculous.

"What's the verdict on that beer, then?" he asked, eyes twinkling with something that looked an awful lot like mischief.

"Well, I can't very well have you rescue me *and* pay for my dinner, then not buy you that beer I promised," I said, glancing down at my phone to check the time. Nine o'clock. I was usually on my way to bed at this time, and I had work in the morning, but... I gave Liam's grinning face a glance, feeling that still-unsettling warmth nestle into my chest when his eyes caught mine.

Apart from it being rude of me to decline after he'd paid for dinner, I found I didn't want the night to end just yet.

"Where would you like to go?"

THE BAR he took me to was up a cobbled side road a couple of blocks away, and from the looks of it, it was a real, old-fashioned pub that someone had attempted to modernize within the past decade. The lighting was pleasantly dimmed and the clientele just the kind of artsy hipsters you'd expect to find hanging out among artisan draft beer on a Monday evening. I stuck out like a sore thumb in my dressy office wear.

"All right then, what'll it be, Mr. Steel?" I said and grabbed my wallet. "What can possibly do just payment for your masterful craftsmanship on my heel?"

Liam's eyes glinted with amusement at my posturing. "Any lager will do."

I arched an eyebrow at him. "Really? You take me to Hipster Haven and don't want a micro brewed, oak-seasoned hop-sensation? How disappointing."

"Fine, surprise me, then," he said, jerking a thumb at an empty booth on the far end. "I'll grab us a table while you order."

To Liam's credit, he didn't even wince when I five minutes later put a pint of *Midnight Wheat, Warming Spices, and a Hint of Vanilla* down in front of him, along with my own chocolate-caramel ale.

"The bartender assured me it would turn your deadened taste buds around to real beer," I said, sliding in next to him when he moved over to make space for me. It wasn't until I was already sat down I realized the small manipulation in getting me to sit next to him rather than on the other side of the table.

"... Liam?"

"Yes, love?" His tone was light as he took a sip of his drink, grimacing at the first taste.

"Is this... this isn't a *date,* is it?" I asked, taking a drink of my own beer as I glanced at him out the corner of my eye.

"Why? Would you mind if it was?" he asked, as nonchalantly as if I'd just asked him about the damn weather.

I nearly choked on the ale. "I—you—I'm *much* older than you." Okay, so the emphasis on "much" was probably going a bit overboard, but it was the first argument my tipsy brain grasped onto.

Liam arched an eyebrow at me. "Yeah? How old are you then, Grandma?"

"Thirty-two," I said, narrowing my eyes at the grandma comment. "What are you, twenty-one?"

This time, I got a full laugh.

"I'm twenty-five, love. Plenty old enough." Without hesitating for even a moment, he let a fingertip brush over the back of my ale-free hand resting on the table between us. It sent a warm rush of sensation up the length of my arm. "When did you last take the time to just enjoy a man's company, Audrey? If I were the betting sort, I'd wager you've let your damn work consume so much of your life, you don't even remember when you last shared a drink with a bloke not on your company's client list."

I opened my mouth to protest—but even as I racked my brain, I knew he was right.

"Look, I've enjoyed the evening. I think you have too. Doesn't have to be anything more than that, if you don't want it to be." Liam flashed me an easy smile and took another swig of his beer, without moving his hand from mine.

I hesitated, eying his fingertips as he drew lazy circles on the back of my hand. Did I? Want it to be more than just a nice evening? My mind flashed back to Eileen's comments about my cobweb-infested vagina, and the way just being around Liam seemed to warm me in the most pleasant way. Twenty-five might be better than what I'd initially shot him to be, but he was still undoubtedly an absolute player.

I knew his type, from when I was still in uni—devilishly good-looking, charming as hell, and completely uninterested in anything serious.

But it had been *so long* since I last had even a halfway decent flirt with a guy. Who said it had to be serious, anyway? I wasn't going to see Liam again—we both knew that—so why the hell shouldn't I cut loose for once in my boring, career-focused life?

Liam's fingertips danced up the length of my arms, raising goosebumps with their feathery brushes. "Of course... if you *do* want more, I'm going to screw you until it hurts to come. I've been fantasizing about shagging you since I first laid eyes on that sweet arse of yours." It was a low, rich growl, so completely different from his normal, carefree tone of voice—and it went straight to my clit.

The fervor with which I lunged myself at Liam surprised even myself.

He just managed to set down his beer before my mouth crashed against his. He grunted, either from impact or surprise, but parted his lips and wrapped both arms around me as I clambered onto his lap and kissed him like I'd never kissed a man before.

Everything was heat and burning need down low in my belly, pulsing through my blood for every beat of my over-excited heart, and then there was the taste of beer on Liam's tongue as I parted my lips for him with a needy moan. He kissed me expertly, meeting my crazed assault on his mouth with long strokes of his tongue and those deviously soft lips cushioning my wild urge for more, more, *more*. More of his kiss, more of *him*.

When I grabbed for his cock and found it hard and eager inside his jeans, he chuckled into my mouth and pulled back just enough to breathe into my ear, "Your place or mine?"

FIVE
LIAM

"Mate, we've arrived." The exasperated voice coming from up the front of the cab finally made me wrestle my mouth from Audrey's hungry lips and glance out the window. We were stopped in front of an indistinct high-rise, and I had no idea how long the driver'd been parked on the curb, waiting for us to stop snogging.

I gave him a wink in the rear view mirror—no doubt he'd gotten quite the show—and tossed a handful of notes at him. Probably overpaid the guy, but my cock was way too hard to try and do math, thanks to the surprisingly fiery little brunette in my lap.

Sure, I'd hoped to get into her panties tonight, but I'd anticipated having to lure and persuade her the entire way. Apparently half a bottle of wine and some dirty talk was enough to get little Miss Prissy Pants to lose her inhibitions.

"Come on, love," I groaned into her ear when she ground down against my crotch to regain my focus. "If we give that poor bloke any more of a show, we're gonna have to start charging."

Audrey made a squeaky little noise and pulled back from me, her face flushing a deep shade of red as she looked up at the rear view mirror. "Oh, God."

Great. Seemed the wine was starting to wear off.

She looked back up at me, and I could see hesitation flicker in her gaze. Yep, someone was sobering up.

I didn't give her time to word some bullshit excuse for why we suddenly shouldn't get naked. Giving her my best smirk I kicked the cab door open and dragged her out, slinging her over my shoulder the second I was out on the pavement. "C'mon, m'lady, let me take you to your castle. Got any dragons in need of slaying on the way?"

Audrey let out a breathless giggle at my antics, her hands finding purchase against my back to stabilize herself as I strode toward the entry door to her building. Relief flooded my system when she handed me the keys and told me her floor—I hadn't been this desperate for a fuck since I hit puberty, despite the couple of girls I'd shagged over the weekend. I was too fucking horny to pinpoint what it was about Audrey that revved my engine so hard, but the feel of her round arse and full thighs underneath my hand had me taking the stairs two at a time.

She made that cute little squeaky sound again when I dropped her to her feet at her front door, and then a moan that went straight to my cock when I pressed my mouth against hers and pushed her up against said door.

Fuck, just kissing her made me lose my mind! Since when had a fucking make-out session robbed me of most of my control? I fumbled with her keys, trying to ram what I hoped was the right one into the keyhole without breaking away from her sweet mouth. She tasted like wine and woman, and I estimated the damn door had about thirty seconds to open before I gave up and just fucked her in the stairway.

But the lock refused to budge as I desperately tried to smash another key into it. For fuck's sake, how many keys did she even have?

"Mmph!"

I ignored Audrey's mewl, letting my free hand slip from her half-exposed tit down her thigh and up her skirt in the hopes of distracting her with a bit of clit play from what was undoubtedly a protest at being fucked against her own front door. She was so warm and soft against everywhere our bodies pressed against each other, and I knew she was gagging for it too. Knew she had been since she'd practically mounted me at the pub.

My fingertips were met with absolutely soaked tights at the apex of her thighs, and I smirked against her lips at the confirmation. Yeah, she was ready for my cock.

I gave up on the damn lock and dropped the keys to the floor so I could grab the crotch of her tights with both hands and free her sweet sex. They tore with a satisfying *rip,* and she whimpered in response, a needy sound that had my cock leaking in my jeans.

"Don't you worry, baby—I'm gonna fill that tight little pussy right up," I growled against her lips.

"Liam!" She drew back to disengage from our kiss and pushed at my shoulders. Reluctantly, I backed up enough to give her a bit of space, though it nearly killed me to separate even an inch of my body from hers.

"Don't tell me to stop." I could barely recognize the deep growl in my voice.

"That's my door."

"What?" I frowned at the laughter in her eyes—she was fucking *enjoying* my torment.

"*That's* my door—you know, *behind* you." She pointed past my shoulder. I took some small consolation in her heated cheeks and breathless voice, despite her obvious amusement at my desperation.

"Don't give a fuck," I growled and dove back for her throat, flicking my tongue at her pulse point as my fingers found their way in behind her panties. "Gonna fuck you right here. Think your neighbors will like hearing you come on my cock?"

"God, no!" She actually sounded pretty shocked at my suggestion, and her small hands returned to my chest, pushing half-heartedly.

I dragged my thumb up through her slick folds and pressed it hard against her clit, hoping she'd forget her protests.

She shuddered against me, and I felt her thighs spread wider, her pelvis tipping up for more. I happily obliged, rubbing it gently.

"God, Liam," she moaned softly. It was the sweetest sound I'd ever heard, and it made me want to hear it again while my head was between her thighs. *Fuck,* but my cock was so damn desperate for her wet heat—I wasn't sure I had the strength to pop her pussy on my tongue before getting at least one good come off inside of her first.

Audrey took advantage of my hesitation and pushed her arms more insistently between us. "Let's continue this inside, okay?"

"Need to have you now, sweets," I groaned against her throat, digging my teeth into her pale skin. "Can't wait."

"Liam," she protested, some of that prim tone from earlier in the day making its way back into her voice. "I don't—f-*fuck!"* Whatever else she'd planned to say was drowned out by her groaned curse as I pinched her clit hard.

I pulled at the pulsing little nub, keeping a firm grip on its base until I was sure she'd lost the will to protest again. Desperate for more but knowing she'd need at least a little foreplay to take me, despite her wetness coating my fingers, I pressed my mouth to hers once more. She parted her lips with a whimper and moaned into my kiss when I switched my grip between her legs to rub her clit with my thumb again. She took the first finger I slid up inside her tight heat like a champ, and I pumped it in and out of her, wishing for the first time in my entire life that my cock was smaller so I could just ram it into her without preparation.

When I gave her two fingers, she started pawing at my chest, but it wasn't like before—she wasn't trying to get me to stop. At three, her pelvis was rocking in rhythm with my hand, and I'd officially run out of self-control.

I pulled my fingers out of her with a wet sound, ripped the hole in her tights a bit bigger, and hiked her skirt up over her hips.

She grabbed for my zipper before I could get to it myself and managed to get it opened. I pulled out my achingly hard cock, lifted her left thigh up over my hip, and lined myself up. Her wet heat kissed my cock head, and I nearly blacked out from the full-body shudder of pleasure.

"Wait!" she suddenly gasped.

"Fucking hell, woman!" I growled, tensing every muscle in my body in an effort to hold back from hilting the girl I'd been aching for for what felt like fucking days.

"Condoms!" she said, her voice shaky with her own admirable restraint. "My bag. We need—"

How the hell had I not thought of that? I'd *never* fucked a bird without a rubber, not once in my entire life. I dove for the black leather handbag on the floor next to her keys and rummaged through it until I found a long string of foil packets. I tore one free, got the packet open and the condom rolled on my cock in three seconds flat.

I grabbed her thigh again, lifting it over my hip, and guided my cock to her opening with my free hand. Without waiting for permission, I drove into her to the hilt.

Every cell in my body was tense, electric pleasure. She was so fucking warm and so fucking *tight;* I couldn't do anything but breathe for several moments as my cock relished in finally being inside her. Her pussy fluttered around me in quick little cramps, already milking me as if she were begging for my sperm. *Fucking hell,* nothing had ever felt this good before.

"Christ! You're s-so fucking big!" Her hoarse gasp drew part of my attention back to her face, and the tight grimace on her beautiful face made me realize she'd probably needed a bit more foreplay.

"Sorry, love," I groaned, hoping against hope I'd be able to go easy on her. Already the initial burst of hot bliss from finally being inside her tight little cunt was fading to a nearly irresistible impulse to start thrusting. *Hard.* "Don't want to hurt you."

"You won't," she said, a note of desperation clear in her voice despite her obvious struggle with my size. "Don't stop. Please. Don't stop."

"I won't," I promised, silently thanking any and every deity who might be listening that she was still willing.

On my first pull out I managed to be slow, but the way her sheath clung to my cock made me snap my hips back harder than I'd meant to.

Audrey yelped and threw her head back against her neighbor's door, and the look of her then—so completely lost in the sensation of my cock filling her pussy—broke the last of my restraint with a near-audible *snap*.

I took her so rough and fast I had to clamp my hand over her mouth to not draw the rest of her neighbors out of their flats when she began screaming and thrashing on my cock like a woman possessed. Her pussy smacked lewdly with every thrust, and I spared her nothing. All my normal consideration went out the window as my brain fogged over with the complete ecstasy of pounding her into oblivion, and all I could sense was the impossible pleasure of having her writhing on my cock. Where she belonged.

I don't know how long I fucked her before suddenly her back arched in a tight bowstring and she clamped her teeth down on my palm and dug her nails into my chest. I didn't even register the pain, because in the same instant her cunt clenched around my cock *hard*, and I lost myself completely.

I pumped her a few more times, groaning like a wounded animal before my balls emptied in an explosion of pleasure so intense my legs nearly gave out.

Her pussy convulsed in a series of tight little spasms, forcing every last drop of semen from my dick while I rocked slowly against her, riding out her orgasm as well as my own.

Only when her sex relaxed completely around me did I still. I moved my hand from her mouth so I could wrap both arms around her body, pulling her off the hard door. "You okay, yeah?"

"M-*hm*." She gave me a groggy smile, and I couldn't hold back a laugh at the completely blissed-out expression playing across her pretty features. Yeah, that was one excellent round of fucking, all right.

SIX

AUDREY

It took a little while before my brain came back from orbit after the mind-numbingly intense orgasm. It returned with a *thump,* and the sudden and highly distressful realization that I'd just fucked a guy right out in my own stairway—for anyone to see. Or *hear.*

Christ, if Mrs. Peterson had been home, she'd have called the police on us for desecrating her front door—and rightfully so.

I wasn't that kind of girl—I'd *never* been that kind of girl, not even in uni. And here I was, thirty-two years old and in a respectable career, with excellent credit score and a drawer full of sensible bras. And I'd let a man I'd known for less than a day screw my brains out basically right in front of all my neighbors! What the *hell* had gotten into me?

Clanking from my kitchen made me bite my swollen

lower lip as a warm mix of embarrassment and pleasure rushed through my veins and rose to my still-exposed chest. I knew what'd gotten into me. *Liam Steel* had gotten into me—literally as well as figuratively.

My nether region was sore from the unaccustomed activities I'd put it through not ten minutes ago, and I cringed at the feel of my fabric sofa right up against my lower lips. Yeah, there was still a big-old gaping hole in my tights and panties where he'd ripped both for better access.

I was *so* not this person. Even sexually liberated Eileen was not this person. And yet... I'd been the one to throw myself at him at the pub. *I'd* kissed *him*.

Had I really been that drunk? I didn't feel more than a little tipsy now, as I sat curled up on my sofa in the faint light from the kitchen spilling through the doorway, but maybe Liam'd just fucked the drunkenness right out of me? It'd certainly been a thorough workout, that's for sure.

Footsteps from the hallway announced Liam's return from the kitchen, and I looked up as his large figure crossed the threshold into the living room. He was carrying two mugs, and when he handed me one he bent to give me a peck on the lips, as if it was the most normal thing in the world. As if we weren't practically strangers.

But he didn't *feel* like a stranger. My body relaxed when he sat down next to me and threw a casual arm over my shoulders, letting the warmth from his body seep into mine from where we were touching.

Why was he so easy to relax with? Even during our date I'd been completely comfortable around him. He made it so easy.

Maybe it wasn't alcohol my brain was drunk on. Maybe it was that intoxicating aura of his that radiated contentedness and *life* in nearly physical measurements.

"Ah-ah, don't give me that frown, love." Liam gave my shoulders a squeeze and offered me a cheeky smile when I glanced up at him. "I'll just think I didn't do my job well enough. Bloody insulting, that."

I blushed predictably and hid my face by taking a sip of too-hot tea. "Don't tease. I can't believe we did that. What if the neighbors had heard? What if they'd come out to check?"

Liam shrugged and took a long drink of his own tea, apparently not bothered by the temperature. "Then they'd have gotten some good wanking material."

"Easy for you to say," I hissed, giving his arm a half-hearted slap. "You don't have to live here."

"You care way too much about what other people think, don't you?" He finished up his tea, put the mug on my coffee table—completely ignoring the stack of coasters—and slid his now free hand up my thigh. "I think you'd find it easier to relax if you just stopped."

I let out a breathless laugh, all too aware of the heat

from his palm through my ruined tights. "It's that easy, huh?"

"It is," he said with a wry smile, and I bit my lip at the way his fingertips were inching up underneath my skirt. "Let me show you."

I fidgeted on the sofa next to him, suddenly feeling way too sober. "Maybe we shouldn't..."

Liam arched a ginger eyebrow at me, not stopping his hand's slow upward stroke against my thigh. "The fact that you're turning all red-faced and shy even after we've already fucked is all the more reason we should. You need to learn how to relax, love, and I'm gonna teach you."

His fingers slipped all the way up, spreading my lower lips apart and delving into my heat. I groaned unintelligibly in response and bit my lip when he stroked my clit with small, precise brushes.

"Liam..." It was meant as a protest but came out as a breathy sigh. *"Oh."*

Maybe he was right—maybe I did need to relax and just go with the flow. We'd already had sex once, so why be embarrassed? Maybe this wasn't something Sober Audrey normally did, but Sober Audrey did spend a fortune on massages and painkillers in an eternal attempt at getting rid of tension headaches. I was pretty sure the last issue of *Cosmopolitan* I'd read while waiting for my monthly massage appointment featured an article about orgasms reducing stress. Judging by what Liam'd just done to me out in the hallway, there was a pretty good chance I'd be fifty shades of zen before he was done.

Liam seemed to sense my resistance dying down, because he withdrew his hand and grabbed my mug, moving it to the table. With that smile of his that made my stomach warm and fizzy still teasing at the corners of his mouth, he placed both his hands on my shoulders and deftly eased me down on my back on the couch. Large but nimble fingers flicked open the buttons of my shirt, and then my plain bra and soft stomach were on display. I bit my lip, feeling a short stab of uncertainty at being bared to his gaze, but one look at his face and any insecurity crumbled and died.

He looked at me with such unadulterated yearning, my skin seemed to heat under his eyes as they swept from my face down my chest to my navel, and back up again. I couldn't remember another time anyone had ever looked at me with such devastating desire, such complete and uninhibited *want*. It made my head spin and my abdomen pulse with responding need.

"You're so fucking beautiful." His voice was rough, urgent. "Do you know how badly I've wanted you all day? And then there you were, in that pub, like a goddamn sign from above."

"I wanted you, too," I gasped. "In the park."

"I know," he said with a smirk. And then he dipped

his head, latching onto one of my stiff nipples as his left hand rounded on the other breast.

I moaned softly at the stimulation, and harder when he began to suck the sensitive tip, hauling it into his mouth with hard pulls of his skilled lips.

Bursts of sensation crackled through my body, culminating between my legs until the ache for attention there grew too great to handle. Whimpering, I pushed his warm hand off my breast and down between my thighs.

Liam chuckled against my breast, but obliged. His nimble fingers danced over my clit, teasing the small nub before he finally pressed down with just the right amount of strength.

"Oh, Liam, *God!*" I moaned as my hips rose up off the couch in blind search for more. "Yes, like that!"

He let me squirm underneath him, keeping my hips trapped by resting his large frame on top of mine while he stroked me just the way I needed. I'd never been with a man who knew exactly what I needed, how hard and where to touch, and in no time I was panting and mewling underneath him, teetering on the edge.

"Please, please, please," I chanted as I bucked underneath his hard body. Every nerve ending blazed with sensation, and I knew if he would just push me that final inch, I'd fall.

"Please what?" he growled, his voice rich and smug and so goddamn *sexy.* It was entirely infuriating. He teased my clit, lightening his touch when I tried to force my hips up for more stimulation, and I cried out in frustration.

"Please make me come!" I shouted, not caring one iota if my neighbors heard. "Oh, *fuck,* please, Liam, *please,* I need to—ohhh*yes! Yes!*" My pleas drowned in a howl of release as Liam pressed down and rubbed me *hard,* snapping the final string tying me to reality. White-hot pleasure burned through my nerves as I writhed and bucked against him, the promised release finally soothing my nerves with waves of ecstasy.

I collapsed down on the couch in an exhausted pile.

"Oh, my God," I mumbled groggily.

Liam's only response was a deep chuckle. He sat up, giving me a moment to come back down.

"You could earn a lot of money as a stress reliever," I said, thinking back to the *Cosmopolitan* article.

Liam barked a full laugh and slid his hands up my torn tights. "I could, could I? Well, love..." His voice lowered to a seductive purr. "I wouldn't demand payment from such a lovely client."

"That's good, because I'm pretty sure I don't earn enough to afford you," I said, unable to fight the sated smile still lingering on my lips as I looked up at him through lowered lashes.

He smirked, and I felt a sharp tug around my waist. When I looked down he was in the process of pulling my skirt and ruined tights off my legs.

"Easier to maneuver," he said with a cheeky wink at my questioning expression.

"We're not done?" I croaked, genuinely surprised. The men I'd been with in the past had very much been done for the night after they came. I was already pretty amazed that Liam had given me another orgasm so soon after his own.

He took my hand and placed it against the fly of his pants. A hard bulge pressed unmistakably against my palm. "Does it feel like we're done?"

I shook my head, the flush in my cheeks more from excitement than embarrassment.

Liam squeezed my hand against his cock, moaning softly as he rocked up against my touch, but just as I was about to offer more, he pulled back and slid to his knees on the floor. When I opened my mouth to ask what he was doing, he lifted one of my legs over his shoulder, spinning me to face him in the process. His hot breath against my exposed mound made the question die on my tongue.

"*Oh.*"

I slumped back against the backrest of the couch as Liam spread my lower lips with his thumbs and proceeded to give me a slow, broad lick all the way from my weeping entrance to my still-buzzing clit.

I moaned incoherently. It rose to a high-pitched squeak when his tongue flicked across the tip of my clit, sending sharp jolts of sensation through the hypersensitive nub of nerves. I felt Liam's amused chuckle at my reaction more than I heard it. He didn't seem the least bit deterred despite my hips' restless squirming.

How he knew just the right pressure and exactly the right ways of worshipping my clit I didn't understand, but, *oh*, he did. He lapped at my lips and circled my clit for a while, teasing my pleasure to mount until it became unbearable. Only when I was clawing at the sofa and chanting, *"Please, please, please,"* did he finally wrap those devious lips around my clit and *suck*.

My scream ripped through the living room and echoed off the walls as my back arched off the couch in a tight bow. Hot, painful pleasure too intense for me to stand wracked my pelvis and shot up through my body and down my thighs in fitful waves. I bucked and cried, trying to dislodge the source of the stimulation, but Liam just wrapped his arms around my thighs and kept suckling my clit in deep, hard pulses. It was agony and it was ecstasy, and I lost myself to the torrent of sensation, fingers buried in Liam's flaming hair as he forced me higher than I'd ever thought I could climb.

When I came, it was with a force pulled from the very roots of my clit.

"Liam!" I screamed as my orgasm made every single muscle in my body clench up, my fingers in his hair forcing him down hard against my pelvis while I rode out the mind-numbing waves of pleasure so intense it

blinded me from everything but Liam's laughing, silver eyes.

When, finally, the agonizing release was over, I slumped back into the sofa, completely spent. Mercifully, Liam eased his mouth off my aching clit, giving my poor nub a much-needed break.

"*Wow*," I mumbled groggily. Then I laughed, a hoarse, wheezing sound, because it seemed like that was now my standard response to him: *Wow*.

How did he know my body better than I did? I'd spent most of that session trying to get him off me, and yet he'd given me the most mind-blowing orgasm ever. I'd never been much into oral sex, but it turned out it was only because I'd never had Liam between my thighs before. Other men usually licked my clit half-heartedly and stopped when I began to squirm, only too eager to continue to the main event. Not Liam. No *siree*.

"You okay there, love?" Liam shot me an amused look, and I realized I was still chuckling.

"Nope. Pretty sure you broke me." I wrapped a couple of fingers around his strong chin and urged him up. He obeyed, resting on both arms above me as he leaned in for a deep kiss. I tasted myself on his lips and hummed in appreciation—and then groaned in protest when one of his deft hands slipped down between my thighs to tease at my still-swollen clit.

Liam laughed when I tried to cross my legs and pulled back, giving me a mischievous smirk. "What are you gonna offer me instead, then, darling? 'Cause I'm right in the mood to lick that delicious little pussy of yours until you pass out."

"I could... could suck *you?*" I offered, feeling the heat rise in my cheeks. I wasn't used to being so blunt about sex, but being with Liam I was quickly learning there was no other way. It was oddly liberating.

"Nah, love." Liam crawled up over me again, forcing me to twist so I was laying across the couch underneath him. His darkened eyes roamed hungrily down my body. "Here's the deal. Either I hold you down and give that poor little clit of yours such a lashing you won't be able to come for weeks once we're done, *or*... you spread those luscious thighs and let me fuck your pussy raw. Your choice."

His hoarsely growled words should not have made goosebumps of excitement break out all across my flushed skin—they really shouldn't. He was a stranger, and I'd let him into my home. He was so much stronger than me he could easily overpower me... but all his promises of forced pleasure did was make my nipples tighten into peaks and my core clench with longing.

Slowly, not breaking eye contact, I spread my thighs for him.

"Good choice," he said, the heat in his voice making shivers of desire run down the length of my spine. With a dark smirk he dipped his head for my nipples and latched on tightly as his hand slid down between my legs again. I whimpered in protest, but he didn't go for my clit. My toes curled on their own accord when he pushed two fingers inside me, curving them just so.

"Ooh, yes! I need you inside, Liam. *Please!"*

He pumped me a couple of times, thrilling his fingertips against my pulsing G-spot until I thought I'd go mad. Only when I was rocking up against him in rhythm with his fingers fucking in and out of my soaked sheath did he relent.

He sat back on his heels, dragging his fingers up through my folds to ghost across my hooded clit before he sucked my fluids off with a pop.

"You taste so fucking delicious, love. Lucky for you, your pussy feels even better wrapped around my cock than it tastes." He shrugged out of his top and undid his jeans with practiced ease. "You ready for it?"

I looked up at the man hovering between my thighs, looked at his chiseled chest and sculpted abs, and that intimidating length between his legs that'd hurt so damn good when he took me up against Mrs. Peterson's door.

"Uhhu." I didn't quite manage to string actual words together, but Liam took my guttural attempt at consent for what it was. With that wicked smile of his still playing on his soft lips he reached for a condom and rolled it on before he spread my lower lips and moved forward.

I bit my lip when his broad head kissed my entrance, and threw my head back with a low groan as he slowly pushed inside. Every nerve in my body was focused on that hot, wet stretch as my pussy struggled to take him inside for the second time this evening. But it was easier this time, even if the size of him still made me grit my teeth and grab at the sofa for purchase.

"God, you're big!" I whimpered, a hitch in my breath when he hilted me smoothly at the same moment.

"*Fuck!*" Liam growled in response, before falling down on top of me, catching his weight in his arms so our skin touched but he didn't squash me. "*Goddamn,* Audrey." He didn't continue, but he didn't need to. The pleasure was written all over his face and echoed through me in deep, pulsing waves where we were so intimately connected. He thrust, and I moaned and slung my arms around his shoulders, needing him to anchor me to reality even as he pushed me toward oblivion.

He peppered my jawline with kisses as I clung to him, the heat of his skin enveloping me as he moved slowly but firmly between my thighs, filling me with his hard girth. It was the purest form of bliss, even as he whispered the dirtiest things in my ear—how he loved the wet sound of my pussy struggling to take his cock, how I was born to fuck... how he was going to screw me until I begged him to stop. Through it all, I gasped my agreement out through moans of pleasure. In that moment, I never wanted him to stop moving inside of me, because this... this was what the true meaning of life was. *Him*.

Liam took me gently until the ache for something *more* grew from a lazy pulse to a deep, urgent throb. I rolled my hips up against him, blindly seeking the source of what would soothe the fire in my blood—and I got it.

With a moan of relief that made me realize he'd been holding back with every ounce of willpower he possessed, Liam snapped his hips down hard between my thighs, making shocks of raw pleasure pound through my core as he finally unleashed his true desire.

My wanton moans turned to screams as the lover between my thighs turned to a beast. He fucked me every bit as hard as he had against that door, making my sofa groan and my pussy smack wetly every time he bottomed out deep inside.

It hurt, but it was the kind of pain that only enhanced the pleasure until it became more than I could contain. And just like I had on the stairs, I came for him.

"*Liam!* Oh, my god, *yes!* Don't stop! Don't... stop!"

He didn't. Even when my climax ebbed, he fucked me through it and straight into another, forcing my pussy to milk his pummeling cock while I cried and came, and cried and came.

Only when my moans turned to whimpers and my pussy had no more left to give did he finally, mercifully, find his own release.

Groaning, he stiffened on top of me for a moment, and I felt his cock swell inside my battered sheath. Then, with a shuddered gasp, he rocked against me once, twice... only to finally sink down fully on top of me, covering my body with his own.

We lay in silence for a while, save our ragged breaths filling the air and the thunder of my heartbeat ringing through my ears. I could feel his pulse where his chest pressed against mine, like a solid, comforting reassurance, along with the sweat glistening on both our bodies and the heat radiating off his skin. I felt so... so complete, as I lay there underneath this stranger who'd taught me things about my own body I'd never have known if he hadn't stopped to help me this morning in the park.

Stranger. I pressed a light kiss to his shoulder and licked the salty flavor of his sweat off my lips. I may only have met him a few hours ago, but nothing about him felt like a stranger as we lay entwined on my sofa in the darkened living room. I looked up and caught his gaze— those amazing, gray eyes so full of *life* and warmth as he looked back at me with a gentle smile curving his lip.

No, in those moments, I was pretty sure no person had ever known me as intimately as he.

SEVEN

AUDREY

An aggressive beeping sound tore me out of dreamless sleep.

I groaned in protest and slapped a hand toward the noise, connecting with my angrily vibrating phone. It was as if the muscles in my arm had turned to Jell-O, and it took me several tries to finally slide the screen in the right direction and turn the alarm off.

"Hmmph," Liam sleepily groaned from behind me, and then a strong arm wrapped around my waist and pulled me close against his warm, hard body. "What's the time?"

"Six," I mumbled, snuggling closer up against my bed partner. "We can sleep half an hour more." I usually didn't take advantage of the snooze button, but then again—I usually didn't stay up until the early hours of the night.

"Mm." I took the sleepy sound as confirmation, and let myself drift away to the comfortable feeling of being held tight.

Only, I hadn't fully fallen back asleep before his large, warm hand began stroking lazy circles against my belly, finally rounding on a breast. Something hard and insistent pressed against my butt, and when the fingers attached to the hand plucked at my nipples, my body slowly began to wake up.

I sighed and stretched out for him as his questing hand delved down low again, this time continuing in between my thighs. My clit was still sore from the unaccustomed amount of attention that'd been lavished on it last night, but Liam's touches were light as a feather and oh so gentle. He stroked his fingertips against my small bud with careful patience until the desire in my body eventually smoldered hot enough to burn away the tendrils of sleep.

The desire pooling between my thighs made me roll over to my back and press my hips up, ignoring the ache in them, blindly searching for more stimulation.

"Yeah?" Liam's voice was still rough with sleep, but the note of lust was unmistakable. It went straight to my already pulsing clit.

"Yeah," I said, finally cracking my eyelids open to look at him. It was still dark in my bedroom, but I could make out Liam's messy hair and wide shoulders as he rested by my side on one elbow. I couldn't see his smile, but I felt it as he pressed a soft kiss to my lips before he shifted on the bed and slipped in between my thighs. Once there, he stretched out on his stomach, and I bit my lip when his hands brushed against my labia before spreading them apart.

We both sighed when his lips pressed against my mound, and my hands went to his unruly hair.

He eased me into it with slow, broad licks against the full length of my slit, only focusing on my increasingly yearning clit when I finally couldn't take the gentleness anymore and pulled him hard against me by his hair.

Liam chuckled at my roughness and gave my hard little nub a small nip in retaliation. The zing of sensation made me arch off the bed with a moan—and that was all the opening he needed. He lashed my clit mercilessly with hard flicks of his tongue, battering it from all angles until I was crying and thrashing underneath him as he forced my body up, up, up. When he finally wrapped his lips around it and sucked hard and deep, I peaked.

"Liam! Fuck, God, *yes!*" My cry rang through the bedroom as my sore muscles clenched around nothing but the ecstasy of release. I slumped down flat on my back, finally letting go of his hair while I tried to catch my breath.

"How do you do that?" I croaked, my mind still hazy

with groggy pleasure. "No one's ever been able to do that. And you... *every* time...?"

Instead of answering, Liam crawled up by body and kissed me deeply. I tasted myself on his lips and sighed into his mouth as his tongue teased mine. He shifted a little so he could rest on one arm without separating our kiss, and I groaned as two of his nimble fingers slid up inside me.

I was still sore from last night, but he was gentle as he pumped his digits in and out of me, testing my readiness and stretching worn muscles. It didn't take long before I spread my thighs wider in invitation and pressed my hips up in instinctive waves.

"Liam..."

He gave my lips one last peck and rolled off, and judging by the crinkling from the bedside table, I knew he was fumbling with the leftover condoms.

Bless Eileen.

Then he was back between my thighs and I bit my lip, anticipating the pain when the wide head of his cock pressed up against my opening.

But he was gentle—much gentler than at any point the night before—and the stretch when he pushed inside barely hurt at all.

Liam stilled for a moment once he was fully inside of me. "God, you feel so fucking perfect." It was a soft rumble. "I could stay inside you forever."

I moaned my agreement.

Our sex wasn't nearly as rough this time—he took me with a slow, unbreakable rhythm, coaxing my climax from my wakening body rather than forcing it out of me like he had every time he'd made me scream on his cock last night. When I came, I clenched around him in sweet bliss, gasping his name as he moaned through his own release and peppered my lips and throat with kisses.

I stared dazedly into the ceiling above his shoulder, my arms still wrapped around his warm, strong torso. The darkness was slowly lightening to a deep gray, and I could make out the outline of his mussed hair as he panted softly against my ear.

I'd never felt like this before—so completely content, from the roots of my hair to my toes. It was a warm, comforting blanket from everywhere his skin touched mine, and it was electric champagne fizz deep in my stomach. He was a stranger to me, and yet he felt so familiar, so *right,* as if being with him was what my brain had been waiting for to finally release all the pent-up anxiety I'd carried around since somewhere around middle school.

"How do you do that?" I whispered into the slowly brightening room. I didn't realize I'd spoken out loud until he lifted his head to look down at me. I could make out the dimples in his cheeks when he gave me a lazy smirk.

"Pure magic, love."

I laughed and rubbed my face against his arm. "At this point, I could believe you."

His smile faded as he looked at me, but it was still too dark for me to decipher the expression in his shadowed eyes. When he bent his head to kiss me, I no longer cared.

His mouth was soft and warm, and as I nibbled on his lower lip I felt his cock begin to stir inside of me again.

Surprised, I pulled my head back and arched an eyebrow a him. "*Again?*"

He shot me an easy grin and rolled his hips, making me gasp and dig my nails into his shoulders from the sudden shock of sensation. "I don't think I'll ever stop getting hard for you, sweets."

"I guess there are upsides to being a cougar," I said, and then cried out when he rewarded my lip with a hard thrust. And another.

WHEN I FIRST HEARD MY phone, Liam had my legs over his shoulders and was driving into me at a merciless pace.

I reached out for my nightstand on pure instinct, but Liam grabbed my wrist, stopping my attempt at answering whoever was calling without missing a beat.

"I'm not done with you yet," he panted. With an

ease I still hadn't gotten used to, he pulled out and flipped me onto my stomach before pushing his throbbing cock back up inside of me with a hard thrust. "If you think answering the phone mid-fuck is a good idea, clearly I'm not doing you hard enough!"

It took me four orgasms and I don't know how much time before Liam finally gave in to exhaustion and collapsed on his back on the bed next to me.

My ears were ringing and blurred dots danced before my eyes as I lay beside him and desperately tried to suck in enough oxygen to not pass out, but I was vaguely aware that I had an insistent grin across my face, and that every single cell in my depleted body was humming with bone-deep satisfaction.

"If—if you plan... plan to make a habit of having sex with... older women...you need to learn to pace yourself," I panted in between gasps for air. "I don't know how I'm not dead."

Liam let out a breathless chuckle. "How *you're* not dead? It hurts when I move! God, woman..." He rolled over onto his side with a theatrical groan and pulled me into his arms.

I sighed happily and cuddled closer against him, content to just feel his body wrap around mine as the endorphins in my body made my blood sing.

If Nirvana was an actual thing, this was it.

The sharp ring from my phone pulled me out of my blissed-out haze with a start. Ignoring Liam's protesting groan, I reached out and grabbed the device, swiping right on the screen.

"Hello?"

"God, Audrey! Are you okay?"

I frowned at the shrillness of the panicked voice on the other end. "Eileen? Yeah, I'm fine. What's wrong?"

"What's wrong? You have a date with a stranger, and then don't show up to work the next day is what's wrong! I thought you'd been murdered!"

I blinked. "What do you mean *'don't show up for work'*?" A horrible sense of foreboding settled in my gut, and I fought my lax body to sit up. "What time is it?"

"Ten thirty. Audrey... what have you been doing this morning?" Eileen's voice gained a distinctly teasing note.

"Shit!" Sheer panic made me jolt off the bed in one jump. A quick glance at my phone's display confirmed the time. "Dammit! I'm on my way!" I hung up, tossed the phone on the bed, and dove for my wardrobe. Only when I was frantically searching through my underwear drawer did it dawn on me that I'd meant to do the laundry last night.

"Running late?" Liam asked, pulling my attention from my desperate attempt at shoving my boobs into a bra that hadn't fit properly for the past ten years.

I cast a look at him over my shoulder—and felt something twinge in my gut at the sight of his unruly red hair and that eternal laugh in his eyes. He was resting on one elbow in my messy bed watching me get dressed, his perfect body still covered in a light sheen of sweat from our sex marathon.

And I knew with sudden and horrifying certainty that I needed him.

Not his sex, not the one-night stand we'd both known this night would be. No, I needed his laughter, his warmth—and that nearly tangible light that seemed to radiate off him like rays of pure, unadulterated *life*. I'd never felt as alive as I had these past sixteen hours or so in his company, and I knew I never would again if he walked out of my life.

It felt like a donkey kick to the gut.

I sank back down onto the bed, my previous panic completely drained by the nauseating realization that I didn't want this to be the last time I saw Liam Steel.

This was supposed to be a one-night thing. Men like Liam didn't do anything more than that—I'd known that when I kissed him in the pub, when he took me up against Mrs. Peterson's front door, and when I fell asleep in his arms from sheer exhaustion several hours later.

But the thought of never seeing him again was unbearable.

"Liam?" My voice wasn't much more than a hoarse whisper.

"Mm?"

I glanced at him again and bit my lip to steel myself.

He looked so completely relaxed, like nothing in this world could ever shake his good mood or quiet confidence, and I wished with everything I was that I could have just a little of his easy strength right about now.

"I... I know this was supposed to be... that this is a one-time sorta deal, but I..." I drew in a deep breath. "Do you think, maybe, we could do this again?"

"I assume you don't mean right now?" There was a hint of amusement in his voice, but also a gentleness that hadn't been there before.

"I... I really need to see you again." I could have swallowed my own tongue. *Not* the kind of thing to say to a player like Liam.

He was quiet for a moment. Then he moved in the bed behind me before one of his large hands engulfed mine completely. I noticed a small scar on his thumb as he stroked it across the back of my hand, then blushed when an image of that same thumb brushing over my nipple last night flashed before my mind's eye.

"I'd like to see you again, Audrey."

The hesitation in his voice hinted that there was more to that sentence

"But?" I asked, staring unblinkingly at the scar on his thumb. My stomach felt like a tight, painful knot.

He was silent for a few seconds. Then he grabbed my chin with his free hand and made me look up to meet his eyes. They had their usual gleam of mischief, completely free of any hesitation now. "But nothing. I'd be pretty fucking stupid to say no to more time in your bed, love."

The tightness in my stomach uncoiled, relief flooding my entire body as he dipped his lips to mine in a kiss that had my heart skipping a beat. I knew he'd considered something before he said yes to seeing me again, but I was too relieved to linger on what it might be.

So long as I knew this wouldn't be the last time I got to feel his light envelop me, I didn't care what had made him hesitate.

EIGHT

LIAM

"Are you *limping?*"

I ignored my twin's amused expression and let my eyes glide over the other people lounging in our shared living room. Our brother Blaine sat with his arm around his redheaded wife on the sofa in front of the TV, and on the floor over by the floor-to-ceiling window, their toddler was busy playing on a square blanket.

"Blaine, Mira," I greeted our guests as I walked from the hallway—doing my best not to limp—and threw myself on the sofa next to them. I couldn't quite suppress the small groan when my worn body impacted with leather.

"It looks like you had a good night," Louis continued, eying me up with a small measure of interest. "Maybe I should give the girl a go after all?"

It wasn't an unusual comment, not for us. We'd

shared more girls than I could count over the years, our identical appearance leaving the lass none the wiser. What *was* unusual, however, was the flare of anger deep in my gut at my twin's casual suggestion. I pressed a hand to my stomach and frowned. Where the hell did *that* come from? We shared everything—women were no exception, so why did the thought of my brother bedding an unsuspecting Audrey make everything inside me feel hot and painful?

"*Louis!* Don't tell me you two still trick women like that." The disapproving hiss came from Mira, but despite her sharp tone, her face displayed exasperation rather than outrage. "You're too old to act like horny teenagers."

Louis' face cracked in a wide grin. "Nah, love, we'll never be too old for that. We can't all settle into domestic obedience like our poor brother here."

Blaine scoffed at the dig. "I think it'd do you some good. I can't wait until some bird finally shows up on your doorstep with a ginger kid or two—that should settle you right down."

Louis and I shared a look and gave a synchronized shudder of horror. We'd made a pact long ago to never, ever get ourselves into a situation where pregnancy might be a possible outcome. As much as we both hated the idea of commitment, of some girl coming between us, neither of us would be able to abandon a kid we'd fathered. The natural solution had been a pact to always johnny up when we shagged a lass.

Except, for the first time in my entire life, I'd almost forgotten the second I'd felt Audrey's soft body against mine.

"If you're angling for a playmate for Aidan, I'm almost positive Marcus will have his girl knocked up by now," Louis said. "You heard anything from him?"

Blaine shook his head. "He'll be in touch when we've figured out how to take care of Dad."

And there it was. The one subject we'd been avoiding for the past two months, waiting for the right moment. After our brother Marcus narrowly escaped the country when he attacked our father to save his fiancée, William Steel had been on highest alert. It had taken a lot ass-kissing before we no longer saw his men lurking around outside our apartment, watching us, ensuring his remaining sons stayed in line. We had made sure to stay away from Blaine, save a few casual meetings in public, so as to not raise his suspicions that we were plotting something.

To make him believe we didn't know he'd killed our brother Jeremy instead of sending him to America to deal with business connections, like he'd told us for the past few years. Knowledge Marcus had shared with us before he'd been forced to flee.

"He's not going to step down," I said to no one in particular.

"We have to kill him," Louis said, finishing my sentence. "A simple hit would be the easiest, but he's keeping Wesley and a few other faithful guys with him at all times now, even when we visit him. And he's never within range of a long-distance rifle. It'd have to be done up close... but there's zero percent chance of making it out alive for whoever does it."

"And then there's the question of Isaac," Blaine said softly. "If Dad dies before we can prove he set Isaac up, he'll rot in prison for the rest of his life."

Isaac. Louis and I exchanged a look, and I knew what he was thinking. Our brother, who'd spent the past nearly two years in jail and refused to see any of us after a drug deal gone wrong. It had been a shock to both of us when Blaine came forward with proof that our dad had set him up to take the fall. Knowing our father had gone after his own blood, killing Jeremy and selling out Isaac, meant none of us were safe—and if there was one thing I wouldn't survive, it was losing Louis. We'd never talked about it, but I knew he felt the same. We loved all our brothers fiercely and would protect them at any cost, but the bond we had with each other was something more than that. He'd been there every day of my life, through all the tough shit, through the death of our mother and every hit we'd been forced to execute while working for our father. Louis had been by my side as I had been by his, and if we hadn't had each other, I knew without a shadow of a doubt we would've been lost in the same kind of darkness that had nearly swallowed up Marcus before he met Evelyn.

I'd always felt guilty for having Louis to lean on when I saw my other brothers struggle with the weight of our shared childhood on their own, but both Blaine and Marcus had pulled through with the help of the women they'd eventually fallen in love with. Isaac had no one. He was entirely on his own, locked up like an animal because our father had betrayed him in the worst way possible within the underworld. Well... the second-worst way. I pressed down the pang of loss at the memory of Jeremy.

"We've also not discussed what will happen once Dad's gone," Louis said. "Our Family's claim to London's throne is already shaky, at best. If we lose our patriarch, it would be nearly impossible to keep it."

"Maybe that's not such a bad thing."

Both Louis and I stared at Blaine as he shifted on the couch. I didn't miss how he pulled Mira closer to his body.

"Have you never thought what it would be like to get out?" he continued. "I know you two hate the darker side of the business, and I..." He glanced at his son playing by the window. "I've got him to think about."

I exchanged a look with Louis. Sure, we'd both wished on a few occasions we didn't have to deal with the bloodier sides of crime, but it was all we knew.

"I don't think there is an out for us, mate," I said

with a soft sigh. "The second the Steel Family loses its footing, every crook in town is gonna be out for our blood. Short of disappearing like Marcus did, we're stuck."

Something passed over Blaine's face, and I frowned.

"You've been thinking about it," Louis said. His voice betrayed my own shock. If anyone was made for the mafia life, it was Blaine. He'd always been ruthless but in control, wielding the power that came with our name with ease. "About leaving London?"

Blaine shrugged and glanced down at his wife. "Only if we must. I know we have obligations to our men, but I won't put the welfare of my wife and son on the line to keep control over an empire built on lies."

"This is our home," Mira said. Her voice was quiet, but had a core of steel as she returned her husband's gaze. "None of us want to leave it behind. I'm not saying you should sacrifice everything to continue being in control of London's underworld, but don't throw it all away in some misguided belief that Aidan and I can't be safe here. We've been safe for a long time now, despite everything that's going on. If you want to change your father's legacy, I know you can do it. Together. But not before he's gone."

I whistled a low tune and saw Louis shoot the curvy woman an appreciative grin.

"Well, well, look who's come around to the criminal side of life," I teased.

"I'm pretty sure I remember a time where you would've literally rather lived on Europe's streets than be part of the Steel empire," Louis continued.

She cocked an eyebrow at us. "If we all disappear, someone else will fill the power vacuum. Someone as bad as your father, most likely. If we stay, we can change things. Try and lessen the violence."

"Leave it to you to strive for a better underworld," Blaine said, an amused tilt to his lips. But he was also looking at her with the same sort of awe I'd seen in his eyes before. Those two were fucking meant for each other, as baffling as it was to understand. Mira had given our brother the light he needed to balance the darkness that came with our world, and he'd given her strength. And for the briefest moment, as I looked at them, my thoughts swirled back to the woman I'd spent the night with and how it had seemed impossible to tell her no when she'd asked to see me again.

Last night had been the first night in months I'd been able to forget all the darkness and betrayal at knowing what our father had done. Somehow, I'd managed to find a moment's respite between Audrey's thighs, and I didn't have the strength nor the will to deny myself. It'd been like having healing salve smeared on a burn, and the relief had been instant and addictive.

"So we stay. And fight. If we can." Louis said, breaking me out of my thoughts.

"Yes," Blaine said after a short exchange of looks

with his wife. "Once Dad's dead."

"Which brings us right back to the how," Louis sighed. "And when."

"I... might know a way," Blaine said. The hesitation in his voice had me exchanging another look with Louis.

"I take it there's a major caveat, since you didn't lead with it?" I asked.

"Yeah." Blaine grimaced. "It involves working with someone we know's gunning for our Family's demise."

I felt my own eyebrows mirror Louis' as he arched one in question.

"There are rumblings that those of our supporters who have fallen away after I turned in the Clerys are gathering around another Family. They're not yet big enough to take us on, but they're hungry for it. If we make them believe there's a rift in our Family, we can use them. It shouldn't be hard, since everyone knows Marcus is in hiding.

"Say one of us go to the other Family, let them know he's considering switching sides to help Marcus and Isaac out. And in return for their help in taking Dad down, we'll give them control over part of London once it's done. That way, we get the manpower we need for a full-scale attack, and don't risk any of our men turning against us mid-fight. The caveat..."

"...is that if they decide to flip on us and warn Dad that one of us is a traitor, whoever goes is dead," I finished.

"Yeah." Blaine looked from me to Louis. "Whoever goes will risk his life. But I don't see any other option. I've been going over this so many times now, I don't see we have another choice."

"Ruling London's underworld alongside another ambitious Family is going to be a challenge," Louis said. He looked straight at me. "But I agree. If one of our rivals are looking to usurp us... this is the best shot we've got."

I nodded. "We'll go. Louis and I."

"You don't have to—"

Louis raised a hand to still Blaine's protest. "Yeah, we do. Your first priority is Mira and Aidan. Liam and I... we have each other. We got this."

"Thank you." The quiet voice belonged to Mira, but when I looked at Blaine, I saw her gratitude reflected in his eyes. Not for the first time, I felt a flicker of horror at how vulnerable he must feel through all this shit with our dad, knowing one wrong move could cost him his wife and child. Sure, they were protected better than the royal fucking family, but if the past few months had taught us anything, it was that William Steel would stop at nothing to keep us all in line.

"It's decided then. Guess we just need to know who we need to pay a visit to in the next few days?" My tone was much easier than I felt. "Who wins the chance to take on London's biggest crime lord?"

"The Perkinson Family."

NINE
AUDREY

Four days.

It'd been four days since Liam typed his phone number into my mobile, four days since we'd parted with the promise of *"soon"*... and four days since I'd been able to take my eyes off my damn phone for more than a few minutes at a time.

But no matter how much I stared at the display, the only texts that'd beeped in over the past few days had been from my sister, my mother, and Pizza Hut. I'd ignored the first, answered the second (yes, I'll come by for Dad's birthday meal), and a half-eaten stuffed crust pepperoni pizza on my coffee table was currently bearing witness to my pathetic staring contest with my phone.

Why doesn't he call?

I growled at my own desperation. I knew why he

hadn't been in touch—a guy like Liam undoubtedly had a very active social life. Getting in touch with the random one-nighter from earlier in the week likely wasn't all that high on his to-do list.

Which meant that... I fingered the display, biting my lip with indecision. It was quite obvious that if I wanted to see him again, I'd have to be the initiator. But how pathetically desperate was that? I didn't particularly want to come across as the needy girl who wouldn't take a hint—I was too old for that.

...Like I was too old to sit by my phone on a Friday night, pining after a guy.

For fuck's sake! I was a grown-arse adult. If I wanted to see a man, I could damn well send him a text and ask him to swing by.

Before I could change my mind, I typed out a quick text and pressed *"send."*

Hi Liam, want to come by when you next have time? Audrey.

There. Short and to the point. Just pure business.

...The business of a booty call. Fuck, had I made it sound like a damn transaction? Why was I so terrible at this?

A sharp beep from my phone jolted me out of my spiraling thoughts. It was from him.

Sure. Be there in 20.

For a moment, I just stared at the message. Shock mixed with elation churned in my gut. I'd not even considered he'd have time to see me on a Friday night, but just seeing the few words he'd typed made every-thing inside me warm up as images of his silvery eyes and the eternal laughter they seemed to hold flashed through my memory. The past few days in work had seemed particularly gray and lifeless—as if the moment he'd left my apartment, the infusion of color and life he'd enveloped me with had disappeared and I'd been left in a deadened, washed-out version of reality. A reality I hadn't known was so empty before he'd given me the briefest glimmer of what I was missing.

Which was absolutely preposterous, of course. We'd shared *one* night. A pleasure-filled night, sure, but even the mind-blowing sex like what he'd shown me really shouldn't make the rest of my life seem empty by comparison. I'd worked hard to get where I was. I didn't need a man to fulfill me. Not even one with a god-like dick.

Maybe Eileen was right. Maybe breaking my extended dry spell with such a vigorous round of shag-ging had given me a mild case of temporary brain damage—something she'd teasingly suggested when she'd found me staring blankly at the wall in front of the copier for the fifth time during the week.

A sharp twinge of excitement down low in my abdomen brought my thoughts back to the present. I'd see him again tonight. In... *"Shit!"* In fifteen minutes!

I jumped up from the couch and took a panicked

look across my messy living room, mentally calculating where my efforts would be best spent.

He's not here for the fucking living room, Audrey.

Decision made to let messy coffee table be messy coffee table, I spun and ran for the bathroom.

I'd just managed to clean my teeth and apply deodorant, and was mid-way through applying a quick layer of mascara when the door phone went with a loud *buzz.*

I squeaked, narrowly avoided to stabbing myself in the eye, and promptly dropped the mascara into the sink.

He's here!

Shit, he's here.

My previous excitement was suddenly overshadowed by a flock of butterflies settling into the pit of my stomach, and I pressed a hand against my top to try and settle them down. *There's no reason to freak out, it's just two adults meeting for some fun.*

But one of those adults had eyes that shone with warmth and light I craved like a heroin addict craves her next fix—and a body carved from goddamn marble.

Somehow, I made it to my hallway and pressed the speaker button on my call box. "Yeah?"

"It's me." Even through the scratchy static, I could hear the eternal smile in his deep voice and that hard Cockney dialect that made my panties dampen in Pavlovian response.

I buzzed him in and unlocked the door—and leaned against it with my eyes closed to try and get myself together. The way my heart pitter-pattered in my chest, you'd think I was a young girl waiting for her crush, not a grown-up business woman who'd arranged a night of passion with a no-strings lover.

Hard raps of knuckles against wood made the door vibrate against my back, and I nearly jumped out of my own skin with a shrill squeak.

"Audrey? You all right?" Liam's voice was muffled by the closed door between us, but the laughter in it was unmistakable.

I internally cussed myself before I turned around, smoothed my top to settle myself—and opened the door.

Liam was leaning against the doorframe, his tall, broad-shouldered figure taking up most of the doorway. He flashed me a crooked smile. "Hey, love."

Before I managed to get my tongue under control to form a reply, he swooped down and pressed a lingering kiss to my lips. The heat from his mouth penetrated my blood and exploded in pulsing waves down through my body until my mind fogged over and my core clenched in rhythm with my ragged breathing.

When he pulled back I stared up at him with wide eyes, mouth half agape.

His wry smile turned to a full grin at my clearly dumbfounded expression. "Can I come in?"

Mutely, I stepped to the side so he could squeeze past me.

Halfway on auto-pilot, I shut the door and turned around to face him again—but the sight of him standing there in his leather coat with that red, unruly hair and easy smile in my hallway after having pined for him for so long left me tongue-tied.

God, I'd missed him.

And I shouldn't have. Not like this. This was way too intense, way too much.

The corner of his mouth hiked up a little higher at my continued silent staring. With an easy movement he shrugged out of his leather coat and dropped it on the small chest of drawers next to the doorway leading into the living room. But instead of taking mercy on me and breaking the silence, he just looked at me with that mischievous smile lurking in the corner of his mouth and simmering heat in his eyes that made my ovaries quiver.

Bastard.

"Tea?" I finally managed, way too loud. I could have slapped myself. Tea? *Really, Audrey? Like a twenty-five-year-old sex god shows up at a woman's doorstep for a cup of goddamn* tea.

A low rumble of laughter made its way up his throat. "Maybe later."

And then, finally, he took pity on me. The heat in his gaze smoldered, some of the mischief slipping to the background. He cocked his head and let those expressive eyes of his run up and down my body, leaving me shivering and too hot at the same time.

Liam took one step toward me, and I took one back, responding to the predatory smirk slipping over his sinful lips. Slowly, in a near-prowl, he herded me backward through my apartment and into my bedroom. I only stopped when I felt the bed hit the backs of my knees.

Liam closed the distance between us and captured my lips in a searing kiss that had me panting and clutching at his strong arms within seconds.

"Liam," I whispered when he finally let me breathe.

An unexpected push and I lay on my back on top of the sheets. My entire body buzzed with anticipation. When Liam shrugged out of his T-shirt and let it drop to the floor, the heat pulsing through my body centered below my navel with a sharp twinge.

"I've missed you," I breathed before I realized I'd spoken out loud.

He climbed on top of me, nudging my thighs apart so he could settle his still jeans-clad hips between them. The outline of his hard cock pressed against my clothed pussy, right where I was aching for him.

"I've missed you, too."

TEN

AUDREY

My head buzzed pleasantly with the echo of several orgasms as I lay sprawled next to Liam some time later, one leg hiked over his thighs and my arm across his chest. I couldn't remember the last time I'd felt so at peace. Well, that was a lie—I couldn't remember a time before I'd met Liam where I'd felt such peace. It was as if he had some magic fix against the constant undercurrent of stress in my life.

I smirked against his tattooed chest and let my fingers dance down his sculpted abs and along the narrow trail of ginger fuzz leading the way to his softened cock. *Magic fix,* all right.

The heavy pole of flesh twitched at my attention, and Liam cracked his eyelids to look down at me. "Again?" Despite his body's obvious interest, his tone was relaxed and lazy.

I giggled and let my hand slide back up to his pecs, flattening across one of the black swirls of ink underneath his pale skin. "Maybe later."

Liam hummed with relaxed amusement at hearing his own words turned against him. "Wuss."

"Chafing is a real problem, you know," I said, trying for a prim tone. It earned me a chuckle and a kiss to the top of my head.

"I don't think you *can* chafe, as wet as you get for me," he said, just a sliver of smugness in his voice.

I huffed, cheeks flushing. He was probably right—the second he touched me, it was as if my abdomen liquified with hot, wet need.

"I'm glad you got in touch," he said after a moment's silence.

I bit my lip, my heart doing an odd flip. "I did ask for your number." And I'd been damn needy about it, too.

"You were still high on endorphins," he said with a shrug. "I figured you'd change your mind once you came back down. Smart girls like you tend to realize they shouldn't make a habit of seeing guys like me."

"Is that why you didn't call me?" I said, and instantly regretted the question. *Way to fucking go, Audrey. Amp up the neediness some more and see how fast he can get his pants back on.* "I mean—"

He silenced me with a finger against my lips. "I know what you meant, love."

I waited for him to continue, to answer my question, but he didn't, and I didn't have the courage to ask again.

"Are you leaving tonight?" I asked instead, somehow managing a casual tone.

"If you want me to, sure." He released me and rolled over onto his side so he could look at me while supporting his head on his hand. His free hand found my bare stomach and stroked across it in a gentle caress. "But I'd like to stay for morning sex."

"I'd like that, too," I said, unable to hold back the smile spreading across my face as I looked at him.

The corners of Liam's eyes crinkled with that innate happiness that had my heart skipping a beat. His hand moved from my stomach to my hip so he could roll me onto my side and pull me in flush against his chest. "Then I'll stay," he said before he dipped his head for another kiss.

It didn't take long for my body to warm against his once more, but when I felt his cock rise against my stomach again and his kiss turned urgent, I pulled back with a laugh.

"How about that tea?" I asked, putting my arms between us when he tried to pull me back in.

"How about another fuck?" he countered, arching his eyebrows at me suggestively.

"Seriously, what kind of pharmaceuticals are you on?" I slapped his roaming hand away from my backside and rolled out of the bed before I succumbed to his all too convincing touch. If I wanted any hope of not being rendered with a permanent limp, I needed at least a small break before the next round.

Liam sighed wistfully and turned over so he could sit up. "No need for pills when you're waving that sweet arse around, love. I've never known a woman as beautiful as you. 'S'far as I'm concerned, the only pharmaceuticals 'round here are whatever amphetamines you're hiding between your thighs."

I snorted, hiding the way my cheeks heated with involuntary happiness at his obvious flattery by turning my back and pulling my thigh-length robe on. "I appreciate the attempt, Liam, but you don't need to feed me bullshit lines. I'm not one of your impressionable girls." I left the bedroom and bee-lined for the kitchen without looking at him. I didn't want him to see how easy it was to listen to all the sweet things he said. It was one thing during sex—it was another to hear them when we both had a functioning blood supply to our brains.

After I finished the tea, I found Liam lounging in my living room, eating one of my leftover slices of now cold pizza with the same carefree attitude as always and not a shred of clothes on. Soft jazz, the old CD I'd left in my stereo from weeks ago, flowed smoothly through the air, and he'd lit a couple of the candles on the sofa table.

"Needed to refuel," he said when I sat on the couch next to him, placing two cups of tea in front of us. He grabbed another slice and held it out for me, and when I took it, he pulled me into his body so I was resting against his side and chest, his pizza-free arm around my shoulders. It felt so good, so natural, and I instinctively relaxed against his warm skin.

"You do know the curtains are open, right?" I murmured in between bites of pepperoni bliss. He was definitely on to something with this refueling idea. My stomach rumbled in appreciation.

"Gotta give your neighbors something to look at," he said with an unconcerned shrug.

"You're not bothered by anything, are you?" I asked, genuinely curious.

"Sure I am." I felt a stroke through my hair, and couldn't hold back a hum of pleasure. "Just never gave two shits about what other people think of me."

"No one?" It seemed like such a foreign concept. As long as I could remember, I'd most definitely worried about what others thought of me, starting with my parents and including my bosses these days.

He made a thoughtful sound. "I guess my brother, Louis. But he and I are basically the same person, so... it's never something I worry about."

"Must be nice," I sighed, not realizing how wistful I sounded before he pushed my chin up with a couple of fingers so he could capture my gaze with his.

"Anyone giving you any bullshit, love?"

The flash of something dark in his otherwise effulgent eyes seemed completely out of place on his beautiful, mischievous face.

"Not really," I said. The memory of the abuse I'd been taking on a daily basis via a steady stream of emails from Perkinson made me wrinkle my nose. "I've got a really horrible client at the moment, but I've always had to measure up to my sister. And I've always come up short, you know?"

"I doubt you come up short against anyone." He sounded so completely sincere that for a moment, I almost believed him. Then reality set in and I flushed and looked down. "Don't do that."

"Do what?"

"Flirt. Flatter." I waved a dismissive hand. "I don't want anything fake, okay? I... being with you is such a breath of fresh air from all the façades. You're so wonderfully genuine. Don't give me cheap lines, like I'm some naïve girl you're trying to get into bed. That's not what I want."

He was silent for a short moment. Then his hand rounded on my chin again.

"Audrey, look at me." His voice was far more serious than I'd ever heard it before. I obeyed on instinct and was caught in his gaze once more. There was so much sincerity in it, it nearly took my breath away

"I'm not feeding you some bullshit lines, love. You're fucking beautiful, driven, and obviously smart as shit. I promise you I'll be nothing but real with you, if you promise me you'll stop thinking you're somehow not measuring up. Not when you're around me. Yeah?"

I stared at him for the longest time, letting his words sink in through the heavy thumping from my heart. Saw the flames of truth in those silver eyes, and knew I'd found the one place in the world I could be free to simply be, if only for a fleeting moment. In the arms of a man I'd thought I'd only ever see once.

My throat was too thick to produce words, so I nodded mutely instead. That was our pact—our promise that existed only in this space between the two of us. No bullshit. No façades.

Liam threw the leftovers of his pizza slice on the table and got to his feet. He held out his hand, and I let him pull me up next to him.

"I love jazz," he murmured, slipping both arms around me. "My mother had this album."

"Is she dead?" The way his mouth tensed when he said *had* made me place my hands on his chest in an instinctual attempt at offering comfort.

"Yeah. Many years ago. I don't remember as much about her as my brothers do, but I remember this. Her love of music." Liam rested his head against mine and held me tighter against his naked form. Slowly, he moved us in rhythm to the music, and I slipped my arms up around his neck.

"I'm sorry," I said, softly so as to not drown out the

melody enveloping our swaying bodies. "How did she die?"

"Shot." He nuzzled his nose against my ear. "It's not a happy subject, love."

"Does it have to be?"

"It usually does. It makes people feel better."

I twisted my fingers in the unruly ends of his red hair that brushed against his nape, making him look at me. "I thought we agreed you'd be real with me."

A shadow of a smile touched his lips, but it didn't have the usual sardonic quality. "We did."

The pure, raw emotion in his eyes made me lift up on my tiptoes to press my lips against his.

Liam moaned into my mouth and tightened his grip around my body. Without breaking our kiss he lifted me up, sliding his strong hands down to grab my backside. I spread my thighs for his hips, and he carried me to the window, pushing me up against the glass.

Breathing heavily now, he ripped his lips from mine and pressed them to my throat instead, kissing down my neck with fevered heat. When he got to my shoulder, he tugged the robe off me. It pooled around my hips and then fell to the floor when he shifted his grip on me, leaving me naked against the cool surface of the window.

"Liam... people can see us," I moaned when he sucked a pebbled nipple into the hot cavern of his mouth.

"Let them watch." His voice was deep and raspy and sent sharp sparks of urgency to my core. Used muscles clenched, and I felt myself dampen for him, my body responding to his need like a finely tuned violin.

I let my head fall back against the window with a whimper of surrender. For the first time in my life, I didn't care if anyone saw me be something less than perfect.

Saw *me*.

Something hot and hard nudged against my sex, and my opening softened in welcome. I bit my lip and braced for what I knew was coming.

He pushed the head of his broad cock inside in one, smooth thrust, and it stretched me so perfectly with its core of steel wrapped in silky softness.

It felt even better than it had before.

"*Fuck*." I clenched my hands uselessly against the impulse to ignore my brain's sudden arrival. "Condom."

Liam's swearing was quite a bit more adventurous than mine. It took him a few deep breaths before he found the strength to pull out and release me.

I slid to the floor with an involuntary whimper of disappointment, but I wasn't alone for long. Liam pretty much sprinted to the bedroom and was back within twenty seconds, foil package in hand. He ripped it open and slid the rubber on, fisting his girthy hardness with one hand. With an impatient grunt he lifted me back up against the window with his free arm and pushed fully inside of me in one smooth stroke.

I whimpered, the back of my head connecting with cool glass once more as my pussy fluttered around the intrusion. My few but thorough experiences with Liam's frankly intimidating size had awakened a previously unknown hunger in me, a hunger to be forced as wide as possible. Something about the sensation of being taken so completely sent my mind spinning and drove my body past the brink of ecstasy.

Still, it was a harsh stretch, and it took me a moment to accommodate him without discomfort.

"Fuck, you feel so good," Liam growled against my throat. "How do you feel so fucking *good?*" He wrapped both arms tight around my waist, settling me fully on his cock as he took my weight. Buried his face at the side of my neck. And then rolled his hips up.

"God! Liam!" His body moved underneath me, forcing inch after delicious inch into my tight heat, grinding against my G-spot on every reverse movement. It was maddening bliss, and I clung to my lover as the world faded to bland nothingness, leaving him my only anchor to sanity.

"*Liam!* Liam, I lo—" He swallowed my voice with a scorching kiss that had my toes curling against his hamstrings and my fingers clutching at his hair. The roll of his hips turned harder, forcing me to focus on only the molten, sweltering sensation of the animalistic ecstasy being pressed into me.

He'd been an intense lover every time we'd joined before, but this time was different. There was something desperate underneath the rhythm of his body, in his searing kiss and in the strength of his grip as he held me to him as if he was scared I'd disappear. It made my heart swell until it ached and my body move against him to bring the relief he was chasing with every thrust of his cock into me.

I don't know how long we fucked up against the window, lost to anything but the desperate yearning wound tight in the gasped breaths between us. I only snapped out of the hypnotic bliss when Liam shifted his grip on me so he could press a thumb against my clit.

"*Fuck!*" My vision exploded and my pussy clamped down hard. My climax came roaring up from the tips of my toes, and when Liam grunted, "*Give me everything, love,*" into my ear, I lost myself. I came screaming his name, my core clutching on his thick length as he gave me the last few, hard thrusts until he joined me with a low moan that sounded somewhere between pain and pleasure.

It was only several minutes later, when I slowly came down to the sensation of Liam softening inside of me and his lips pressing gentle kisses to my shoulder, that I realized I'd almost told him I loved him.

ELEVEN

LIAM

It was only just past sunrise when I rolled out of Audrey's bed to look for my pants.

I found them within seconds and pulled them on as quietly as I could so as not to disturb her.

She lay curled up on her side with her dark hair spread out over the pillow in a messy fan and most of her soft skin covered by the duvet. There was still an imprint in the bedding next to her where I'd been holding her close all night.

Looking at her made my chest tight, and I rubbed distractedly at it before I turned to find the rest of my clothes.

I'd done this thousands of times before—gotten out of bed after a hot night with a bird before she ever woke up, if I wasn't in the mood to deal with any promises I may or may not have made while in the heat of the moment.

Neither of us had said anything last night, but what'd happened between us wasn't just a regular shag. I'd screwed plenty of girls, many of them more than once, and nothing had ever felt like last night. I couldn't put words to why my heart felt too light and too heavy at the same time, but I knew that at some point during that fuck, we'd crossed a boundary. As I'd laid with her in my arms after, listening to her breathing turn slow and steady, I'd felt... at peace. More than the kind of satiated relaxation I always got after a good shag. Different from the instinctive sense of calm I got from having Louis near me.

It was the kind of peace I'd seen in Blaine's eyes when he looked at Mira as if it was just the two of them in the world, and the implication made my gut clench.

I couldn't afford to care for a girl right now, not with how fucked up everything with our Family was. If anyone found out about her, she'd be in constant danger.

And then there was the fact that neither Louis nor I had ever really been too bothered about any of the girls we'd been with.

We'd had so many one-night stands and short affairs neither of us would likely be able to recall even a third of the women's faces. Many of them we'd both been with without their knowledge. The one thing that was always a guarantee was that, by the end of it, it was just Louis and I. Even with our large family, even when our mum was alive, to some extent it'd been just me and Louis from the day we were born. We were two parts of the same whole, and if something ever dented the bond we shared, I wasn't sure I'd ever be whole again.

No. Whatever it was about Audrey that felt so good, I'd need to put a stop to it right the fuck now, or things would get too complicated. I didn't like complicated, especially not when I was already trying to orchestrate my own father's goddamn murder.

I walked over to the bedroom door, intent on getting out of there and away from the turmoil of unaccustomed emotions rolling in my gut, but something made me hesitate before I stepped over the threshold. I glanced at the sleeping woman over my shoulder and my chest tightened harder around my lungs.

I'd never really worried about what the girl I ditched felt like when she woke up alone. Most of them probably expected it—I knew I didn't exactly give off the most commitment-happy impression. But Audrey would be hurt, I knew that much. She'd clearly not had a no-strings fling before.

I grimaced at the memory of how she'd asked to see me again—told me she needed it. I should have said no then. I was going to, but the vulnerability that had radiated off her despite her best attempt at seeming unfazed had kicked me in the gut like no amount of tears from other girls had ever managed to. And hell, I'd *wanted* to see her again. Badly.

Fuck.

I walked back to the bed, to her side, and bent to gently shake her bare shoulder. "Audrey."

"Mmm." She groaned in protest but cracked an eyelid. "Hmm?"

"I have to go," I said.

She frowned, clearly fighting the haze of sleep. "Is something wrong?"

"No, love. Just need to go deal with some business," I fibbed. "Just go back to sleep."

"Mmm," she agreed, her eyes closing as she buried deeper into the pillow. "See you later."

"Yeah," I lied. "See you later." I bent to brush a kiss over her temple. She sighed in response, and my chest constricted again.

When I shut her front door behind me a moment later, an elderly lady was just getting out of the door opposite Audrey's, a small, poofy dog on a leash by her side. A flash of our first night against that door made my lips twitch.

"Lovely morning to be doing the walk of shame, eh?" I greeted her with a wink.

Her lips pinched up as a scandalized look passed across her round face. She looked me up and down with obvious disdain. "I see Miss Waits has taken to bringing ruffians home. That's what comes of young women living on their own—they start keeping questionable company. Not that you would care what having your sort loitering on the premises does to the property value."

She ignored my amused grin with a huff as she turned away from me and started down the stairs.

I trailed after her down the stairs, both hands in my pockets. "Sure, love. Property value's nothing to joke about. Not that I necessarily agree that a bird getting a bit of action will crash the market. Does your flat lose value every time your husband gives you a good roger-ing, hmm?"

We'd reached the ground floor. The old biddy turned around to me, and I thought she was gonna give me a good tongue lashing. I didn't notice her bag in her leash-free hand before she'd swung it at me with a surprising amount of force for her age. It hit me square in the face with a heavy thump.

"You need to learn respect for your elders, you delinquent! I shall be having words with Miss Waits about her taste in gentleman callers." She turned her back to me with another look of disdain and exited the building with her head held high and the poofy dog in tow.

I rubbed my sore face, chuckling despite what felt like a shiner beginning to bloom around my left eye. Okay, so maybe I'd deserved that, but *damn*.

"DID YOU GET INTO A *FIGHT?*"

I sighed at the incredulous tone in my twin's voice when I entered our kitchen and saw him sitting by the cafe table with a cup of coffee.

"Nah. You're up early. Or is it late?" I walked to the coffee machine and poured myself a mug.

"Mate, you're sporting a black eye. There's no way we're going to pretend that's not a thing. What the hell happened?" His lips quirked up at the corners. "Did one of your lady friends spot you out with someone else?"

I grimaced at the uncomfortable twang in my chest at the thought of Audrey. I determinedly pushed it away. "Some old biddy called me a delinquent and smacked me with her handbag." I sipped the too-hot coffee and rested against the kitchen counter. "I had it coming."

Louis snorted with amusement. "I'm sure you did. Ah, what I wouldn't have given to see that."

"Harsh." I put my coffee-free hand to my chest in mock-hurt. "And you call yourself my brother."

My twin grinned, his eyes twinkling. "Where were you, anyway? New girl, or the little prude who made you limp earlier in the week?"

"Same girl."

Something in my voice must have tipped him off,

because his smile faded somewhat and his eyes narrowed. "What's going on?"

Bloody twin-bond. Sometimes it was really fucking inconvenient that lying to each other was nearly impossible. "Nothing's going on. What about you? Hooked up with someone I should have a go at, too?"

I wasn't expecting the twinge of disgust in my gut at uttering that question, and I hid my frown from Louis by taking another sip of coffee. Since when did the thought of fucking a bird Louis had pulled give me anything other than a mild thrill from knowing she'd never realize she was getting screwed by both of us?

Fucking hell.

Louis gave me a long look, and I knew he wasn't buying my "nothing" claims, but he obviously decided against pushing me. For now. "Well, I figured one of us should probably get some rest before we try and get the Perkinson on board tomorrow, so no."

I bit the inside of my cheek at the subject change. "We're really doing this, aren't we? Setting Dad up."

"Yeah." Louis dragged his fingers through his messy, ginger hair, and I knew the pained expression on his face perfectly mirrored my own. "We have to. None of us are safe as long as he's alive."

"I know," I said, pushing down the wave of sadness. We'd both felt the sting of William Steel's leather belt growing up, but I knew our older brothers—especially Jeremy—had run interference, oftentimes taking a beating to save us. As a result, we hadn't felt as much of his infamous violence on our own bodies as our brothers, and I knew we had a better relationship with our father than they did as a result. But any lingering sense of family bond to him had died when we learned what he'd done to Isaac and Jeremy.

Everything for the Family was the Steel motto, and we'd done so much terrible shit over the years to protect our father's interests, up to and including killing men who'd betrayed the Family. Justifying it with unwavering loyalty to the Steel name. But it'd all been a lie.

The man we called Father had murdered his eldest son and betrayed another, and in doing so, he'd killed any justification we'd clung to in order to do the work he expected of his sons. There was no more Steel Family—not as long as we let a monster rule us.

"You must forgive me... I find myself mildly skeptical that the mighty William Steel's favorite sons would waltz into my home and ask my help in assassinating their beloved father... I'm sure you understand." Brian Perkinson, the patriarch of the Perkinson Family, steepled his fingers as he regarded Louis and I from the other side of his wide desk.

I managed to conceal my grimace with a smirk. We hadn't exactly "*waltzed in.*" Getting into Perkinson's estate for this meeting had been a fucking *Mission Impossible*-style endeavor, to make absolutely sure no one saw us entering.

"Our father's reputed to be many things, but *beloved's* never been one of them," I said.

He arched an eyebrow at me. "Perhaps not. But the Steels are quite famous for their motto... *Everything for the Family,* isn't it? Now what could possibly have made you two forget that pretty little proverb?"

Louis and I exchanged glances. It wasn't easy, saying it out loud to someone outside of the Family. To someone who'd spent the past few months looking for a way to overthrow the Steel empire and likely kill all of us in the process.

"He had our brother murdered. Double-crossed another and let him rot in jail. None of us are liking the possibility that we might be next on that list." Louis' voice was quiet, but firm. "We still stand by our Family motto, Brian, do not think anything differently. It's he who's chosen another path."

Perkinson whistled low. "Well, I'll be damned. So that's what happened with Isaac? I did wonder why William seemed incapable of pulling the right strings to get him off with a slap on the wrist. And the murder... Marcus?"

"No," Louis said.

"Jeremy," I continued, steeling myself against the gut-punch of pain talking about the loss of our oldest brother still delivered.

"He covered it up by telling everyone he'd left for the States to deal with some overseas business. Marcus fled the country to avoid a similar fate," Louis finished.

Perkinson leaned forward a bit. The interest was clear on his shrewd face. "And you have proof of this?"

I lobbed a folder on his desk. "Of the Isaac thing,

yes. There was a recording of our father ordering Jeremy's murder."

"It was lost in the fight with Brigs a few months ago," Louis said.

"Hmm." Perkinson flicked through the folder, an eyebrow arching as he got to a couple of CCTV print-offs. Finally, he closed the folder and looked at us.

"All right. Say I believe your motive. I take it you're here because you need manpower. What do I get out of putting my men's lives on the line?"

"Forty-five percent." Louis said.

"You will rule London with us and our brothers. Once our father is dead," I continued.

"Seems to me you have quite a long ways to go before your father is, indeed, dead. If you want my help with it, how about we say seventy-five percent." Brian Perkinson leaned back in his chair and raised both eyebrows at us. "Because if you'd had any other choice, you'd never have sought outside help for this little endeavor."

"Forty-five." Louis' voice was as cold as the steel our Family was named for. "Because if you say anything other than yes, you know you'll never get a foothold in this city. We know you've been trying for months to find a way to take our Family out. Wanna know why we haven't smacked you down yet? Because you're no threat to the Steel empire. You haven't got the strength, Brian, and you never will. Not without us. We only come to you because the other minor Families have gathered around you. It's a courtesy. We could easily have gone to any of their patriarchs and offered them the same deal, and you fucking know they'd snatch it up with both hands and turn their backs on you. And, once the dust's settled, they'd be the Family who got to rule alongside us. Wanna continue playing in the gutter like a rat?"

"Or are you ready to step up to the fucking silver platter we're offering you?" I finished, folding my arms across my chest and leveling him with my best *Steel* glare. I knew my twin and I had a reputation for being the most easygoing of William Steel's sons, but any British criminal worth their salt knew you only pushed a Steel so far.

Brian's eyes narrowed and his jaw tightened, but after a few seconds, he nodded. "Fine. Forty-five percent. But I need to see some commitment from you before I lend you so much as a cup of fucking sugar."

Louis and I exchanged a glance. We'd expected as much.

"S'long as we can keep it below the radar, you've got the Steel empire available, Perkinson. What do you need?"

He pulled out a folder from a drawer in his desk and slid it across. I opened it and saw a printed-off picture of a man's face on top of a small pile of papers.

"I need this guy gone. And I need you to see to it, personally."

I pressed down the numb sensation spreading from my gut to my limbs. A hit. Of course he wanted a hit. It was the number one way of showing loyalty in our world—once you took a man's life for someone, they had you in their palm.

"What's he done?" Louis asked, when I couldn't take my gaze off the picture. He looked like your standard thug: bad skin, broad neck, cold eyes.

"Thought he could skim a couple of thousand off the top on the latest heist he did for me. I need to send a signal to the rest of my men. You know how it goes."

We did know. It was just how it went in our world—a life was not worth more than a measly few thousand pounds, not when loyalty was on the line.

I'd killed before for the same reason—both Louis and I had. And every single time I'd hated it with every fiber of my being. I'd done it, because it was "*for the Family.*" Or so I'd told myself, when I'd wake up in the middle of the night with the memories of men I'd murdered haunting my dreams.

This time, it'd be a man who'd never crossed me in any way.

I stared at the picture and wished with everything I was that I could have been someone else.

"We've got a deal." Louis' voice didn't betray the emotion I knew was tightening his chest as he leant over the desk and shook Perkinson's hand. I knew he felt like I did, though we'd never talk about it—I knew we wouldn't. Talking about it made it too fucking real.

I also knew he always cried in the dark solitude of his room after a hit.

I dragged my eyes from the image, inviting the numbness to spread into my chest as I looked at our new ally. If we wanted to save ourselves and our brothers from our father, this was something we had to do. *For the Family.* Only this time, it wasn't a meaningless motto spoken to keep us in line.

"We'll take care of it."

NORMAN WALLIS SAT SLUMPED in the chair we'd tied him to not twenty minutes ago, blood and brain matter leaking from the hole in his temple.

He'd begged for his life. They didn't always. Sometimes they threatened and cursed, and that was so much fucking easier to deal with.

I glanced at Louis, who slung back the first of what I knew would be many drinks, leaning against a crate in the abandoned warehouse we often used for this part of the business.

"Jeff's on cleanup," I said, purely to fill the silence that'd echoed through the space since Norman had uttered his last plea.

"Please, I have a son," had been his last words. I didn't know if it was true or not. Not that it mattered.

I looked at the gun in my hand and bit my lip at the faint tremble making it shake in my palm.

The far door into the warehouse slid open with a rumble and Jeff stepped through, his helper Fred in tow. They were carrying plastic wrapping and buckets filled with what I knew to be chemicals.

"I'm off. See you in the morning, yeah?" Louis looked at me over his shoulder for the shortest moment before he nodded at our men and strode off.

I stared after him, wishing he'd stay and knowing how fucking terrible it would be if he did. That was the one downside of our twin-bond—that we always knew, without a shadow of a doubt, what the other was feeling. And right now, neither of us wanted to feel anything. Even if the darkness seemed to press in all around me, and I needed him so fucking bad. He was my safe place, the only peace I knew, and *fuck,* I needed peace from the horror screaming in my brain more than I needed the air in my lungs.

An uninvited image flickered through my brain.

I breathed out through my nose, frowning at the floor as the memory of how fucking good I'd felt with Audrey in my arms last week. How confoundedly calm I'd been. At peace.

No.

No fucking way.

I'd already made my decision when it came to her. My world was too dark, too bloody dangerous. And this kind of shit was exactly the reason why I needed to stay the fuck away from her. She was way too gentle a woman to get dragged into my shit, just because I needed to hold someone to get through the night.

I threw my gun on the nearest wooden box and flexed my tensed hand to erase the feeling of the metal against my palm.

A soft thud from where Jeff and Fred were rolling the body into a black tarp drew my attention, and I bit the inside of my cheek until I tasted blood as I saw them roll Norman Wallis up like a dead fish.

If he did have a son, he'd never know what'd happened to his father. There'd be no body to identify, no grave to visit.

No final resting place for the man I'd killed to save my Family.

"Liam?" I stared up at the redhead outside my door and wished I was wearing something other than my ugly pajama pants and food-stained T-shirt.

I hadn't heard from him in almost a week, he hadn't responded to the text I'd sent after three days of obsessively staring at my silent phone, and I'd thought... I'd thought I'd never see him again. But here he was, leaning against my doorframe in that casual way he had, as if I hadn't just spent a week trying to desperately glue my broken heart back together.

"Hey, love," he said, and then he reached for me. His hot lips crashed against mine with a desperate urgency I hadn't expected, and I opened my mouth for him on instinct when his tongue swept against the seam. He pulled me close against his body, his hands curving around my backside until all I could feel was his heat and the hardness of his body against mine.

Only when he dipped his hands into my pants did I find the will to pull away.

"Liam—"

"I'm sorry I didn't call," he interrupted, his hands tightening around me as if he couldn't bear to let me go. His gray eyes, dark with a desperation that didn't reflect pure sexual need, swept over my face, the plea in them impossible to ignore. "I'm so sorry."

"What's wrong?" I asked, worry making its way through the shock of seeing him and the ache of longing in my stupid heart. "Did something happen?"

"Nothing you can't fix," he said, his voice hoarse. When he pulled me tight against himself and buried his nose in my messy hair, I didn't resist. Not until his hands delved back into my pants.

"Liam... I can't," I mumbled into his leather coat as I clasped onto his wrists to stop his advances. "It's that time of the month."

He pulled back enough to frown down at me. "What do you mean?"

I arched an eyebrow at his obvious ignorance. Guess a player like him rarely hung around a girl long enough to experience that side of things. "I'm on my period."

"Oh." His stroking hands didn't stop, but he gave me a quick glance. "I don't mind. I just..." Liam paused, regret flickering across his taut face and he finally stilled. "You're not feeling good, are you?"

I gave him a pained smile. Apparently the dark circles under my eyes were more pronounced than I'd thought. "Sorry, no. I won't be up for that sort of thing for a few days. If you'd called first, I would have—"

He touched a hand to my cheek, silencing me. "I know, I'm an arsehole. I'm sorry, Audrey. I didn't mean to just show up on your doorstep like this."

Something had happened. As he stood in my doorway, that inner joy he'd always seemed to radiate was gone, and he looked so... lost. Scared.

I reached out and grabbed his hand. He followed me when I pulled him into the hallway and shut the door after him, but when I began guiding him to the bedroom, he stopped, still with his large, warm hand clasped in mine.

"No, you're not up for it, love. It's okay."

I sent him an admonishing look and tugged on his arm until he followed me again.

"Audrey..." he said once I stopped next to my bed. Despite his objection, I could hear the longing in his voice.

I raised up on my tiptoes so I could press a gentle kiss to his lips, and then I sank to my knees in front of him. Comprehension dawned on his face, and the look of gratitude flittering across his features nearly took my breath away.

I hadn't done this with him before, despite the many times he'd brought me over with his skilled tongue. He hadn't asked, and I'd been too busy recovering from the onslaught of sensations he poured over my body whenever we'd been together to think of it. But now... The sound his zipper made when I lowered it made anticipation trickle down my spine. I pulled his already half-hard length out, and he breathed a harsh gasp that made me clench. My abdomen gave a small spasm in warning, making me grimace at the dull pain.

"You okay?" Liam closed his hands around my face, tipping it up a bit so he could catch my gaze.

"I'm fine." I turned my head to kiss his palm and then, I wrapped my hand around his cock. "Just relax and let me take care of you."

Liam hissed in response and released my face.

He felt heavy and so warm against my palm. The silky soft skin grew taut as he rapidly grew to full size, pulsing in my hand with the deep thrum of his heartbeat.

Smiling at his obvious need, I swiped my tongue out and gave him a lick from the frenulum, up over the broad rim, and around the head before I opened my mouth fully and took him in. My jaw protested at having to open so wide, but the raw moan that tore from Liam's throat drowned out any discomfort. When I moved my head further down, his hands found my hair.

"Audrey." It was a hoarse whisper, and when I

glanced up, I saw his eyes were clenched shut, his whole body tense with strain, but the hands in my hair never pulled or forced. He just kept them there while I moved my lips up and down his thick shaft, tangling in the messy strands as he moaned.

I didn't tease him, could sense he needed the release rather than prolonged pleasure, so I worked his cock rhythmically, up and down, over and over, until his breathing was fast and shallow and his hands tugged on my hair.

"I'm close," he grunted, and I was about to move away and finish him off with my hand when I looked up and saw the intense *pain* in his eyes, so completely raw and unfiltered it hit me like nothing had before.

Logically, looking back, the instinctual urge to soothe whatever it was that hurt him so badly shouldn't have made me want finish him with my mouth, but for some inexplicable reason, it did. I wanted him to give me his pain, his desperation, his torment, until he had nothing left, and so I sucked him hard while he groaned and came.

The salty taste of his essence filled my mouth, making me swallow on reflex as I stilled my movements and braced against his thighs.

"Audrey..." His voice was softer now, but still ragged with his panted breath. "You didn't have to do that."

I let his softening cock slide out of my mouth, giving the head a peck before I looked up at him. "I wanted to."

He released my hair and stroked a thumb over my lips. And then his face cracked with grief and he slumped to his knees in front of me. I don't know if he reached for me before I reached for him, but soon, he clung to me while sobs wracked his strong body.

I held him for the better part of an hour, silently stroking his back until eventually, his sobs quieted and turned to slow, deep breaths.

"Do you want to talk about it?" I asked when he finally pulled his head up from my shoulder to look at me.

"I can't." Liam's gaze locked in mine, and my stomach flopped at the emotion in his eyes. But it wasn't pain anymore. It was something else, something that made my heart ache.

"I'm sorry I came to you like this. After not calling for nearly a week. You deserved better."

I shrugged, trying not to show him how much I'd longed for him, like some stupid teenager with a crush. "It's okay, it's not like we're anything more than friends with benefits, I get it."

Liam shook his head and reached for my hand so he could interlock our fingers. "I thought we agreed there wouldn't be any bullshit between us."

I opened my mouth to protest, but he continued before I could. "I'm not good at this. I've never... I've not cared for a girl like I do you before. I don't know how to be your boyfriend."

Boyfriend.

The word hung in the air between us, suspended by the silence as my heart took an extra couple of beats.

"Do... do you *want* to be?" I asked, unable to quell my incredulous tone. One thing I'd been certain of from the very first moment I saw Liam Steel was that he was a player. Multiple women, no commitments... everything about him screamed that I should stay away, that he wasn't what I was looking for. And yet I'd known I needed him like I needed the sun since that first date.

And I'd known I was in love with him since our last night together.

I'd tried to suppress it, because I knew only heartbreak lay down that path. Until he stood in my door with pain written across his face. Pain, and a yearning that mirrored my own.

Boyfriend.

Liam grimaced. "Audrey... I'm not one of the good guys. And I don't want you to get hurt."

"I think it's too late for that," I said softly. "I... there's something about you that I..."

"I know. I feel it too." He rubbed his free hand across his face and drew in a deep breath. When he looked at me again, there was more of his old self back in his gaze. "I need you to tell me... if you could choose... if you'd never met me that day in the park, you'd continue on with your life as always, and you'd be safe. Or... we were together, but... something awful might happen. You might get hurt. Which would you choose?"

I wrinkled my nose at his cryptic question. "Something awful?"

"If King Kong suddenly climbed the Eye, or giant spiders roamed the streets," he said, as if that explained anything.

"Ew. Giant spiders, really?" I shuddered.

Liam made a vague hand gesture. "It was the worst I could come up with off the top of my head."

I sighed. "I'd probably take the spiders. But I'd also never leave my apartment again."

He smiled, but there was a touch of strain in the set of his sensual lips. "I need you to be sure, love."

"Why? What's this about, Liam?"

He rubbed his face again and exhaled deeply. "It's about me being a selfish fuck. I don't want to leave you alone, even though I know I should. It's not fucking fair! I've never felt like I do with you in my arms, nothing's ever felt this goddamn *right*, but I... if you get hurt because I can't stay away, then I..."

"I can't even tell you, that's the most fucked up thing. Just know that... if we keep seeing each other, I can't promise you... There is a very real chance you could end up getting hurt. And I need you to tell me that that's not a risk you're willing to take. I need you to tell me to leave, because I don't think I can do it if you don't."

I put my free hand on top of his and looked into his eyes, searching for what I'd been too scared to even hope to find there. Until tonight. And I found it. This was the man I was meant to be with. This redheaded player with his easy smile and his demons he couldn't tell me about. This was it. *He* was it.

"Liam, I don't care. I just want to be with you."

"Audrey—"

"No. I don't care. No bullshit, remember? You asked me to choose, and I did. I pick you, spiders and all. Just promise me... promise me this isn't just some fling for you, okay? Because I..." I paused, not quite capable of saying the words even though everything inside me ached to tell him. But it was too much, too soon.

I love you.

"If we're doing this, I want it to be the real deal. I can't... I can't do casual."

He smiled then, but despite the relief in his eyes I saw the sadness in the set of his full lips. "I don't want casual, either. But I wish you'd choose differently."

I shook my head, pinching my lips with determination. "It's not a choice."

"I know," he rasped, before he pulled me into a kiss. It was soft and tender, and it made warmth flood through my veins and fill my blood with a happiness I couldn't remember ever feeling before. When he withdrew, there was nothing left of the confusion and worry in my body. Only the warm buzz of the joy I'd always felt whenever he was near me.

"So we're doing this?" I confirmed.

"Yeah," he said. "We are."

I gave Liam a wide smile before I climbed into his lap. My *boyfriend's* lap. "Guess that means you're coming with me to my dad's birthday dinner, huh?"

FOURTEEN
LOUIS

"Where are you off to?" I raised my eyebrows at my twin as he walked into the kitchen, wearing a pressed shirt and smart jeans. Not completely unusual attire for him, but he looked somehow... neater than usual. And he was fiddling with his cuff, like he usually did when he was nervous.

"Audrey's dad's birthday," he said with a grimace.

Audrey.

My stomach dropped with uncomfortable foreboding. The little prude he'd picked up from a pub a few weeks ago. I hadn't asked, but I knew that's where he'd been sleeping most nights this past week. With *her.*

This was the longest he'd ever been with a girl before—that either of us had, and I wasn't stupid. He liked her. Fuck, he was going to a goddamn family birthday with her now? He more than liked her.

Worry mixed with something else, something dark and painful I didn't want to prod further twisted in my gut. We both knew we couldn't afford distractions right now, and getting attached to a bird was about the dumbest fucking thing he could have done. Soon as you cared for someone, they became a weakness. Just look at fucking Marcus—he'd only narrowly avoided death because he lost his head when his girl was in danger.

If that happened to Liam...

The dark thing in my gut clenched and snarled at the thought.

If that happened, I could lose him.

"You've been seeing her a lot lately," I said, keeping my tone casual.

He shot me a quick glance, and I could tell from the look in his eyes that I hadn't managed to hide my worry completely.

"Yeah. She's a good distraction."

"Mmhm," I hummed, not buying it for a second. Multiple birds were fine distractions—one was fucking trouble. "You in love with her?"

If I hadn't known him so well, I would have missed the millisecond his fingers froze against his cuff.

"Nah, it's nothing serious. Don't worry." He gave me a brilliant smile before he turned his back on me and headed to the hallway, grabbing his leather jacket on the way. "See you later!"

The front door slammed shut behind him, and I frowned into the silence that settled in our shared flat.

That was the first time my twin had ever lied to me.

I PARKED FAR ENOUGH AWAY from the door Liam had disappeared into that when he came back out again ten minutes later hand in hand with a woman, he didn't spot me. Not that he would have noticed much, the way he was looking down at her as if there was only the two of them in the entire fucking world.

The dark thing in my gut twisted when he stopped to brush a lock of her hair away from her forehead. The look on his face, then... of complete and utter worship. He loved her. He loved her the same way Blaine loved his wife, the same way Marcus loved the girl he threw everything away to be with.

It was like a mule-kick right in my sternum, and I had to clench my hands around the steering wheel until my knuckles turned white to keep myself from keeling over at the strength of the panic that tore through me at that look.

A tsunami of emotions warred inside that black pit in my gut, but at the root of it all was all-consuming, mind-numbing *fear*. Fear of losing the one person in this world that had kept me from giving in to the violence and despair that was our birthright. Fear of being left alone when she either got my twin killed, or if... I breathed deeply when the wave of jealousy so hot it burned my esophagus clawed its way to the surface.

If this was it for him, if that girl was to Liam what Mira was to Blaine, or Evelyn to Marcus... Then even if we somehow made it through the fight against our father, I would still lose him. It wouldn't be him and me against the world anymore. She would take my place, and I...

I knew I'd never survive that.

FIFTEEN

LIAM

Audrey's parents lived a couple of hours outside of London in the sort of neighborhood I'd always mocked: white-washed villas, roses in the front garden, and Audis in the driveway. It reeked of upper middle class and weekend golf trips.

I glanced to the woman next to me, conscious of her bouncing knee and the way she was worrying her bottom lip. "Nervous?"

She flashed me a quick smile. "A little bit, yeah. I know it's silly. It's just... I want them to like you. And they're so judgmental. Is that awful to say? Everything's got to be a certain way, or it's not up to their standards."

"Miss Waits, are you implying I'm not every parent's wet dream?" I shot her a teasing smirk that had her giggling and finally releasing her poor bottom lip.

"I'm implying that you're very obviously not a rich

banker looking to settle down and give my parents two point four grandkids so they can show off to their friends at the golf club."

I huffed. As far as I was concerned, bankers were about the only people more corrupt than my Family. "Ah. They don't appreciate a man who can give their daughter multiple orgasms, then? Pity, I was gonna lead with that."

Audrey's smile vanished, a look of abject horror taking its place. "Don't even joke about it. Liam, you can't say stuff like that to them, okay? They're not..."

"Fun?" I finished, arching an eyebrow at her. "Concerned about your happiness?"

She flushed a light shade of pink and looked down. "I'm sorry. I don't mean to push all my issues onto you. I know it's ridiculous—I'm thirty-two years old and I still crave my parents' approval. I just never lived up to their expectations, or to my sister's golden life, and it still messes with me sometimes."

I took one hand off the steering wheel to brush her cheek. "Hey, calm down, love. You're fucking amazing, and if they can't see that, they're right thick. I don't care if they like me or not—but I do care that you're happy. I'll be on my best behavior, promise."

The corner of her lips quirked up, and my heart gave a happy spasm. Fuck, she was so goddamn beautiful when she smiled.

"You know, the thing I love about you is that you're

exactly the opposite of what I was brought up with. I don't need you to be on your best behavior—I just need you to be with me."

My heart pounded harder in my chest once more, and I sank back in my seat with a soft sigh. It'd been a week since we'd started an actual relationship, and every moment we'd been together had been so fucking easy. When I was with her, even the shit going on with Perkinson and the plotting with Blaine and Louis felt like a distant nightmare. Audrey was my safe haven.

If impressing some pricks who thought their daughter needed to fit into some godawful mould of mediocrity would make her happy, then I didn't mind playing along.

The Waits' house was a detached villa like all the others in the neighborhood, with green privet hedges surrounding a lush garden. I pulled up in front of their driveway and parked the Jeep within view of the villa's large windows. Telling Audrey to wait, I slipped out of the car and walked around to her side, opening the passenger side door and offering her my arm.

She giggled as she let me help her out, flashing me a happy smile before we turned toward the house, and my heart did an odd flip in my chest. I might just be fronting to give anyone looking a good impression, but being like this with Audrey... like an actual couple... it felt amazing. Like everything was just right.

She rang the doorbell once we made it to the front

door, and it was opened so quickly I knew the woman opening it had been looking out the window at us as we approached. Nosy bird.

She looked a bit older than Audrey by a couple of years, with the same dark hair and brown eyes. Her sister, I guessed, even though they didn't share the same amazing arse.

"Hey, Mel." Audrey leaned in to give her sister a cheek kiss. "Mel, this is Liam. Liam, Mel. My sister."

"Me*lissa*," her sister corrected as she shook my hand. "Forgive my sister, she's not always good with proper introductions."

I arched my eyebrows a millimeter at the unnecessary insult, but before either I or Audrey could say anything, another woman came fluttering into the hallway.

She was older still, with immaculately cut shoulder-length hair in what would've looked like a natural blonde, if it wasn't for her age. She was small and thin with features like Melissa, but the smile on her face was all Audrey. Their mother, I guessed.

"Mum," Audrey said, confirming my suspicion as she hugged her. "I want you to meet Liam Steel. Liam, this is my mother, Margaret."

"Ah, the boyfriend?" Margaret extended a hand and I shook it, stopping myself from giving her a sturdy *"business"* greeting the second before I closed my fingers. The only time I was usually shaking hands with people was during meetings with other mafia Families. They usually involved quite a bit of strength—another way of displaying dominance.

"Yes," Audrey confirmed. Her slight hesitance and the quick sideway glance she gave me made me fight back a smirk. Yeah, I wasn't used to being called *"the boyfriend,"* and we hadn't put what we were into exact terms. It was obvious Audrey wasn't quite sure what I'd think of being labeled her boyfriend, but—somewhat to my own surprise—I didn't mind it one bit.

"A pleasure to meet you, Mrs. Waits." I noticed Audrey's impressed side-glance. Someone clearly didn't expect me to be the kind of guy who knew how to kiss up to my girl's parents. I gave her mother my best smile as I patted her hand still resting in mine.

"Oh, please, call me Margaret." A faint flush warmed her cheeks, and she pulled her hand back with a slightly jolted movement. I shot her a wider grin, suppressing the urge to give her a knowing wink. Somehow I doubted Audrey would appreciate me teasing her mum about falling for the infamous *"Steel-twin"* smile. It wasn't often on purpose, but quite a few women we'd shagged over the years had fallen into our beds because of it. And more than one had been at Audrey's mother's age.

"Come in, Peter and Sally are here, and the Joneses and Smiths." Margaret seemed to have regained her bearings and ushered us into the living room. "Phil? Come greet your daughter and her friend."

I arched an eyebrow at Audrey upon hearing her mother's title for me in the slightly larger group of people filling the living room. She shot me a grin in return. "I'm too old to have boyfriends. Women over the age of twenty-seven have *husbands* or *friends*," she explained in a hushed tone as a balding man about Margaret's age made his way toward us with a jovial smile and a glass of amber liquor in his hand.

"Audrey." He hugged her with his drink-free hand before looking at me, his smile fading somewhat. "Mr. Steel."

"Mr. Waits," I greeted, offering him my hand. The handshake I got in return made my bones groan. Apparently it wasn't just in the mafia world you displayed your dominance with a handshake. Clearly Audrey's dad was somewhat less enthused about meeting me than her mother had been.

"My daughter tells me you own a couple of businesses," he said, and I got the distinct impression of getting evaluated by an opponent. "Aren't you a little young to run a business?"

I ignored the dig at my age—no wonder Audrey'd been focused on the few years' age gap between us if this was where she came from—and gave him my best smile. "Audrey's been much too generous. It's a family business—I only own a part of it."

"Oh," he said, a slight gleam of interest showing in his gaze. "So you come from a good family, then? What do you trade in?"

I suppressed a snort at the suggestion that my family was any kind of *good*. Sure, we might still have a tentative grasp of London's underworld's throne, but I was pretty sure no man would be thrilled to know his daughter was dating a mafia son. "We do a few things. I'm mainly involved in the nightclubs and bars."

"Hm." The hesitance on his face was clearly visible —apparently nightclubs weren't quite fancy enough, but the promise of family money was seemingly still strong enough to spare me his full scorn.

It was interesting to watch, on some level. I'd known Audrey was pretty uptight from the first moment we met. I'd never thought much about why. Seeing her family, and especially her dad, made it pretty clear her messed up ideas of what was important in life came from them. It baffled me how they could look at a woman like Audrey and never think she measured up— but then again, my Family had its own yardsticks that others would think fucked up. If you were a Steel, you'd better be tough and know how to handle a situation —*any* situation—or you were toast. It didn't matter that Louis and I hated the darker sides of the business, or that they'd driven Marcus nearly fucking insane. Our father had raised us to rule or die.

I guess by comparison I could give Audrey's dad a bit of slack—if only for Audrey's sake.

Still smiling, I wrapped an arm around Audrey's midriff and pulled her in closer against me. "Of course, my family was thrilled when they heard about Audrey. She's the smartest bird I've ever met—and they seem to believe that she will give up her job and put that brain of hers to work for us if I manage to keep a hold of her."

I knew I'd won him over when his lips finally pulled up in a genuine smile. "Oh, of course. She is a very smart girl, her mother and I've always said as much. Tell me—Liam, was it? Do you golf?"

"I HAD no idea you were *this* good at schmoozing."

I shot Audrey an amused grin before refocusing on the road. She was in the passenger seat with her bare feet on the dashboard, eyes closed as she carded her fingers through her now loose hair.

"You can say it—I completely won them over. I am, in fact, a god when it comes to handling your parents."

"I don't know about *god,*" she teased. "But yes. You were very good. Thank you."

"My pleasure. Figured it'd be easier on you if they didn't hate your *friend*. I draw the lines at golfing, though." I pulled up outside Audrey's apartment complex and drew the handbrake. "Your stop, milady."

"Want to spend the night?" She sent me a smile full of promises that made my cock awaken with a spasm. "I do believe you've earned a reward with that performance."

"You have no idea how much I want to take you up on that offer," I said, mentally cursing the nighttime gig my father had set up for us. "But I have to get to work. Raincheck?"

"Maybe," she said, giving me her best shit-eating grin. "If you accept my dad's invitation to go golfing."

"You little witch," I growled, but couldn't hold back a laugh at her cheek. The difference between her demeanor now and before we went to her dad's birthday party was like night and day, and something in my chest felt light with the knowledge that I'd caused that. I liked making her happy about as much as I liked fucking her— it just hadn't really dawned on me before now that the two could be separated. With a teasing scowl, I slipped out of my seatbelt so I could lean over and kiss her soft lips.

She parted hers beneath mine and wrapped her arms around my neck, enveloping me in her sweet warmth. *Fuck,* but kissing her got me so goddamn hard! My cock ached to escape the confines of my jeans, and I mindlessly let a hand slide to her breast, squeezing the plump flesh gently. I was halfway starting to consider how to get her convinced to get into the backseat with me when she pulled back with a breathless laugh.

"I think we better stop now, before one of my neighbors spots us and calls the cops."

"Fucking Mrs. Peterson," I growled, earning me another laugh.

"Thank you, Liam." Audrey grasped both my hands in hers, the smile slowly fading as she looked at me with so much sincerity my heart gave an uneasy flutter in my chest. "Truly. Today... it meant a lot."

I smiled softly. "I'd do anything for you, love."

She kissed me again, harder this time. Her need fueled my own, and by the time we finally separated again I was halfway on top of her, my hand fully up her skirt and underneath her knickers.

"You sure you don't want to come up?" she breathed.

"Oh, I fucking *want* to," I groaned. *"Fuck."*

Audrey let out a breathless laugh and gently shoved my hand away. "But work. It's okay. Come see me tomorrow once you're off work?"

"Oh, I will." I reached up to tweak her peaked nipple pressing against the fabric of her dress before I pecked her lips and slumped back in my seat. "Sleep tight, love."

"Bye, Liam," she said, giving me that smile of hers that had my heart beating faster in my chest. *Fuck,* I was so goddamn addicted to that woman.

I waited on the curb for her to get safely inside the building before I released the handbrake and put the

Jeep into gear. But just as I was about to pull away, my phone beeped in my pocket.

Expecting an update on the job we were meant to be doing later I pulled it out to see a new message from Louis.

Get home now. Dad's here. It's bad.

SIXTEEN
WILLIAM STEEL

Of all my children, my two youngest sons had always been my favorites. I know they say you're not supposed to have favorites, but let's be honest here... every parent does. And mine were my two mischievous twins, with their red hair and easy laughter that reminded me so much of their mother—bless her soul.

Granted, it wasn't a hard list to top these days.

I nodded at Louis as he handed me a cup of tea before he slumped down in the leather sofa across from me and sprawled out. "So what brings you by, Dad?"

"Oh, just catching up. I heard through the grapevine that one of you has a girlfriend now? After the disaster with your brother, I thought it best to check in." My "*grapevine*" shifted from one foot to the other behind me. What had the world come to when a man could trust his employees more so than his own flesh and blood?

The twins might be my favorites, but neither of them had taken a bullet for me. In fact, I was pretty sure one of them had been the one to nearly kill Wesley a few months ago, to save their traitorous brother. I hadn't mentioned it to my right hand man—I didn't need him getting distracted with idle thoughts of revenge. And, as much as the thought of my own blood saving the worthless scum who's turned on his own father for a girl made me grit my teeth with anger, I knew my sons were loyal to each other. So long as they were more loyal to *me,* we didn't have a problem.

Besides—no matter how loyal Wesley was, he'd never be a Steel.

Still, being Steels didn't mean I trusted my two redheaded sons to pick my side over the rest of their family's'. Not after how every single one of their blasted brothers had betrayed me over the past few years. So, I'd had Wesley keep surveillance on them.

But if one of them had truly been dumb enough to fall for a girl, maybe I could pull Wesley back to focus on more pressing matters. They were smart enough to know a woman was the easiest way for an opponent in this game to control you. No man with half a brain would hand over his heart if he was about to attempt mutiny against the Steel empire—not even one of the two impulsive twins.t to attempt mutiny against the Steel empire—not even one of the two impulsive twins.

But of course... if they *had*... controlling them both would be so easy, any plans to overthrow me were dead on the stalk. There was no way either of them would do anything that might harm the other.

"A girlfriend?" Louis' ginger eyebrows shot up in amusement. "Not to my knowledge. But I'll text Liam to swing by and tell you as well, if you'd like."

I nodded and leaned back in the comfortable arm chair. Family ties were so much easier to put up with when you could control them. "Please do."

"HEY, DAD." Liam gave me a carefree nod as he walked in the door, then glanced at my right hand man. "Wesley."

"Dad was saying how he wanted to check in to hear more about this *girlfriend* one of us apparently picked up," Louis said from his position on the couch. "Seeing how Marcus' bird turned out to be a bit of a safety risk."

"*Girlfriend?*" Liam's eyebrows shot up as he sat down next to his twin, an identical expression of bemusement spreading across his face. "You hiding something from me, brother?"

"I was just about to ask you the same thing," Louis quipped.

"Sorry, Dad, no girlfriend. I'm afraid you're gonna have to stick with Blaine's kid, if you were hoping for an upcoming expansion to the Family." Liam gave me a teasing smile—the little bastards knew I'd had to swallow my words about my grandson's mother whoring around across the European continent when the kid came out looking like a fucking carbon copy of Blaine.

I narrowed my eyes at his lip, but didn't bite. "Huh, well that is odd," I said, motioning at Wesley. "From the pictures I've seen, it certainly looks like it—though I couldn't say for sure who she belongs to."

Wesley dropped the first photo on the coffee table in front of them. It was of a brunette girl's naked back pressed up against a window. One of the twins had an arm wrapped around her and his head resting against her shoulder.

"Aw, that's real nice, Dad. You got him spying on us shagging now? That's not creepy at all. Are you planning on getting it framed, too?" Liam looked at me with a grimace.

"Since when did sliding your dick between a willing pair of thighs mean we had a girlfriend?" Louis asked, an eyebrow arched. "I reckon we've got close to a thousand at this point, then. Gonna be hella expensive in birthday presents."

"And Christmas," Liam agreed, shaking his head at me. "Honestly, don't you have anything better for him to do? The other Families not causing enough trouble at the moment?"

Wesley dropped another photo on the table. This one you could see the girl's face. She looked up at whichever twin accompanied her, the look of adoration plain as day. And he... even the flat photograph captured every ounce of love written so clearly across his features you had to be blind not to see it.

Wesley put another photo on the table—the two of them laughing and holding hands. And another. Kissing tenderly.

"I'm sure you can understand how I became a bit *concerned* that there might be just a tiny bit more to this girl than your usual tarts. These three pictures were taken over the span of a few days. As far as I'm aware, you don't often keep seeing these ladies." I smiled cooly at my sons, who'd both grown remarkably quiet as they stared at the pictures. "So? Is there something I need to know about? I would hate for either of you to do anything irrational, should our enemies come across her."

"Nah, Dad," Louis said, the same casual indifference in his voice as before. But I saw the half-second's panicked look in his eyes when he first saw the second photo. "She's nice and all, but nothing more than a quality lay. We swap, once in a while. Always do, with the good ones. That's why there are multiple pictures."

"Swap?" I asked, staring down Liam who—if I wasn't mistaken—had a slightly ashier hue than before.

"We both fuck her," Liam clarified, giving me a smirk. "You don't let pussy like that just get out of your bed without offering your favorite brother a go, too. I'm sure you'd have done the same with Louisa, if your brothers were still alive. I've heard how she squeals more than once, and you know what they say about the loud ones."

"Don't be crass. She may not be your mother, but she still deserves your respect."

Louis rolled his eyes and flicked the picture of him— or his brother—penetrating the young woman up against a window toward Wesley. "Oh, sure. We're the ones who are crass. Seriously, Dad, you could just have fucking asked instead of having Wesley creep around outside her windows with a fucking camera. I may even have a video somewhere, if you really want a close-up of the action."

I raised my hand when he demonstratively pulled out his phone before getting up from the chair. "Thanks, that won't be necessary. We should get going."

"You sure? It's got her in face-down doggy. From what Jeremy said that one time he spied on you and Mum, that's your favorite."

I gave my obnoxious offspring a stern look before I turned toward their door. Wesley followed behind me like a faithful shadow, leaving the pictures behind as a silent reminder of the power I now wielded over them both.

He didn't speak until we were in the car, pulling away from the twins' flat.

"Do you want me to keep checking in on them when they go to her place?" he asked, eyes on the road. He was always vigilant, that one. Part of why I liked him more than my sons. He was reliable—faithful.

"I don't think that'll be necessary for the time being, Wesley." I smiled thinly as I looked out the tinted window from the backseat at the Thames below their expensive high-rise. "That girl is more than just a fling. And now they know I know. They won't be causing us any problems. If they do... well, now you know who to start cutting slices off to get them to fall back in line."

SEVENTEEN

LOUIS

"What the fuck were you thinking?" I rounded on my twin, anger at his idiocy quelling some of the nauseating fear that'd settled in my stomach since our father showed up. "Why would you paint a big fat target on your back by keeping on seeing that girl? If he didn't buy the fib about us both screwing her, he's got his hands firmly around your balls now. And I fucking doubt he bought it, if Wesley's been spying on you. Do you even know how ridiculously in love you look when you're around her?"

"How do you know what I look like around her?" Liam asked, folding his arms across his chest.

"Because I fucking followed you this morning, you dumb prick. You lied to me. To *me!* Did you think I wasn't gonna look into what the fuck's going on with you? How could you be so careless? How could you fall in love? You

fucking saw what it did to Marcus!" I was aware I was shouting, but I didn't care. Ever since our father had stepped
through our front door, I'd imagined a thousand times over
what my life would be like without Liam in it, and it felt
good to finally release all the pent-up panic at him.

"Fuck, Louis! Don't you think I know how
dangerous it is? I was selfish, okay? I was selfish, and I
put her in danger—"

"Fuck her!" I interrupted him. "I don't give a shit
about *her*—what I do care about is you not getting yourself bloody killed. Do you remember how fucking close
Marcus was to dying? Fully-fucking-*dying?* Because he
wanted to save his girl. And this Audrey bitch, she's got
no clue about our world, does she? Evelyn knew, she
knew how to deal, and she *still* almost cost our brother
his life!"

Anger ignited in my twin's eyes and he pointed at
me with so much vehemence it made me blink. He'd
never looked at me like *that* before.

"Don't you *ever* insult her again. This is not her
doing."

I threw my hands up. "No, it's *your* fault! What the
hell do you want me to do, start preparing my best man
speech?"

Liam shook his head, the anger still evident on his
face. "Just stay the fuck out of this, Louis. You don't get
it. You can't." And then he turned his back on me and

walked toward his own bedroom. Leaving me alone in the living room with my anger.

"What's so special about her anyway?" I called after his retreating back.

He didn't answer.

"Don't fucking see her again, Liam!"

The sound of his bedroom door slamming was the only reply I got.

"LIAM?" The brunette woman in the door looked up at me, her eyebrows meeting in a frown.

She was a pretty girl, I'd give my twin that, with her full lips and chocolate eyes, and her curvy figure was right up both Liam's and my alley. But she wasn't anything special—we'd both screwed hundreds of girls who'd be considered far more beautiful than her. What the fuck was it about her that had Liam so twisted up? He hadn't spoken to me in the three days since our blow-up, and he'd been a right moody prick around our men as well.

"Hey, love." I pushed my twin out of my mind, stepped through the doorway and, giving Audrey a trademark smirk, bent to kiss her. Thoroughly.

She breathed a small, startled gasp before our mouths connected, but when I brushed my tongue against the seam of her lips she opened them and allowed me to deepen the kiss.

Warm, sweet heat rushed into my lungs and pulsed through my body. Her lips were so soft against mine, they made my head spin and my cock rise to the occasion in record time. I groaned into her mouth with unexpected pleasure, the vague notion that I'd definitely found the reason for Liam's obsession making its way to the forefront of my mind. Damn, she had me so fucking hot, I was more than ready to skip foreplay and get her on her hands and knees on the nearest bed. Or floor, for that matter.

And then, as if she'd been able to read my mind, she pulled away, raised her hand and smacked me across the face with enough strength to make my head turn.

"You absolute fucking prick!"

I rubbed my cheek, surprise mixing with the hot sting blooming out from my left cheek. When I turned back to look at her, there was absolute murder in her eyes.

"Wha—?"

"You think you can just dump me via fucking *text*, refuse to answer any of my attempts at getting a goddamn explanation—and then stroll up to my door *three fucking days later* and kiss me like... like *it's no big deal?*" Her voice broke on the high pitch at the end and she shot a look out into the hallway, probably to see if her screeching had brought any of her neighbors' attention down upon us.

As if summoned, a chain rattled on the door opposite Audrey's flat, and an old lady peered out into the hallway, mouth pinched. "Miss Waits—"

"I'm sorry, Mrs. Peterson," Audrey interrupted her. I was surprised she could sound so apologetic, the way her teeth were clamped and her hands clenched into fists with her anger. "We'll be quiet."

Before the old bat could respond, Audrey'd shut the door behind us. She returned her focus on me, her eyes narrowed with anger.

Huh, seemed Liam had actually been smart enough to break things off with her. I briefly considered making my excuses and leaving, but... the way Liam had been acting, I didn't have any confidence in his ability to stay away.

Which meant I needed to do what I'd come here for: screw her so many times Liam would wake the fuck up and realize she was no different than any of the other girls we'd shared before. And in the end, it'd be me and him again, and Audrey would be nothing but another bird who'd spread her thighs until we'd had our fill.

Just looked like I had a bit of charming to do before she'd let me into her bed.

"I'm sorry, love," I said, reaching for her face. She smacked my hand away and gave me a glare that might have made my persistent erection shrivel up, had I truly been the one to bring down her fury. "That wasn't how I meant it."

"Not how you meant it?" she hissed, her tone incredulous. With shaking hands she fumbled her phone out of her sweatpants pocket and thrust it in my face. "Then what the hell is this?"

I took it, quickly swiping to her messages. I pressed Liam's name, and saw several unanswered texts from her to him. Pleading with him to answer her. Asking him why. Telling him he promised.

An uncomfortable knot grew in my stomach as I scrolled up, and up. We'd both been with so many women, there'd been a few broken hearts along the way, even though we never made any promises. I'd been on the receiving end of angry texts a time or two, but I'd never really been too bothered. Because I knew I'd never promised a girl more than a bit of fun and some orgasms.

That wasn't what Liam had done to Audrey. I didn't know what he'd promised her, but just from the look on his face when I saw him with her, I knew it'd been more than he'd ever promised a girl before.

When I finally got to Liam's text, the knot in my stomach didn't ease up.

Audrey—I can't see you again. I'm so sorry.

I looked up from the phone at her again, internally cringing. Not gonna lie, the urge to pack up and flee was pretty overwhelming, but I knew I couldn't. For Liam's sake.

"Look, I..." I rubbed the back of my neck with my phone-free hand. "I'm really, truly sorry."

"Sorry? You're *sorry*? God, Liam, you just pushed me out of your life with no warning, no explanation... and now you're *sorry*? Why am I even listening to you? Get out!"

The small woman pointed at the closed front door, her eyes promising me all kinds of pain if I didn't obey. But I wasn't about to leave. I couldn't. So I did the only thing I could think of—I grabbed her wrists in both hands so she couldn't slap me again and forced my lips to hers.

"Mmph!" Her muffled squeal died when I pushed her up against the wall and deepened the kiss. My blood rushed through my body in a wave of heat as her sweet taste overwhelmed my senses once more. Her curves ground into me, from her thighs over her stomach and to her full breasts, and again I got the overwhelming urge to just spin her around, rip her pants off, and take her until the urge to fuck like a goddamn beast had been quelled.

Sharp pain in my lower lip snapped me out of it. I pulled back and stared down at the woman who'd just bitten me. We were both breathing heavily, and despite the still-angry glare she leveled at me, I saw something more in her gaze now. Desire. Yearning. She wanted it, too, even if she wanted an explanation for Liam's text more. I gave her the first fib I could come up with.

"Audrey, I'm sorry. I got scared. I know I hurt you, and you didn't deserve that. Please, just give me a chance to make it up to you."

She was still glaring at me, but I could see uncertainty flicker in her chocolate gaze now. "Scared?"

"Scared," I said, stroking her wrists with my thumbs. "I've never been in a relationship like this before. Or at all, really. I know I didn't handle it well. I'm sorry."

She stared at me for a moment longer, but then her shoulders slumped in defeat. "I knew I shouldn't have taken you home to meet my parents. It was too much, too soon."

Bloody right it was too much. I still couldn't believe Liam had gone for that, but I grabbed onto her softened stance with both hands. Slower than before, and softer, I closed my mouth over hers again. She only hesitated for a moment this time, and then her soft lips moved against mine, the tip of her tongue brushing against my lower lip where she'd bitten me before.

When she melted against me, I released her wrists and grabbed her around the hips. She moaned softly into my mouth, and my cock gave an achy spasm in response.

Yeah, sex was so back on the table.

I reached down to push a hand into her pants and found her panties already damp with excitement. I stroked her lips through the clinging material until she bucked her hips out for more. Then I slipped my fingers underneath the hem of her knickers and finally touched her soft sex.

Audrey moaned into my mouth and reached up to undo my jacket. She managed to get it opened and shoved off my shoulders—forcing me to pull my hands from her panties—and then she went at my shirt, clawing more than she unbuttoned, but I didn't care. When the ripped garment was finally off and her soft hands slid up my bare skin, I shivered under her touch, my cock pulsing with need to have her stroke it instead. Then she dug her nails in and scratched.

"Shit." I ripped my lips from hers, thinking I'd hurt her, but the absolute blaze of lust that met me when our eyes locked told an entirely different story.

"*Fuck. Me.*" She slid her arms around my torso and dug her nails into my back, pulling me close against her body. "Now."

"So that's how you want it?" The bite of her nails made my lips curl up in a smirk. Looked like the little prude wanted to get her anger at Liam's abandonment out with a bit of hate-fucking. I was so down for that.

Not waiting for her reply, I grabbed her by the hips again and lifted her up, forcing her to spread her knees for me. She did, locking her ankles behind my lower back and sliding her arms around my neck for purchase.

I slammed her up against the wall, hard enough to make her grunt on impact, and then I was on her. I went for her throat, closing my lips and teeth around the creamy column of her neck and biting down, making her moan and pant as I bit, kissed, and licked at at her exposed skin. I rolled my hips between her thighs, rubbing my achingly hard, jeans-covered cock against her clothed pussy, reveling in her the heat and her small mewls when I got her in just the right spot.

"Liam... bedroom!" she panted, pulling at my hair to get my attention.

I grunted and tightened my grip around her midriff before I pushed off the wall and looked around for her bedroom. Thankfully, the bedroom door was slightly ajar, and I spotted an immaculately made bed through the crack. I carried her there in five long strides, threw her down on the bed, and kicked off my jeans and boxers.

Audrey rose up on her elbows so she could look at me, and her pink tongue peeked out to wet her lips as her eyes roamed hungrily over my form. Under less desperate circumstances, I would have let her look a little longer, but I didn't have it in me this time. Every cell in my body screamed to taste her, fill her, *take* her, and I wasn't going to wait any longer.

I was on the bed in seconds, and had her T-shirt and pants off before she could do more than gasp. Her knickers followed, the waistband snapping when I ripped them off her with a careless tug, and then she was laid bare for me. Naked and vulnerable... and so fucking gorgeous, I couldn't do anything but stare for a few breaths.

She was the pinnacle of womanhood, with the generous swell of her round hips, soft stomach, and full breasts crested by peachy-pink nipples begging to be sucked. Her pretty face was flushed with excitement, those pink lips parted with her pants and her brown eyes dark with pure lust. For *me*.

And between her thick thighs spread in invitation, her small sex was open, begging for me with a delicate sheen betraying a desperation to match my own.

I fell down between her thighs and wrapped my lips around her clit with no preamble, pinning her legs down when she bucked from the sudden onslaught. And then I sucked. Deep and strong pulls, like it was a piece of hard candy. I'd usually ease into it with a new girl, figure out what she liked and slowly rev up the stimulation until she was falling apart underneath me, but that wasn't gonna happen with Audrey. Everything about her lush body begged me to *take,* and I wasn't capable of going slow. Not when my cock ached for every second I wasn't inside her, and every instinct hardwired into my body roared with need to *fuck.* Only the desperate urge to taste her beautiful cunt before I buried myself balls-deep in it had saved her from getting rough fucked without any foreplay whatsoever.

"*Fuck, L-Liam!*" I felt her hands in my hair, simultaneously attempting to push me away and draw me closer. "It's too much! S-stop. Slow down. *Fuck!*"

I ignored her cries for mercy, listening only to her body as it writhed and thrashed in my grip. I knew she was close, could tell from the rhythmic waves of her mound against my mouth, and I wasn't about to ease up before she gushed for me.

My persistence was rewarded within minutes. Audrey broke off mid-cry, every muscle in her body tensing as her back arched off the bed. I sucked her clit hard one final time, releasing one thigh so I could push two fingers into her, ramming her g-spot with more force than finesse... and she *broke*.

Her pussy clamped down on my fingers at the same time as her pelvis jolted hard against my lips, and then the most haunting scream I'd ever heard from a woman ripped from her throat as her whole body spasmed once, twice... only to finally collapse down on the mattress in a boneless heap.

Slick heat covered my fingers and flooded her splayed lower lips, soaking the bed. I eased off her clit and licked at her folds, the scent of her pleasure going straight to my lizard brain. She tasted fucking delicious, and if I hadn't been so desperate to fuck, I'd have happily stayed down there for hours.

But I was, more than I'd ever been in my entire goddamn life.

I found a condom in my jeans pocket and slipped it

on before I returned to the bed, kneeling between her thighs. She moaned incoherently but didn't open her eyes when I brushed a hand through her short curls.

With a smirk, I fisted my cock in one hand and pushed it against her splayed folds before she had a chance at gathering herself after her orgasm. When I shoved in to the hilt in that first push, however, her eyes snapped opened and her body arched up off the bed,

"God damn, you're so fucking tight," I hissed, drowning out her mewl at the sudden and rough penetration. Wet, warm heat clamped down hard on my cock, making sparks of raw pleasure flicker across my skin and burn in my blood. *Fuck,* she felt even better than she tasted.

"Oh, God, Liam," Audrey moaned underneath me. Her fingers clutched at the bedding and her beautiful tits rose and fell with her hard gasps. "Nothing feels better than your cock!"

Seemed the little prude liked it rough. I was more than happy to oblige.

I wrapped my arms around her thighs and slung both over my shoulders so I could raise up above her, resting on my arms next to her head. And then... then I gave her everything I had. All the anger and fear I'd felt for my twin since he found her, all the resentment boiling in my gut for how she'd tried to take him away from me... I took it all out on her wet little cunt. I fucked her harder than I'd ever fucked anyone before her, pounding my anger and lust into her tight heat so hard the smacking of flesh was only drowned out by her desperate cries.

She was wild underneath me, bucking and clawing and screaming like a banshee. My skin stung form her nails, but it only fueled my desperate need to take her harder, faster.

Some time later, when she came on my pummeling cock with a pained wail, I let her ride out the hard spasms before I flipped her onto her stomach. She huffed into the pillow, but didn't protest when I grabbed her by the hips and pulled her up on the knees. Instead, she arched her back and pushed her arse up, presenting her swollen, well-fucked pussy for more.

No wonder Liam had been so enthralled. Audrey may have looked like a prim and prudish woman, but when it came right down to it, she loved to fuck more than any girl I'd known. If I'd been even halfway as rough with the last bird I'd bedded, she wouldn't have let me back inside of her for a week.

"Dirty little thing," I growled. "Begging for my cock like a trained whore, even after I've fucked your cunt into a slobbering mess."

To my delight, a wanton moan escaped her at my crude remark, and she spread her thighs wider.

I smirked and got into position between them, rubbing over her puffy lips in appreciation before I sunk my cock back into her velvet heat.

"Fuck, yes," I groaned when her pussy gripped me tight again, and that unquenchable ecstasy of being inside her crackled through my blood like electricity once more. "You were fucking born for this."

"Liam..." It was a hoarse whimper, her voice rough from screaming.

I smacked her arse in response, making her jolt up on her hands, grabbed her by the hips, and gave her a full, deep thrust.

She moaned, a raw, mewling sound, when my broad head kissed her cervix, the new position allowing me to go deeper than I had before. I adjusted a little, ensuring I wouldn't hurt her, and then I pulled her back onto the full length of my cock. *Hard.*

This time, her moan came out in an explosive exhalation, quickly followed by a long, broken cry as I let my instincts take over and fucked her with every ounce of strength in my body once again.

There was something about being inside her that short-circuited my brain with the dual assault of nearly painful pleasure and an animalistic need to *take*—to claim her soft little body until all she knew was *me*. All that mattered was her and I, and that insatiable hunger in my very bones I knew on an instinctive level she was the only one who could quell.

I don't know how long I fucked her doggy-style on her bed, but when her keening became frenzied, I came out of my pleasure-fueled insanity enough to reach around her bucking hips and rub her clit.

It was enough to push her over. Her arms gave out underneath her and her pussy locked down tight around my still-thrusting clock, nearly forcing me to still with the strength of that first spasm.

I groaned incoherently at the mind-numbing bliss, digging my fingers into her hips when white sparks of raw pleasure blurred my vision of her thrashing body. And then, like a fucking dam breaking, I finally *came*.

Only it wasn't like a normal orgasm. It was so much more, and the power of it nearly made me pass out on top of her. I think I was roaring like a beast, but I honestly wasn't aware enough to be sure. Everything was heat and *relief* and fucking ecstasy, and the only thing I sensed with absolute certainty for what felt like minutes on end was the tight, wet grasp of her pussy milking my cock for every ounce of my essence.

When my conscience finally floated back into my body, I was lying on top of her back, both of us sprawled out on the bed and still panting for air.

I raised up a little, making sure I wasn't squashing her, but unwilling to move off her completely. She felt so absolutely perfect against my body, her smooth skin sticky with our combined sweat, but I didn't care. I'd never felt better in my entire goddamn life, nor anywhere close to this relaxed. It was as if she'd drained every ounce of tension and every drop of fear and anger right out of my dick, along with what I was pretty sure was the biggest load I'd ever blown. As far as I was concerned, she had an actual miracle cunt between those lush thighs of hers.

"Fuck," I murmured, bending my head to nuzzle at her wild hair with my nose. "Don't think I'll be able to see straight again for at least an hour. That was the best goddamn sex I've ever had."

I don't know what I'd expected she'd reply to that, but the broken sob I got sure as hell wasn't it.

"Shit, did I hurt you?" Sick dread replaced my floating sensation of complete elation in the blink of an eye. I lifted off her, pulling my cock out of her softened pussy as gently as I could while praying I hadn't done any permanent damage.

Fucking hell, what the fuck was I thinking? I'd been too rough—much, much too rough.

"Audrey, where does it hurt?" I kneeled down by her side and gently turned her head so she looked at me. The tears brimming her eyes made my gut twist.

She shook her head and pulled away from my grip, rolling onto her side with her back to me so she could hug herself. "You didn't hurt me."

"The fuck I didn't," I said. "You're ain't fucking crying for nothing. Tell me what I can do, love. Tell me what I did."

"You left," she whispered.

"Huh?"

"Is this what you really want? Just tell me. I can't do it again—I can't fall for you again, if what you're here for is just sex."

She sounded so broken, it tore at my gut. I reached for her without thought, wrapping my arms around her in a feeble attempt at stopping her tears.

I didn't know why, but the next thing I said was: "No, love. That's not why I'm here."

EIGHTEEN
AUDREY

Liam was still lying next to me when I woke up some minutes before my alarm the next morning.

He was fast asleep, sprawled on his back with his right arm wrapped loosely around me.

I was resting on his shoulder, and had been for most of the night, as far as I could tell. We'd fallen asleep like that. After he'd comforted me and promised me...

My heart gave an achy spasm in my chest at the memory of last night. When he'd been standing there in my doorway, I hadn't been able to stop myself from hoping... Even though I'd known I should kick him out, that same stupid part of me that'd fallen for him in the first place had panged with wild hope.

Careful to not disturb the sleeping man, I eased out of his loose grip and sat up to flick the bedside lamp on and turn my upcoming alarm off.

I was so goddamn stupid.

I'd let him into my bed again. And yes, he'd apologized and promised, but he'd done that once before. And then he'd broken my heart.

And here I was again, exactly like on of those young, naive girls I'd told him over and over again I wasn't, allowing myself to fall for the same promises once more.

I glanced to my side and pressed a hand to my chest at my heart's painful throbbing at the sight of him.

He looked so peaceful in his sleep, so innocent. His ginger hair was a fiery mess on my pillow, his pronounced muscles relaxed. The ebb and flow of his slow breaths raised his wide, tattooed chest up and down in an inviting rhythm, and I fought the yearning to climb back underneath the covers and press my ear against his ribs to listen to his heartbeat.

I'd had my share of teenage love and broken hearts, but nothing... nothing had ever felt like this. Being with Liam was like finally being whole... and at the same time, so completely broken I didn't know how I'd ever be able to piece myself back together if he left me again.

When, I told myself, forcing the thought to seep through my mind and take hold of my heart with its chilly grip of despair. There was no point in pretending like everything was going to work out when I knew deep down that there was no way it could. He might want to, but he was too young, too free-spirited to give me what I needed.

And what was that, anyway? Vows of forever, a small house outside of London, and two-point-four kids? Weekends at the golf club?

As charming as Liam had been with my family, I knew that wasn't him—and it never would be. So why was I even doing this? Why was I staring at his sleeping face and wishing with everything I was that I could see us ending up together in the long run?

Because you let yourself fall in love, you fool.

The feeling of despair made me push off the bed with an aggravated huff—only to stumble the second my feet hit the floor and I tried to make my legs take my weight.

Damn, that hurt.

Dull, throbbing pain echoed through my core and radiated through my limbs. It took me several deep breaths while I rested against my night stand to be able to push myself upright without wincing.

I knew he'd been rough last night, but I apparently hadn't realized *how* rough. Not that I'd minded one bit while it was happening. I'd wanted it hard—I'd wanted to scream all my anger and hurt out underneath him until my orgasms finally quelled the sense of betrayal.

I hadn't foreseen having to limp around like a novice rider the next day.

Eileen was going to have a field day.

I managed to get myself ready for work and dressed without waking up Liam, and I was thankful for it. I didn't have the strength to face him right now. It was better like this.

I left him a note on my pillow, telling him to make sure the door was latched when he left, and then I quietly shut myself out of my apartment.

Hopefully whenever I next saw him again, I wouldn't break into tears and beg him to love me the way I'd been so close to doing last night.

NINETEEN
LOUIS

I'd never let myself out of a bird's flat without her still being soundly asleep and clueless to the fact that she'd wake up alone. Or with Liam, instead of me.

But then again, everything with Audrey seemed to be a first.

I'd certainly never spent post-sex bliss comforting a crying girl before, that was for damn sure. Nor had I ever felt like such an absolute fucking prick as I had while she'd sobbed in my arms. She loved Liam, that much was painfully obvious. Not in the puppy-dog way many of the girls we bedded crushed on us, either.

No, she full-on fucking *loved* him, and I'd made Liam's dismissal of her so much worse with my little stunt. I might not have known why my stupid twin had gotten in so deep with with this girl, but I cursed him for it all the way home from Audrey's. Did he love her, too?

Was that why he was being such a moody arsehole about it?

A sickening fear mixed with my general sensation of self-loathing. If... if he hadn't been forced to cut ties with her because of this thing with our dad, would she have been it for him? Was she the woman he was supposed to marry?

The woman he was supposed to leave me for?

I'd always known the day would come, even if I'd done my best to deny it. As I'd seen first Blaine and then Marcus lose themselves to the women they fell in love with, I'd known the time was drawing near when Liam would find his other half. The one that would replace me.

It'd always been him and me—he was as much a part of me as my own fucking hand, but *love*... That was the one thing that I couldn't fight back against.

In my most shameful moments, I'd secretly hoped it'd be me who found love first, even though I knew I never would. There would never be anyone who could replace Liam for me. But the alternative...

If Audrey was really Liam's true love, like Mira was Blaine's and Evelyn was Marcus'... Then one day, when we'd finally gotten rid of our father and stabilized our hold over London, he would find her again.

No.

I couldn't lose him. Not yet. Not when everything

I'd ever known was already such a fucked up mess and bound to get much, much worse.

Playing Audrey like this might've been an arsehole thing to do, but even if Liam somehow managed to stay away from her until it was safe for him to be with her again, I wasn't about to let her take him from me after all was said and done. I had to show Liam she wasn't the one. And so, I had to keep up the charade a little while longer.

I sank down on the leather sofa in mine and Liam's shared living room and fished out my phone. I'd snuck her number off her phone while she was sleeping and blocked Liam's number and replaced his with mine in her phonebook. Someone should really tell her to put a PIN on her phone.

Love, you got anything planned tomorrow evening? I want to take you out.

The small pang of excitement in my gut as I pressed *"send"* surprised me, but it probably shouldn't have. Crying aftermath aside, fucking Audrey had been the best damn sex of my entire life. No wonder a small part of me was looking forward to seeing her again, despite how shitty I felt about deceiving her. It was funny, really, on an abstract level. Before I'd met her, I hadn't been particularly looking forward to fucking her, but I hadn't felt bad about manipulating her, either. She'd just been a troublesome piece of arse, a means to an end.

Fucking Liam. Why the hell couldn't he just have screwed her once and let that be it?

WHEN AUDREY OPENED the door to me at half past ten the next night, I wasn't prepared for the gut-punch of desire that made my jaw drop at the sight of her.

She'd dressed in a black, tight-fitting dress that hugged her curves in all the right places and displayed her magnificent tits with a plunging neckline. Pieces of shimmering jewelry enhanced her clavicle and delicate earlobes, and her lush brown hair was piled on top of her head in an intricate up-do. Her pretty features were enhanced with makeup in the best of ways, with dark red lips that made me ache to kiss her.

"You look fucking amazing," I said. My voice was hoarse even to my own ears.

The way she lit up at my compliment sent another stab of urgent need through me. She was so impossibly beautiful when she smiled like that, with complete sincerity and happiness. Was this what Liam had seen straight from the beginning? Where I'd seen an uptight, pretty-but-plain woman, he'd seen this fucking goddess I'd somehow missed at first glance.

That smile did it for me. I shouldered my way through her door and pulled her in tight as I kicked it shut behind me. She managed a startled laugh before I swallowed her breath with a heated kiss and grabbed her by the arse so I could pull her pelvis flush with my own.

She was so warm and soft in my grip, and perfectly pliable as I molded her against my own body. Her cherry-flavored kiss sent sparks of desire through my blood, ramping up my lust until I wasn't capable of holding it in any longer. But when I moved to press her up against the nearest wall while simultaneously hiking up her dress, she pushed me away with a small huff.

"I thought you were taking me out." Her dry tone almost covered the look of hurt and uncertainty flashing through her eyes as she looked up at me, lips still slightly parted and her chest heaving from our kiss.

"Well, yeah, but then you went and opened the door while looking like a fucking goddess," I countered as I reached for her hips again. "And now I'd much, *much* rather stay *in*."

"Oh." She relaxed her shoulders so she was no longer pushing me away, but the look of disappointment on her face made me hesitate. And then, finally, it clicked.

"Oh, shit, you thought I was taking you *out*-out?" I took in her pretty makeup and sexy dress and mentally slapped myself. Of course she'd been expecting a fancy club and some dancing.

"Don't worry about it, it's my mistake," she said, pulling away from me. Her shoulders slumped the tiniest bit as she turned around and headed for the bath-room. "We can stay in. I'll just get changed—help your-self to some wine if you want, there's a bottle in the fridge."

"Hang on, love." I grabbed her by the shoulder, halting her retreat. She didn't look at me, but her intense disappointment cut straight through me like a near tangible thing. I spun her back around and nudged her chin up with a finger to make her meet my gaze.

She really was a gorgeous woman, even without the makeup. Her chocolate eyes seemed to shine with their own light, even now, as she was obviously fighting-and-failing to hide her disappointment. And for a moment, I wished I could have taken her out. To *Red,* or *Eleonore,* two of the posher clubs my Family owned. Given her the VIP treatment, because a girl like Audrey deserved the fucking best.

I blinked, pulling myself from my ridiculous thoughts.

Even if getting seen with her wasn't a terrible idea—which it was—I wasn't here to fucking *date* the girl. I only needed to get her comfortable enough with me that I could show Liam she wasn't the one for him—that she was just like the other girls who'd never know nor care who of us was between her thighs.

Which probably also meant I should take her to where I'd originally planned for us to go, instead of fucking her up against the nearest available surface. She was pretty leery of me, for obvious reasons, so making her think I just wanted to screw her wasn't the best of ideas, either.

"I do want to take you out. It's just not something that requires heels and makeup. I'm sorry I didn't make that clear when I texted you. We should go."

She frowned. "What should I wear then?"

"Sportswear if you have it, leggings and trainers if you don't," I said.

Audrey's frown turned deeper. "Sportswear? Where exactly are we going?"

"It's a surprise." I offered her a wide smile. "But it'll be worth it. Trust me."

She hesitated for a little while, but then nodded and turned back around. "All right. Wait here while I get changed, then."

AUDREY LOOKED up at the huge cathedral with complete confusion as I stopped her by an unlit part around the back. St. Paul's Cathedral, with its white walls and trademark dome, was a stunning piece of masonry from the eighteenth century and quite a bit of a tourist attraction—during the day time. At night the roads surrounding it, particularly at the back, lay quiet and more or less abandoned. I'd taken us to a particularly shaded part as well, to avoid pulling random passersby's interest, too. As far as it was possible in a city like London, we wouldn't be interrupted for what I had planned next.

"It's closed," she said, obviously still having not clocked on to my intentions. "Did you mean for us to go in?"

"Not exactly. How are you with heights?" I shot her a cheeky smile.

"I usually don't mind them, why?" She looked as confused as ever.

I swung my backpack off and reached in for the gear I'd brought. When I pulled out the two harnesses and rope, her cute frown of confusion deepened.

"What's that?"

"That, my dear, is climbing equipment." I jingled the metal-and-nylon gear in front of her.

"I don't underst—" her voice broke with a startled gasp when she finally grasped my plan. "You're joking!"

"Wouldn't dream of it, sweets." I gave her a wink and then shook the harness I'd brought for her free, easing it around her hips and between her thighs before she shook herself out of her stunned stupor.

"Liam, what the hell? Are you insane? You want us to—to *climb* a *building?*"

TWENTY

AUDREY

"Not just any building. This cathedral." He finished trapping me in the harness, tugging sharply on several loose ends before he slipped into his own. He looked way too comfortable with it, and at the back of my mind, I wondered if I was about to discover exactly what sort of activities had given Liam his amazing body. "The view's amazing from up there. I betcha you've never seen London like you will once we're up."

I blinked, still sure he was having me on. "I've been up the Eye before. You know, during the opening hours, safely cocooned in one of the cages. Like a normal person. I'm not doing this."

"Why not?" The way he looked at me, with that eternal smile on his lips, made me bite my lip. He sounded like he truly didn't believe there was a good reason not to freakin' climb up a several centuries old—

and very tall—religious building, like it was something all couples did on date night.

"Uh, how about because it's dangerous? We could fall."

"Nah, love." Liam gave my harness a playful tug, making me stumble closer to him. He wrapped his arms around my body and kissed the top of my head before I could straighten up. "You're all safe. This'll make sure you don't get hurt. Besides, you'll be with me. I'd never let you fall."

I swallowed at the smoldering fire in his eyes, willing my ovaries to calm the heck down. I wasn't going to let him talk me into this ridiculous idea just because a single look from him could fry my ability to think straight.

"It's illegal," I countered. "And did I mention an all-round terrible idea? I'm not exactly some gymnastics god here. You might be able to Spider-Man a building, but I'm not. And besides, why do you even *want* to do this? Just tell me one good reason!"

Liam nudged my chin playfully again and then stepped away, looking up the cathedral. "It's an easy climb, and I'll help you. Trust me, love, if you want to, you can. And as for the why..." He looked back at me, and for once, the smile was gone. Something more solemn, but so sincere it nearly stole my breath away, glowed back at me from his shadowed eyes. "When was the last time you felt truly free, Audrey? You work an office job, your life revolves around figures and numbers. I bet you follow all the rules, like you have done since you were sitting at the front row of your class, hand up to show the teacher what a good girl you were.

"Do you even know what it feels like to be free? Do you ever look up at the sky and wonder who you'd be, if you'd been allowed to choose? That's what's up there, love. Freedom. And it's waiting for you to come and fucking take it. So come. Take it. With me."

I was vaguely aware of the tears blurring my vision as I stared at Liam. Maybe if I'd been able to look away from his burning gaze I could have retreated behind my normal shield of rationalization. I could have huffed and argued that there was no way some illusive sense of *freedom* could be found at the top of a bloody building.

But as his gaze bored into mine, it felt like he *saw* me —saw my very essence, and every hope and every dream I'd abandoned along the way as I molded myself to become the person my parents thought I should be.

"How do you know?" I whispered, my throat constricting around the words. "How do you know me so well?"

He reached out and brushed a thumb against my cheek, capturing a trailing tear. "We're all caught in the same bullshit, love. Of who we're supposed to be—of expectations we think we have to fulfill. When I need a reminder of what truly matters, I come here."

I nodded, wiping the last few stray tears from my

face and stepped up the the side of the building. Someone who could see me this well... I wanted to follow him wherever he would lead.

"Okay. Show me how."

MY INITIAL FEAR of being caught by police and then having to explain to them why I was trying to climb up a cathedral was quickly replaced by something much more life-preserving once I got more than two meters up the white wall. I clung to the handholds Liam had shown me before he climbed up ahead of me with an ease that suggested he wasn't bothered by such mundane things as gravity. I wasn't even that high up yet, but the realization that if I fell once I got just a little higher, it was only this much-too-thin-looking nylon rope attached to Liam that'd save me from certain death was hard to shake.

As if on cue, the rope secured to my harness shook a bit and I glanced up. Somehow, Liam had already made it to the first roof several meters above me, and he'd apparently found something to tie his end of the rope to.

"Need a hand?" he called.

"Yes." I'm not sure my small squeak was actually audible up from his vantage point, but the way I clung to my small perch without moving must have clued him in to my state of mind. Scraping sounds from up above made me glance back up, only to see his strong form climbing back down the building—this time without a rope.

"What are you doing?" I squeaked once he made it down by my side. His fingers dug into the furrows as if it was second nature to him to hang off buildings like a damn monkey, and he looked completely unfazed as he shot me a grin.

"Coming to your rescue. You've been clinging on to this poor ledge for about ten minutes now."

"No, I mean, where's your rope?" I hissed. "What if you fall?"

"I won't fall, Audrey." His expression turned serious, and I got the sense it was to calm me down. Like he knew I was teetering on the edge of hysteria. "I've done this climb dozens of time. It's easy."

"Easy?" I gasped. "How tall is this damn cathedral anyway? Nothing's easy about it."

"Sure it is. Was it hard to get where you are now?"

I reluctantly shook my head—after Liam had shown me how, it'd been surprisingly easy to climb the few meters. The old wall had plenty of handholds and ledges to grab onto.

"Well, the rest of the climb is just as easy. You just have to focus on one step at a time. Come on, Audrey, you can do this, I know you can. You've come this far— don't give up now."

I took a deep breath and gritted my teeth. He was

right. I'd made it this far. If I gave up now, I knew in the core of my being that I would regret it for the rest of my life. I wasn't sure what exactly I was looking to prove with this climb, but inside my chest, a tight feeling of longing ached for me to continue.

Shakily, I reached up for the next ridge above me.

"That's it, now find the hold just above your left knee with your foot. A little further to the left. There."

Liam climbed next to me this time, showing me where to hold when I couldn't find purchase and encouraging me every step of the way. I focused only on the wall and on his voice, placing my hands and feet at the furrows he pointed out as I pulled myself up one step at a time. It felt like we'd been on that wall forever when finally, the roof spread out above me.

"This is the tricky part," Liam said, his voice cheerful. "Once you get up, make sure to find your balance before you try to stand. The wind is a bit strong."

"Uh-huh," I managed through gritted teeth. My arms were shaking from the unaccustomed exercise, and sweat made the wisps of hair that'd pulled free from my ponytail stick to my face. When I wiped it against my arm while reaching for the roof, my foot slipped.

I yelped and scrambled for purchase, adrenaline kicking in with a burst of raw power, but before I could think anything more than, *"oh, shit!"* Liam's arm wrapped around my hips and arse, steadying me.

"Easy now, I got you," he said. "The foothold's just a

little to your right, about a foot and a half up. A little more. There you go."

I managed to find the small ledge I'd missed before and pushed up. Liam boosted me the last bit above the balustrade and suddenly I was on my hands and knees on the gently sloped roof.

"Oh, my God, I did it!" I gasped. My entire body trembled from the still-lingering adrenaline, but I felt absolutely unstoppable.

"Told ya it was easy." Liam's cheerful voice was followed by a smack against my backside as he joined me on the roof. When I looked up, he pulled a water bottle from his backpack and handed it to me. "We'll have a little break before we climb the dome."

Normally, I would probably have protested against the idea of continuing up. I'd already proven I could do it, so why continue even higher and add more risk? But that was the entire point of this little excursion, I was starting to realize. We were doing it simply because we could. Leave the rationale and rules on the ground— tonight, with Liam as my guide, I was experiencing a different side of life.

It was as intoxicatingly freeing as everything else about him had been since the day we met.

The climb up the pillars toward our final destination, the balustrade balcony surrounding the dome known as the Stone Gallery, was much harder than the initial walls had been, but I was determined now. Liam helped me every step of the way, guiding me and occasionally pushing me when I couldn't reach a particularly high hold, and just over half an hour after we'd made it to the first roof, I scrambled over the stone balustrade and fell onto the balcony in a graceless heap with a victorious, albeit breathless, laugh.

I'd done it. I'd climbed all the way up St. Paul's Cathedral, without dying or getting arrested. I'd actually done it.

"Come look at the view with me."

I looked up at Liam, who scaled the balustrade with quite a bit more finesse. He held a hand down to me, that warm smile of his playing at the corner of his mouth as he looked at my splayed form.

I groaned and took his hand, letting him carry most of my weight as he pulled me to my feet.

It was breathtaking.

London's skyline stretched out before us with its many lights. There were taller buildings to be sure, but none close to us. It was just us and the open sky, and the city with all its stress and rules far below. And I felt... free.

Something pressed against the insides of my chest, as if fighting against the confines of my ribcage. I breathed deeply, big gulps of air, filling my lungs until I thought they might burst.

Free.

Only riding a horse at a full gallop across the meadows when I was a kid had ever compared to this.

"How did you know what was up here?" I whispered, not looking at the young man by my side who'd shown me what I'd been missing all along without knowing it. I wasn't sure I could, because if I looked at him right now, I knew I'd never be able to hold back the flood of emotion bubbling up inside of me and threatening to burst out.

"Me and my brother, we always used to climb the trees in our garden to get away when things got too rough at home. Every problem seems so small when you're up high. It's only your own strength that matters then. When... when things got worse, we climbed higher. I've been scaling buildings since before I hit puberty."

"When your mother got shot," I said softly, grabbing his large hand in mine. I knew what he meant from the emotion in his voice—it was the same as when he'd first told me about how she died.

Something in the small gasp of air that escaped him made me finally look up at him. He was staring at me with pure shock, and I frowned in confusion.

"What?"

"He told you?" he said, his voice not much more than a whisper.

TWENTY-ONE
LOUIS

"Who told me what?" she asked, her flushed face pulling into a confused frown.

He'd told her. She knew about our mother and how she died.

For the longest moment I couldn't do anything but stare down at the small by my side, who knew about my most painful loss because my twin had shared it with her. We never spoke about her, with anyone. Hardly even each other. The loss had been too painful to ever fully process, even if we'd been too young to understand at the time.

But Audrey knew.

And for some reason, it shook me to my core.

"Liam?" she asked, clearly worried by my sudden shocked silence. "Who told me what?"

"Sorry, I... forgot you knew about that," I said, shaking my head to dismiss my odd outburst.

"I guess you haven't told that many people," she said, giving my hand a gentle squeeze.

"No one," I said. "No one before you."

She bit her lip and gave my hand another squeeze. "Do you want to tell me how it happened?"

I opened my mouth to tell her no, but something about the way she looked at me made me hesitate before I could get the words out. There was so much emotion in those beautiful brown eyes of hers, so much trust, and for reasons I could never explain, right then I wanted nothing more than to tell her everything. With a certainty that shook my very foundation, I suddenly knew that I wanted her to see all the pain of my mother's death and everything that'd happened around it.

But if I did that, I would have to explain about my Family. What we were. What I was.

"I can't," I said softly before I reached for her cheek with my free hand and brushed a stray lock of hair away.

She smiled up at me, a sad little tilt of her lips, and pressed her cheek against my hand, like a cat looking for affection. "Whenever you're ready, I'm here."

I finally got it, then. What Liam saw in her.

It wasn't her beauty, or even the ridiculously addictive sex. It was this... this *thing* inside of her that lit up like a fucking sun and called out to me with more power than a siren's song. It was gentle and beautiful and *warm*, and it was everything I'd needed since the day my mother died. That place inside of me where the feeling of safety and *home* had been ripped away. I thought it'd been destroyed for good, but it wasn't. It'd been here, with her, all along.

She was supposed to be mine. Not Liam's.

Mine.

The city seemed to fade away into nothingness as I stared down at the short woman who held the key to everything I'd never known I needed. Some part of me must have known all along, I realized with faint amusement. Why else would I have taken her up here, to a place I only ever came alone? It hadn't been pure physical attraction that had me aching for her the moment our lips touched that first time I went by her flat.

She was the one.

"Liam..." Her voice was hoarse and raw, and from the look of shock and desperate yearning on her delicate features, I knew she could see the emotion playing across my face as clear as day.

"I love you, Audrey," I said. It was ridiculous, of course. I'd only known her for a few days. It didn't matter, though, because it was true. I loved her, and there was nothing I could do to change that.

She made a small noise in response, like a wounded bird's broken cry, and then her face cracked with a sob that seemed to come from all the way down the depths of her soul.

"I love you too," she gasped.

I don't know who moved first, but the next second, she was in my arms. She felt so perfectly solid, so completely real. I bent my head to kiss her lips, and she parted hers in eager response. She tasted saltier than she had before, and I realized she was crying as she clung to me. I pulled her closer to me, moaning with the desperate need rising inside me like a phoenix from the ashes of everything I'd thought I was. This was it. *She* was it.

Audrey's hands on my drawstring waistband and her urgent mewls turned the swell of emotions inside of me carnal with the suddenness of a shifting forest fire. I groaned into her mouth and reached for her sex. The harness made it more awkward to get her pants pulled far enough down her thighs to allow access, and I had to spin her around to lean against the balustrade to manage.

She whimpered and arched her back once I finally got her harness off and dropped her leggings to knee-height, pushing that deliciously full arse back against me to display her needy little cunt.

I growled at the sight of it, of *her*. She was such a fucking goddess, and I needed to be inside her more than I needed air to breathe. With a few desperate snags of the nylon harness around my own hips, I managed to get it shifted enough to pull out my already hard and aching cock. I slipped a hand between her legs, rubbing her sex until she slicked up enough to allow entry, and then I spread her lips and *thrust.*

"Yes!" The note of pain in her broken cry hinted that her pussy could have used a bit more foreplay, but the way she pressed herself back against me, swallowing me to the root despite my roughness, told me she'd needed this as fervently as I did.

Fuck, she felt so goddamn good around me. She was hot and tight, her muscles fluttering against my hard length in tight little spasms as her pussy adjusted to me. I could spill my very soul inside of her.

I fucked her with all the desperation and all the bone-deep intensity roaring inside me, fucked her with my hands on her hips, pulling her back against me so she was forced to take me to the hilt again and again, and all the while she begged me for more, more, *more!*

We were meant to be together, meant to be one, and as I took the woman I loved with everything I had and everything I was as London's lights gleamed around us, I felt more alive than I ever had before. No adrenaline kick would ever compare to the tight, wet heat between Audrey's thighs, no music to her gasped moans of pleasure, and no alcohol to the roar of blood rushing in my ears as I pumped her full of cock. She went wild beneath me, scratched her fingers bloody on the stony banister, and screamed her agonized pleasure out across London's rooftops.

When my climax came, it came with hers.

Her pussy's hard, milking spasms and her sweet cries of ecstasy made me lose the last remnants of control. I roared as my balls released and I *came* like I'd never come before. I clutched at her hips while white-hot pleasure crackled through every nerve in my body, blinding me to everything but the city's lights below and around us.

I rocked blindly against her, filling her with the last spurts of my seed and relished in her soft moans as she, too, came down from her high. Finally, my vision returned and I stilled, pressed up tightly against her backside. I slipped my arms around her waist and hugged her close to my chest, wanting that moment to last forever. This perfect point in time where everything was as it was supposed to be. Her and me, and this endless well of bliss of our bodies releasing to each other.

"I love you," she whispered into the empty air in front of her.

I nuzzled my face against the back of her neck and kissed her cheek when she turned her head. "I love you too."

"It feels so odd to hear you say that," she confessed. "I never thought..."

"That I'd wake the fuck up and realize?" I sighed, burying my nose in her hair. "I'm sorry I'm such an idiot. If I'd been any kind of smart, I would have realized the moment I first saw you."

"I don't think I'd have been particularly receptive," she said with a small giggle. "I was so stressed out, I wouldn't have noticed if the Prime Minister came dancing through that park wearing a tutu and clown shoes."

A jab of something sharp and unpleasant dug into my blissful haze, and I frowned against the side of her cheek. I vaguely recalled Liam mentioning he'd met her in a park when he first saw her. That's what she was referencing—the first time she met Liam. Not me.

I pushed down the sting of absurd jealousy and buried my nose in her hair to breathe in her scent. She smelled like fresh air and sex and *me,* and right now that was all that mattered. I knew at some point I'd have to come back down to Earth and figure out a way to get us through this clusterfuck I'd unwittingly created. I couldn't pretend like I was Liam forever, nor could I risk her safety like Liam had by being careless and getting caught coming out of her building too many times.

And then there was the whole issue with my twin.

An ugly twinge of guilt made me breathe deeper to let Audrey's calming scent drown out the reality that waited for me once I allowed myself to start thinking again.

He cared for her, that much was obvious. Might even be in love with her. I didn't dare think about what kind of consequences my betrayal would have for our relationship. Because it was a betrayal now, I knew that without a shadow of a doubt, and if I thought too much about it, sick fear threatened to spill in over my wall of contentment.

"Can we sit down for a bit? My legs are like jelly, and I'll need to be able to climb back down soon." Audrey's voice drew my attention back to her, and I smiled, grateful for the distraction.

"Sure. If you're that much of a wuss," I teased. I eased my mostly softened cock out of her swollen pussy and fixed my pants, covering myself.

"Easy for you to mock—it's not you who've just been screwed silly by something the size of a damn water bottle while trying to not fall over the railing to your death," she grumbled. She tried to pull her leggings up, but got caught in the tangle of the harness.

I smirked at her irritated huff and reached down to help her, twisting the harness out of her way and was able to sneak a quick tickle over her clit in the process. She smacked my teasing hand away, but managed to pull her pants up to cover herself and snap the harness back into place. With a small sigh she then slid down on the stone floor of the balcony encircling the dome and leaned back against the banister. "Why is sex with you always so exhausting?"

"Is that a complaint?" I asked, arching a teasing eyebrow at her as I sat down next to her so I could pluck her off the floor and slide her onto my lap, sparing her backside from the cold stone.

She grinned, her teeth gleaming white in the darkness. "Hardly."

"That's what I thought." I wrapped my arms tighter around her and leaned back against the railing with a contented sigh. She wasn't the only one who was knackered, but I wasn't surprised. Sex with Audrey drew every flicker of tension from my muscles and mind more effectively than any massage could have—not to mention the sheer force of it all. So far, I seemed incapable of fucking her with anything less than my full strength. It was a good thing she was built well, or I'd have been afraid to break her in half every time I bedded her.

"Liam?"

"Hmm?" I hummed, obligingly braiding my fingers with hers when she lifted my hand.

"Do you want to come to a work thing with me next Friday?"

"Don't think there's much I wouldn't want to do with you," I said honestly. "What is it?"

"Oh, that dumb party I've been moaning about a few times. You know, with my nightmare client. It's a black tie event."

"Sure," I agreed. Not gonna lie, the memory of how she'd looked in that black dress she'd opened the door in earlier this evening flickered through my mind. I could stand to suit up if I got to see her in something like that again. Besides, it'd be nice to take her out, even if it was just for her work. It wasn't exactly something I could do around any of my own places before my father had been dealt with—or I'd talked to Liam.

As if she could sense where my thoughts were going, Audrey said, "Liam?"

"Hmm?" I grunted, wishing she'd not used his name just then.

"What happened to your scar?"

I frowned and glanced at her. Her brows were knotted in a confused frown as she stared at my hand. "What scar?"

She touched my thumb. "The one you had right there. I know it's the right hand, too."

I looked at my hand. It had a few scuffs and calluses from the climb and general work, but there wasn't any scars. Never had been. But before I could ask her what on Earth she was on about, I remembered.

Liam.

Liam had a scar there, from some fucker who'd managed to catch him with a broken bottle in a bar fight several years ago.

TWENTY-TWO
LOUIS

I'd lost count of how many birds I'd shared with Liam without them ever knowing we'd swapped along the way. No one had ever had the slightest idea they were seeing two different people instead of just one. No one apart from our mum had ever noticed any of the few minuscule differences between us, not even our father or any of our brothers. When we'd been younger we'd often pretended to be each other, just for the hell of it or to get out of trouble, and did it occasionally to this day even if it wasn't for the thrill of fucking a girl who thought she was with someone else.

Even our tattoos were absolutely identical.

And yet somehow, Audrey had noticed a tiny scar vividly enough to know that something wasn't quite right.

Shit.

"It... sometimes disappears into the skin when I'm a bit chilly," I lied, fighting back the sudden urge to hide my hand from her.

"That doesn't sound like any scar I've ever heard of," she said, her frown deepening as she studied my thumb. "And your hands are pretty warm. They always are."

"Well, then it's obviously magic," I said, managing a smile as I tipped her chin up to break her study of my skin. "I'm a wizard, love."

She giggled and made a face at me, and I bent to kiss her, hoping to break her interest in my missing scar. It worked, thankfully, and I felt a wave of relief when she flicked her tongue against my lips, obviously well and truly distracted.

"If I fuck you again while we're up here, I'm not sure *I'll* be able to climb down again before dawn," I mumbled against her mouth when her hands began to search for my crotch.

She broke off with a small laugh. "Okay, good point. But can we stay for just a little longer? I don't want this evening to end yet."

I nodded, bathing myself in the love from her eyes. As far as I was concerned, I could have stayed up there for the rest of eternity.

"I CAN'T GO to Perkinson's thing tomorrow."

It was the first thing I'd said to my twin since he slammed the door on me more than a week ago, partly because he'd ignored me since then and partly because I'd felt guilty as fuck since...

Since I'd betrayed him.

The irony that I'd been scared of Audrey coming between us because he was falling for her, and now knowing that *I* was the one to let her split our unbreakable bond, wasn't lost on me, but I wasn't ready to dwell on it. Not yet, when there was so much at stake. No, I might as well enjoy the constant sensation of bliss in my chest whenever I thought about her for a little while longer—the stars should know she was the only ray of light these days.

Liam looked over his shoulder at me from the mug of coffee he was brewing. The dark, haunted look in his usually so silvery eyes cut me like a knife.

"He's expecting us to show up," he said. Even his voice was off, though I doubted anyone but I would ever notice. "There'll be a few key players who need to see his Steel connection."

Fuck, was this still about Audrey? Or was it everything else getting to him? Brian had asked us for quite a few favors since that first hit, and we'd both been working hard to make absolutely sure it stayed below the radar. There was only so much pull we could wield without our dad finding out. He wouldn't mind us "bettering connections" with an old, wayward ally, which was what we'd write our presence at Perkinson's party tomorrow off as, but the second he found out we were siphoning any sort of resources... We'd suffer the same fate as Jeremy had.

"He'll be happy enough as long as just one of us shows. I've promised to show up to this thing, but..." I bit the inside of my cheek as I looked into my twin's eyes. He was hurting, bad. As much as I didn't want to stand Audrey up, I couldn't turn my back on him, either. "But I can cancel, if you need me there."

"Nah, it's fine." Liam turned his back on me once more and finished making his coffee. "I got this."

"You sure?" I asked as he turned to leave the kitchen, mug in hand.

"Yeah." He left without another word. The sound of the door to his room closing behind him was the last I heard of him for the rest of the night.

TWENTY-THREE
AUDREY

"Well, well, Miss Waits. I had my doubts about you, but this isn't looking too shabby."

I managed a stiff smile in acknowledgement of Gregory Perkinson's praising tone as he took in the venue for his much-anticipated vodka launch. I say "much anticipated" mainly because I was anticipating the hell out of getting it over with and hopefully never having to work with him ever again.

"I'm glad you are pleased so far," I said as two poker dealers with only tassels covering their nipples walked by on their way to the casino section of the warehouse I'd managed to transform into a suitable party venue. Finding twenty-five staffers willing to work in their undies had almost been a breeze in comparison to getting the concrete-and-steel building turned glamorous enough to not get me fired.

"People should start arriving in twenty minutes or so, and we'll pull the curtains from the stage for the grand reveal of your vodka," I began, wanting to make sure my difficult client wasn't going to mess up my carefully made schedule.

"With the *Playboy* girls?" he interrupted me.

"Yes, with Lianne and Suzette." I was pretty sure my stiff smile was slipping into a pained look, but he was too busy eying the two poker dealers as they set up behind their tables at the other end of the large space to pay my facial expressions any mind. "You'll let everyone know the casino's open and we'll let people mingle and play. The caterer will serve everyone canapés and vodka throughout the night, and the... the *dancers* will be performing on the five platforms you can see spread throughout the room." I nodded to indicate the nearest platform adorned with a pole. "And the jazz band is just setting up now. Is your security team ready?" He'd insisted he'd hire his own security for the launch. I was pretty sure he was having delusions of grandeur about his vodka debut, the way he'd been so insistent that he "needed to trust the men on the door with his life, so he'd take care of it," but with the kind of money he was pouring into my company, my bosses had told me in no uncertain terms to give him whatever he wanted.

That was also the explanation for the rehearsals I'd sat through to find sufficiently "classy strippers" while my lucky colleagues had enjoyed their business reports and meetings back at the office.

Not that I was bitter, no siree. Just because I'd spent years of blood, sweat and tears, first in school and then working my way up in Caslik Consulting, only to find myself relegated to errand girl for an overgrown teenager who wanted the "best strippers in town" for his stupid vodka party. Which businesswoman didn't dream of finding herself surrounded by pasties in order to advance her career?

"They're checking the perimeter as we speak and will set up before everyone starts arriving," Perkinson said, with an air of importance that had me biting my lip until I tasted blood to keep from eye rolling. "I'll best get 'round back to set up and see the girls. I'll catch up with you later, Miss Waits."

I managed to force my cheeks into another smile when he turned his attention back to me. "Sure thing, Mr. Perkinson. I'll do the last rounds out here."

THE NEXT HOUR or so was so hectic I barely had time to breathe. There was a reason I hadn't gone into event planning after university, and it wasn't just because you apparently risked hosting launch parties with more naked breasts than a maternity ward. Only the knowledge that Liam had promised to show up kept me from going crazy while the hundreds of guests filed into the warehouse as I dashed around, making sure the serving girls had the right amount of vodka in every glass, the pole dancers had chalk readily available, and the loo was stocked with toilet paper.

It was well past Perkinson's speech before I finally had a moment to myself. I staggered into the main room, which was now filled with smartly dressed men and women, jazz and the classiest strippers London had to offer. I waved over a topless waitress and snatched a shot glass filled with Perk Vodka from her tray.

"Thanks," I said. "And sorry, again, about the, eh, uniform."

She smiled. It wasn't the first time I'd apologized to the female staff I'd hired for this event. "You would be surprised how many of these gigs I've had. Men and breasts—they're really just big babies. Tips are great, though."

I laughed, feeling a bit better about it. She had a point. As I looked out across my venue, it was quite obvious that a rather large section of the male attendants were pretty much hypnotized by the amount of feminine beauty on display. "I bet. Thanks again for the vodka."

She winked and headed off with the tray toward a cluster of middle-aged men, and I wandered off looking for Liam.

It didn't take me long to find him—his flaming red

hair lit up like a beacon by one of the tables in the center of the room. When I got closer, I frowned as I recognized Gregory Perkinson by the table, too. There was an older man sat between them and four broad-shouldered, muscular men hung around behind. They looked like the kind of hired muscle a Bond villain would employ, and I had the vague thought that Perkinson was taking his theme a touch too far. But mainly, I was just shocked that it looked like Liam knew him.

I possibly shouldn't have been. I knew very little about Liam's social life, but he had said he owned some nightclubs. Of course a guy like Perkinson would know nightclub owners.

"Liam—" My smiling approach to the table was abruptly intercepted when one of the big goons behind him put a massive hand on my shoulder, effectively stopping me mid-step.

"That's far enough, little lady," the hired muscle grumbled.

I stared up at him, mouth open in shock just as Liam and the two other men by the table turned around at the disturbance.

"You better get your hand off me *right* now," I hissed, my outrage at being manhandled by some body-guard for hire at an event I'd planned swiftly overtaking the shock of it all. "I'm the damn event planner, you moron!"

The big goon cast a glance to his side at Liam—who was staring at me with wide eyes.

"Audrey?" His voice was rough in that way it got when he was holding back emotion, and despite my anger, I felt myself flush with happiness. He'd sounded about the same when I'd opened the door wearing my little black dress last week, and I'd picked out the violet gown I was wearing tonight hoping for a similar reaction.

"Hey. I didn't realize you knew my client, Mr. Perkinson." I batted the goon's hand off and brushed my fingers across Liam's shoulder in silent greeting before I turned to the third man and held out my hand. "I'm Audrey Waits, the event planner. Pleased to meet you."

He smiled widely at me and got up from his chair. "So I see. You've done a marvelous job, my dear. I'm Perkinson senior—Gregory's my son. And you know young Steel?"

"Yeah, we're... together." It was still too odd to call him my boyfriend. I'd been too busy with the launch to see him since that night on top of St. Paul's Cathedral, but I knew without a shadow of a doubt that we were together now.

Liam got up from his seat and put his hand on my shoulder, nodding at the bodyguard who'd stopped me. "Come, love, let's get some fresh air."

"Okay." I smiled at the two Perkinsons, happy that I'd get a bit of alone time with Liam before I'd have to get back into the fray. "If you'll excuse us for a moment. Everything's running smoothly, but I'll be back in in ten minutes."

Gregory looked miffed, but when he opened his mouth to say something, his father cut him off: "Ah, young love. You go enjoy your girl, Steel. We can always talk business later."

Business? I frowned at the cool, calculating look in the elder Perkinson's eyes as he looked me over, but Liam's warm hand on my shoulder pulled my attention away. I guess it wasn't too surprising that Perkinson senior gave me the creeps—he'd supposedly raised his pig of a son, after all.

Liam led me through the throng of people with a hand on the small of my back, out through the carpet-lined hallway, past the toilets, and toward the side exit. Only when we were outside in the cool air did he stop.

"I've missed you," I said as I turned toward him, wrapped my arms around his neck, and pressed my lips to his. It'd almost been a full week since he told me he loved me, and I'd ached for his touch in the days that'd followed.

Liam seemed to freeze for a moment, his lips stiff and immobile against mine. But then, as if he suddenly came back to himself, he let out a soft groan and kissed me back so tenderly, it made my heart flutter. His arms came up to rest around my waist, letting me feel his protective strength underneath the expensive-looking suit. His kiss was so different from last we parted, like he was reacquainting himself with my taste, and yet entirely the same, the way he moaned with want for every brush of our lips against each other.

"I've missed you too," he whispered hoarsely in between kisses. "So fucking much."

I moaned happily, my thoughts beginning to flicker in the direction of finding somewhere private for a quickie, when Liam pulled back with a suddenness as if some sort of spell had been broken.

"What the fuck are you *doing* here, Audrey?" he said, his face so serious it made me blink. "The Perkinsons are bad men."

I snorted. "Yeah, no kidding. It's not like I *loved* putting on an event that involved ordering spare nipple tassels, but I kinda had to. I like being able to pay rent and all."

"*He's* your nightmare client," he said, as if it was a complete revelation. "Fuck, Audrey, if I'd known..."

I shrugged. "Not much to do about it. Hopefully I won't have to work with him after tonight, though. Hey, how do you know him and his dad?"

Liam released me with one hand and rubbed it over his face. "No, you don't understand— *Fuck!* Okay, this is what we're going to do. Wait here for me. I'll make your excuses, say you've come down with something, and then I'll take you home."

I frowned, pulling back from him. "What? No. I

can't leave now, I'll get fired. What are you so worked up about anyway? I've made it this far, I can handle a few more hours."

He brushed his hand against my cheek so gently then, and my protests died at the way he looked at me, with devotion and regret so pained it took my breath away. I didn't understand why he was so upset, but that look in his eyes was impossible to argue with.

"Trust me, love. Just this once."

Dazedly, I nodded.

He touched his fingertips to my cheek again. "I'll be back in a moment. Wait for me here. Don't go anywhere without me, okay?"

I stared silently at his retreating back before he disappeared in through the side door, leaving me alone among the parked cars next to the old warehouse. His absence left an odd sort of chill that surpassed the mild evening breeze. I shuddered and folded my arms across my midriff at the prickling awareness against my skin. Something was obviously not right, the way Liam was acting, but for the life of me I couldn't understand what had him so on edge.

But I trusted him, and right now, that was all that mattered.

"Audrey!"

I jolted at the sound of my name and peered out among the parked cars. Liam's flaming hair and smiling face came into view just as he rounded a parked Audi.

"My God, woman. You look fucking fantastic."

I stared at him as he crossed the last few meters of tarmac and wrapped his arms around my body, instantly shielding me against the chill.

"I'm really sorry I'm late. I hope you saw my text—I had to run a last-minute errand." The ginger man bent and pressed a kiss to my stunned lips, teasing his tongue across them before he realized I wasn't responding properly. "Love, is something the matter?" His smile was gone once more, replaced by a concerned frown.

"You—how did you get around there?" I blurted, too confused by his magical appearance at the exact opposite way he'd disappeared only moments before to ask what the hell he meant by being late.

His frown eased a little, a teasing smirk slipping over his devious lips. "I drove, love. You doing okay? Need me to help you with some stress relief? I'm sure we can pull a quickie in my backseat before this nightmare client of yours misses you."

"W-what? Didn't you just...?" What the hell had happened to his apparent rush to get me out of there not moments ago?

My question got cut short when the back door opened once again—and Liam stepped out.

The man by the door looked up and our eyes met—and his entire body gave an odd sort of jolt.

I stared at him for two long seconds before I looked up at the man who still had his arms around me. They were identical.

"L-Liam?" I whispered.

It was an odd sort of sensation—like I was halfway floating above my own body, looking down at myself and the two men who looked so much alike that for a moment I thought I was seeing double.

The man whose grasp I was in turned halfway to see what I'd spotted—and froze, the color in his faze draining.

"Louis?" the redhead by the door asked, his brows locked in a frown that suggested he, too, wasn't quite comprehending the situation. "What are you—" His eyes slid over me again, and his voice broke off.

"W-what... what's going on?" I didn't recognize my own voice—it was too high-pitched and tense. *Louis. Not Liam. Louis.*

It was the sound of that name—the name that wasn't Liam—that finally made it click.

"You're twins." Numbly, I fumbled for his hand. He let me lift it up so I could see his thumb. His scarless thumb. I'd known something was off about his explanation at the time, but I'd brushed it off. Because I'd trusted him, and I'd never thought...

"You're *twins*," I said again. The numb shock in my chest threatened to crack and crumble away when hot, painful understanding lanced through my abdomen like a knife. They'd... shared me? Taken turns. Like I was a damn amusement ride.

Never bothering to tell me I was losing my heart to someone who wasn't real.

"Audrey..." It was the man without a scar—Louis. He reached for my cheek, but I backed away from him. From both of them. I stuck my finger up between us like a weapon and pointed it first at him, and then at Liam by the door.

"Don't you *dare* say my name!" It came out in an angry hiss, even though everything inside of me was agony from the monumental sense of loss and betrayal. None of it had been real. "You've had your fun, you sick bastards. I never want to see either of you ever again, you hear?"

"Audrey." This time it was Liam. He took a couple of steps toward us, his face drawn with tension. "Listen to me—"

"*No!*" I screeched. "No! I am done, you hear? No more bullshit excuses! I'm *done!* What kind of sick perverts are you? I loved you, you sick pricks! I *loved* you, and you *let* me! Whatever you have to say, I don't want to hear it! Leave me alone!"

When I spun around and ran into the parking lot to find my car, neither of them followed.

"I DON'T KNOW what to say, Audrey. You left your client's event not even halfway through—we're lucky Mr. Perkinson isn't leaving Caslik. What were you thinking?" Lennard Blue, my department manager, looked at me through his half-moon glasses with a nearly paternal disappointment as I did my best not to cower from the other side of his imposing desk.

"I'm really sorry, Mr. Blue. I think it was food poisoning." I managed to keep my voice even, despite the pang of pain even the mention of last Friday brought with it. I'd cried pretty much non-stop throughout the weekend, so at least I knew I looked as crappy as someone who'd had food poisoning for the past few days. It was only the threat of losing my job if I didn't show up that somehow made me able to crawl into work Monday morning—where I'd promptly been called into Mr. Blue's office.

"You know there's no excuse when it comes to this important a client. I'm sorry, but I'll have to place you on probation for the next three months. You could have cost the company a lot of money." Mr. Blue leaned back in his comfortable-looking leather chair and steepled his fingers. "Don't make any more mistakes, or you'll be having a very serious chat with HR."

"But, sir," I protested, shocked by the severity of my punishment. I'd expected a stern talking-to, but probation? The event had gone smoothly, despite my disappearance halfway through. "I couldn't—"

"That's enough, Audrey," he interrupted me. "You're very lucky you're not looking at a dismissal notice."

If I hadn't felt so completely crushed already, I'm not sure I would have been able to rein in my outrage at the injustice of it all, but as it was I only just managed to hold back the tears as I nodded silently and left Mr. Blue's office.

Eileen waited for me with a cup of freshly made tea in our shared office. She'd heard—as had the rest of the office—about my meeting with the head honcho. At the sight of me, her comforting smile fell. "Was it that bad?"

"I'm on probation," I croaked as I sank down in front of my computer.

"*What?* That's ridiculous! Clement Smith fobbed off his last client's meeting to get a damn pedicure, and it cost them hundreds of thousands. He just got told not to do it again!"

I sniffled into my mug and shrugged half-heartedly. "Smith's a senior account manager. There're different rules, I guess."

"Screw that, Audrey! No one works as hard as you, and you've been here nearly as long. They can't do this to you."

I don't know if it was Eileen's outrage on my behalf that finally cracked the thin shield I'd pulled up around me to be able to make it into work today, but suddenly, I couldn't hold it together anymore. With a loud sob, I surrendered to the tears.

"Oh, honey." Eileen got off her chair and hurried to my side to wrap her arms around my shoulders. "It's going to be okay. It's just a dumb job."

"I-it's noh-ot!" I sobbed into her shoulder. "It-it's Liam, too."

"Liam? What now? I thought it was going well between you two, the way you've been beaming this past week."

"I thought so too," I sobbed. And then I told her the whole, humiliating story, from how I'd taken him home to see my family to climbing St. Paul's Cathedral and falling in love with what turned out to be a couple of twins who'd just been having some fun on my expense.

"Really? Twins?" Something about Eileen's tone was way too excited. I gave her a baleful look before I blew my nose, and she replied with an apologetic grimace. "Sorry, I know you're hurting, honey. It's just... are you sure it was just a game to them? It *sounds* like they really liked you, too. Maybe they just didn't know how to suggest—"

"Stop it, Eileen," I sniffled. "This isn't some weird fetish porn, okay? It's my life, and I let them ruin it because I'm so pathetically needy and *stupid*. I actually thought—I thought I'd met *the one*. As if life is a damn romance novel."

My friend patted my hair and sighed. "I know it sucks, sweety. It'll get better soon, I promise."

IT DIDN'T. By the time Friday rolled around, I was still as miserable as ever. I couldn't even escape into my work as I'd always done when something got me down, because every moment at the office was just another reminder of how unfair my probation was—and the instance that had brought it down upon me.

I was so lost in my own misery that it wasn't until I got off the subway on my way home that I realized I was being followed.

There was something about his reaction when I turned my head and caught the stranger's gaze that made all the small hairs on my body stand on end—something in his cool eyes and the way he quickly averted them when he realized I'd noticed him.

My heart sped up to double its regular pace, kicking my lizard brain into hyper drive as I realized he'd been there since I left work. He'd been outside my office, had followed me across the park and down the Tube, always just outside my field of vision, but close enough that the instincts currently screaming in my head knew it wasn't just a coincidence.

Making a snap decision, I got out of the line to the bus and jogged the few yards to the taxi ramp, quickly hailing a cab. Whoever he was and whatever he wanted, I wasn't about to find out.

I slumped back against the backseat of the taxi as the driver pulled out into the traffic, throwing my stalker a last look out the window. He looked visibly irritated as he watched me drive off.

Nothing about him had seemed even remotely familiar—he had the sort of bland face most people wouldn't notice in a crowd, thinning hair, and was wearing a trench coat and carrying a leather briefcase. Nothing about him had stood out in London's busy business quarter or on the Tube.

So why the heck had he been following me?

No matter what outlandish scenario I tried to think

up, nothing made sense, and in the end, I settled on the conclusion that he'd just been some creeper who'd taken a shine to me for whatever messed up reason some men had to stalk women. Who knew, perhaps he was into misery.

I'd almost put the incident out of my mind when later that evening, I happened to glance out my living room window, the one Liam had made love to me up against, and saw my stalker staring back up at me from the pavement down below. And he wasn't alone. A big, burly man wearing a leather vest stood by his side, bulging arms folded over his chest as he stared up at my window, too.

Behind them, just down the road, a nondescript white van was parked.

TWENTY-FIVE

LOUIS

"Liam—"

My twin shot me the same kind of nasty look he'd given me for the past week the few times we'd been in the same room. He'd hardly been home since then, and I'd only caught him this time because I'd camped out on the sofa and he just so happened to be on his way in to change his clothes. *"No."*

It was the only thing he'd said to me when I'd tried to explain—*no.* It was really all he had to say, because I knew what he meant: *No,* he didn't want to hear my explanations, *no* he wasn't ready to forgive me... *no, we* weren't going to be okay anytime soon, if ever.

I knew I deserved every fucking ounce of loathing he had for me right now, but it didn't mean I was going to give up on him without a fight. I couldn't go to

Audrey and try to sort out the hurt I'd caused her before I knew Liam would be okay. Or at least until he knew why I'd done what I'd done. I owed him that much, and I had to believe it'd be enough. Maybe not right now, but in the long run... I had to believe he'd forgive me some-day. The alternative was too painful to even consider.

"Look, I know you're pissed at me. You have every right to be..." I began. But Liam just shot me another look of utter contempt and continued on his way to his room, ignoring me. I wasn't going to give up that easily, though; not this time. It'd been a full week, and clearly giving him space wasn't helping any. So I got up from the couch and caught him before he left the living room, stopping him by placing a hand on his shoulder. "I'm sorry, mate, we *have* to talk about this. Now."

He spun around then, brushing my hand off in the process. "Oh, we do, do we? And you think you get to tell me when I'm ready to talk, after the stunt you pulled? Go fuck yourself, Louis."

"If not for us, then for Audrey," I interrupted him. "It's been a week—it's not fair on her. I know you care for her—"

He snorted. "She doesn't want to hear it any more than I do—don't you think I've tried to call her and explain it was my idiot twin's idea of a joke? God, Louis! I was gonna... I was gonna find her again, once this fucked up mess with Dad's been sorted. I was gonna *marry* her, and you—" He stopped himself from finishing that sentence, but I saw it all in his eyes as he glared at me. He thought I'd... cost him his true love.

I shook my head. "It's not what you think—she's not supposed to be your wife, Liam. I know what I did was shitty, and I'm sorry. It was never meant to end like this—"

"The fuck do you know about what she's supposed to be?" Liam interrupted me with a nasty snarl. "You still think this is all about you and me, don't you? That's why you tricked her, isn't it—to prove to me she's just another piece of arse? Well, you can go fuck yourself, Louis. If you truly were my other half, you'd fucking *know* how important she is to me. But instead, you *broke* the one good thing that's ever happened to me. I'll *never* forgive you for what you did, Louis. *Never.*"

The vehemence in his voice hurt nearly as much as his words themselves, but in the middle of my despair, my own anger rose. Why was he so fucking quick to think the worst of me? Was his trust in me really that fragile, after all we'd been through together? From the day we were born, it'd been him and me against the world—and he wasn't even willing to fucking hear me out?

"I know she's not meant to be your wife because she's gonna be mine, you fucker," I yelled. "I fell in love with her, okay? Yeah, I was afraid you'd get yourself fucking killed, the way you were acting, so I was gonna show you she was just another girl. I didn't plan for this to happen, but I can't change it now. I *love* her, Liam. And she loves me, too. I'd give anything to have done this any other way than how it went down, but I can't change what happened."

Liam stared at me in shocked silence for two full seconds. Then his face twisted with absolute fury. "*You? You* love her? Get the *fuck* out of here!"

Whatever else he was about to say got drowned out by the sharp chirp of my phone going off. I glanced at the display, and my heart skipped a beat at the name that flashed against me.

Audrey.

I held a hand up to silence my twin and flicked the answer button.

"Audrey? I was gon—" My voice died at the sound of her broken voice.

"*Liam?*"

"It's Louis, love," I said, the sound of my twin's name on her lips making my chest constrict unpleasantly. "You okay? You sound..."

"*Someone's watching my flat. He followed me home from work, and I... I'm sorry to call you like this, but I don't know what else to do. I tried the police, but they don't have time to come out. I wouldn't have called, but... I'm really scared.*"

I could tell she was, from the shaky note in her voice

and just the fact she'd called me. She'd made it pretty damn clear she wanted nothing to do with either of us last Friday. Then the implication of what she'd said set in. Someone... someone followed her home.

If I'd been even halfway convinced it was a run-of-the mill stalker, I'd still been over there in a heartbeat to make sure she was safe, but the timing of this incident was way too convenient. A week after our underhanded partner discovered her ties to us and suddenly someone was hanging around her work and following her home? Yeah, there was zero chance this was a coincidence.

"I'll be there in twenty. Don't open your door for anyone else, got it? And if they try to force their way in, you call me immediately. Not the police—me."

I was already moving toward my bedroom when the call disconnected.

"What's going on?" Liam called after me just as I closed my hand around the gun I kept stashed in my underwear drawer. His voice carried the sick dread currently roiling in the pit of my stomach.

"Fucking Perkinson's put a tail on her," I growled as I stormed out of my bedroom and headed for the front door. "Someone followed her home."

"Bloody hell." I didn't have to look behind me to know he was following as I headed down the stairs to the parking garage. Seemed making sure our girl was safe was one thing we could still work together on.

"I DON'T SEE ANYONE," I mumbled to Liam as I slid out of the Jeep's driver side.

"Let's check 'round back," he said, waving me along as he snuck up to the side of the building.

We moved soundlessly along the side of Audrey's high-rise, making it to the communal area between it and another building. The space was covered in darkness, and I squinted into the shadows, searching for a clue.

"There," Liam hissed, nodding his chin in the direction of some shrubbery. One of the shadows broke free from the bushes and I saw the outline and first one man, then another. They'd spotted us, too.

"Oy!" Liam shouted, breaking into a run. I was right behind him, the weight of the gun in my hand a solid comfort. I'd always hated shooting people, but knowing these pricks were hanging around Audrey's made me feel a hell of lot calmer about the prospect than usual. Whatever they were here for, it wasn't anything good.

The two by the bushes didn't wait for us to catch up to them. They turned around and sprinted off into the night.

We took up pursuit, but they had too much of a lead. They made it to a white van parked up on the side of the pavement and drove off with screeching tires before we could catch up to them.

"Fuck!" Liam pulled the fingers of both hands through his hair as he stared after them. *"Fuck!* I should never have let her alone when I fucking *knew* Perkinson would look into her!"

Neither of us mentioned the other option—that it was our dad's men scouting her out, still. As bad as it was that our supposed ally was spying on our girl, it would be infinitely worse if Dad hadn't bought our fib about her just being a bit of arse.

I didn't respond, just turned around and walked with long strides to the entrance to Audrey's building. She answered the door phone after a few moments, her voice shakier than normal.

"Yes?"

"It's me, love. And Liam. Let us in."

The lock buzzed open, and I followed my twin up the stairs. Audrey opened her door as soon as we knocked, but with the chain on. Smart girl—even if that wouldn't have stopped a made man determined enough to make her an insurance policy.

Her wide, brown eyes flickered from Liam's face to mine before she closed the door again. We could hear the chain rattling, and then she opened it again. There was so much doubt and pain on her face at the sight of us, but right then, it didn't matter. Not when we didn't know if those men were gonna return with reinforcements.

"Grab your toothbrush, love." Liam pushed in past

her and cast a look around the flat—and instinctive reassurance that her home was safe enough for now. "You're coming with us."

TWENTY-SIX
AUDREY

Of course, I refused.

All the way down the stairs and while one of the twins basically lifted me into the backseat of their parked Jeep. I still came with them—the two men who'd ripped my heart out not a week ago, whom I'd sworn I'd never call again when I curled up to cry late at night in my lonely bed.

But I *had* called them when I was scared and didn't have anyone else to turn to. And they'd come. Both of them.

So I followed them when their faces told me things were so much worse than I feared, even as they refused to answer any of my questions and only kept repeating that it would be okay.

"You know who they were, don't you?" I asked as the twin behind the wheel pulled away from my building. It was the only explanation I could find to the way they were acting—that they somehow knew who had been following me, even if it made no sense.

"We have a pretty strong suspicion," the non-driving twin said from the front passenger seat. His voice was as grim as I'd ever heard either of them.

"You don't have to worry, Audrey," the other redhead said. "We'll sort it."

"I don't have to worry?" I repeated, incredulous. "Some creep followed me home and... and stared at my windows all night, like a complete psycho, and then his buddy shows up. And now you two are insisting I drop everything and just flee with nothing but my tooth-brush... excuse me if I find it pretty fucking hard not to worry! For the last time—would you please tell me what's going on?"

I saw them exchanging looks, but neither said anything.

Feeling both irritated and powerless, I fell back against the backrest with a frustrated sigh. "Fine! I guess it's not like you're in the habit of being honest with me anyway."

THE TWINS' flat was in one of the old converted industrial buildings along the river not far off where I'd met Liam that morning my heel broke.

I hadn't seen either of them flash their money at any point in the time I'd known them, but when I stepped into their shared flat, it was pretty obvious their net worth was way above mine. Way, *way* above.

The flat was spacious and effortlessly trendy, with bare brick walls, glowing parquet floors and a view across the Thames that would have taken my breath away if I'd been even a little less out of it. The decor, however, spoke clearly of the amazing space being occupied by two bachelors. A large, black leather sofa dominated the living room we stepped into, and most of the wall facing it had been taken up by a flatscreen TV.

"I'll call Blaine, give him an update," one of the twins said to the other. I didn't know who—seeing them next to each other like this, without being able to check their hands for scars, I couldn't tell the difference.

"And Perkinson?" the other asked, quirking an eyebrow. "I don't much feel like swinging by and asking him what the fuck he's playing at. Can't trust he won't cut his losses and have us executed if we show up without backup."

"And with backup, Dad's bound to find out," the first twin mused. "Fuck."

Perkinson? I blinked—twice. *My* Perkinson? "E-executed?" I croaked.

One twin reached out, stroking a hand comfortingly up along my back. His touch felt so natural, it took me a moment to remember we weren't like that anymore. I pulled away from his comforting hand with a glare, and a flicker of pain crossed his handsome features before he pulled his focus back to the problem at hand.

"You're going to hear a lot of things that won't make a lot of sense to you. We get it's scary, love, we do, but the less you know, the better."

"Don't you think it's a bit too late to hide it from her at this point?" the other twin broke in. "They showed up at her fucking flat."

The first twin glared at his brother. "She didn't ask for this shit, Louis."

"No, but she got it anyway, didn't she?" Louis snapped. "This is what fucking happens when you're a part of our Family, and the sooner she knows the full truth, the sooner she'll know what's at stake here."

"*She* is not a child," I said, my tone about as frustrated as I felt at being kept in the dark. "And if you know why those creeps have anything to do with my client, I think I have a right to know."

The redheads exchanged a long look, and I got the distinct impression they were coming to some sort of agreement.

In the end, Liam exhaled deeply and sank down on the backrest of the sofa. He rubbed his hand across his face before he looked at me. "Fine. Just... know that I never meant for you to get involved in any of this."

"Brian Perkinson, Gregory's father, is the patriarch of a mafia Family. We've been working with them, but after they saw you at the vodka launch last Friday, they must've realized they could use you to get an upper hand over us. At least, that's we think," Louis said.

"That's the good option," Liam muttered.

Fear so intense it reduced my irritation and general worry about my own safety to ashes swept through me as I stared at them. As angry and hurt as I was from what they'd put me through, the part of me that'd fallen in love with their light and vitality was shocked to the core that they'd gotten mixed up with mafia types, of all things.

"Jesus fuck," I whispered, pressing my hand to my mouth as my mind raced for any knowledge I had about the kind of criminals they'd gotten themselves tangled up with so I could try and look for a way out for them. Unfortunately, my spotty knowledge of the criminal underworld came from TV shows. "How did you get messed up with the mafia? *Why?* There's gotta be a way to get you out. Do you owe them mone—" The dark look that passed between the twins made my frantic thoughts still. "What?"

"Audrey..."

"We're not messed up with the mafia."

They both looked at me then, the expression on their faces identical masks of complete and utter seriousness. It looked so alien, so wrong on them.

"We *are* the mafia."

"What?" I whispered, sure I must have heard wrong.

"The Steels are one of the strongest Families in London's underworld."

"Our Family used to rule the city, but... There's a war coming. The Perkinsons were our allies."

"But we suspect that's not the case anymore, if they had you watched."

I looked from one to the other as they talked, looking for even the slightest hint of insincerity. I found nothing. My head was spinning, and I slid down on the backrest next to Liam when my legs threatened to give in.

"You told me... you owned nightclubs," I whispered.

"We do," Liam said resignedly. "Louis and I... we try to spend as little time as we can with the bad shit. We spend most of our time with the nightclubs."

"But... but you *do*... do the 'bad shit,' too?" I asked. I looked at them and tried to reconcile the happy, gentle man I'd thought I was falling in love with with two mafia sons. "You... hurt people?"

A look of regret was mirrored in both their eyes.

"Sometimes." Louis' voice was soft. "When we have to."

"Oh, my God." How could I have gotten them so wrong? I'd thought... but of course, they'd fooled me with who they were as well, so why not *what* they were?

They hurt people.

I got up from the backrest and walked toward the front door.

"Audrey..."

"Don't."

I ignored their calls, intent on the doorknob. I couldn't be a part of this—I couldn't get any further involved, no matter how much my soft, stupid heart was refusing to believe they were truly evil. Even if their own words confirmed what they were: criminals. And not just hackers, or identity thieves, or perpetrators of some white collar crime like that. They were *mafia*, of all things.

A large hand closed around my shoulder the second my fingers touched the door handle.

"We can't let you leave, Audrey."

I spun around and looked up into Louis' gray eyes. They were darker than their normal silver, and the emotion in them pulled at something deep inside of my chest. I pushed it aside.

"What, am I your hostage now?" I sniped, wrapping all my hurt and anger with them for all the lies they'd told around me like an armor. "Are you going to *hurt* me if I leave?"

"*Never.*" They spoke at the same time, the denial immediate and fierce. Louis' stormy eyes turned darker, as if there mere suggestion was the deepest insult they'd ever heard.

"But if we let you leave, whoever was watching you will snatch you up," Liam said.

"And trust us, they *will* hurt you, if for no other reason than to show us they're serious. And we'll never allow anything to happen to you," Louis finished. He didn't release my shoulder until I let my fingers fall away from the doorknob. And even then, he stayed by my side until I stepped away from the door.

As scared and angry and overwhelmed as I was, what they were saying was making too much sense to ignore.

As much as they'd lied to me, they'd come for me the second they'd known I was in danger. As I looked at them, these two men I'd never known as well as I thought, I knew without a shadow of a doubt that they wanted me to be safe.

"Okay," I said, folding my arms across my chest as I looked at them. "What do we do now?"

"*We're* not doing anything," Liam said, his eyebrows arching high on his forehead.

"Liam and I will make some phone calls. *You'll* do nothing," Louis finished. "Are you hungry? I think we have some bread in a cupboard or something."

"I ate, thanks," I snapped. My irritation with once again being pushed out of the loop was possibly irrational—it wasn't like I'd have any idea what to do about rival mafia wars. Ignoring the both of them, I marched over to the couch and sank down in its soft plushness. It might be hideous, but at least it was comfortable.

"Feel free to watch TV," Liam said. He leaned over to get me the remote and stroked a couple of fingers along my cheek as he did. He shifted away before I could move my head from his touch.

I flicked on the giant flatscreen and tried to ignore the longing jab that still went through me whenever either man touched me.

TWENTY-SEVEN
LIAM

"Liam?"

My consciousness slowly seeped back at the achingly familiar voice speaking my name. For a moment, while the haze of sleep lifted, I thought I was back in Audrey's bed, and the warm sense of completion that filled me made a lazy smile spread on my lips. "Mmh?"

"The bread's moldy."

I frowned, the comfortable feeling lifting as I became aware of the painful kink in my neck. I grimaced and stretched, feeling leather underneath me rather than my comfortable mattress. I wasn't in Audrey's bed—I was on the living room sofa, and the realization made last night's events come rushing back like a flood of proverbial shit.

My eyes flew open and I looked up into Audrey's

pretty face. She had sleep-messy hair, but she was fully dressed in the same set of comfortable jogging pants and T-shirt she'd been in last night. I hadn't stripped her when I'd carried her into my bedroom last night after she'd fallen asleep on the sofa to *Two and a Half Men* reruns, figuring she'd probably not appreciate being naked around either of us at the moment. Similar reasons was why I'd slept on the sofa. Normally, I'd have bunked with Louis, but that wasn't in the cards at the moment. As much as we needed to work together to ensure Audrey's safety, I hadn't forgotten what he'd done. And I doubted I ever would.

"What?" I croaked, coughing to clear my throat.

"The bread—it's moldy. I'm starving, and you literally don't have anything else to eat in the house." She arched an eyebrow at me. "I assume I'm not supposed to do a quick croissant run."

"Oh, sorry." I pushed the blanket off and sat up with a grimace at my stiff neck. "We usually keep something around, but..." But neither of us had had the mind to shop in the past week.

I rubbed my neck. "I'm just waiting for a call from our brother—he's got some spies out, keeping tabs on Perkinson. Once he's given us the all-clear, I'll get some food for us, love."

"Okay," she said, her voice flat. With a sigh she sank down in the armchair to the right of the sofa. "You didn't have to give me your bed. I could have slept on the couch."

I snorted. Fat chance I'd make her sleep on the damn sofa. "It's all right."

She didn't respond, but she didn't leave, either. I looked over at her, and my chest tightened at the sight of her pretty face. I'd missed her so goddamn much, it'd been nearly unbearable. Only the promise I kept repeating to myself that I'd find her again once this shit with our dad was over—and somehow convince her to give me another chance—had made me strong enough to pull through.

When I'd seen her at Perkinson's event, I'd been too floored by her unexpected appearance to do what I should have done—quickly diverted her to ensure Perkinson never suspected she was more than a distant acquaintance. But I'd been so wrapped up in the rush of emotion her nearness brought up, I didn't manage to react. And when she'd told him we were *together*... I'd been too confused at her apparent disregard for the break up between us that I hadn't kept a sharp enough eye on Brian.

A least her reaction to seeing me there was explained when I saw her in Louis' arms moments later.

The acid fury in my gut returned at the memory of how utterly... How completely *in love* she'd looked as he held her close, the way *I* was supposed to. The way I had been, until I'd realized how much danger I was putting her in. I'd thought I could keep her away from my world, but I'd been wrong. So I'd given her up, because I couldn't keep her safe any other way, even though it nearly killed me. I knew my text would have fucking broken her heart, and that I'd promised her... But I'd had no other choice.

And then Louis... My fucking *twin*—the one person I'd always been able to count on... He'd brought her right back into the danger zone for his own selfish, fucked up reasons.

She hated us both now. I didn't know what lies he'd told her to get her to look past my text, but she sure as shit was blaming me in equal measure for his deception.

"I didn't know he went to you," I said.

She gave me a dark look. It spoke of so much mistrust, it made my chest ache.

"I didn't know he was pretending to be me," I said. I needed her to know.

"I'm sure. That's why you never called to straighten it out after I found out, right? Makes perfect sense."

God, she was so hurt. It was clear to see, through her armor of anger. She'd been hurt so fucking much, and as much as I wanted to blame Louis for it all, I knew it'd started with me. When I left her, after promising I wouldn't mess her around. Then what she'd said set in, and I frowned.

"I called you. Multiple times."

"You didn't." She fished out her phone and lobbed it

at me. "Check the call records, why don't you? Neither of you called."

I swiped right to open her phone and pressed her call logs. There were no incoming calls from my number this prior week. I bit the inside of my cheek when it occurred to me that she didn't have a PIN on her phone.

He wouldn't have...

I navigated through her phone until I got to the list of blocked numbers. Mine was the only one on there. When I checked, I recognized Louis' number by my name under her address book.

That absolute piece of *shit*—

My own phone chimed, pulling my attention from the renewed surge of betrayal rising in the pit of my gut. One glance at the display revealed Blaine's name. Finally, some news. I answered with a swipe of my thumb.

"Dad knows. Wesley's on his way. Get out—now."

Blaine's voice was stressed, and his toddler was fussing in the background, but the warning made it through my own frustration and anger like a bucket of ice water.

Dad knew.

I was on my feet and headed toward Louis' room without missing a beat, pushing aside the sensation of marrow-shattering fear. We'd been prepped for this since Blaine and Marcus told us what our father had done to our two older brothers.

"Perkinson?" I asked as I pushed Louis' door open. "Louis, get the gear. We've got to go."

"Yes. He flipped. My guy said he'd been scared as shit you'd come for him and figured his only chance was going to Dad. I'm getting Aiden and Mira out. We'll have to have radio silence for a while. I'll contact you when I can—you still got the burner?" Blaine was all business. I could hear him moving around on his end, and Mira shushing their kid. Then the sound of car doors slamming and an engine roaring to life.

"Yeah, we've got it. One hour, 10 p.m., every Sunday."

"Stay safe. Both of you." Blaine's voice cut out as the call ended.

My twin sat up in the nest of blankets on his bed, his usual morning grogginess quickly wiped away as he looked at me. "He knows?"

"Yes." It was all I had to say. Louis was in motion, heading for closet with a look of determination writ across his features. One I knew perfectly mirrored my own.

I turned my phone off and shoved it back in my pocket—we'd have to wait until we were out of town to get rid of them—and jogged to my own room across the hall.

Audrey stood by the crossover between the living room and hallway when Louis and I came out from our rooms less than thirty seconds later, her arms wrapped around her midsection with her brows knitted in a frown. "What's going on?"

"We've gotta go, love," Louis said. He put the arm not loaded down by a heavy trekking backpack around her shoulders so he could steer her toward the front door. "Right now. Get your shoes on."

She did as he said, but the confusion was clear on her face as we herded her down the stairs, Louis' arm never leaving her shoulders. He was protecting her, I realized, with a start that managed to make its way even through my grim sense of urgency to get out of London before our father's right hand man got to us. And despite my anger with him, despite how fucking betrayed I still felt at what he'd gone, and fucking *furious* I was at his claim to love my future wife... I found that right now, when the only priority was to make sure she was safe... it felt as right that he had his arm around her as it would have if it'd been my own.

The twins drove us North out of London in their Jeep, but after three hours of back road driving they finally pulled into what looked an abandoned farm. They still hadn't explained what was going on, but after the revelation of what they were, I didn't much care to push for details. The less I knew, the better my chances to make it out alive.

My perspective changed somewhat abruptly, until Louis jumped out of the passenger side and walked over to open the gates of what looked like an ancient barn that could topple over at any moment, and Liam drove the Jeep—with me still in the back—into its dark interior.

"Is this where you'll both reveal you're also crazy mass murderers, and this has all been a ruse to lure me to your remote Farm of Torture?" I was only halfway joking. Sure, I still had an innate trust that whatever was going on, they were doing their best to ensure I'd make it through safe and sound, but come on... a fucking *barn?*

"I'm sorry, love," Liam said as he put the Jeep into park and pulled the handbrake. "I know you must be confused as fuck. Just... let us get to safety, okay? We'll explain, if you want us to, once we're not running anymore."

I frowned at him. "We're still running? We're in the middle of nowhere. No one's around for miles."

He scoffed. "It takes a hell of a lot more to shake a man like our dad."

"Wait... your *dad?* I thought we were running from Perkinson?" My hesitation at getting further involved was brushed away by the revelation that for whatever reason, we were running away from their father, of all people. "Isn't he... I thought... Aren't mafia Families supposed to be super loyal?"

I caught his grimace in the rearview mirror as he unbuckled his seatbelt and slid out of the Jeep. "This isn't a TV show, love. My dad's nothing that can be confused with *loyal.*" He spat the word out as if it tasted foul on his tongue.

Seemed I'd hit a sore point. But then I guessed it would have to be, if they were actually *running* from their own dad. For the first time since they'd told me what they were, the creeping notion that being in a mafia Family perhaps wasn't the happiest of lives niggled at the back of my mind. Even though they'd deceived me, I was pretty sure the vital, vibrant man—or men, I supposed—I'd fallen so hard for were real enough. At least partly. No one could fake the kind of aura that'd pulled me in like a moth to a flame. But that obviously wasn't all there was to them. I'd seen that clear enough when Liam—or Louis, I wasn't sure—had come to me so distraught I'd pushed my own discomfort aside to comfort him the only way I knew how.

What would it be like for someone with the kind of light and warmth both twins carried at their cores to grow up inundated with violence and crime?

I pushed the disturbing thought aside and crawled out into the barn. Right now was definitely not the time to think about such things.

Louis was waiting for me. He grabbed my hand before I could trip off the vehicle and lifted me down. Ensuring I didn't fall, like he had the night we'd climbed St. Paul's Cathedral.

No, definitely not the time for such contemplations.

I stepped away from his grip and looked around the darkened barn. It smelled like damp, rusty metal and moldy hay. The gaps in the ramshackle walls let in enough light to let me see a few lumps underneath tarps scattered around between piles of old hay and ancient farm tools.

Liam walked to one of the tarp-covered shapes and pulled off the cover with a crinkly rattle, revealing a nondescript station wagon. It was the newest-looking thing in the barn by several decades, but it was still a sad downgrade from the Jeep.

Louis covered the Jeep up with the tarp, then proceeded to pull out his phone and smash it with a rusty hammer he'd picked from the floor. Liam handed him his phone, and he repeated the process until there were two small piles of plastic and glass next to each other in the hay.

They both looked at me, and I inadvertently pressed a protective hand to the pocket that held my phone. My last anchor to a life that'd never involved made men or a need to flee the city. "Surely that's not necessary?"

WHEN WE CROSSED the border to Wales in a third car somewhere close to midnight, but only after having crisscrossed a good part of England to throw off anyone still on our trail, I was feeling pretty damn dejected. It might have had something to do with the fact that I hadn't had anything to eat other than three power bars all day, but I'd kind of given up holding it together since the twins made me surrender my phone. It was as if seeing my last connection to what I'd thought was reality smashed to pieces in front of me had finally made me realize how utterly and completely terrifying my situation was. I was far away from home, with two men I might trust to try and keep me safe but honestly didn't know—two criminals, no less—and the mafia on our trail. The fact that neither Liam nor Louis said more than a few words to me or each other, and how their wildly uncharacteristic brooding filled the car with nervous energy, made it perfectly clear that they were worried too.

We drove into the mountains along completely dark, winding farm roads for what felt like forever until finally, Louis pulled the car to a stop deep into what turned out to be dense woodland. When I crawled out, wincing as I got to stretch my cramping legs for the first time in hours, I could hear rushing water somewhere to my right, but I couldn't see more than a hand ahead of me. Even the stars were blocked out by the heavy canopies above us.

Both twins flicked on a flashlight each. Liam handed me his, before he pulled out his heavy rucksack from the boot of the car and held out his free hand to me.

I hesitated to take it, and he snorted at my reluctance.

"The river you can hear to your right is at the bottom of a steep drop, and it's got some nasty rocks around this bend. You familiar enough with the area to know where to step to avoid falling to your death?"

I narrowed my eyes at him, but relented. I wasn't much of a hiker on the best of days, let alone in pitch darkness after the most distressing day of my life. "I don't even know where we are," I muttered as I slipped my hand into his. The warm, safe sensation that coursed through me when he closed his fingers around mine was as comforting as it was unwelcome.

It didn't take more than ten minutes hiking through the uneven terrain for me to become grateful for Liam's hand. Not that I saw anything of the supposedly deadly drop somewhere to our right, but his firm grip saved me from more than one twisted ankle. Roots and rocks seemed to pop up from the ground every few inches. Both twins moved across the uneven ground like damn mountain goats, even weighed down by their heavy packs, and I got the distinct impression that buildings weren't the only thing they climbed in their free time.

Free time from their criminal day job. Christ.

It felt like we'd walked for-absolute-ever when the woods finally opened up and the twins slowed to a stop.

The stars spread out above us like the most stunning patchwork ever, and despite my exhaustion and general unease, the sight of it made me gasp in in awe. I wasn't much of a camper, to put it mildly, and it'd been a very, very long time since I'd seen the night sky without city lights dimming its jaw-dropping beauty.

"We're here," Liam said. He gave my hand a small squeeze, and I pulled my gaze from the stars above to settle on the clearing in front of us. I couldn't see it all in the illuminated cone from my flashlight, but it looked like we were standing in front of an ancient shack consisting of uneven rock walls and a patchy roof with a small chimney sticking up. It could have been taken straight out of the early Middle Ages—even though I was pretty sure they had doors even back then. This little shack just had an opening in the side with nothing to cover it.

A sinking feeling settled in below my ribs. "We're *where*, exactly?"

"Home sweet home." Louis sounded awfully cheerful all of a sudden, and I had the feeling it was because of my less than thrilled demeanor. I shot him a glare that he completely ignored as he moved into the shack and let his flashlight move around the small space. "Ah, we're in luck. No rats' nests, and the firewood's still here from last time we came."

Rats' nests? I turned my head to stare at Liam in horror. Surely this was some kind of joke.

"It's a mountain bothy," Liam explained. "They're set up around the country for anyone to use. This one hardly ever gets any traffic, so we picked it for our emergency plan. We'll be able to hide out here until Blaine gets in touch, without our dad finding us."

No wonder it never got any traffic—I looked back at the small hut and shuddered. I don't know what I'd expected, but it certainly wasn't *this*.

The last—and only—time I'd been camping, I'd been seven. My dad had gotten the great idea to take the family to a campsite on the coast. We'd stayed in a nice camping wagon, but my mum had complained about the communal showers and tight living quarters non-stop for two days until he finally gave up and drove us all to the nearest hotel. I wasn't a nature girl in any way, shape, or form.

But then again, not getting killed by the mafia might rank higher than comfortable accommodation, I told myself as I drew in a big breath and finally walked inside. Even if only slightly.

The hut had a dirt floor and a small fireplace. And that was it.

Louis was currently kneeling in front of said fireplace, messing with some tinder. It didn't take him long to get a small fire started that lit up the tiny space. It was maybe ten by six feet, with the open doorway located at the other end to the fireplace.

Liam dropped his heavy pack next to Louis' by the far wall and stretched his strong body with a sigh. "Right, let's get some food on. You hungry, Audrey?"

"I could eat a horse." I rubbed a hand against my growling belly. "But if all you've got are more protein bars, I'll pass."

"Nah, we packed actual food." Louis flashed me a smile. "And coffee... No horses, though."

The promise of coffee made me perk up just a little. "Okay, great. Hey, where's the bathroom?"

Liam rummaged through his pack and pulled up a small shovel and a roll of brown toilet paper that he held out toward me. "Turn left once you're out of the bothy—the forest is more even in that direction, but don't go too far."

I stared at him. "You have *got* to be kidding me."

He looked genuinely surprised for a moment, but then lit up in a grin when my horrified expression finally clicked. "You're a proper city girl, huh?"

"Well, yeah, if by '*proper city girl*' you mean '*definitely not going to dig her own goddamn toilet out of the ground*,' then sure."

"I can come along and dig it for you, if you really prefer," Louis offered from his crouch in front of the fire. The slight gleam of amusement in his eyes told me he was definitely enjoying my horror.

"No thanks," I hissed, snatching paper and shovel out of Liam's hand. "I've got it."

The twins' chuckle followed me out into the dark clearing.

They both shot me amused looks when I came back in a few minutes later, but thankfully didn't comment on my traumatized expression as I plopped down on the rolled out square of tarp they'd placed on the floor a little ways off from the fireplace. A small pot was resting on an iron ring over the flames, and food-smells from it made my stomach growl. A kettle hung from a hook on the iron ring—probably where our coffee would come from.

"How long do you think we'll have to stay here?"

Liam shrugged. At least I thought it was Liam—they'd both moved after I left, and I wasn't close enough to check their hands for scars. "A while. Our brother Blaine will be working on a plan while we hide out here—he's got a larger network than we do."

I wanted to ask what would happen after their brother pulled said plan together, but frankly, I didn't think I had it in me. Not tonight. Too much had happened in the past twenty-six hours, and I couldn't stomach anymore. So I propped myself up against the rough stone wall, ate the plate of beans and sausages Louis offered me, and tried not to think about what the future held.

It turned out to be much easier than it'd been during the car ride here. The late time of day—or night—the food, and the crackling of firewood all worked to melt the stress from my body until my eyelids grew heavy and my limbs felt like lead.

"Ready for bed?" one of the twins asked, his voice softer than usual. Probably so as not to stir me from my near-comatose state.

I nodded and he rolled out a sleeping bag on top of the tarp and unzipped it for me. "Climb on in."

I kicked off my shoes and obeyed with a pleased hum. It didn't even matter that I was laying on a dirt floor only covered by a tarp—my mind switched off the moment my head touched the ground.

TWENTY-NINE
AUDREY

I cared a lot more about my lack of mattress early the next morning, when I woke up to every muscle in my body aching from the rock-hard surface I'd been sleeping on all night. I was also sweating buckets, thanks to going to bed in my clothes, and when I rolled over with a groan to try and ease some of my discomfort, my elbow hit solid flesh.

That's when I realized I wasn't alone in the sleeping bag.

Whichever twin had climbed in beside me after I'd fallen asleep grunted at the impact and then proceeded to roll over and wrap his arms around my midsection.

"Stop that!" I hissed, just as desperate to escape his body heat as I was dismayed at the uninvited closeness to one of the men who'd tricked me so gruesomely. It was one thing to trust them to keep me safe from their mafia ties—the intimacy of waking up in the same sleeping bag was something else entirely. Especially when I felt something hard begin to grow against my backside.

"What?" the redhead grumbled as he nuzzled his nose in against my hair, obviously still mostly asleep. A few feet away, on the other end of the tarp, the other twin cracked open a pair of sleepy, silvery eyes at the disturbance. He was, thankfully, in his own sleeping bag.

"Touching me!" I pushed at his arms until he released me and then fought my way out of the confining bedroll. I scampered to my feet, wincing at my sore back's protests, and placed my hands on my hips as I glared down at both of them. My less than quiet awakening had seemingly pulled them both out of their slumber. They looked like identical, sleep-mussed images of confusion.

"*Why* were you in my sleeping bag?" I asked the twin whose grasp I'd just escaped.

"We only prepped for two," he said, hiding a yawn behind his hand. "One of us had to bunk with you."

I opened my mouth to lay into him, but nothing came out. All right, so that was a pretty good reason. Not that that made my foul mood much better. I was still hot and sticky and sore all over, and judging from the light shining in through the open doorway, I'd had less than six hours' sleep after what'd been the most stressful and traumatizing day in my entire life. What I needed was a shower. And coffee.

"I need to wash, but I'm afraid to ask about the bathing facilities," I said, glancing from one twin to the other. They'd both stripped down, it seemed, from what I could see of their bare, tattooed torsos.

"I'll come with," my bed partner sighed. "Sleeping with you was like holding a damn toaster oven all night." He climbed out of the sleeping bag, and I was somewhat relieved to see his maroon pair of boxer shorts. That is, until I noticed the unmistakable bulge in them. Quickly, I looked away, only to catch his twin's amused gaze. He'd clearly seen what I'd been looking at.

With an irritated huff I grabbed my toothbrush and stomped out of the shack, hoping the flush I could already feel spreading across my cheeks would die down before any of them woke up enough to start teasing me.

Maroon boxers came out a few moments laters, still only dressed in his underwear and with a towel over his one arm and what looked to be a bar of soap, some toothpaste, and his own toothbrush in his hand. He stretched, making all those taut muscles in his abdomen and chest roll in the most mesmerizing way. He looked like a big cat waking up after a nap. A disturbingly sexy cat.

I looked away before my cheeks could heat up again.

"Nothing like waking up in nature," he said with a happy sigh. "Come on, I'll show you where we bathe."

Clearly someone hadn't woken up with a sore everything.

Damn youth.

I shuffled after him through the small clearing that housed our shack, ignoring the stunning beauty that surrounded me. I was way too sore and way too grumpy to appreciate the lush little enclave, the woods surrounding it, and the mountaintops lining the horizon as far as the eye could see.

Maroon led me through the trees until they gave way to a calm, slow-moving river.

"It's the same river you heard when we were walking up. It's just much safer in this part—you can swim if you like, but only here. It's got some nasty undercurrents further down, and a lot of sharp rocks." My bed partner dropped his belongings on the shore and stuck a toe in. "Refreshing!"

I wanted to bitch about the fact that he clearly expected me to wash in a goddamn *river,* but given the fact that I'd had to squat behind a bush to pee last night, I just didn't have any more fight left in me. With a resigned sigh, I grabbed the toothpaste and sat down to clean my teeth.

Next to me, Maroon dropped his boxers—giving me an eyeful of his perfectly sculpted arse—and then *ran* into the goddamn water like an over-excited Labrador. I squealed as ice-cold river water splattered me and got a deep laugh in response before he finally—

at the middle of the river—dove headfirst into the water.

"You jerk!" I growled when he finally popped up again, red hair plastered to his scalp and eyes sparkling with mischief and pure zest for life. I hadn't seen that expression on either of them for more than a week, and despite my general annoyance—and soaked top—seeing it now made something in my chest warm.

"Come on in—the water's great," he said, splashing in my general direction, but without hitting me this time.

"Yeah, it's not." I held out my wet top for emphasis. "It's colder than a melted glacier."

"Unless you plan on smelling like ripened cheese, you'll have to come in eventually," he teased. "We won't see a hot shower for a least a month."

I paled. "A *month?* You're joking."

The twin's teasing smile fell for that look of serious-ness they'd both had all day yesterday. "It's going to take Blaine some time to figure something out. We'll be here for quite a while. And after that, we may have to move to another safe location. I know this is a lot for you to deal with, love, and I'm sorry. I tried to protect you from all this shit, and I know I've failed."

"But... my job," I croaked when it finally fully sunk in that I wouldn't be back to my regular life for quite possibly a very long time. "I can't just disappear. They'll fire me! I have to call them, I have to let them know—"

"I'm sorry," he repeated, and from the look of him, he truly was. "You can't. Perkinson knows where you work, it's not safe to get in touch with them."

"But—"

"Your job is not more important than your life, Audrey." His voice was suddenly stern, demanding obedience. It was such a sharp contrast to his usual self, it finally cracked through the last defense I'd put up around myself to get through this insanity. With a rush of startling clarity, I finally understood that my life would never go back to how it had been. If I even made it through alive, I'd never go back to my old job, I'd never gossip with Eileen over piles of reports, and I'd never get the promotion I'd killed myself to get for the past three years.

My career was over. You didn't just take off for more than a month with no warning or explanation and not have it go on your permanent record. Everything I'd worked for for as long as I could remember was over.

The twin was as surprised by my tears as I was. When the first deep sobs broke free of my awfully constricted chest, he flinched as if the sound caused him physical pain. Then, without hesitation, he came out of the water and onto the shore to wrap me up in his wet embrace.

I leaned in against his chest, not caring that he soaked me through with cold river water, just grateful to be held as everything I'd held dear seemed to fall apart and leave me feeling so naked and alone I could barely stand it.

All my life, I'd worked myself to the bone trying to get the perfect career, and within a day it had been stripped from me, leaving me with nothing. I was nothing without my job—it was my entire identity, my entire life. I couldn't even imagine what my parents would say when they found out their youngest daughter had ruined her prospects. It wasn't like I'd be able to tell them it was because I'd somehow gotten involved with the mafia. No, I was completely on my own now.

Except for the twins who'd caused this disaster in the first place.

As I cried my eyes out on the redhead's shoulder, I had the vague realization that I wasn't angry at them for dragging me into this. Angry that they'd deceived me, yes. Angry and scared that *they* were mafia—yes.

But not angry that they'd inadvertently lost me everything I'd ever worked for. Because... because the only way they could have avoided it was if we'd never met at all.

As I clung to the twin whose name I wasn't even sure of, I knew I'd never been truly alive until the day I met Liam. I didn't know why, or even how, but I knew it was the truth.

"You okay?" he murmured against my ear when my tears finally stilled.

I nodded shakily. The coldness of his wet flesh was

finally starting to seep through my emotional state. My clothes were soaked now—there was no way I could leave them on, or I'd risk getting sick. I pushed against his chest and he released me.

"I need to wash. And I might as well give my clothes a quick rinse too. I've been wearing them for nearly two days and I didn't exactly get a chance to pack any spares."

He didn't say anything as I slipped out of my clothes, but I could feel his eyes on me when I stood naked—and freezing—by the side of the river. I fought back a blush at the knowledge of his attention—he'd seen me naked before, and I'd just been cuddled up against his bare form as if it was the most natural thing in the world. Now was not the time to get bashful.

I washed my clothes as quickly as I could, using the bar of soap he'd brought, and then forced myself to wade out in the freezing water. It was even colder than I'd thought from the splashes I'd received, and I squealed the entire way until I slipped on a smooth river stone and plunged under.

When I came up again, gasping and spurting water like a lost orca, deep, masculine laughter rang through the quiet woodland.

"Prick!" I shouted. I didn't turn around to glare at him, knowing full well I'd just get another eyeful of his naked body if I did. His only answer was more laughter.

I washed up as quickly as I could, with my back

turned to the near shore to preserve just a smidgen of modesty. That's probably why I didn't realize we'd gotten company until I was on my way back to dry land.

I looked up from the riverbed once I was almost all the way to shore and reasonably certain I wouldn't slip on any more stones, and the sight that met me made me stop in my tracks, still ankle-deep in cold river water.

Both twins were sitting on the grass by my wet clothes, watching me. The brother who'd brought me to the river was still gloriously naked and sporting an erection—the other was dressed, but I was pretty sure I saw a bulge in his jeans before I managed to quickly avert my gaze again.

"For fuck's sake! Don't you two have anything better to do than creep on me?" I hissed.

"Not really, no." The newcomer shot me a cheeky smile and tossed a towel at me. "You'll find the WiFi reception out here is pretty poor."

"Ha ha." I wrapped the towel around myself, then folded my arms as the cool air made my skin break out into goosebumps, and leveled the clothed twin with a glare. I wasn't feeling another accidental take of bared penis, so I purposefully didn't look at his naked mirror image. When he opened his mouth again, the mirth was way too prominent in his silver eyes to ignore. I bent for my wet clothes and toothbrush and stalked off without giving him the chance to continue. They might have forgotten what'd happened between us in the panic of suddenly running for our lives, but I hadn't. I wasn't about to subject myself to more of their teasing charms and pretend like they hadn't broken my heart.

We might have to live together in this camping version of hell, but I wasn't going to let their natural humor and charm pull the wool over my eyes ever again.

BUT AS THE DAYS PASSED, it became increasingly obvious that both their moods were far from the warm, joking demeanor I'd come to know.

The first day, I assumed it was a natural reaction to our circumstances, and I was too wrapped up in how miserable I was myself to pay it much mind.

By the second night, I realized there was more to it than just the stress of the situation.

I was feeling kind of off, so I'd curled up in one of the sleeping bags to rest for a bit after dinner—another exciting meal consisting of tinned beans and bland meat —but the rough ground felt harder than normal, and my muscles were already sore. I was too uncomfortable to fall asleep, so I just lay there with my eyes closed, feeling sorry for myself.

"It's time to turn on the phone," one of the twins said.

"I know." Ruffling as one of them searched through

their bag followed, and shortly after, the tune of a phone being turned on.

"Do you think there's any chance Blaine's found a way in yet?"

"No."

The first twin sighed, an irritated sound. "This isn't getting any easier by your refusal to speak in more than one-syllable words."

"Why would I? There's nothing to talk about that requires anything more," the second twin snapped.

"The hell there isn't." The first twin had lowered his voice, but the frustration in it was still evident. "We're stranded in fucking no-man's land for God knows how long—with *her*. What do you want us to do, fucking ignore each other?"

"Not like it's out of character for you to ignore when something you do is shitty," twin two said.

"For fuck's sake, Liam," twin one—Louis—growled. "*You* were the one to call Dad's attention to it in the first place! I was trying to help. I couldn't predict it'd end like it fucking did!"

"*I don't want to hear it.* Do me a fucking favor and just fuck off," Liam said, and there was so much vehemence in his voice, it made an unexpected wave of hurt on his twin's behalf bloom in my chest. I'd never known either of them were even capable of so much anger, and it tore at my heart. I didn't know what'd gotten between them, or even how their usual relationship was, but this seemed so terribly *wrong*. I had no idea why my reaction to something that really didn't include me in any way was so strong, but tears welled behind my closed eyelids.

Louis sighed, a dejected sound this time, and I could tell he'd gotten up from the noises from the other end of the shack where he and Liam had relocated to not disturb me while I tried to sleep. Moments later he slipped into the sleeping bag behind me. His strong arms closed around my midriff, pulling me in against his bare chest, and pressed his face against the back of my hair. Hugging me, like a child would his favorite teddy bear.

It felt…. It felt like it had when we'd been together before I learned the truth—back when everything had seemed so perfect. He was so warm and comfortable, and I couldn't fight the sense of complete and utter calm that settled into my body at his embrace. The fact that he thought I was asleep, that I knew this wasn't some ploy to try and seduce me, let me push all the anger and hurt aside for just a few moments.

I knew I shouldn't have responded like this to being held by either twin, but right then, I didn't have the strength to fight against it. If being held by Louis for just a little while could make some of my misery ease, then it had to be okay. Just this once.

I fell asleep to to the steady sound of his breath rising and falling against my ear.

THIRTY

LOUIS

The sun had only just breached the horizon when I
woke up on the third day after our escape from London.

Audrey was still snug in my arms, like a warm, solid
reminder of why I'd done what I had to my twin.

It'd hurt so fucking much to hear the hatred in his
voice last night. He kept it together around Audrey, we
both did, and I guess I'd stupidly thought that meant we
could start to slowly work it out. I'd been so wrong, and
it'd cut me so fucking deep to see how much the only
person I'd ever shared anything real with hated my guts.

Well... the only person besides the soft woman still
sleeping soundly in my arms.

I kissed her still T-shirt-clad shoulder and wished
she'd be comfortable enough around us to sleep naked,
but knew it was too much to expect. I hadn't had a

chance to try to sort anything out with her yet, and as much as everything inside me ached to have her hold me back, I knew I had to clear the air with Liam first. I owed him that much, after how terribly I'd betrayed him.

Even if he was being a royal prick about it.

I pulled my arm back from where Audrey had been using it as a pillow all night, careful not to disturb her even as the limb prickled with pins and needles from having been forced into the same position for so many hours.

She murmured disapprovingly in her sleep, but settled down when I pushed my T-shirt from yesterday under her head. Both Liam and I'd only brought one change of clothes, and it needed a wash, but would do as a pillow for now. She obviously wasn't much of a camping enthusiast, and I'd noticed how stiffly she moved after a night on the tarp. If we'd had any idea she'd be coming along back when we packed in case of having to leave town, we'd probably have found some way of making things a bit more comfortable. But we hadn't known, and she was stuck with what little comforts we could provide with the bare minimum we'd brought.

It was also why I was getting up at the bloody crack of dawn, despite the yearning to stay snuggled up with Audrey for a few more hours. We'd packed food for two people to live off for a month, no more, and fishing gear to make that stretch a while longer if necessary. With Audrey here, we'd have to start fishing much sooner. Liam and I might be okay with living off a low-calorie diet for a week or two, but I wasn't about to let my future wife starve.

I slipped fully out of the sleeping bag, lamenting the loss of Audrey's warmth when the cool morning air wrapped around my bare legs and torso. But when I moved to grab my pants and spare T-shirt out of my pack, I noticed something dark and sticky covering everything from my navel and down across my thighs in viscous splatters. It looked like... blood?

My brain froze for half a second when I realized what it was. I was covered in blood. But I felt fine...

Audrey.

I'd never felt terror as deep into the marrow of my bones as I did when the truth hit me like a ton of bricks.

It wasn't my blood—it was Audrey's.

Frantic, I ripped the sleeping bag off her to see where she'd been hurt as I called out for my twin. It didn't matter that we weren't on good terms then—all I could process was that Audrey was in trouble, and I needed him.

"Liam!"

My shout didn't just wake my twin with a start— Audrey sat up with a spasm, her eyes wide and unfocused as she looked at my frantic attempts at getting her legs free from the sleeping bag without jostling her too much. It was splattered with blood, too, and so were her knickers.

"What's going on?" Liam was out of his own sleeping bag and by my side before Audrey could even get out a startled, *"What the hell?"* his brows knitted with concentration as he took in the scene. The second he noticed the blood, he turned white as a sheet.

"Baby, you're bleeding," I said, trying to speak as softly as my panic would let me. "Where does it hurt?"

"It doesn't," she said, alarm making its way to her voice, too. She tried to see, but Liam pushed her down on her back and pressed a hand on her shoulder to keep her still.

"Best if you don't move, love," he said, his voice rough with the same choking terror I felt thrashing in my gut. He looked at me, and I saw naked panic in his eyes. "We've got to get her to a hospital."

I nodded, feeling sick to my core. Neither of us knew how far away the nearest hospital was, and we had a thirty minute hike to get to the car. Not to mention the risk of being seen in public—our father's reach was very long, and even in Wales we couldn't be certain. But that was just a risk we had to take.

Working together, we began to gently ease Audrey's underwear down her thighs. If we could, we'd have to stem the bleeding before we tried to move her.

However, we didn't get very far before Audrey made a squeaky little sound and swatted our hands away with surprising strength. "Stop that, you imbeciles!" she hissed. "Right now!"

"Audrey—"

"I'm not dying, what the actual fuck!" She pulled at her panties, managing to wedge them back up to cover her fully. "I obviously got my period. What's the matter with you?!"

Liam and I stared at each other in numb disbelief. The adrenaline was still coursing through my veins, making it hard to fully grasp what she'd said.

Liam looked at the blood-soaked sleeping bag to where she was covering her smeared crotch with her hands, a mix of embarrassment and fury on her pretty face. "Are you sure? It's so much blood..."

"Yes, I'm fucking sure!" Audrey pulled her legs underneath her and scrambled to her feet. "God, have you two ever had a biology class?"

My twin and I stared mutely after her as she stomped out of the bothy. My heart was slowly starting to regain its normal speed, and my head felt light with relief as the adrenaline started to wear off.

"She is going to hate us forever, isn't she?" Liam said. A snort escaped him, halfway between amusement and exasperation. "Fuck."

"In our defense, it's a little startling to wake up in

what looks like a crime scene," I offered, rubbing my hand across my face with a sigh. "She's gonna need those feminine product things—I don't suppose you happened to pack anything that can substitute?"

Liam shook his head but headed for his pack. "The gauze from the first aid kit will have to do."

"Bet she's gonna love that," I muttered.

We found her by the river, waist deep in the water. When she saw us, she turned her back on the shore, but not before we'd seen the embarrassed flush on her face.

I kicked my boxers off and left them next to her bloodstained clothes, and then I waded out toward her while Liam dipped the sleeping bag in the river to rinse it out.

"You okay, love?" I asked Audrey when I got out to her. She still had her back turned to me, and for a moment I thought she might try to ignore me. But then her shoulders sank and she lost her stiff posture.

"I'm really sorry," she croaked, still without turning around. "I didn't know—"

"Don't be daft." I put my hand on her shoulder and made her turn around to face me. She did so reluctantly, and when I finally made her look at me, she looked so mortified, as if she'd done something wrong. "It's just something that happens to birds, isn't it? Nothing to do about it."

"I guess you did sit through a biology class or two," she muttered, clearly trying to make light of the situation. I gave her a wry smile and—ignoring her startled protests—pulled her into a hug.

"Ugh, stop that!" she hissed, but her hands on my torso only pushed for a moment. Then she relaxed and let me hold her, even if she did still grumble under her breath.

"I'm only allowing this because you're warm and this river is liquid ice," she warned.

I pecked the top of her hair, ignoring her little huff in response. I'd been so fucking scared she'd die on me or something, I needed to feel her just breathing against me for a little bit.

Audrey let me hold her for a minute or so before she finally wrested free of me. "The water is giving me cramps," she said, in way of explanation, before she waded back in against shore.

I followed her with my eyes and caught Liam's dark stare. He'd watched me hug her, obviously, and from the looks of it, he wasn't pleased.

I felt a stab of guilt, but the sooner he realized she wasn't supposed to be with him, the sooner he'd be able to get over what I'd done. Maybe.

It wasn't like he minded too much that we took turns sleeping with her at night, anyway. We'd not discussed it, but it'd seemed like the natural solution. And, strangely, I didn't really mind seeing her in his arms. I just didn't like going to sleep alone when I could see them together mere feet away.

AUDREY SPENT the rest of the day trying to keep her distance from both Liam and I, and it was obvious she wasn't feeling too good. I felt like shit for not being able to make her comfortable, but there wasn't much to do about it.

Except when I came into our makeshift home around seven that night with the fish I'd spent the last hour gutting and cleaning for our dinner, she was lying curled up on her side with her head in Liam's lap. He was stroking her hair and speaking softly to her, random stories from old fairy tales our mother used to read to us when we were little, as far as I could tell, and she looked... peaceful.

He'd managed to do what I hadn't, and the hot stab of jealousy in my gut at the sight of them felt like pure acid.

I don't know why I hadn't thought of that before... why the idea had never even crossed my mind. I'd known she was meant to be mine since the night we climbed the cathedral, but I hadn't paused to think that maybe... maybe, if given the choice, she'd... choose Liam.

He was the one she'd fallen for first, after all. She'd thought I was him when she told me she loved me.

What if Audrey didn't want me? What if she wanted Liam?

"Your turn to cook," I snarled, throwing the fish at my twin with more force than was necessary.

He caught them and gave me a glare. "I'm busy."

Audrey sat up, wincing as she did. Judging from her worried frown, she'd picked up on the animosity between my twin and I. Not that it was hard—I hadn't managed to hide it this time.

"I can cook, it must be my turn."

"No." We cut her off simultaneously.

"You're not feeling well."

"Lay back down, love."

"No, I'm f—" Her protest was interrupted when Liam forced her back down on the sleeping bag she'd been resting on

"Don't be daft, you're not getting up just because my brother's being a twat."

I snarled. *"I'm* being a twat? You fucking wanker."

It felt good. I didn't even care what I was shouting about, but finally giving air to all the pent-up anxiety, guilt and—yes—anger that'd been gnawing at my gut for so long was fucking blissful. "Why don't you take some fucking responsibility for once?"

"Me?" Liam hissed. He got to his feet, and from the look on his face, he too was more than ready to lay into me. Fine. I was happy to accommodate. "You're the bloody idiot who's pretending like he did nothing wrong, when you're the fucking reason we're out here in the first place!" he shouted, tossing the fish back at me.

"I'm the reason? If you'd fucking kept it in your pants, none of this would have happened! Dad would never have known about her!"

"That's fucking rich, coming from the idiot who brought her right into the middle of a fucking mafia event," Liam snarled back at me. "Perkinson wouldn't have known where to look if you hadn't, you massive tit."

"Stop it! Both of you, just stop it!" The shout came from the floor, and we both stopped mid-shouting match at the absolute pain in Audrey's voice. She was still sitting down, but she was looking at us with tears in her eyes, her fists knotted in the sleeping bag. It absolutely broke my heart to see her that upset, especially when the numbing realization that I'd caused this set in.

"Why are you fighting?" she sobbed. "I'll cook the stupid fish!"

"It's not about the fish," Liam said, his voice much softer now. He knelt down next to her and wrapped his arms around her shoulders. Much as I wanted to, I couldn't blame him—I had the same urge. I sank down next to her, too, and put my arms around her midriff, hugging her to me as gently as my twin did to him.

"I know it's not about the fucking fish," she hiccupped, rubbing at her eyes, but the tears were still coming. "Is it because of me? Is it because you had to throw away everything to get me out of London?"

She was so far off, it made me snort. She really had

no idea how much we loved her—and it tore at my heart. I wanted to tell her so badly that I loved her, that I was so fucking sorry... but I knew I couldn't. Not now. She wouldn't hear it, and Liam... As angry as I was with him at the mere thought she might prefer him over me... he was still my brother.

"No, love. It's nothing like that," I said, softening my voice in an attempt to make her stop crying. It only halfway seemed to work. "We're both just stressed."

"We didn't have to leave London because of you," Liam continued. "If Perkinson could flip on us the second he saw we had a weakness in you, he would have flipped on us regardless. At least we knew to keep an eye on him this way."

I caught his eye for a moment—I hadn't thought that through before now, but he was right. If we hadn't set a spy on Perkinson after the incident at Audrey's flat, we wouldn't have known to leave London before it'd been too late. In some fucked up way, this whole mess between us and her had quite possibly saved our lives.

"Could you both please just stop it, then?" she sniffled from her cocoon between us. "This sucks hard enough as it is. Having you two fight—it's too much."

"Yeah, we can do that, love," Liam said.

"Don't worry about it," I added, giving her a small smile when she turned her tear-streaked face toward me. "We'll be good."

Keeping an uneasy truce with my twin wasn't going

to be easy, but I didn't care—and from the looks of him, neither did Liam. When our eyes locked again, I knew he was thinking the same as me—if she cared enough about us to ask us not to fight, that had to mean there'd be a way to win her back.

And I was going find it before he did.

THIRTY-ONE
AUDREY

If I'd been more used to being on birth control, I'd have remembered to pack a sachet of pills along with my toothbrush when Liam and Louis brought me to their flat back in London. Unfortunately, I'd only started them after Liam—at least I thought it'd been Liam—and I'd almost forgotten a condom for the second time. A good choice, as it turned out, since I only remembered about such things as protection well after my time with his twin atop St. Paul's Cathedral.

But sadly for me—and Louis and the sleeping bag we'd shared—I hadn't had the presence of mind to bring my pills with me on our impromptu camping trip, which had led to probably the most mortifying experience of my life yet.

If the twins hadn't been so completely cool about it, once they'd made sure I wasn't hemorrhaging to death, I probably would have never come back out of that river. But they were, and even went out of their way to try and make me comfortable—going so far to comfort my emotional outburst when they started shouting at each other.

I cringed and glanced at the nearest twin at the reminder of how my hormonal insanity had gotten the best of me and I'd started *sobbing* like a child.

They'd obviously both done what they could to make me stop crying again, and there'd been peace in our little camp since then. They'd even cooked the fish together, most likely in an attempt at proving things were fine and I didn't have to start blubbering again.

My face heated from the shame of having broken down like that—but dammit, I couldn't help it! My hormones were all out of whack, thanks to the unauthorized birth control break, and I had zero control over my emotions.

All I cared about right now was to try and make my cramps settle down, and ideally not burst into tears again for the next four to five days. Earlier, Liam had sat down on the tarp where I'd been curled up with a massive case of cramps, put my head in his lap without asking, and started telling me stories like I'd been a little kid. A part of me had known I should be furious, that I needed to keep my distance, but... most of me had just enjoyed being cared for. So I'd let him stroke my hair and pretended like all the messed up things between us were just a bad dream. Despite the cramps, it'd been amazing.

"You ready for sleep?" one of the twins—I thought it might be Liam—asked me when I started nodding off in front of the fire some hours after the sun had set.

"Yeah," I yawned—and then frowned when I remembered the still-wet sleeping bag that Liam had washed in the river this morning. It wouldn't be dry for probably a few days. "But... what are we going to do about the sleeping bag? Did you bring any blankets?"

He shrugged and got to his feet to stretch. "Nah, we'll just share."

I blinked. "Share? All three of us? In *one* sleeping bag?"

"Sure," his twin said, a small smile lurking in the corner of his mouth at my obvious hesitation. "It'll be nice and snug."

I opened my mouth to protest, but quickly shut it again. I was the reason we only had one sleeping bag right now, and what was the alternative? Someone sleep on the bare tarp.

"You might want to ditch the T-shirt," the first twin suggested as he got out of his own pants and shrugged his top over his head. "It's gonna get warm between us."

"Why do *I* have to be in the middle?" I grumbled, but I was too exhausted to put up much of a fight. It wasn't like they hadn't both seen me topless before, anyway. Heck, I'd even let Louis hug me while we'd both been completely naked earlier because there'd been nothing sexual in it. He'd just offered me comfort, and I'd been grateful for it.

"Because you're much nicer to hug than Louis," Liam said with a teasing quirk of his eyebrow, confirming my suspicion of who was who.

Louis snorted from the sleeping bag, where he'd already gotten comfortable. He opened the zipper and pulled back the top part, inviting me in.

I slid out of my pants and, hesitating for only a moment, pulled my T-shirt off as well. To both twins' credit, I didn't catch them staring like they had the first time I'd been bathing in the river.

Louis wrapped his arms around me as soon as I was laying down, enveloping me in warmth. His arms brushed against the underside of my breasts, and despite how incredibly unsexy I felt, it still sent a small twinge of the non-crampy variety through my abdomen. Up until now, my conscious closeness with either man had been very limited, but there was some-thing undeniably intimate in snuggling up like this. Knowing he was awake while our bodies were inter-twined, without much fabric between us for modesty. Flashes of the many times I'd been naked with one of them before, in my flat when I'd had no hesitations over being intimate, helpfully sprung to the forefront of my mind.

It didn't get any better when Liam slid into the

sleeping bag and pressed his entire, gloriously hard body against my front.

"Comfy?" he asked me with a wink when I flushed at being sandwiched between the identically sexy men I'd been so attracted to since first sight. Thankfully, my cramps kicked in before my body got too carried away, effectively quelling any and all desires for anything other than sleep.

Instead of answering, I nuzzled my face in against his collarbone and closed my eyes. It didn't take long before I was fast asleep, wrapped up in strong arms and the comforting scent of burning wood, fresh air, and man.

IT TOOK two days for the sleeping bag to dry, which meant two days of going to sleep and waking up completely entangled with both twins. They'd stopped arguing, even going so far to have small conversations now and then, but it was still obvious that there was some point of contention between them. The only place they seemed to shed it completely was when we were squeezed together at night. It was as if that time was sacred somehow, our one time of the day where we all pushed every stress and aggravation aside to just be. There was something about being embraced by them so intimately that helped calm both my cramping body and uneasy mind, and I found that for those hours, it was easy to forget how they'd tricked me and what they truly were.

Once the other sleeping bag dried, I silently mourned the loss of our nighttime cuddling, but I needn't have. Come evening, Louis moved the fresh sleeping bag across the tarp and opened the side up on both of them, allowing them both to hold me like they had for the past few days—just with a bit more breathing room. We didn't talk about it, but deep down, I knew we all needed this small sanctuary.

Days turned into weeks, and our lives in the mountain bothy became routine. The twins fished daily to stretch our supply of canned goods, but otherwise, there wasn't much to do than wait for it to become Sunday. For one hour on Sunday night, one of the twins would turn on the old-fashioned phone they'd brought, and we would all wait in vain for it to ring.

All that spare time gave me a lot of time to worry about what my parents were doing—if they'd declared me missing, if I'd been officially fired from my job yet... and what I'd do once everything got back to normal. If it ever would. For every day that passed, my resolve to not ask questions about what had brought us here withered away a little more. I might not have wanted to get involved with any mafia-related business, but the longer we were hiding out in the Welsh mountains, the more obvious it became that I was already in the deep end, whether I liked it or not.

So on the third Sunday, after Liam came back from fishing further upriver, I finally caved.

"We need to talk," I told them as he walked into the stone hut we'd called home for three weeks now. It was a rainy day, so both Louis and I had stayed inside for most of it, tending the fire and watching the gray blanket of misery out the open doorway.

"Sure. What about?" Liam threw the fish in the empty pot next to the fire and proceeded to strip down so he could towel off. He'd been soaked through while fishing, and his red hair was plastered to his forehead and making small rivulets of water splash down his face and back.

"Everything," I said, doing my best not to look at his perfect arse as he stepped out of his jeans. When I finally forced myself to look away, I saw Louis looking at me with a knowing smirk, and flushed predictably. Thankfully, he didn't call me out on my perving.

"Starting with why we've been hiding out from your dad, of all people, for the better part of a month. I want to know everything."

"Are you sure?" Louis glanced at his twin before he looked back at me.

"Yeah, I'm sure. It's becoming increasingly obvious that this isn't just some nightmare that'll go away if I just pretend like it's not real for long enough. So I think I have to know—don't you?" I sighed, steeling myself. "Please. I need to hear everything."

"All right." Liam, now with a towel wrapped around his waist, sat down on the tarp opposite me, a few feet from Louis. "Our father, William Steel, has ruled London's underworld for years. Our brothers and us... we grew up in it. About three years ago, our brother Isaac went to jail for what we thought was a drug deal gone wrong. It was unusual, because our Family has a lot of pull. He wasn't supposed to get locked up, but he did. For twenty-five years, no parole. Has refused visitors ever since."

"Some time after that, our eldest brother Jeremy was sent to America to solidify business ties over there. Or so we were told. No one heard from him. Fast forward a bit, and Blaine and Marcus, our two remaining brothers, come across proof that our father's behind it. He double-crossed Isaac to get him locked up, and... he killed Jeremy." Louis shook his head, as if the memory of their father's betrayal caused him physical pain. I couldn't blame him.

"We've been working with Blaine to try and find a way to get rid of our father once and for all," Liam continued. "None of us are safe while he's still around. But doing so isn't exactly easy, especially because if he goes down while Isaac is still in jail, Isaac will rot his life away in there. The alliance with Perkinson was meant to give us the firepower we needed, but we still needed a way to save Isaac."

"And then the prick went and flipped on us," Louis finished, disgust in his voice. "If we make it out of here alive, I'll kill him myself."

"Is it that easy for you?" I blurted. "Killing?" I didn't know why, but the thought made me so angry. Or, strike that, I did know why. The two of them—they'd always seemed so full of *life*. The thought of them taking one without an ounce of mercy made the sense of betrayal flare up again. How much had been a lie? All of it?

"It's never easy." Liam's voice was soft. "Never. But sometimes, there's no other way. This is one of those times. If we don't, we will sign over our own lives, our brothers'. Their wives, and Blaine's kid."

"Yours," Louis whispered, regret plain as day on his beautiful face.

My stomach lurched. *"Mine?* But I—" I was about to say I wasn't involved in any of this, but then I remembered the two men who'd watched my windows late at night. I wasn't hiding out in the wilderness for no reason. I took in a deep breath to calm myself. I'd asked to know everything, and throwing a tantrum would just convince them I wasn't strong enough to handle the truth.

"Have you killed before?" I asked. It was the one thing that'd looped in my mind over and over since they'd told me what they were.

"Yes." The pain on Louis' face was mirrored in his twin.

"The night I came to you, I had to kill a man." Liam's voice was so hollow, it made my chest ache. I'd never thought I could pity a killer before, but I remembered what night he meant. I'd never seen so much agony as I had on his face when he cried in my arms that night. They weren't cold-blooded killers, that much was certain. Something I hadn't realized had been coiled tight in my chest eased as I looked at the sorrow written across both men sat in front of me. They might have been mafia, but they weren't ruthless. They were criminals, but they were still...

Still what, Audrey? Still the men who tricked you into falling in love with a lie?

"Why did you trick me?" I hadn't meant to ask. I'd promised myself I wouldn't give them another chance to lie to me, but seeing them like this... so open and vulnerable... it pulled on me with an urgency I could hardly grasp. I *needed* to know—I needed to understand how everything I'd felt for them could have been such a massive lie.

Liam looked to his side, at Louis, his brow arched in challenge.

His twin looked sick, but he raised his gaze to face me. "I was scared," he whispered.

"Scared?" Somehow that confession made the rage I'd felt when I'd first realized they'd tricked me come roaring up from the depths of my very core. That part of me who'd felt the betrayal the deepest cried out, and I scrambled to my feet. "You were *scared?* What the fuck kind of explanation is that?"

"Let me finish," he said. His voice was still low, but there was firmness in it. He glanced at his brother, then returned his focus to me. "Please."

I clamped my jaw shut, glaring at him, but managed a short nod.

"Our father had someone watching us. He saw Liam with you, and I... The way Liam was acting, going to see your parents, behaving like a smitten teenager, I was afraid what would happen if our father threatened you. Our brother Marcus nearly got himself killed defending his girl, and I couldn't..." Louis drew in a deep breath and shook his head as if to clear it of horrible images. "I couldn't bear it if Liam got hurt because of some girl."

It hurt, hearing him call me that—*"some girl."* I tried to ignore the irrational emotion as I stared at Louis. This wasn't even the man I'd fallen in love with, not at first. Why did I care if he called me "some girl"?

But that night on the cathedral balcony... that had been Louis. Not Liam. That night had changed everything.

Who was I even in love with? The shock of that thought hit me like a ton of bricks. I didn't know which of them my stupid heart ached for, because I'd fallen in love with both of them, thinking they were one man.

"I decided to show him you were nothing special—just another girl," Louis continued. "So I went to you and pretended to be him."

"When?" I rasped out. "How long did you pretend?"

"Since Liam broke up with you. I was the one who convinced you to give me another chance. It's been me since."

I shook my head at the onslaught of emotion. Somehow knowing was even worse. "Why? Why the fuck did you do that? He'd already... he *left* me. Why did you make me fall for you, too?" I faintly realized I was shouting, but I didn't care. I stood over him, hands balled into fists, daring him to make excuses for what he'd done.

"I wanted to make sure... If he wavered, I needed him to know what he thought he felt wasn't real." Louis' voice was still quiet in the face of my anger, but he kept his gaze locked in mine despite his obvious regret.

"That's so cruel." I couldn't hold back the tears anymore. They fell down my cheeks, and I wiped at my face, as the hurt echoed through me. "I was so fucking *broken,* and you pretended to... You pretended to be him, to want to make amends, just to... You *slept* with me and held me while I cried..." I shook my head, unable to continue.

"I know. And I am so sorry, Audrey," he said, his

voice finally raising from a whisper. "I was scared and I was cruel, and I am so fucking sorry."

"I didn't know he was pretending to be me," Liam said. "If I had, I'd have put a stop to it."

I swung around to level my glare at him. "How fucking noble of you," I hissed. "You dumped me with a one-line text after you promised... I thought you apologized to me and tried to make it up, but it was your brother. Your twin, who was just using me to protect *you,* was the one to apologize for how absolutely fucking cruel that was!"

Liam paled in the face of my anger, but didn't relent. He got to his feet too, towering over me. "I was trying to protect you! Dad had to believe you meant nothing to me, or you would've been in danger."

"And I? Did I have to believe I meant nothing to you, too? Because that's exactly what that stupid text made me feel." He reached for me, but I pulled away. "You could have done it gently—you could even have bloody told me what was going on. But no, you broke my fucking heart, you absolute prick!"

Despite my tears as I shouted at the man who'd hurt me so gruesomely, it felt good to finally get it all out. Even while I'd thought he'd come back to me, the lingering mistrust for what he'd done still festered in my chest.

"I would have come back—once you were no longer in danger."

I scoffed. "That's really nice, Liam. And, what, you'd have expected me to just take you back? How long would you've been out of my life for at that point?"

"I did it because I fucking love you, Audrey!" Liam was shouting too now, the frustration and hurt plain on his face. "I thought he might hurt you, and I panicked, okay? Being away from you... it wasn't fun for me, either. All I wanted was to crawl back and beg you to forgive me, but I couldn't. If the choice was between never being with you again or seeing you hurt because of my Family, I had to choose to leave."

"You could have told me," I insisted, wiping harder at the tears that kept falling faster and thicker down my cheeks in rivulets.

"Told you what? That I am in the mafia? You wouldn't have fucking run, if you'd had a choice?"

I opened my mouth to deny it, but then I remembered my horror when I'd finally found out what they were. Yeah, I probably would have run.

Then what he'd said finally sank in. He'd said... he loved me.

I'd thought he'd told me before, but that was Louis. I turned to his twin, eyebrows knitted in a frown as I took in the emotion in his eyes. "On that balcony..."

"I meant every word," he said, his voice quiet but rough. "I've loved you since our first night together. I didn't admit it to myself at first, because it was fucking ridiculous—I'd known you for mere hours. But I know you're meant to be mine, Audrey. There's only you, and there only ever will be, regardless of what you choose."

Regardless of what I choose. I blinked when the implication finally set in.

They wanted me to... choose between them?

THIRTY-TWO
AUDREY

"This is crazy—*choose?* Are you really asking me to *choose* between you?" I stared from Louis to Liam, mouth open. The tears finally stopped from sheer stupefaction.

"I love you," Liam said, softly this time. "I know you've felt our connection since day one, too. And if none of this bullshit would have happened, there would be no doubt in your mind. You would never have been with Louis—you would have been with me."

"But it *did* happen," Louis said, his hand coming to rest on my shoulder. I was too numb with shock to brush it away this time. "And I was the one you said you loved. *Me.* I know you saw me, even if you didn't realize at the time. Like I saw you. *I* love you, Audrey."

I shook my head. "What even gave you the thought I'd be with either of you, after what you *both* put me through? You had your reasons, I get it, but *you* tricked me—" I pointed at Louis, and then turned to his twin. "—and *you* broke my heart. And you're both fucking mafia! What—*mmph!*"

My indignant tirade was cut short when Liam pressed his lips against mine, hard. Behind me, Louis wrapped his arms around me underneath my breasts and pulled me back against his body. His lips skimmed up the back of my neck, nibbling at the tendon there as his twin kissed me with such overwhelming passion, it took my breath away.

I parted my lips, more on instinct than any deliberate decision, and moaned when his tongue swept in to stroke mine. Heat mixed with the zings of sensation from my nape where Louis' lips and teeth danced over my sensitive flesh, tightening my nipples and making me pant into his twin's mouth.

I'd missed this so much. The yearning from their kisses that pulled on my heart so perfectly, and the teasing seduction from the hands caressing up and down my sides and Louis' lips against my neck that had my body aching within seconds.

Some distant part of my mind tried to protest, tried to shout at me to stop—that this was so wrong on so many levels—but I pushed it away. I didn't have the strength to withstand this, nor the will. I'd been so scared and so heartbroken for so long, and everything inside me ached for what the twins' heated touches promised: sweet release.

When Liam pulled back, Louis turned my head with a finger and captured my lips with his. His kiss was as passionate as his brother's, as filled with desperate yearning and proof of the truth in his declarations of love.

It overwhelmed me, consumed me, and I kissed him back with every ounce of my being—every ounce of the confusing swirl of longing warring in my chest to break free. The only thing that was clear in my mind as they tore my defenses down with every kiss, every touch, and every gasp of breath was that I loved them. Both of them.

Their hands stroked my body, down my sides and up underneath my top. Rounded on my breasts, rolled my nipples and pulled my pants and underwear down my hips.

Liam pressed scorching kisses to my stomach, trailing down over my navel while Louis ravaged my mouth with so much passion it made me moan and clutch at the twin who knelt in front of me.

The first kiss to land on my mound made me gasp and jerk, but Louis didn't release my lips. He flicked his tongue against mine and cupped my breasts in his large hands, tweaking the stiff little peaks as his brother opened me up with his thumbs, exposing my pulsing sex to his hunger.

Liam's first licks teased my inner lips and ghosted around my hooded clit, making me moan and squirm as he groaned with appreciation.

"I've missed tasting you, love," he whispered before he closed his lips around my clit.

I groaned, almost losing my balance, but Louis' grip kept me upright as Liam lifted one of my legs over his shoulder, anchoring me by clamping onto my backside with both hands. And then he sucked me.

I thrashed between them, lost in sensation as they plundered my mouth, my nipples, and my pussy in one. They didn't relent, their grips on my body only tightening the more I writhed, until suddenly and with the force of a flood, I came between them.

Only then did they break away from me, both breathing hard, and I thought this crazy, desperate moment of yearning and lust was over. I was wrong.

Liam eased my leg off his shoulder, but not before he got my pants and panties off me completely, discarding them before he let his hands run up my thighs.

I opened my mouth to protest, to suggest we calm down and talk things through before we continued down a path we'd likely regret, but Louis shattered my thoughts into a million pieces when he pinched my nipples hard enough for me to mewl, then proceeded to strip my top off while I fought back against the mixed sensation of pain and pleasure.

"You're so fucking beautiful." I didn't know who rasped it out so hoarsely it went straight to my clit and abused nipples, but I saw the unabashed look of lust and longing on both their faces. I didn't struggle when they pushed me to the ground and spread me out on top of a sleeping bag, nor did I protest when Louis stripped down and climbed between my thighs, his heated gaze intent on my now swollen and open sex.

He was gentler than his brother had been, easing my still-zinging nerves into it with long, broad licks up the length of my slit without touching the pulsing nub up top. Slowly, my pussy came down from its first orgasm, and I rocked my pelvis up against his tongue for more. I was rewarded with rapid lashes right on my clit, but before I could do more than jerk and gasp, Liam's lips closed around a nipple and *sucked.*

My gasp turned to a deep groan at the dual assault. I grasped for purchase, my fingers twining in flaming hair, and was rewarded with deep chuckles and more of that unyielding stimulation.

"You have such magnificent tits, love," Liam groaned as he turned his attention to my other breast. I moaned incoherently in response, because just then Louis slipped two fingers inside of me, curving them after my G-spot. Deep, scalding pleasure roared up along my spine, making me jerk and thrash, and when he switched the lashes for thorough suckles that went right to the root of my clit, I came. *Hard.*

Both twins stayed latched to my body for the dura-
tion, forcing me higher and over the peak again—and
again, letting me scream until my throat burned before
they finally pulled back.

I came down slowly, with a floating sensation fluttering through my body from the tips of my toes to the
roots of my hair. Blearily, I looked down at Louis, who
gave me the smuggest smirk I'd ever seen on a man. And
that's after knowing the two of them for a while.

He wiped the clear sheen I'd left on his lips and
chin with a hand and popped a finger in his mouth to
suck off the leftovers. His eyes fluttered shut, and the
moan of pleasure that rumbled out of his chest made my
toes curl.

"All right there, love?" Liam pulled my attention
from his brother by putting two fingers under my chin so
he could turn my head. He looked somewhat amused at
my dazedness, but the burning desire in his stormy eyes
was the far greater emotion. It made still-buzzing
muscles down low in my abdomen clench with want,
despite my well-sucked clit's pleas for a timeout.

"Uh-huh," I breathed, humming when he pressed a
languid kiss to my lips.

"That's good," he whispered, his voice husky and
filled with unmistakable lust. "Because I'm going to
screw your pussy raw. You have no fucking idea how
sexy you look when you come for us, do you?"

I could only whimper in response as Louis slipped

three fingers up inside of me as if on cue, pumping me slowly but oh so thoroughly. When he thrilled his fingertips over my pulsing G-spot, I cried out and arched up for more.

"I think she's ready," he said, that smug smile still evident in his voice. Probably because I was so soaking wet even three of his fingers moved with relative ease in my tight sheath. He pulled them out and slapped his palm down between my widespread legs, smacking my swollen pussy none too gently. I jolted and moaned, the sting lancing through my molten flesh and blazing through already tensed nerves.

"Get on your hands and knees, love. I ain't asking twice," he rumbled, the laugh in his voice gone as if it'd never been there, replaced by rough urgency.

I scrambled to get my jellied limbs to obey, somehow twisting around on the sleeping bag so I ended up facing Louis.

He smirked down at me and wrapped a hand around my jaw, gently teasing my lower lip with a thumb. "Guess that'll do. Open that pretty mouth for me, baby."

I did, nipping at his thumb and flicking my tongue across its tip when he dipped the digit into the wet cavern of my mouth. But my teasing came to a stop when Liam rubbed a hand up along the slit of my pussy from behind, tapping my clit with his fingertips before he spread my lips open, exposing my entrance.

"God, you're wet. You want this, don't you, you dirty slut? You want to suck my brother while I fuck your sopping little cunt into oblivion, don't you?" he growled. The heavy pressure of his other hand pushed down on my lower back, forcing me to arc my arse in a lewd invitation. "Guess what, love? You'll get exactly what you need."

Every ounce of blood in my body burned at his words, and I whined a wordless confirmation around Louis' thumb.

"That's what I thought." Liam's growl was followed by thick pressure against my opening. I cried out when my body's resistance gave way and he sank the full length of his cock all the way up inside of me, hilting me with one smooth push. I'd still struggled a bit with their size the last time I slept with Louis, and it'd been weeks since either man had last penetrated me. It hurt to take Liam now, even after all the foreplay, but it was a good kind of pain. When his hips slapped against my arse with a wet smack, I was so perfectly, excruciatingly *full*, all I could do for a few moments while my body adjusted was pant. Liam groaned behind me, the pleasure he got from being inside of me unmistakable.

"Fuck, you feel so goddamn perfect," he moaned. "How do you feel this fucking *perfect*?"

Within moments, the deep, dull pangs from stretched flesh melted into nothing but pleasure as my pussy fluttered around the intrusion, remembering how to mold itself after a cock this fat. Liam knew as well, could feel my body yielding, and dug his fingers into my hips to anchor himself. And then, he thrust.

The thick slide made me cry out, but no sooner had I opened my mouth than Louis pressed his hard cock in between my lips. I loosened my jaw and let him rock fully into my mouth, flicking my tongue around the crown of his head and the frenulum underneath on its way in.

Louis hissed, pulling me closer by my jaw until his fat cock nudged at the back of my throat. Had it been anyone other than the twins, I would have panicked and gagged, but not with them. Even in this primal a stage, or perhaps because of it, I knew neither man would ever hurt me. So instead of pulling away, I relaxed and let the thrusts from Liam fucking me guide Louis' cock as deep as it could go without entering my throat. There was still a good bit outside of my lips, but Louis didn't seem to mind. His eyes were half-closed in obvious pleasure as he rested his hands in my hair, guiding me down on his cock again and again.

I rocked between them, clenching at the sleeping bag beneath me with both hands in order to stay in place the harder the twins moved, buffeting me back and forth like a leaf caught between two stormfronts. The slick sounds of hard cocks fucking wet flesh mixed with the smell of sex and groans of pleasure, filling my world until I was blind to anything but the scarlet-tinged haze of being taken by the two men who'd stolen my love and broken my heart.

I don't know how long I was on my hands and knees between them like that, lost in my own bubble of pleasure and endorphins, but when Liam reached underneath me and pinched my clit, I came back to with a shriek.

Louis groaned, undoubtedly from the vibrations around his cockhead still lodged deep in my mouth, and kept my mouth on him by tightening his grip in my hair when I tried to pull away. "Ah, ah, love. You can have your clit rubbed and still suck my dick," he purred, thrusting a little harder for emphasis. "Pull away again and you're gonna get off with my dick down your throat."

I tried to shoot him a warning glare, but just then Liam pinched my clit again, hard, and pulled on it with sharp little tugs that shot pangs of pained ecstasy down my thighs and up my spine, making every muscle in my body spasm. I screamed around Louis' cock as Liam tortured my aching clit and fucked my pussy with every ounce of strength in his body, panting growls of pleasure into the air behind me for every time his cock hilted in my convulsing sheath.

Gone was Louis' warning, and I desperately tried to pull my lips off his cock to control even some of the excruciating pleasure bursting through my body and mind. His fingers in my hair didn't give me an inch, and when Liam forced me forward with the impact of his hips slapping against my arse and I screamed as he ground his fingers against my clit with enough strength to make me see stars, Louis pushed his cock deeper than before. The burning stretch as he entered my throat came at the exact moment my orgasm hit me.

I tried to scream, but no sound came, tried to thrash against the violent roar of devastating bliss ripping through my core and pulsing through my nerves to every cell in my quivering body, but their hands kept me from fighting. They both cried out in my place, hands tightening on my hips and in my hair as Louis fucked my throat for one, two, three thrusts before he came, spilling his seed deep before he pulled out.

I swallowed because I had no other choice and gasped for air, but didn't have time to think before Liam's punishing pounding of my still twitching pussy ripped my attention to him. I cried out brokenly and was rewarded when too many fingers tweaked my pebbled nipples and rubbed my aching clit to another, pained orgasm.

Liam came with me this time, roaring his pleasure as I sobbed underneath, shuddering in the throes of climax. When he finally stilled behind me, his bruising grip on my hips easing, I sank down on the sleeping bag in a boneless heap, too exhausted to move so much as a finger.

Liam stayed inside me, his strong body resting on

top of mine, though he took enough of his own weight to not squish me.

Louis sprawled out next to us, tangling our fingers. "You okay, love?"

"Uhhu," I managed to grunt. I turned my head so I could look into his eyes. They were brimming with pure, unadulterated happiness. "But maybe give a girl a heads-up next time, eh?"

"I did," he said with a cheeky smile. "And you took it like a champ."

"Next time?" Liam rumbled above me before he ghosted a kiss to the side of my cheek. "Someone ready for seconds?"

I gave a halfhearted snort. "It was a figure of speech. There's no way we're doing that again anytime soon."

"Really?" Liam asked. He sounded way more intrigued than he had any business doing.

"No way at all?" Louis continued, and the devilish gleam in his eyes was unmistakable.

I groaned in vain protest. "Please. Don't."

"Don't what?" Liam purred into my ear. He nuzzled at my cheek with his nose and flicked his tongue out to tease my earlobe.

"Lick your sweet little clit until you beg for more?" Louis finished. He rolled over so he could sit up on his knees, a predatory draw to the tilt of his lips.

I grimaced. My clit was still pulsing from Liam's

rough stimulation and the orgasms they'd wrung out of me only moments before. "God, no."

Liam snorted and sat up, still keeping his slowly growing cock deep in my sheath. "Pretty sure it's the first time I've heard that one."

"How about this, then—You suck us hard and we won't hold you down and force you to get off on our tongues until you're raw," Louis said. This time, the hungry growl in his voice was unmistakable.

Soreness aside, the dirty suggestion made my pussy clench arduously on Liam's cock. His hard length pulsed in response, filling me more insistently.

"Hm, feels like she's not entirely opposed to that idea," Liam hummed. He gave me a playful thrust, making me whimper, but then pulled out. "Which is it going to be then, love? Suck us off, or have your clit forced to give up a dozen or two more orgasms?"

I was pretty sure I wasn't going to go free once I'd gotten them hard, but as enticing as their other offer sounded, my clit *was* pretty sore. Plus, as reluctant as my tired body was, I couldn't deny the thrill of wondering what they'd come up with next. I forced myself to roll over and sit up, turning my head so my lips bumped into Louis' cock. He wasn't fully hard, but he wasn't fully soft, either. Their lack of refractory period had been a lot to deal with when it'd just been one of them. This time, I just hoped I'd still be able to walk once they'd finally had their fill.

Louis smirked down at me and slid his cock into my mouth when I obediently parted my lips. "Good girl," he groaned.

I flicked my tongue around his crown and took him deeper, and he swelled to full size before I'd managed to do anything else, forcing my jaw apart.

"God, you're so good at sucking cock," he groaned, stroking my cheek as he pulled out. "Ready for more?"

I nodded unthinkingly, the taste of him still buzzing on my tongue and making my pussy long to be filled. I wasn't sure what it was about these two, but being with them had me aching for more even when my body was weak from too many orgasms already.

Louis moved down between my legs, swapping places with his twin. I opened my mouth for Liam, eager to please him too even though he was already fully hard from watching me with his brother.

Liam slipped in between my lips with a rumble, filling my mouth with the tangy flavor of our combined releases. Had he been anyone else, I wouldn't have enjoyed it—but he wasn't. And I did.

I sucked his cock clean, humming my appreciation as he petted my hair and told me I was *"such a good girl"* while Louis stroked his hand up and down my swollen lower lips, preparing me for more without touching my sore clit.

Only when Liam pulled out of my mouth, his cock

hard and pulsing, did Louis guide his cock to my opening and push in to the hilt.

I groaned, falling down on my back at the feel of him. It didn't hurt this time, not after how thoroughly Liam had fucked me just moments before, and the rush of pleasure was instant.

"That's it," Louis murmured as he lowered himself above me, letting me feel his weight as he rolled his hips between my eagerly spread thighs. "Take me just like that. All the way inside."

I moaned for more and he sped up, the slow undulations quickly turning to hard thrusts. I clutched at his shoulders and mewled, lost in the pleasure. I could feel my body trying to climb, slowly this time, and tensed up to chase the ecstasy I knew would come if he kept pumping me like this. How I'd wanted to stop before was beyond me—being with them felt so good; why would I ever want it to end?

"Turn her over." Liam's voice was a faint echo in my haze of pleasure, but then that wonderful thrusting stopped and Louis rolled us over so I was suddenly straddling him.

I growled in frustration and moved my hips, eager to chase the promise of bliss I'd been nearing, but Louis wrapped his arms tighter around me, stilling my movements.

"What—"

He kissed me, swallowing my irritated protest. His

lips were soft and so scorching, my mind turned blank. I parted my lips for his questing tongue, and when Liam's fingers slid down my back to my upturned arse, I mindlessly tried to arch up for more of his titillating caresses.

"That's it, good girl," he whispered behind me. "God, you're so beautiful." He grabbed my arse in both hands, squeezing the plump flesh. "So fucking perfect."

I was so lost to his caresses and Louis' tongue, my mind only snapped back when his fingers slid from my cheeks down to my pussy, stroking the lips spread around his brother's thick cock and wedged a tip of a finger in alongside it.

"*Oh!*" I tore my lips from Louis, grimacing at the unexpected stretch. "W-what are you doing?"

"Shh love, he's just making you feel good," Louis murmured. "Relax. And trust us. We'd never hurt you, you know that."

"*Uh-huh,*" I whimpered, because just then Liam slid his finger all the way in, and quickly slipped a second finger in alongside it. Even though I'd been nice and relaxed to take Louis' cock without pain, the extra girth of Liam's fingers stretched me farther than I'd been before, and my pussy protested with a weak little spasm around the intrusion.

Louis groaned low in his throat at the added stimulation and kept his arms locked around my body so my beginning struggles to pull away came to nothing. He held me still for Liam as he slowly fucked his fingers in and out of my tight sheath, murmuring how much he loved me against my ear when I began to pant at the stimulation. And slowly, it started to feel good.

The slight pain turned to nothing but that deep, feminine pleasure of being *filled*, and my pussy gushed slick, coating them both to ease penetration. I rocked back, eager for them to move, and was rewarded with a rumble of appreciation from both men.

"Ready for more, love?" Liam asked, and I closed my eyes when his lips skimmed over my shoulder while his fingers still thrust gently in and out of my splayed pussy.

"Yes. Please." *Oh, yes,* I was more than ready for them to pick up the pace and bring me to the elusive orgasm that'd been flirting with my pulsing nerves since Louis slid inside of me. I rocked back, trying to make the twin underneath me move too, but instead of complying, he just grabbed my hips and held me perfectly still as Liam slipped his fingers out of me.

"Why?" I was vaguely aware I was whining, the frustration of losing stimulation when I wanted more too much to bear.

But before I could protest too much, Liam slipped his hands up over the curve of my hips, holding me firmly in place... and then something hard and much, *much* broader than his fingers nudged at my opening where I was already fused with Louis.

My eyes flew wide open and my breath hitched in

my throat when it finally dawned on me exactly what they had planned.

"Oh, my God, you're not serio—*oh! Oh!* N... no-*ow!*" My panicked protest died on a pained groan when Liam, using his grip on my hips for leverage, forced the fat head of his cock up *inside* of me.

The stretch was far too much, far too *big*. I fought against both twins' hold in my attempt at escaping the excruciating penetration. All it got me was a light swat to my backside before Liam pushed his cock deep.

I couldn't even scream. Everything was tension and heat and pleasure so intense it bordered the realm of agony. I was so *full!* So utterly and excruciatingly... complete.

Maybe it was the adrenaline, or maybe it was just the sensation of feeling the twins' bodies enveloping me, protecting me even as their cocks forced me so wide I could do nothing but rest on Louis' shoulder and gasp for breath. But as I lay there, shuddering in their arms as they moaned my name and hissed with the intensity of my pussy's grip, I'd never felt more *whole* in my entire life.

"God, you're so fucking amazing, Audrey," Louis groaned beneath me. "Fuck!"

"You doing okay, love?" Liam gasped, the strain in his voice evident.

I could only whimper in response. Was I doing okay? I didn't know—I hardly knew my own name, let alone if the deep, pulsing strain at the core of my body where their cocks opened me up wide was from pleasure or pain.

"I think she needs a little convincing still," Louis said. He skimmed his lips along the top of my head and now my turned neck, nibbling at the sensitive spots there.

Liam bent forward to kiss my opposite shoulder, and as he did, he slipped one hand around my hips and down to my exposed clit, brushing gently against it.

I jolted, my pussy contracting around the cocks filling it on instinct, making me cry out as the muscles strained futilely against the intrusion.

"Shh, I'll be good," Liam whispered hoarsely in my ear as he ghosted his fingertips over my aching clit in small circles. "Relax. We only want to please you."

"Trust us, Audrey," Louis murmured into my other ear. "We'll make you feel so, *so* good."

I whimpered again, this time in surrender. Even as my body struggled to accept them, I knew they were right. Whatever issues we may have had, neither man had ever brought me anything than mind-numbing pleasure in the bedroom. And having both of them together, *inside*... nothing could ever compare.

Slowly, I relaxed between them. My straining muscles softened one by one as a wave of calm rolled through me until my fitfully spasming pussy finally accepted the brutal invasion. And just like that, the agony of being opened too wide was gone, replaced by nothing but deep, smoldering pleasure.

I gasped at the unexpected rush of *need* that followed. God, all I wanted—*needed*—at that moment was *more*. More sex, more pleasure... more of *them*.

"More!"

A deep chuckle vibrated through me from above and below.

"There we go."

"Good girl."

And then, blessedly, they gave me exactly what I needed.

Louis moved first, sliding his long, thick cock halfway out, only to thrust it back deep the next moment. He set a slow, even rhythm, letting me feel the full length of his cock rub against my frontal wall and swollen G-spot again and again and again, while Liam teased my clit with gentle precision. I moaned and shuddered, unable to keep my grasp on reality. The world tilted and faded until there was nothing but Louis' thrusting cock and that deep, burning stretch of both my lovers forcing me so incredibly wide, all the way to my very core.

That's when Liam began to move, too.

My orgasm was so instantaneous, I didn't get to prepare myself for it. One moment I was panting and whimpering with pleasure, the next my back arched of its own accord as every single nerve in my body crackled with bolts of ecstasy so intense I could do nothing to fight them. My body contorted between the twins as I rode their cocks over wave after cresting wave, each climax bringing me higher and higher as my pussy fought to contract enough to bring an end to it. But I was forced open too wide, my muscles unable to rein in the excruciating force of their pounding cocks forcing my orgasm to rise like a tide, with no end in sight. For every time I screamed out in tormented bliss, they would only fuck me harder, the seesaw motion ruthless in its relentlessness.

I came until every contraction of my exhausted pussy around their too-thick cocks made me cry from pain. I came until my world was nothing but the hard pounding between my legs, my pulse drumming in my ears in the same rhythm as the men I loved gasped their pleasure in the shared air between us. And still, they fucked me, like rutting beasts addicted to the pleasure they found between my legs.

I don't know how long they took me. Time didn't have meaning in my cage of molten flesh and agonized rapture. I'd long since stopped counting my own orgasms, the peaks blurring into one, long, continuous climax in my hazy mind when, finally, first Liam and then Louis stiffened, their moans deepening as their hands clutched my body tighter.

The rush of semen flooding my gaping pussy felt like a soothing balm as it coated my cervix, and I groaned with relief while my body slowly stilled. The spasms in my core seemed to ease with every rush of their seed until I had nothing left to give. There was only peace. Peace, and the bone-deep knowledge that I had found my place in the world—between these two men. Forever and always.

"You okay, love?" Despite the thoroughly sated note to Louis' voice, a sliver of worry made its way through as he brushed a thumb against my tear-stained cheek.

"Was it too much?" Liam asked. He was laying on top of me, pressing me into his twin's chest with most of his weight, and I felt him nuzzle his face against the crook of my neck.

I sighed, content to my very toes. *Was it too much?* I would have said yes, before. The agony of it, the exhaustion... it had felt like too much, like I couldn't contain the pleasure they were forcing into me. As if I was about to come apart at the seams from the intensity of their combined lust.

But now?

As I lay between them, sated all the way into my very bones, and felt their synchronized heartbeats against my chest and my back, I knew what had happened was exactly what I'd needed to finally understand.

"I love you," I whispered.

THIRTY-THREE

LIAM

It's funny how the arguably filthiest thing I'd ever done to a girl was also the one thing that finally cemented a few undeniable facts for me.

One—Audrey was mine. There was no other way to describe it. As fucked up as it sounded, somewhere along the mind bending fuck we'd just shared, I'd felt something click into place that'd been permanently out of whack, even back when I was first with her. Perhaps it was because I'd finally said it out loud, had let her know how I truly felt, without holding back like I had before. Whatever the reason, the strong sense of everything finally being right hummed in my chest.

And two—Louis loved her as much as I did. I'd seen it in his eyes while he was with her—felt it in the way he moved within her. He loved her with every ounce of his heart.

I love you, she'd said. But to who? And did it matter? If she chose one of us, the other would be broken. Being without her for that week had damn near torn me apart. Facing the rest of my life without her? I clutched the sleeping woman in my arms tighter at the sickening sense of dread the mere thought stirred in my stomach. But if she chose me instead of Louis... I glanced over at my dozing twin. He had his arms wrapped loosely around her, too, and his face nestled in the crook of her neck. I was still pissed at him for what he'd done, but I got it. He'd been terrified of losing me, and I'd have likely done something similar in his place. And he was still my twin—my other half. The thought of seeing him ripped apart if Audrey chose me felt as sickening as if I had to suffer her rejection myself. And if she chose neither...

I stroked a hand through her tangled hair and tried to block out that particular train of thought. If I had to choose between seeing her with Louis and never seeing her again, I'd pick the former every time. At least that way I'd get to be around her.

"This is pretty fucked up, huh?"

I glanced up from Audrey's sleeping face at the whisper from my twin. He was watching her too, before he looked up catch my gaze.

"Uh-huh," I agreed. I looked down over her naked body so entwined with ours and snorted. I hadn't even paused to think how incredibly messed up this had to look from the outside. I'd fucked Louis' women before, but never at the same damn time as him. Fuck, I'd not batted an eyelid at feeling his cock move against mine inside of her. It'd felt... natural. All of it had. Even this, now, when my desperate longing to show her how much I needed her had been quelled and all that was left was this complete sense of peace.

"Feels pretty good, though."

"Yeah," he said, his gaze ghosting down to where our legs were tangled with hers. "That's the fucked up part."

I wanted to ask him what he meant, but just then Audrey made a small mewling noise and her eyelids flickered open.

"Morning, love," I said, swooping down to peck her mouth before she could regain her bearings.

"Sleep well?" Louis asked, pressing his lips to hers in a quick kiss as soon as I pulled back.

"Y-yeah. Thanks." She looked from him to me, and then she fucking *blushed.* For someone who'd spent a good solid hour-plus getting screwed silly mere hours earlier, it was pretty fucking adorable. You'd think once she'd had both our dicks in one go, modesty would be out the door, but apparently not.

"Did you? Sleep well?" She did her best to not look too much at us as she sat up, extracting herself as subtly as she could. Even her voice was detached, as if she hadn't just woken up in the aftermath of a sex orgy.

Would probably start talking about the damn weather any moment now.

Louis let out a snort. "A prude 'til the end, eh, love? You're actually trying to pretend like nothing's out of the ordinary here, aren't you?"

I grinned, pushing my worries aside for later. I could always fret about what would become of this fucked up little love triangle of ours when shit actually had to be dealt with. Right now, in our little camp with reality pleasantly far away, I was going to enjoy what happiness came our way. And waking up with Audrey after an afternoon's debauched sex? Yeah, that ranked pretty fucking high up there on things that were worth smiling about. "What's the matter, love, not brushed up on your post-gangbang etiquette?"

Audrey's blush turned crimson. She hid her face in both hands with a squeak that made both Louis and I laugh.

"Shut up! It's not funny!" she hissed from behind her hands.

"It's pretty hilarious, yeah," Louis said. He sat up next to her and pressed a kiss to her shoulder. "Relax, love. It's just us—there's nothing to be ashamed of."

"Easy for you to say," she grumbled, still hiding behind her hands, but her shoulders seemed to relax a millimeter or two. "I'm not exactly used to... to this sort of thing."

"You think we are?" I was genuinely amused by her

assumption that Louis and I woke up naked with a bird between us every other Sunday.

"Well..." Audrey finally lowered her hands to give me a shy glance. "Aren't you? You seem so... comfortable."

"Would you listen to that—bird thinks we're complete perverts," Louis teased. Then he sighed and stroked a hand up her back before snaking an arm around her middle. "We're comfortable because it's you, Audrey. Why be ashamed when what we did felt so good?"

"Contrary to what you might think, we've not bedded a girl together before," I added, trailing my fingers along her lower back in gentle circles. She seemed to relax a little under our touches, though the heat in her cheeks was still very much present. "Taken turns without her knowing, sure, but never like this."

"So... what you did to me, pretending like you were just one guy, that's *normal* to you?" Her voice turned just a little sharp, and Louis shot me a dirty look behind her back.

"We've done a lot of shit we're not necessarily proud of, Audrey," he said softly. "But this? Not one of them."

"Oh." Audrey finally let her hands fall to her lap. "I... don't know what to do now."

"Don't do anything," Louis said, giving her a small squeeze. "It's late. I'll cook us some dinner, and we can just..."

Pretend like everything is going to be okay. I knew what he wanted to say, but he didn't finish. Saying it out loud would break the walls down around our small bubble of peace. On the other side of this waited a lot of death and heartache, but right now, we could have just a few moments where everything was all right. Just the three of us.

"Okay," Audrey whispered, and I knew she understood it, too. It was a silent pact—a pact to ignore all the horrors that awaited us for just a little while longer.

She lay back down, cuddling up against me when I offered her my shoulder as a pillow. Louis sighed happily and let his fingers trail over her full backside in a gentle caress. But when he dipped them further down, she jolted and shot him a glare over her shoulder. "I thought you were cooking dinner."

"I was. But your pussy is so pretty." The purr in his voice made my own cock stir with interest at the implied suggestion, but Audrey was having none of it.

"Absolutely not! I'm starving, and I'm still really sore." She crossed her legs for emphasis, and Louis pulled back with a sigh.

"Fine, fine. I guess you earned a break." He got up and stretched lazily, heading to the smoldering fireplace.

We ate in front of the fire and, when Louis' wristwatch showed ten, we switched on the burner phone.

It went off the second it caught signal, the loud

ringing making all three of us jump. I gave Louis a quick look before I picked it up and pressed *"answer."*

"Yeah?"

"Liam?"

I blinked at the voice coming through the scratchy reception. It wasn't Blaine on the other end—it was Marcus. I hadn't heard from him in months, not since he fled to America with his wife, and hearing his voice made an unexpected jolt of happiness shoot through me. He may have been crazy as fuck, but I'd kind of missed his looming presence.

"Yeah, it's me. Louis is here too. Are you and Evelyn all right? And Blaine and his family?"

"Yes."

Relief flooded through me at the confirmation and I opened my mouth to ask specifics, but was cut off before I had the chance.

"We don't have much time. Listen and be quiet." So his phone manners hadn't improved much. I grimaced, but didn't argue.

"You need to get to Isaac. Tell him the bird's safe. Tell him he has to give you what he's got or we're all fucked, got it?"

"What do you mean we're fucked—do you have intel on Dad?"

"Liam, do you understand?" my brother snapped into the phone.

"Fucking calm down," I growled. "Yeah, I get it, but

how are we supposed to get to him? He's been refusing visitors from day one."

"*Figure it out. And do it now—if you're not in and out of there by midday tomorrow, we're done.*"

"Marcus, what the hell is going on?" Sure, I knew shit was already on fire, but the urgency in my older brother's voice was a distinctly next level. "We need to know what the hell we're dealing with."

"*He's hiring the* смерть. *If we don't stop him before he drops off the payment tomorrow at noon, we're all dead.*"

THIRTY-FOUR
AUDREY

The ride back to London was as tense as our escape had been three weeks prior. The only difference was that this time, I actually knew what was happening.

They'd tried to keep it from me, to tell me that everything was going to be okay and not to worry, but I'd been through too much to take it this time.

So they'd told me. About getting their brother Isaac to talk being the only thing that might save them from certain death, about the futility in trying to run from a death sentence placed on you by this *Smerts* gang their brother had mentioned.

Perhaps in another life, if my heel hadn't broken that day in the park, I would have watched the news one evening while eating my takeaway dinner and shuddered in relief at the announcement of London becoming a bit safer now that two made men were dead.

But as I sat on the backseat of the inconspicuous car they'd used to throw their father off their trail, I knew I would never, ever, let anyone hurt the twins.

It'd all become so painfully clear, somewhere in the tangle of limbs and multiple orgasms. I loved them. Both of them. I hadn't been able to figure out who I'd fallen for, because it wasn't one or the other—it was both of them.

My heart ached as I watched them quietly discuss their options in the dim light of the oncoming vehicles while Liam drove us closer and closer to the city we'd only narrowly escaped from. We'd had a careful truce, after our debauched afternoon of pleasure. It hadn't been said in words, but we all knew that in that hut in the Welsh mountains we got to pretend like everything was going to be okay. It didn't matter that they were mafia sons and that their father was looking to kill us all —and it didn't matter that they'd both fallen in love with the same girl, who would never be able to choose between them. We'd just been. The three of us.

I'd never thought I'd miss that damn hut or the uncomfortable tarp and claustrophobia-inducing sleeping bags, but as I saw the countryside slowly give way to buildings, I wished with every fiber of my being that we'd had just one more night together.

Because even if we made it out of this alive... there would still never be a happy ending for us.

I wiped the tears sliding down my cheeks as

discreetly as I could and took a deep breath. I had the rest of my life to mourn the loss of the two men who had finally shown me what it felt like to truly be alive. Right now, we had more pressing matters to focus on.

"I should go."

Louis looked at me over his shoulder, a frown creasing his forehead. "Go?"

"To see your brother. You two need to keep a low profile."

"Absolutely not!" Liam spat at the same time as Louis hissed, "Are you *mad?*"

"You say he's rejected visits from your entire family since he was sentenced. Maybe he won't refuse a stranger who says she has news about his girl."

"There is zero chance we're letting you waltz into a prison, Audrey," Liam said. The possessive growl in his voice made my heart pitter-patter, but I shoved the idiotic emotion aside. This was too important to let them baby me in their effort to keep me safe.

"If your brother truly has information that can stop your dad, don't you think he's being watched? Your father's men will be much more familiar with you—it'll be easier for me to slip in unnoticed. Besides, how do you plan to get Isaac to even see you?"

"We'll think of something. We're not risking your safety." Louis' tone had the sound of finality.

"No. Enough's enough. I know I'm not used to your big, scary mafia world, but I'm done being babied. I'm already stuck in the mud with you—it's too late to try and keep me out of it. Besides, if you two idiots get yourselves killed because you were too stubborn to let me help you, then who's going to stop your father from coming after me?" I made my voice as stern as I possibly could as I caught Liam's gaze in the rearview mirror. "I am going to visit your brother. You two need to figure out how exactly your father is planning on delivering that money, and then you need to stop him."

"Audrey, it's too fucking dangerous. You're not doing this, and that's fucking *final!*"

BELMARSH PRISON CONSISTED of a multitude of stark buildings loosely connected behind a tall fence made of concrete and topped with barbed wire. I walked up to the gates and the guard building, the faint sense of victory over winning the argument with the twins evaporating at the sight of the guard's grim face and the looming shadow of the compound behind the fence. I'd been able to convince Louis and Liam that it was too important to attempt to stop their dad from delivering the payment to the Russians for them to spend any more time trying to get into the prison unseen *and* get their brother to talk in the end, only because I emphasized the likelihood of what would happen to me if they weren't around to stop him. It'd been a half-victory though, since

Louis was *somewhere* keeping an eye on me, leaving Liam to try to stop their dad on his own. Not a solution I'd been happy about, but it was the only deal I got.

"Hi, I'm Lana Clarke, here to visit Isaac Steel." I held up the fake ID they'd managed to get me at six this morning when they'd woken up some poor guy named Sam in the Southeastern part of town who they apparently trusted. He didn't look particularly trustworthy to me, with his shifty eyes and food-stained vest top, but he'd produced the ID in an hour and given me some of his wife's clothes so I wouldn't look like I'd just come in from the wild. I'd also been offered a shower, but after glancing at the mold growing in his bathroom, I'd politely declined.

"Visitation slip?" the guard grumbled, and I fumbled the printed piece of paper out of my pocket and handed it over. He typed in the relevant number and finally handed it back to me. "Proceed to reception."

Did that mean Isaac had agreed to see me? I thanked the man and followed the arrows leading to the visitation center once the heavy gates clanked open.

I waited in line with the five other women who'd shown up this early on a Monday morning for a female prison guard to pat us down and check our pockets and bags for offending items such as hair clips, bracelets, and gum.

"Do not leave the assigned table until asked to do so by a guard. Keep noise levels low. Any aggressive behavior will lead to immediate removal and your visitation privileges being revoked indefinitely. Do not pass the prisoner any items. You must comply with any and all instructions from members of staff," the woman droned in a voice as engaging as an infomercial as she patted me down. Once we were all checked, she opened the metal door separating us from the visiting area. "You have one hour."

It was a large room with a high ceiling, painted pale green with the exception of the upper half and ceiling, which were both a depressing shade of beige. The floor was covered in blue institution-strength carpet that was uncomfortable to step on, even through the soles of my shoes. There'd been a clear attempt at modernization, but there was no escaping the depressing weight smothering Belmarsh like an invisible blanket. It was a max-security prison, and no amount of cheap paint could hide that.

There were a good thirty tables set out across the room, and I sat down at the one allocated to me. A few minutes later the door at the far end of the room buzzed open, and men in gray uniforms began to file into the room.

My nerves, which I'd managed to keep in check up until then, broke through my iron control and I clenched my fists in a desperate attempt to calm them again. I couldn't afford to lose it now—if I didn't manage to convince the twins' brother to give up whatever information their other brothers thought he possessed, I risked the two men I loved getting killed. And likely me along with them.

He was one of the last to walk through the doors, but I recognized him instantly. I'd thought he would look like the twins, but that wasn't the case. Apart from his height, the obvious strength of his body despite the shapeless prison garb concealing his wide shoulders and narrow waist, and the sharpness of his jaw, Isaac Steel looked nothing like Liam and Louis. His hair was jet-black and his chiseled face devoid of any and all emotion. Where there'd always been a nearly visible energy crackling off either twin, their brother was a void. And yet I knew he was a Steel from the way he moved—self-assured yet softly, like a stalking panther.

When he sat down in the chair opposite me, I noticed his eyes were as gray as theirs, but they couldn't have been more different from the men I knew. There was no happiness, no mischief in his gaze as he stared at me. Just silent, dark *danger*.

Suddenly, and with a rush that went straight to my lizard brain, my nerves were on high alert from more than the importance of this meeting. I'd gotten so used to the twins, I'd never stopped to consider that maybe not all mafia sons were as gentle as them. It wasn't until I saw their brother that it dawned on me how truly safe I'd felt with them, even when I'd first learned what they were.

Yeah, there was about a zero percent chance I'd have let a man like Isaac Steel take me to the middle of nowhere, no matter who was after me.

I felt his eyes on me, scrutinizing me. Looking for deceit, I guessed, as I pulled myself together and returned his gaze.

"Isaac Steel? I'm Audrey Waits. Thank you for meeting me." I was proud of how even my voice sounded, despite my heart pounding in my throat at his unsettling stare.

"Visitation form said Lana Clarke." His voice was a deep timbre, with the same cockney accent as the twins.

"I know. I had to use a fake name. Your father might be on the watch for me."

If he was surprised that his father was looking for me, he didn't show it. "If my father is looking for you, a fake name isn't going to keep you safe."

I nodded, wetting my lips. "I'm starting to get that."

A small pause and then he asked, "The visitation form said you had news about Ellie. Is she dead?"

The way he said it, with no emotion whatsoever, I could almost have believed he didn't care one way or the other. But when I shook my head, he exhaled softly, and I realized he'd been holding his breath waiting for my answer.

"I was told to tell you that she's safe."

His eyes narrowed. "By who?"

"Marcus. I am here on behalf of Liam and Louis."

He cursed under his breath and made to stand up. "We're done here."

"No, wait." I reached forward to put my hand on his tattooed forearm in an instinctive response to the panic flaring in my chest. If he left now, we were doomed.

Isaac stared down at my hand, and it took everything in me not to flinch off him.

"We need your help. Please, please don't go." I spoke as quickly as I could, the pleas bubbling from my lips as fear gripped my spine.

To my great relief, he paused, but his eyes were narrowed to slit. "You've got thirty seconds."

"Your dad—your brothers found out that he killed Jeremy and got you sent in here. They were working on finding a way to get rid of him and get you out, but... he found out. We all had to flee London while Blaine tried to use his spies to keep tabs on your father. That's how we learned he's going to put a hit on us all. Some gang called Smerts?"

"Смерть," Isaac corrected. He sighed deeply and rubbed a hand through his dark locks. "They're not a gang, love. They're the most dangerous assassins in the world. Sorry to be the one to tell you, but if you've been marked already, you're as good as dead. Nothing I or anyone else can do about it."

"But we haven't—according to Blaine's spies, it won't happen until midday today. Marcus said... Marcus said you could help us. That you know something that will get him to back off before it's too late," I said, gripping his arm as if clinging to him would somehow make him care enough to tell me what I needed to know. "This girl—this Ellie. Is she why you're in here? Did your father use her against you somehow? She's safe, Isaac. But your brothers are not. I'm not. Please."

"You say you're here on behalf of the twins. What are you to them?"

I was taken aback by the directness of his question, but as much as I didn't want to get into the complicated relationship I had with his brothers, he had a right to know. "I'm their... their girlfriend." Or as close to a girlfriend as a woman could be when stuck in a love triangle.

Isaac hummed, as if it was the most natural thing in the world that I'd not specified one twin, but included them both. "And from the looks of you, you're a typical middle-class working girl, aren't you? Take your career seriously, never broken the law. Had dreams of a white picket fence and barbecues in the garden with your neighbors, before those two off-railed your life."

How on Earth he could read me that well I had no idea—I'd just gotten back from living in the wilderness for weeks, and my current attire borrowed from Sam's lady friend didn't scream middle-class, to put it politely.

When I just stared at him, he obviously took it as confirmation and continued, "If you're here, talking to me, you're the girl they expect to marry. They trust you.

But I'll wager the twins never meant for you to get involved in our family shit, and that they're both pretty fucking panicked at how much danger you're in. Probably tried to hide you away when you said you'd come see me so they could avoid my father's eyes and ears a little longer. Am I close?"

I nodded mutely. Apparently, he knew his brothers well.

"You know what I'd do in their place, Audrey?" Isaac leaned in over the table a little, fixing me with gray eyes that should have reminded me of the twins but didn't. "I'd fucking lie through my teeth to save my woman. Even to my own brother. I'm sorry they were stupid enough to get you involved in our family shit, I truly am. They should have known better. But I'm not risking Ellie's life for you."

"And your brothers' lives? Do they mean as little to you? Because they're out there, risking their arses to save *you*. They could've taken your father down when they realized how evil he was, but they didn't... because that would leave you to rot in prison for the rest of your miserable life. Instead, they're risking everything to try and stop the man who put you in here. Your brother Blaine—he's got a wife and a child. And still he didn't take the easy route. Liam and Louis could've left the country, but they didn't. *No one* abandoned you—and you're telling me you're refusing to help them because they might *lie* to you? I wonder what Ellie would think of you, if she knew what a coward you are."

I hadn't meant to lose my temper at him, but the unfairness of his claim that the twins would lie about something like that made my blood boil. I moved my hand from his arm and stared him down, too furious to be rattled by his disturbing gaze.

"He told me he would peel her skin off." Isaac's voice was soft, but devoid of emotion. "Strip by strip, while she was still alive. And video it for me to watch. Have you ever met my father, Audrey?"

I shook my head, mute from horror.

"He doesn't *look* evil. But you can still tell—that part of us who recognizes monsters will know him for what he is. I am in here because I know my father's secret, and I was stupid enough to tell him I knew.

"Have Louis or Liam ever told you how he used to beat us? So brutally we'd have bruises for weeks and months? How he used his belt for any slight, perceived or real?"

I shook my head again.

"I guess they wouldn't. Maybe they don't remember. They were very young, and we tried—my brothers and I —we tried to interfere when he went after them. You think I don't love my brothers enough to sacrifice my life for them? I do. But not hers. Never hers. So if they don't put him down, and if he finds her again... I will kill you. And Mira and Evelyn. There is nothing and no one who will be able to stop me. So tell me, Audrey. Do you still want me to tell you his secret?"

The complete sincerity in his stormy eyes made a shiver of ice travel down my spine. But his threats didn't matter. If he didn't tell me, we were as good as dead anyway. "Yes."

Isaac leaned back in his chair, hands clenched into fists on the table. "He had our mother murdered. She was working with the cops to try and get him locked up for good—because of the beatings. He didn't touch her, but she wanted us to be safe. And since you don't divorce a mafia patriarch... she went to the police. He found out. This is why Jeremy's dead, too. I was stupid enough to tell him, and he didn't have a weakness to be exploited. So our father set me up on a drug deal, had Wesley shoot a man with my gun, and told me to take the fall or he'd come for Ellie."

"Who's Wesley?" I did my best to keep my mind clear, despite the horror of his tale. To have grown up in a home with so much violence... But I had to keep my head on straight if I was going to figure out how we could use this information to get out of this mess.

"My father's right hand man. He's been with the Family for the past twenty years. Done all the horrible shit dear Dad didn't want to do himself."

"Do you think he was involved in your mother's murder?" I asked as the first threads of a plan began weaving together at last.

"I know he was. It was in the files of the detective who was working with my mother. Dad eventually found out who he was and had him killed, too, but I got to the files before he did. Everything's in there. Every dirty family secret."

"And where are those files now?" I asked, unable to conceal the urgency churning in my gut.

Isaac breathed out, a small huff of air. His lips pulled up in a wry, joyless smile. "The one place that son of a bitch never dared to desecrate. They're buried at Highgate Cemetery. In my mother's grave."

THIRTY-FIVE

LIAM

I knew going on my own was a terrible idea. Whoever Dad had sent to order our hit, it would have been infinitely better if we'd been two to take him down. But that would have left Audrey alone, without any way of getting help if our dad's men recognized her.

As I crouched on the rooftop of the warehouse across from where I knew the London contact for the смертьs had his domain, I felt just a sliver of anger at Marcus and Blaine. They'd both left town, leaving Louis and I as the only hands we had in the city right now, because they wanted to protect their birds. Meanwhile Audrey, who'd hardly known what the underworld was up until a few weeks ago, was neck deep in it, and except for maybe tying her up and hiding her away in one of Blaine's safe houses, there was nothing we could do to change it. Of course, they didn't know we had a woman involved.

So fucking stupid.

If I'd been any kind of smart, I'd have kept on jogging when I saw her flailing around in the park that morning. She'd been safe.

Flashes of yesterday played for my mind's eye. Of her moans and whispered words of affection as she writhed between us. The time she'd held me while I cried after having killed a man. Holding her hand as we went to see her parents together, like a normal fucking couple. Guilt gnawed at my stomach as I stared at the alleyway below, because I knew I didn't want her to be safe. I wanted her to be with me more than I wanted to know she'd never get hurt by my dark world.

Selfish fuck.

I growled at my idiotic angsting and pushed it away. It didn't matter what I wanted, because right now I didn't have a choice about it anyway. And if I didn't focus, we'd all lose our heads.

I waited for more than an hour on that rooftop. When a car finally pulled up, it'd started to rain and I was soaked through. At the sight of the driver, however, my adrenaline picked up, and I forgot about my discomfort.

I'd have known that face anywhere. Wesley was a large black man in his forties, and he'd been with our Family since his late teens. Or with our father, more precisely. He'd been unquestionably loyal to our father from the day Dad killed his abusive stepdad. According to Marcus, he was also the man who'd been sent to kill Jeremy. Of course he'd be the one to order a hit on us, too.

I quickly slipped across the rooftop and down the side, climbing down the wall where Wesley wouldn't be able to spot me. When I crept around the corner, gun drawn, he'd finally made it out of the car and was holding a brown leather briefcase in one hand. Undoubtedly the blood money our father was willing to spend to get rid of us.

He didn't notice my presence until I pressed the gun against the back of his skull and growled, "Hello, Wesley."

Wesley stiffened, his muscles bunching underneath his black wool coat as he slowly raised his arms. "Louis," he greeted. "Or is it Liam? I never could tell."

No surprise there; our own father had never been able to tell the difference.

"Doesn't really matter, does it?" I tapped him with the gun. "Give me your keys."

He obeyed, and I quickly unlocked the boot and motioned for him to get in.

"I won't fit," he protested. "That boot wasn't made for anyone over 5'10"."

"You and I've both seen bigger men than you fit into this exact car. Get in, or I'm putting a bullet through your skull. Your fucking choice." I moved closer to make sure he complied, but that was exactly what Wesley had been waiting for.

The second I was within range, he threw his elbow back into my ribs hard enough to wind me.

I keeled over with a groan, but managed to twist away before his fist impacted with my face. When he went for my knees I was ready, and I kicked him hard across the thigh, making him stumble forward and right into the line of my fist. It connected with his chin, but as he spun around, he aimed a kick right at my stomach.

I flew backward, dropping the gun like a fucking untrained kid as pain exploded through my body. He was on me instantly, grabbing for the weapon while trying to hold me back.

I kicked, hitting him the gut, but not with enough power to get him off. He swung again, and I managed to block his punch, but I wasn't fast enough to recover, and his fingers closed around the handle of the gun.

"You can fucking forget about it!" I punched him in the elbow just as he pulled back to aim, which is the only thing that saved me from getting shot in the chest. The gun went off, quieted by the silencer I'd attached to its barrel, and pain lanced through my right bicep.

"Fuck!" I gritted my teeth to work through the pain, using the spike of adrenaline to land a blow to the side of Wesley's face hard enough to send him to the ground and off my body. He didn't recover before I'd wrestled

the gun out of his hand and pulled back to aim it at his head.

"Move, I fucking dare you," I growled.

Wesley froze, eyes trained on the gun. For five long seconds, all that could be heard in the alleyway was our ragged breathing and the falling rain splattering against the ground and the tin roofs above us. When I was sure he wasn't going to fight again, I got to my feet, biting the inside of my cheek to keep from crying out at the pain in my arm.

Putting enough distance between us that he wouldn't be able to surprise me again, I turned to the car and quickly fired two bullets into the boot, creating a couple of air holes and decreasing the resale value by tens of thousands. I smirked, knowing how pissed my dad got when the "company cars" got damaged.

"Get in the fucking boot, or suck on a bullet. Last chance," I snarled at my father's right hand man.

This time, he complied without a word.

I WAS LATE PULLING up at the safe house where I'd arranged to meet up with Louis and Audrey, a fact that was very much cemented when Audrey stormed into the garage the second after I'd pulled in and threw herself around my neck before I'd gotten fully out of the car.

"I was so scared you'd been hurt!" she said, her voice raw with emotion. "You're so late. What happened?"

"Complicatio—*ow!* Fuck, Audrey, be careful." I flinched away when she inadvertently grasped onto my arm where I'd been shot.

Her brown eyes widened in alarm—and when she spotted the blood seeping through my coat, her face turned pale as a sheet and she released me as if she'd burned herself. "Oh my God, what happened? Do you need a doctor? Oh God, Liam, what can I do?"

"Shh, calm down, love it's just a flesh wound." I nodded at Louis, who stepped out into the garage and awkwardly put my uninjured arm around Audrey's shoulders. "Got a present in the boot. Be careful, it's a lively one."

Louis arched an eyebrow in question and accepted the keys from me. "Please tell me it's not a Russian."

I snorted. "Didn't get hit in the head so no—I haven't kidnapped a fucking assassin." I grimaced as pain throbbed from my wound, reminding me I probably needed to have a look at it sometime soon. "You good?"

"Yeah, go sit down. I'll be in to stitch you up in a moment." He grabbed my gun from the car and walked around the back. "Audrey, get him inside, will you? And don't let him try to bullshit about just needing a Band-Aid. There's enough blood here that he's gonna need stitches."

I glared at my twin when Audrey turned, if possible,

even paler. "Don't stress, love, I'll be fine," I said, forcing a smile.

"Stop trying to play brave!" She grabbed me—with surprising strength, I might add—around the waist and guided me away from the car and to the door that led into the safe house, letting me support my weight against her body. It was a relief not to have to carry my full weight myself, and I frowned against her soft hair as she led me inside. The adrenaline was starting to leave my body, and it was getting harder to ignore the pain spreading from my right arm. Maybe that bullet wound was a bit nastier than I'd assumed, after all.

The house was a tiny one-room shack and not very well-lit, leaving shadows to play over the peeling wallpaper from the single, naked bulb hanging from the living room ceiling. At the far end was a sink and a stove, as well as an ancient-looking fridge, and in the corner next to the door that led to the stairs was a rickety-looking old sofa with mildewy cushions and an equally awful-looking armchair.

Audrey led me to the sofa, helped me sit down, and immediately began to fuss with my coat to get a look at the wound.

"It's fine, love, I promise," I repeated, doing my best to calm her down. She'd obviously not had a lot of experience with the kinds of injuries that came with being in the mafia, and she looked like all the blood was about to make her hurl. "Really, just sit down. Louis will have me fixed right up in a moment."

She ignored my protests and eventually managed to get the coat off. The small gasp that escaped her made me look down at the wound and grimace. It'd been bleeding more than I'd thought, and there was a deep groove in the torn muscle. No wonder it hurt like a bitch.

"Louis!" Audrey screamed at the still-open door to the garage before she grabbed her own top and ripped a large chunk of fabric out of it. She pressed it firmly against my wound with both hands, ignoring my flinching, and shouted for my twin again.

"*Louis!*"

My brother came in the door before she managed to call a third time, herding Wesley in front of him with the gun pointed firmly at his back. He'd tied his hands behind him with duct tape and gagged him as well— both things I hadn't had the time for when leaving the смертьз'.

"Is it bad?" Louis asked her. He nudged Wesley forward so he could lean over to look. Audrey took the pressure off my arm for a moment to show him, her eyes big and fearful as she looked at my twin for guidance.

"Well, shit," Louis grumbled. "That's gonna leave a scar. Just keep the pressure on, love. And if he faints, slap him. I'll be down in a second, just tying this prick up upstairs."

"Will he be okay?" she whispered, and I realized she thought I was dying. My heart gave a sappy spasm of joy at the despair in her voice. If I hadn't been in so much pain, I might have felt bad about enjoying her fear.

"Yeah, don't worry. He's tough as old leather." Louis gave her a wink, probably to try and make her feel better, and then led Wesley out the door and up the stairs.

We could hear them walking around upstairs, the scraping of a chair and something—or someone—heavy being pushed into it and the murmur of Louis' voice.

"Don't die on me."

I blinked at the sound of Audrey's voice and turned my head to look at her. Tears rimmed her beautiful brown eyes, catching on her lashes as she stared at me with undeniable fear—and so much love, it made my heart pound heavily behind my ribs.

"I couldn't bear it if you died. I love you so much. Don't die."

"Audrey," I whispered. Awkwardly, I moved my uninjured arm to put my hand on her shoulder, giving it a squeeze. I wanted to hug her against my chest, but I couldn't move enough to do so. "I'm not dying. I promise, love. I'll never leave you. No one's ever getting between us—no one and nothing. You're the only thing that matters, love."

The tears in her eyes overflowed at my words, and then her lips were against mine, kissing me with a desperation I'd felt ever since I'd been forced to break up with her.

"I love you, Liam," she whispered in between salty kisses. "I love you. I love you."

It was only when I pulled back to breathe some moments later that I noticed Louis watching us from the doorway, a look of dark regret clear on his so familiar features.

When he saw me looking, he forced a smile and walked over to where they'd left our camping bags. "Ready to get stitched up, brother? Isaac left us with a lot to discuss."

THIRTY-SIX
AUDREY

I still felt queasy from watching Louis stitch his twin up with the needle and thread they'd brought in the First Aid kit, but once the bleeding had stopped and Liam no longer looked like he was about to pass out, I did feel a lot better.

After dinner, he also no longer looked close to death like he had when he'd gotten out of the car. I'd been so terrified that he'd actually die on me.

I lifted the hand he still had wrapped around mine from while he was being sewn up and kissed his knuckles, grateful that we were all safe, at least for a little while longer.

The love in his eyes at my small gesture of affection made me smile, despite the severity of the situation.

"You actually got Isaac to meet you?" Liam asked.

He sounded impressed or surprised, I couldn't quite tell which. Maybe both.

"Your dad threatened him. If he'd allowed any of you in, or talked with you on the phone, he'd have killed Isaac's girlfriend. Ellie. Gruesomely."

"Ellie?" Liam's face displayed clear surprise this time. "She's his girlfriend? You sure?"

I shrugged. "I mean, he didn't call her that, but... I just assumed. Why?"

"She's an old childhood friend of his and Jeremy's. Used to come around back when mum was still alive. They stopped seeing each other right around when when Isaac turned eighteen," Louis said. "Doesn't matter, though—whatever the case, she's safe, and Dad's lost his hold over Isaac. So he spilled the beans on Dad's secrets."

Liam arched both eyebrows at his twin. "Yeah? How bad is it?"

"He had Mum killed," Louis said softly. "She was working with a cop to gather enough dirt on dad to take him down. So he murdered her."

The expression of complete and utter grief that'd passed across Louis' features when I'd first told him now mirrored on Liam's face. He shook his head, his lips parting as if to speak, but no words came out.

I squeezed his hand to offer him what comfort I could, like I had for Louis. "Isaac got a hold of the cop's files without your dad knowing. He buried them in your mother's grave. There might be enough evidence in there to threaten your father to back off on the... the assassins." I wasn't going to try to pronounce that foreign word again.

"But not enough to take him down, or that cop would have already done it," Liam said, his voice raw with anger. "So we're right back to where we started. *Fuck!*"

"Not necessarily." I looked from him to Louis, my stomach tight from what I was about to suggest. "Isaac said Wesley is your dad's right hand man. I assume that's the Wesley we have tied up upstairs?"

Louis nodded, a small frown appearing between his brows. "What do you have in mind?"

"Does he have family? Someone he cares about?" I took a deep breath. "Someone he would consider betraying your father for to keep safe?"

They both stared at me in complete silence, and with expressions so horrified you'd have thought I'd sprouted horns.

"It's the only logical option we have left, as far as I can see," I said. "Do you have any other way of getting close enough to your dad to end it?"

"Do you know what you're saying, love?" Liam asked, his voice soft. "What the outcome of your plan would be?"

"He'd kill your dad," I said, sounding much more certain than I felt. But this was the only outcome—or it was the only outcome that didn't end with us dead, rather than the monster who'd tormented his family and forced us into hiding.

"That's if things go according to plan. If they don't... then we'll have to start cutting slices off an innocent man whose only crime is loving the wrong guy. If Wesley refuses, we have to show him we're serious," Louis said. His voice was also gentle.

"You both need to stop treating me like I'm this fragile china doll," I said, simultaneously irritated and thankful for their obvious concern. "We need to make it out of this alive, and it's time to stop being delicate about it. I might not have grown up in the mafia like you two, but what we need right now is a strategy. And that—that I *can* do. This is no different than a hostile business takeover." Minus the need for actual murder and blackmail. "And as much as I don't want to see an innocent man get hurt... I'd much rather risk a nameless person than one of us. Do you think your dad would have spared *me,* had you not gotten me out of London before he could get to me? If you don't step up and play the game as cunningly as he does, we'll lose."

The twins were silent for a beat as they exchanged a long look, and I got the sense they were nonverbally communicating with one another. Finally, Liam looked at me, a small smirk lurking at the corner of his mouth. "You're right. It's a good plan."

"And to think we've tried to shield you from our

world," Louis continued. His lips were pulled up in a reflection of his twin's smile. "You were bloody born for this, weren't you?"

"Our little mafia princess," Liam said, his voice teasing—but there was also an undeniable measure of respect.

Louis stretched. "I guess I'll go tell Wesley the happy news. And then we'll go grave robbing."

THIRTY-SEVEN
LOUIS

"You sick sonuvabitch!"

It turned out Wesley wasn't nearly as thrilled about having his lover threatened as he'd been about spying on ours. I cocked my head at the tied-up criminal on the rickety chair in front of me. His eyes were wild with anger, his muscles bulging in a futile attempt at getting free. "You touch him, I'll cut that girl of yours to fucking *pieces!*"

"It sucks to be on the receiving end, doesn't it?" I asked him while I cleaned my nails with the tip of my hunting knife. "Wanna hear the funny part? Audrey's the one who came up with this plan. I know she doesn't look it, but she's tough as nails, that one. How about your Roger? Think he'll be tough, too, if we start slicing bits off him to send to you?"

Wesley didn't respond; he simply glared at me with all the hatred of a trapped bull.

"See, I'm not so sure he will. So here's my proposal to you, Wesley. You put a bullet in my dad's brain, and me and my brothers will leave your boyfriend alone."

"I'll never betray William," he growled, tugging on his tied wrists once more. "Not like you and your ungrateful fucking brothers. Bunch of twats, the lot of you. You never deserved to be born into the Steel empire."

"Ah. Yes." I sighed melodramatically and let the blade of my knife dance across my knuckles. "You always did envy us, didn't you? Sucking up to my father so much and yet you always knew... you'll never be a Steel, no matter how many of us you kill. I appreciate that you're in a bit of a tough spot, so I'll give you a couple of hours to mull our offer over: Do you give up dad, or do you give up the only person who actually truly loves you? Because make no mistake, Wesley—William Steel does not love you. He is incapable of love."

Without waiting for him to answer I stepped behind him and undid the bindings that tied him to the chair, but kept the duct tape tying his wrists together in place.

"Where are you taking me?" he demanded as I poked him in the back with the very tip of the knife, ushering him toward the door.

"Out for a little late-night excursion. You put a

bullet in my twin, so I'm afraid that means you're gonna have to help with the digging."

———

LIAM DROVE. Despite his wounded arm, he assured me he could drive just fine, and to be honest I'd have rather had him by the wheel than in charge of our hostage anyway. Wesley was a big guy who'd been trained by the same men me and my brothers had—if he spotted a weakness, he'd go for it. So I spent the car ride to Highgate Cemetery in the backseat with a gun aimed at him.

Unfortunately for me, I could still catch glimpses in the rearview mirror of the small looks of adoration Liam shot Audrey's way. When she put her hand briefly on his while he was changing gears, it took all my willpower not to look away from Wesley so I could no longer see them in my periphery.

The image from when I'd walked Wesley into the shitty safe house to find Audrey on the couch with Liam was seared into my brain. She'd told him she loved him. And I'd believed her.

It wasn't so much the words themselves as it was they way she'd said them—the absolute desperation on her face when she'd thought he might die.

Yeah, she loved him. She loved him like you'd love your soulmate. Like I loved *her*.

She'd made her choice, even if she hadn't fully acknowledged it yet.

I fought against the black chasm of despair opening up like a gaping maw in my chest. I couldn't wallow in my own misery—not now. She might have chosen my twin, but I still loved her until it ached. And I loved him —and Isaac and Marcus and Blaine. I needed them all to be safe, and until they were, I couldn't dwell on the hollow pit of agony where my heart had once been.

AS SAVVY AS Audrey was with the business side of the mafia, she still needed quite a bit of training on the physical aspects. I caught myself thinking of which fighting styles would be best to teach her so she could defend herself while I pushed her delectable round arse over the cemetery's high fence. Without thinking, I let my fingers find the seam of her pants and brush up against the heat between her thighs.

"Stop that, you bloody pervert!" Audrey hissed from her precarious perch atop the fence. With a glare in my direction, she pulled her leg up and then managed to slide down the other side without further help.

The realization that I wouldn't be the one to help her settle into life in our Family stabbed through my gut like a fucking icepick, and I forcefully shoved it aside before I scaled the fence myself.

Not now.

The cemetery was pitch black, save for the light from the London skyline faintly illuminating the edges of the old graveyard. Liam switched on his flashlight and we began walking the familiar path to our mother's grave.

I'd been here plenty over the years. Leaving flowers. Asking for guidance.

We'd been very young when she was killed, but I still remembered her funeral as if it was yesterday. It'd been the worst day of my life.

Anger boiled in my gut at the knowledge that our own father was the reason she was gone. He'd murdered the woman he'd proclaimed to love, the only person who'd ever looked out for us, all to preserve his power. *His fucking power.* It was all that'd ever mattered to him, in the end.

Everything for Family. What a load of shit. The woman who'd given her life to try and save us from his violence had proven a far stronger portrayer of our family motto than the man who'd beaten it into us every day of our lives.

We walked through the graveyard in silence, Liam's flashlight illuminating the gravel path and the old trees lining it. Even that prick Wesley was quiet, though I wasn't sure if it was out of respect for where we were going, or because he was scheming up some plan to try and escape. Probably the latter. I poked him in the back with the barrel of the gun to remind him what'd happen if he got any ideas.

"It's here," Liam said softly, more to Audrey than to me, as he stopped in front of an achingly familiar slab of marble. I could recognize that tombstone anywhere.

"Eleonore Steel," she read from the stone. She didn't speak the next words out loud, but I could see her mouthing them out to herself in the cone of light from the flashlight. *Mother and wife. Forever missed, never forgotten. With love, we say goodbye. With love, we will reunite.*

"She died so young," Audrey whispered. With an anger that surprised me, she turned to glare at Wesley. "How can you work for a monster who killed the mother of his own children?"

"She was weak. She betrayed the Family," Wesley said, his voice as cold and detached as ever.

"To save her kids. Are you telling me you won't do anything you can to save the ones you love?" She looked him up and down, contempt clear on her face at his unmoving features. "I pity you. And whoever you've told your heart belongs to. Clearly you have nothing to give them but hatred."

"Big words for a woman who so easily threatens an innocent just to get her way," Wesley hissed. "You think spreading your thighs for these two pricks means you know anything about their Family? About love? You will never be more than second best. You will never mean as much to them as their own flesh and blood."

"That's enough." Liam pulled his knife and sliced through Wesley's bindings before shoving a shovel into his hands. "Dig."

Wesley stared from the shovel to the grave, then back to Liam. "You're not serious?"

"Deadly." Liam stared unblinkingly at him.

"I thought you were supposed to have canonized the woman, and now you want to dig up her *grave?*"

I'd never thought Wesley had any limits with the despicable shit he'd do, but apparently, grave robbing was over the line even for him.

"We're doing this *because* we loved her, you twat. Maybe she didn't die for nothing after all. Now get digging—I ain't telling you again." I cocked the gun in warning.

It took Wesley and I a good hour before I finally hit something hard with my shovel. I froze for a second when the metal scraped over something decidedly wood-like, but quickly realized we weren't deep enough down to have reached the casket. I sucked in a breath of relief. As much as I wanted to believe that whatever Isaac had hidden away would somehow justify losing our mother, I didn't want to come face to face with her casket. The day they'd lowered it into the ground had been more than enough for me.

"Whatcha got?" Liam asked, leaning over the edge of the grave to peer into the shallow hole we'd dug out.

"Looks like a wooden box of some sort," I said, bending to pick it up.

It was indeed a wooden box. Varnished but undecorated, just slightly larger than an A4 sheet of paper, and maybe six inches tall. I bent to pick it up and brushed the caked dirt off its lid. "I think this is it."

I handed it to Liam, and he flicked the lid open and grunted in confirmation at whatever was inside. "Looks like it."

"Put it in the car," I instructed, turning back to Wesley with a grim expression. "We'll need to get this filled as quickly as possible."

Liam handed his flashlight—and, very demonstratively, his gun—to Audrey, leaving us with the clean up. I had my own weapon at hand, but knowing Wesley, it was good if he knew there was more than one gun aimed in his general direction. I didn't know if Audrey had ever held a gun before in her life, but as long as Wesley thought she might have a chance of shooting him before he could overpower me, we'd be good.

Whether it was due to Audrey's watchful eye or not, he didn't try anything, and we got the grave filled back up and smoothed over quicker than we'd dug it. There wasn't much to do about the bare soil where lush grass had grown until tonight, but I made a silent promise to Mum that I'd come back with some grass seeds and fertilizer once we'd sorted out Dad. And roses. She'd loved roses, Marcus had once said, so those had been my flowers of choice when I came to visit her grave.

"What's keeping Liam?" Audrey's voice pulled my attention to her. She was looking back in the direction we'd come, a note of worry in her voice.

I glanced at my wristwatch and cussed. It'd been more than half an hour. He should have well been back by now.

"Come on, best go ch—" It was only the faint flicker of movement I caught out of the corner of my eye that made me move to the side just in time for Wesley's shovel to impact with my shoulder and neck instead of my skull.

I crashed to the ground with a grunt, pain exploding through my body from the impact. He'd put all his weight into that swing—if I hadn't moved just then, I'd be dead, my skull cracked like a grape on the ground.

As it was, I was pretty sure my shoulder was broken. I gritted my teeth against the nauseating wave of pain and looked up just in time to see Audrey take aim and fire.

The bullet went way wide, chipping a small piece of the marble tombstone.

"Nice fucking try," Wesley snarled. He swung the shovel again, smacking the weapon out of her hand and sending it and the flashlight flying in between the graves. A metallic smack followed by complete darkness announced the flashlight's death; murder by tombstone.

"Audrey," I gasped. "Run!"

She obeyed—thank the stars above, she obeyed. But my relief at the sound of her hurried footfalls disappearing off toward the gate was quickly interrupted when Wesley's shovel smacked down full-force on the ground right next to my head.

I rolled, grunting from the pain in my broken shoulder, and kicked into the darkness. My foot connected with something solid, and Wesley huffed as I swiped his ankles from underneath him, sending him crashing to the ground. I tried to get on top of him, but was too hindered by my shoulder to make it before the large man had recovered. Too late I went for my gun, but Wesley beat me to it. He ripped the weapon from my belt and I heard the click of the safety being uncocked.

Cussing, I rolled again, cringing when I landed on my broken shoulder, but it was just in time.

A shot rang through the night, so close to my head it was deafening, but he didn't hit me. I scrambled to my feet, narrowly avoiding the second shot, and threw myself further in between the graves.

Wesley shot one more time, but this one was wide off. He didn't know where I was hiding, and in the darkness, it'd be impossible for him to tell. I heard him swear under his breath when he realized, but my momentary relief came to a dead halt when the sound of his feet hit the gravel, and he set into a jog. In the same direction Audrey had disappeared.

My heart gave a spasm as cold dread filled my lungs. *Oh, no. No, no, no.*

I didn't think—didn't care that my shoulder was screaming in agony as I scrambled to my feet. All I cared about just then was that an armed man, an enemy, was chasing down the woman I loved.

As soon as I took a step forward to run after them, my foot hit something metallic. "Thank fuck," I whispered into the night air as I bent and let my fingers close around the familiar handle of Liam's gun. It was the same model as my own. I didn't bother putting it away as I took up chase after Wesley, biting down on the pain when every step sent jolts of agony shooting through my shoulder.

The further I ran without seeing any of them, the more my anxiety gnawed at my gut. Where was Liam? He didn't have a gun to defend Audrey with, but I knew she'd still be infinitely safer with him than on her own.

Fuck, if only—

My thoughts came to an abrupt halt when I rounded the final corner before the gates next to the fence we'd climbed. They were open, but that wasn't what made icy fear freeze every muscle in my body. I came to a stumbling standstill as I stared at the people illuminated by the single street light outside the cemetery.

A dozen men stood on the other side of the gates.

One of them held Liam with an arm twisted up behind his back, a gun pointing at his temple. Audrey stood close by him, but the person holding a gun to her head was my father. By his side, Wesley stood with the smuggest look as he stared me down, and I wished I'd killed him when I'd had the chance. Everything inside of me itched to put a bullet in his brain. I'd never wanted to kill someone so badly before.

"Just in time." My father's cold voice rang through the quietude, sending sharp spikes of fear through my body. "But you two were always my *dependable* sons, weren't you?"

He had them both. The two people I loved more than anything else... *he* had them. The man who'd had his own wife and child murdered in cold blood.

I looked across his row of men and knew I could do nothing against them all. Even if my father didn't have guns aimed at Audrey and Liam, there were just too many for me to take down. So I did the only thing I could. I raised my gun and aimed it straight at my father's head.

He laughed. A short, disparaging bark, and then he yanked Audrey's head backward by her hair, displaying her vulnerable throat.

"You've got some balls, son, I'll give you that," he sneered. "Wanna see if you can press the trigger before your twin and the girl are dead on the ground?"

"You won't hurt them." I knew I sounded much more self-assured than I felt.

"No?" My father cocked his head at me. "It seems to me you have been conspiring with your brothers to take me down. Involving low-lifes like the Perkinsons in Family affairs... And this little tart, whoever the fuck she is. And now here you are, waving a gun in my face. Tell me again why I shouldn't kill them both? Maybe you and your brothers will fall in line when they get some concrete proof of what exactly happens to anyone who crosses William Steel."

"Like you killed Mum? And Jeremy?" I bit back. "You betrayed your own blood. I think you've more than proven how little you can be trusted." I turned my attention to his men. "You hear that? He killed his own wife and child. You think he'd hesitate to kill *you*? Or your families?"

"Don't bother. Unlike my own ungrateful offspring, they understand the meaning of loyalty. Your mother was a traitor. And I guess what they say is true—if there's something wrong with the bitch, there'll be something wrong with the pups. I should have killed you all when I learned the truth about her."

I dared a glance at his men, and on their faces I saw the truth. They might be scared my father would turn on them, but that was exactly what kept them in line. No one would help me save my twin or my love. So there was only one thing left for me to do.

"Take me instead. If you let them go, I will come with you willingly. You can do what you want with me —make me an example for the whole city. I'll do whatever you want me to, say whatever you want. And I won't struggle when you execute me."

"Louis!" Audrey's gasp was filled with terror.

"How very *noble*," my father spat. "Fine. I accept. Your life for theirs... as long as your twin promises compliance, now and forevermore."

"Louis, no! No fucking way!" Liam's voice was furious, but when I looked at him, I saw the panic in his eyes.

I lowered my gun until it hung limply by my side, not looking away from the man I'd shared my whole life with. Who meant everything to me, along with the woman who loved him, not me. "Yes. This is how it has to be. This way I get to die knowing the two people I love will find happiness together."

"How do you think we could ever be happy without you?" Liam asked, and the first sliver of despair finally showed in his voice. He knew, too. He knew there was no other way now.

"I know the love you share. I know because I feel it too. But she's supposed to be yours, Liam, I understand that now. She was yours first, and she will always be yours first. So please. If you want my sacrifice to mean anything, concede to him. Accept his terms. And live a long life with her by your side. Maybe pop out some ginger babies and name one of them after me." I tried to crack a smile, to show him everything was all right, but it was impossible. The absolute devastation I saw in my twin's eyes was too real to wish away with a joke this time.

"Louis, no! Louis, look at me!" Audrey sounded so desperate, and as much as I yearned to see her sweet face one last time, I knew I couldn't or I'd lose my nerve. I wanted to be with her more than I wanted to breathe, but it wasn't possible. And now, at least I could give her up knowing it would save them both.

Slowly, with one final, lingering look, Liam nodded. Then he turned his gaze to our father. "I will follow your leadership, now and forevermore. If you let Louis give... give his life for Audrey's and my own, I will be by your side and under your rule until I take my last breath."

THIRTY-EIGHT

LIAM

"There is nothing we can do, love. He won." I didn't have the strength to look up from where I was sitting on the couch in the flat I'd shared with Louis, my head in my hands. Everything inside me was still numb. It'd been just over half an hour since my father's men had escorted us here and taken up guard outside the building. Nothing'd been said, but I figured they'd be staying there until Louis was dead.

Louis. A pang of raw pain made it through the numbness, but I viciously pressed it down. If I allowed myself to think his name, if I thought about what was going to happen, I'd never survive it. And I had to. For her.

"Bullshit!" Audrey hissed. She'd been pacing back and forth in the living room like a caged lioness since we'd gotten home. "There has to be something, Liam. There *has* to be! We can't just let him..." Her angry voice died down to a broken sob, and she collapsed onto the sofa next to me. "We can't let him die. We just can't."

I didn't respond, because what was there to say? We have to?

"Liam. Look at me." Gently, she wrapped her hand around my arm, squeezing. "Look at me. Right now."

Slowly I lifted my gaze to hers. Her beautiful eyes were red-rimmed and panicked, but there was also a fire in them that I knew no longer existed in mine.

"We cannot let him die. We won't. You hear me? We'll find a way."

"What way, Audrey? We won't be able to leave the flat, we don't even know where he's taken him. We have no way of getting in touch with my brothers. And I have to protect you."

Her face twisted with renewed anger. "Protect *me?* No! This is bullshit, and we promised each other no bullshit. I'm not just going to sit here and let him die because I need to be protected from your world. I've had a gun aimed at my head, visited your brother in jail, and been chased through a cemetery by a hitman. Protecting me isn't an option here. Not when his life is on the line!"

"I can't lose you, too!" I hadn't meant to shout, but it came out like a roar. "You're all I have left! I can't—I *won't* lose you as well!"

Audrey cupped my face. She looked into my eyes, and in hers, I saw my own sorrow mirrored. "You won't. I promise you, I won't let your father take me from you. But we're going to get him back, Liam. Tell me you're with me."

I placed my hand atop hers, savoring the sensation of her palms against my skin. "I am with you always, my love," I whispered, my voice breaking under the weight of too much emotion. "And if there was a way to save my twin without losing you, too, I would do it in a heartbeat. But if I get you killed, his sacrifice will mean nothing."

"You won't." Determination set in on her pretty features, and she stood back up to begin pacing once more. "Tell me about the... *Smerts*."

I blinked. "The смертьs? They're Russian assassins. They have no loyalty but to the person who pays them, and once you've been marked, they will end your life. There's nothing anyone can do to stop them. If one fails, another will take his place until the job is done."

"How much do they cost?"

"Audrey, no. We do not get involved with them. Ever. They're too dangerous. If something goes wrong, they will turn on you like it's nothing. And they will kill every man, woman, and child in a family. Entire bloodlines have been erased from history because some foolish man who thought he could get rid of his enemies stiffed them on payment or insulted their honor." I got to my feet, too, the mere thought of bringing the смерть taint into my family—and hers—causing icy tendrils to creep up my spine. "You hire them once, they will always be a shadow hanging over your family name. For generations upon generations."

She turned to look at me, and I saw steel in her eyes. "Then we don't insult them, and we pay them what we owe. I don't give a shit about either of our families' names, Liam. What I care about is saving your brother. And you. You think either of us will ever get over losing Louis like this? And what will happen once he's gone and you're supposed to come to heel by your father's side? The man who murdered your twin? I ask you again—how much do these assassins cost?"

Slowly, I exhaled and I looked at the woman in front of me. She was undeniably still the same woman I'd been so attracted to the first time I saw her, with her lush curves and pretty face. Even the fire in her gaze I'd recognized that first time she'd let me in between her thighs, but it'd been nearly hidden—muted embers smothered by her upbringing and attempts to live by society's rules.

"You've changed, love," I said softly, though I wasn't able to keep the pride out of my voice.

"I have," she said. "I'm no longer scared of what people think of me, because it doesn't matter. The only thing that matters is what *I* think of me. You taught me that. You and your brother. And *I* would not be able to live with myself if I sat idly by while the man I love dies for me. And neither would you—I know that much."

Slowly, I nodded, because she was right. In the end, I would do anything for the people I loved the most. And that was her. And Louis.

Even call down the смерть taint.

"You're right. I'll call them."

THE RUSSIAN on my doorstep was as tall as me and as wide as my brother Marcus. His icy blue eyes were devoid of emotion, and when they flicked to my side, I had to quell the urge to step to the left and shield Audrey from his sight.

"Mr. Steel," he said, a hint of accent in his deep voice. "Mrs. Steel?"

"No, no, we're not married." Audrey sounded a bit flustered, but she quickly gathered herself. "Please. Come inside."

I stepped aside and the Russian walked in. His gaze roamed the living room before landing on me once more. "I believe you said the matter was of some urgency?"

"Yes. My brother—my twin—is being held by my father, William Steel. I need to get to him before it's too late."

The Russian arched an eyebrow at me. "We are assassins, Mr. Steel. We do not rescue people. If you do not have a target for me, you have wasted my time."

"We do have a target," Audrey said, her voice sharp. "William Steel. But we need him dead before he kills Liam's twin. An organization with a reputation like yours is capable of working within time limits, I'm sure."

The assassin cocked a brow at her. I wrapped an arm around her and stared him down, ensuring he knew she was under my protection. But he didn't take offense to her sharpness.

"We do. For the right price."

"And that is?" Audrey asked, sounding every ounce the businesswoman she'd been trained to be. An errant thought that she could do quite well for us once we'd taken control of London again flickered at the back of my mind.

"What is the deadline?"

Audrey glanced at me.

"Two hours. He'll want to display Louis to the Perkinsons and the other families to show them the true power of his wrath before he kills him," I said.

"Then our price is five million pounds," the Russian said. "Up front."

"I can get you five hundred thousand up front. The rest I won't be able to get to before he's dead," I said, a knot of ice forming in my gut. Of course they wanted upfront payment—it's why our father hadn't managed to secure the hits on us. If that payment had made it to them, we'd be having an entirely different meeting with the смертьs than we currently were.

"The price is five million up front," he repeated, voice impassive.

"Five hundred thousand now—six million and five hundred thousand after," Audrey said. "You know it's a better deal than what you'll get if you turn us down. And you know the Steels are good for it, especially after their father is gone and they inherit the empire."

The Russian narrowed his eyes ever so slightly at her. "The смертей do not negotiate."

"I'm sure that's not true," Audrey countered, as calmly as if this had been a regular business meeting. "You are an organization who takes monetary compensation for your services. I am certain you will want the best price possible for your work. What we are offering is the best price. The alternative is you leave here with nothing—an outcome neither party will be pleased with. I take it you already expended some effort getting past William Steel's men guarding this building? It would be a shame if that was in vain.

"Of course, the alternative is you take the deal, and the guaranteed seven million we are offering, and everyone benefits. Well, everyone but William Steel... Tell me, did you not have a business deal with him fall through yesterday?"

The assassin stared at Audrey with a blank expression for three long seconds while the silence stretched between us, and my adrenaline spiked as I prepared myself to defend her, gunshot wound be damned.

Then he turned his head to look at me. "How much for the woman?"

Audrey went pale as a sheet next to me, but despite the circumstances, I couldn't hold back a grin. "Sorry, she's not for sale. I plan on marrying her once this matter with my father is settled."

"Pity." He looked back at her, his eyes sliding up and down her curvy figure once. "She could be useful." He looked back at me. "Seven million. Five hundred thousand now."

I shook his hand, suppressing a wince as the firmness of his grip sent bolts of pain up my wounded arm. "Deal. Wait here."

When I left the room to find the five hundred grand Louis and I'd stored away in case of an emergency, Audrey practically stuck to me like glue. Once we were out of earshot in the kitchen, she whispered, "Did he... did he really offer to *buy* me?"

I smirked. "Sure did. You should be proud—it takes a lot to impress a смерть."

"But why?" She still sounded horrified, but I guess she wasn't exactly used to a world where human flesh was traded as commonly as drugs and weapons. Not that we'd ever partaken in the slave trade—even mafia

Families had limits, and that one even our father hadn't crossed.

"Who knows? Either he wanted you to do business negotiations for the organization, or he found your bossiness as hot as I do. Wanna ask him?" I playfully lifted my brows before I knelt down to reach up under the cabinet that hid our safe. It was a bitch to get to, but it was well enough hidden that no one would think to look for it there.

"God, no!" She was silent for a little while while I struggled with the combination.

"Liam?"

"Yeah, love?"

"You said... you planned on marrying me."

I paused, my fingers stilling on the dial. "I do."

"I—"

"We'll talk about it after," I said softly. I knew what she was about to say. That things were so complicated between the three of us, how could I possibly talk about marriage? But everything we'd been through, the night the three of us had shared in the bothy in the Welsh mountains... it changed nothing. There would be heartache, I knew that, maybe even a lifetime's worth, but I would always want to say my vows of forever to this woman, of that I was certain.

But right now, I had to focus if I wanted any chance at saving my brother, because if he died, nothing would ever matter again.

"After," she agreed. "Once Louis is safe."

"WHY IS IT ALWAYS WAREHOUSES?" I muttered.

Audrey looked at me from behind the wooden pallet where we were both crouched.

Even in the shadows shielding us from detection, I could see the question on her face.

"Every time there's a liquidation planned, it's always in a fucking warehouse," I explained, though I was aware my irritation with the location was ridiculous. And not really the point, regardless, but it was a lot easier to focus on than the knowledge that somewhere in there my twin sat, hurt and alone, with a gun aimed at his head.

"Easier clean up." The way she said it, so matter-of-factly, I couldn't help but snort.

"Fucking mafia princess indeed." I gave her another glance, this time more appreciative. In some ways, she was calmer about the darkness in our world than Louis and I were—and she'd only been privy to it for a measly few weeks.

She smiled grimly, not taking her eyes off the front of the warehouse where a couple of my dad's men were standing guard. "I'm done being a delicate flower who's too scared of the world to bite back. They took Louis from us. They're going to pay."

"Yes," I agreed. Her deadly tone fueled my own anger, fanning it through my blood until it blessedly quelled the fear and uncertainty that'd been gnawing at my gut since Louis surrendered to our father. "They are."

THIRTY-NINE

AUDREY

It took several minutes before the men guarding the entrance to the warehouse turned their backs in favor of a couple of approaching cars, and Liam waved me forward.

In a shock of recognition, I noticed Gregory Perkinson in the passenger side of the front car just as they pulled up. To see my nightmare client under such circumstances was beyond surreal, but I didn't have time to waste on the rush of emotion the sight of him inspired.

I hurried after Liam in a bent-over run and threw myself around the corner of the warehouse just as the the sound of opening and closing car doors announced the newcomers' arrival.

Liam put a hand on my shoulder and wordlessly

told me to stay put. Then, quickly and soundlessly, he crept forward, still in a crouch, toward the far end of the warehouse. I could see the outline of a man pacing down there, oblivious to our presence.

Quicker than my eyes could follow, Liam leapt up from behind the man, put both hands on his head, and twisted.

A bolt of nausea shot through me at the faint *crack*. The man dropped like a sack of potatoes.

Liam turned to where I was hiding and waved me forward.

It was an odd sensation—while I'd known they were mafia for some time now, and they'd told me they'd killed before... somehow actually *seeing* Liam break that man's neck rammed home how little I'd truly known of the man I'd fallen in love with.

But the truly surprising part was that, as I stepped over the body on the ground to join him, it didn't bother me. I'd seen a man get killed, and I felt nothing but a passing moment's discomfort, my focus still solidly on saving Louis and casualties be damned. This man, though nothing more than a grunt, would still have caught and hurt us if Liam hadn't taken him out.

It's funny, the things you never have to learn about yourself when you work an office job and spend your nights in front of the TV. I'd always considered myself a compassionate person, but as I snuck in the side door the now dead guard had been standing in front of, I realized that I was the kind of person who'd feel nothing at taking someone's life if it was between them and someone I loved. It was an oddly liberating sensation.

The side door led to the main room, but fortunately someone had stacked several pallets and crates around it, creating a perfect hiding spot.

Liam waved me over to a crack between two crates and I bit my lip at what I saw. The warehouse was very big, but it was nearly halfway full of grim-looking men. Mafia, I assumed. All here to see the twins' father show them what happened to anyone who crossed him. Even his own blood.

It took a little while for me to spot Louis, the angle of the crates narrowing my view of the other end of the warehouse, but when I did, my heart dropped.

He sat on a chair on top of a small dais with his arms and ankles tied. Blood dripped from a split eyebrow and a busted lip, and pain was etched across his face. Next to him, Wesley had a gun casually pointed at his head. He said something we were too far away to hear, and Louis grimaced in return, his lips moving in reply. Whatever he'd said, Wesley didn't seem to appreciate it. He thwacked the butt of the gun against Louis' shoulder, hard, making him cry out before he clamped his jaw shut in defiance.

That cry silenced the room. Everyone turned their

focus to the dais, hushed silence gathering over the crowd of what looked to be at least fifty people.

And then I saw him. The man who'd caused so much evil.

William Steel was a handsome man for his age, with iron-gray hair and the same square jaw and broad shoulders as his sons. I hadn't had time to appreciate how much of their father was in the twins the first time I'd met him, and it'd been too dark to really tell. But the physical appearance was all they'd inherited from him. As much as they might be capable of killing, I knew without a shadow of a doubt that neither Louis nor Liam would ever be capable of the kind of evil their father had unleashed upon their entire family.

He strode up on the dais with confident steps, stopping on the other side of Louis to where Wesley was standing, and turned to face the crowd.

"Friends. I want to thank you for coming here on such short notice. Tonight is a historical night for London, and I would hate for any of you to miss it. I know relations between many of us have been tense for some time now, and so I thought it important for you to see with your own eyes how I will stomp this.... *rebellion* out once and for all.

"The Steels have ruled London for decades, and while I'm sure many would love to see us de-throned, I also know most of you would agree that we have run the

city with a fair hand. Until my sons took it upon themselves to ruin the empire my Family's built from within."
William reached out and grabbed a handful of Louis'
flaming mane, yanking his head back. "Lies. Corruption.
Deceit. Treason. This is what I've put up with from my
own kin these past few years. *Everything for the Family.*
It seems my sons have forgotten their code of honor,
along with their principles. And so it is with a heavy
heart that I announce a death sentence on my youngest
child. It is my hope that his brothers will see reason and
come to heel once they understand that William Steel
does not suffer betrayal from anyone—not even his own
blood. If they don't... they will suffer the same fate.

"And as for the rest of you..." He released Louis' hair
and pointed over the crowd with two fingers. "There
have been whispers of overthrowing the Steel empire for
two years now. Yes, of course I know. And I know that
every single person in here has been a part of these
conspiracies."

Murmurs rose from the gathered men. William
silenced them with a hand gesture.

"It ends tonight, or you will find that I am not the
only one to lose a child. Know that any conversation you
have about overthrowing my rule, I will learn of. Know
that the punishment will be swift and merciless. Too
long I've allowed this bickering, even in my own house.
No more. It is my hope that tonight's execution will

underscore just how serious I am—and that we can all walk away from here with a new understanding and a prosperous working relationship going forward. Wesley?"

He nodded at the large man by Louis' side, and panic exploded in my brain when I realized what was about to happen. Right now. I'd assumed the assassin would be here in time, I'd assumed everything was going to be all right. It hadn't occurred to me that we might fail. Even after the cemetery, I'd had an unshakable faith that in the end, we would all be safe.

That faith came crashing down as I saw Wesley slowly raise his gun. We were too late.

No, no, no!

I grabbed Liam's arm, willing him to do something—anything—to make this stop, but I needn't have.

He slipped out from behind the boxes and raised the gun he'd taken from the guard whose neck he'd broken, aiming it at Wesley within the blink of an eye.

But before either man could shoot, a resounding bang made everyone turn toward the warehouse's front doors.

It took me a little while to realize what had happened. More men stood in the now broken-down doors. Maybe twenty of them, guns trained on the people inside. It wasn't until I spotted two distinct figures I realized help had finally arrived.

I'd never seen the twins' brothers before, but one

look at the two raven-haired men leading the group of newcomers, and there was no doubt in my mind who they were. They were as big as both the twins and Isaac, one of them perhaps even more so, and their grimly set features were undeniably from the Steel lineage.

"Nobody fucking move," one of them, the slightly smaller one, shouted. "Anyone flinches, they get a bullet between the eyes. Do not draw your weapons. Do not be a hero. You will die."

You could have heard a pin drop, the silence spreading across the warehouse was that deafening. Until William Steel pulled his own gun faster than the human eye could follow and pressed it against Louis' temple.

"Blaine. Marcus," he said. "How nice of you to join us, though I am unsure what you thought you'd accomplish here. You won't be able to get a shot off before your brother is dead. You and I both know you don't have the balls to sacrifice one of your own. An unfortunate taint left over from your mother's influence, I'm saddened to say." His eyes flickered to Liam. "Ah, and I see you didn't take our little chat last night seriously, either. Who is it going to be, then, Liam? Wesley? Me? No matter who you shoot, your twin will die. But you can still live. You and that girl you seem so fond of. Lower your weapons—all of you. Only one of my sons has to die tonight. The choice is yours."

No one moved.

I looked from the Steel brothers to their father, and across the sea of made men between them, and I knew this wouldn't end well. The longer Liam and his brothers hesitated, the sooner someone in the crowd would snap and draw his weapon, and all hell would break lose. And I would lose Louis—and possibly also Liam.

Moving carefully, I slipped out from behind the crates to stand by Liam's side. He was too focused on his father to pay me any mind, which was probably for the best. However, I caught Wesley's eye, possibly because I was the only one moving in his field of vision. He glanced at me—and I stared back. Willing him to remember what we'd promised would happen to his boyfriend if he didn't comply.

Something in my expression must have shone through, because he kept his eyes on me for several moments.

I raised my hand and tapped my fingertips against my temple. *Think.*

At that moment, I swore to myself that if either of my twins got hurt from this, I would personally find his lover. And I would end him.

Wesley tore his gaze from mine, and my heart sank at the same time as my fury boiled in my veins. He thought my threat could be dismissed, that I didn't have the strength to carry through—

The gunshot echoed through the warehouse, like a

singular thunderbolt. Deafening as it echoed off the metal walls.

I—and everyone else—stared at the dais. William Steel lay lifeless on the floor, crumpled in a heap next to his tied-up son. A red mark leaking a thin trickle of blood was visible on his temple.

Wesley lowered his gun without taking his eyes off his former boss's body.

Liam was the first to move. He walked to the dais in long strides, gun at the ready. When he got there, he turned to face the crowd.

"William Steel's reign over London has ended. It has ended because he caused harm to the Steel Family, to his own kin. He killed our mother, he killed our brother—and he tried to cull the rest of us, too. I want you all to remember this night. Remember that anyone who attempts to harm the Steel Family will die.

"My brothers and I have taken over the Steel empire, and we expect absolute and complete loyalty from anyone who wishes to do business in our city. Traitors will be dealt with. Harshly. Does anyone have any objections to our claim? Now is your time to speak up. Now is your *only* time to speak up."

Only silence followed his words.

"Very well." Liam nodded at his brothers at the back of the crowd, then turned to untie Louis.

The two dark-haired brothers moved through the throng. From my vantage point, it took me a moment to realize that they were gathering up people, and it wasn't until they'd herded the small group of five men up to the dais that I saw exactly who they were: The Perkinsons.

Loud murmurs rose from those who remained in attendance, one voice rising above the others to shout, "What's the meaning of this?"

"As my brother said—we do not tolerate traitors," the Steel brother who'd spoken before said. "The Perkinsons betrayed us. We offered them forty percent of London for their support, and they accepted—only to sell us out to our dear father the second our backs were turned." He kicked Gregory in the back of the knees, making him stumble to the ground. Perkinson senior went willingly, a look of grim acceptance on his face. A couple of the others struggled, but were quickly—and painfully—subdued.

"I still expect payment in full."

I jumped at the lilting voice sounding right behind me and spun around to come face-to-chest with the Russian assassin. He leaned against the pallets Liam and I'd been hiding behind, both arms crossed over his chest without taking his cool gaze off the dais.

I arched an eyebrow at him and forced my speeding heart to settle down—as much as was possible with the lethal killer this close. "You didn't fulfill the job you were hired to do."

"I would have. But you contracted another to do my

job. I do not appreciate being beaten to a kill, Miss Waits."

So he'd learned my name, then. I frowned, trying to ignore the unsubtle indication that he knew who I was now. "We didn't hire anyone else. That man was his right hand."

"Yes. And he shot his master—the man he's worshipped for so many years... because *you* told him to." The Russian finally took his disturbingly cold eyes off the front of the room and settled them on me. "When he hired my organization to kill his sons, I researched the family. I always do. That man has been loyal to the point of idiocy for two decades. And yet one gesture from you, little bird, and he turned like a rabid dog. So yes, you contracted another to fulfill my job, and I will have my agreed payment." His gaze flickered down my body once, but there was no heat in it when his focus returned to my face a second later. "Be thankful I find you *interesting,* Miss Waits. I could easily have taken offense to your lack of faith that I'd honor our arrangement."

"There's nothing interesting about me," I squeaked, my composure waning in the face of his chilling presence. As far as I was concerned, anything that would make him take notice of me wasn't something I wanted. At all. Especially not when the twins weren't there to save me from committing a potentially lethal faux pas.

Something that could have been the ghost of a smile

curved the corner of his mouth. "Oh, I disagree." He reached underneath his coat and flicked out a small, white business card that he held out toward me between two fingers. "And so would my organization, should you be so inclined."

I took his card out of reflex. "Thanks, but, um, no offense, but I don't really think the life of an assassin is mine. Also, I don't speak Russian. I am very flattered, though."

He snorted, and this time I was pretty sure a smile touched his lips. "The choice is yours, of course. You could attempt to choose one of your Steel men and see if they can bear to be parted. Their bond is quite *famous* in the underworld, you might say. My best guess, you will ruin them both. Or, you can go back to your old life. Get up every morning, put on your work attire, and travel to a job you know deep down will never fulfill you. I've seen your true face tonight, little bird. You've tasted the other side now, and you know this is where you belong. Between murderers and thieves. You're good at it. And what's more... you like it. That feeling of power when a man dies because you will it? When you find yourself craving another taste... call."

The Russian straightened up, his glacial eyes finally leaving my petrified face to sweep back over the crowd. "Remind your Steel men to pay what they owe before the sun sets tomorrow evening." He didn't bother looking back, and when I blinked, he was gone.

Slowly, and dazed from the surreal encounter, I turned back to look at the dais. Liam had gotten Louis untied and was supporting him as they stood next their two other brothers, with the five Perkinson men kneeling in front of them, all facing the crowd.

"Under my father's rule, all five of these men would have died for their crimes," the Steel brother who'd forced Gregory to his knees said, his voice echoing through the warehouse. He tapped the back of my former nightmare client's skull with the barrel of his gun. "Surely they were part of the conspiracy, no? If and when we find proof of this... That will still be the case under our new leadership. But..." He moved the gun to Brian's head. "You cannot always blame a son for his father's sins."

The second gunshot of the night rang through the warehouse. I cringed as Brian Perkinson fell to the floor with a thud, half the back of his head missing.

The raven-haired man turned to the remaining four, who looked visibly nauseated. "You have a choice to make. Seek revenge for your patriarch's death and end his days like him—on your knees—or take the mercy you've been shown tonight and realign your Family with the Steels."

"We—we choose you." Gregory's voice was hoarse and hardly recognizable with the new tone of servility that'd certainly never been there during any of my meetings with him. "The Perkinsons will serve your Family now, and forevermore."

A shout went through the crowd, like a wave of sound as the fathered mafia Families let their support be known:

"Steel! Steel! Steel!"

"Well, that's what you get when you run off like a damn hero to sacrifice yourself. What the fuck were you thinking?"

I sat in the comfortable armchair in the twins' flat, looking on as Liam cared for Louis' injuries with far more gentleness than his words let on. His hands moved over his twin's bruised and battered flesh as carefully as if he'd been a newborn, pouring peroxide on wounds and smearing ointment on bruises.

"You know I couldn't lose you. Either of you," Louis said. His voice was still cracked and hoarse, and the thought of what'd been done to him to make it sound like that made me want to cling to him and sob into his neck like a child. But something held me back. Something had *been* holding me back ever since we'd left that warehouse a few hours ago. I wanted to kiss them, confirm with my own hands and lips that they were both going to be all right and that we'd truly made it through this nightmare. But I hadn't.

"Do you think I'd survive losing *you,* you fool?" Liam asked, his voice too raw with emotion to hide the pain. He dabbed disinfectant on the two stitches he'd put in his brother's eyebrow to close up the gash there. "It's always been you and me. *Always.*"

And there it was. The reason I couldn't give in to my desperate urge to climb onto the couch with them and tell them how much I loved them.

The Russian's words echoed in my head as I stared at the two twins who'd changed me so fundamentally I could barely recognize myself. The men who'd stolen my heart and broken it into two equal parts.

You will ruin them both.

As I looked at them on the couch, their bond was so visible it may as well have been a physical entity. They truly were two halves of a whole. An entity. I'd gotten between them, an outsider who didn't understand, and it'd nearly broken both of them. In the end, if I ever chose one and not the other, they would both wither and die, and the life and laughter I'd first felt when I met them would be gone. Because of me.

"We'll need to get you to the hospital with that shoulder," Liam said, breaking my inward spiraling thoughts.

"It'll be fine on its own," Louis protested.

Liam leveled him with an unamused stare and a cocked eyebrow. "It's bad enough we both have to add to our tattoos with all these new fucking scars—I am not adopting a hunchback so we are still identical when your shoulder sets wrong because you're a massive knob-head and didn't go to the fucking hospital." He looked at me, his face smoothing and his voice gentling. "You wanna come, love? Or do you need to sleep? The flat's secure—we've got men watching it."

My heart clenched as I looked into his gray eyes. The love in them was unhindered by the exhaustion painted across his handsome face, and I wanted so much to give in to my stupid heart begging me to stay. I wanted nothing more than to climb into bed and sleep the horrors of the past few days and weeks away, only to wake up in a warm embrace and a world where every-thing was okay—where I'd get my happy ending, because that's how fairytales turned out. You slay the dragon and get the prince, and live happily ever after.

But that wasn't how our story would end.

"I..." I looked from him to Louis, and fuck, it hurt. It hurt more than anything I'd ever had to do, but I *had* to do it. If I was selfish, if I stayed, then it would only hurt them both infinitely more in the long run.

"I'm not coming with you. And I'm not staying." I drew in a deep breath and got to my feet, locking my knees when my legs wobbled. "I think it's best if we end this now, before it's too late."

The look of shock on both twins' faces was identical. "Audrey, no—"

"I know it's been brutal, love, I do." They both got to their feet, Louis a little slower than Liam thanks to his broken and battered body. They reached for me, trying to assure me, but I stepped back. I couldn't stand the thought of their hands on me, because I knew if they touched me, I wouldn't be able to find the strength to break away. Not now, not ever.

"But it's over now. I swear on everything that's holy you will never again be put through what you've been these past few days."

"We can protect you now, Audrey. You're safe. We don't have to hide anymore. No one will touch you."

I looked down, unable to keep looking at the desperate plea in both sets of gray eyes, and fought against the tears threatening to spill over. "It's not that. You know it's not."

"Then what? What can we do?"

I looked back up, losing the battle against the tears. They slid down my cheeks, fat streaks of translucent pain. "This doesn't end well. I can't choose between you. I love you both... so much. And I can't bear to see you fall apart. If I come between you, *this*... your bond— I'd ruin you, both of you, and I couldn't live with that."

"Audrey, no, that's not—" Louis reached for me with his good arm, but I flinched away.

"You of all people know it is," I said, looking at his many injuries. "You knew it at the cemetery—you gave your *life* because you knew there's no way the three of us could ever be happy. Do you think he could be happy knowing you were broken? Could *you*? If I choose you, can you live with the knowledge that your twin is hurting because of us?"

I saw it in his eyes, the moment he understood the truth in my words. Pain so intense it echoed in my own twisting gut flashed across his face. He didn't say anything, but he didn't have to. He knew I was right, and the evidence was written all over his beautiful, broken face.

Drawing in a deep breath to give me the strength I needed, I turned and walked toward their front door.

"Audrey."

It was a whisper. I didn't know from who, and I didn't turn around to find out.

"I don't think we should see each other again. It... it would hurt too much," I said, my voice as broken as my aching heart. "Goodbye."

"HONEY, why don't you call your old job. I bet they'd love to have you back. Maybe you're not feeling well because you need to get back to your old life."

The thing about returning after several weeks of

being a missing person is that your parents tend to get pretty clingy.

Not that I could blame them, or minded, when they asked if it "wouldn't be better" if I moved home for a little bit. I'd predictably lost my job after not giving them any notice about my extended absence, and with no income, I'd happily accepted moving back home with my parents for a little bit while I figured out what to do next.

It'd also been nice to have someone doting on me while I tried to get over the heartbreak I'd caused myself. They weren't particularly understanding about that part, having decided that "that boy" was the reason I'd gone missing. Both my mother and father got in a huff just at the mention of Liam's name, so I didn't talk about him. Or Louis. At least it made not thinking about them, and how much I missed them, a little easier.

However, I hadn't been back a week before both my parents began trying to push me back into my old job. My old life. The old Audrey-mold they'd so carefully crafted while I was a kid eager to please everyone around me. And I... I found it no longer fit.

The Russian had been at least partly right—one thing that'd come out of my brush with London's underworld was that I knew I no longer belonged in an office. I didn't belong in the corporate world, and I didn't want to spend the rest of my life bending over backwards to please people who would never respect me or my work.

"For the six-hundred and twentieth time, Mum, I'm not going back to my old job. I wasn't happy there. And I very much doubt unemployment causes nausea." I pushed my bowl of half-eaten cereal away and got up from my seat at my parents' breakfast bar to clean it up. I *was* feeling pretty terrible, and I really wasn't in the mood to argue about my future yet again. It was hard enough to try and figure out what the hell I was going to do about my life now, when everything I'd thought I wanted was a career that no longer meant anything to me. Having to fend off my concerned parents on top didn't exactly help matters. Nor did the persistent nausea I'd been waking up with for the past few days.

"I'm just concerned about you, Audrey," my mother said as she watched me with tented eyebrows. "We both are. And your sister, too. You were so happy in that job— and you were working on a promotion. And then you just up and leave with that... that young man, only to come back... It's like you're a different person. What happened to my sweet Audrey? The one who was so focused on her career and knew what she wanted in life?"

I closed my eyes for a brief moment, focusing myself. This had been a long time coming, and it was about time that she heard it.

"I'm not a different person, Mum. I'm exactly who I've always been. It's just that I was never really allowed to be *me*. I was supposed to be this mini-version of Mel, and I tried. I really, really tried. But I wasn't happy, not at all. I hated that job, I hated having to suck up to superiors who never valued my inputs and constantly overlooked me when it was time for promotions.

"I don't know what I want to do with my life, but I know it's not going to be anything like it was before. *I'm* not going to be like that. This is me—the real me. I'm not perfect, and I probably won't be much to show off at the golf club, but I hope I'm good enough. At least, I'm good enough for me." I gave my dumbfounded mother a smile and kissed her cheek before I turned to rinse out the bowl and put it in the dishwasher.

When I went to leave the kitchen, she called after me. "Audrey."

I turned, hand on the door frame.

"You'll always be good enough for me. Always."

I clung to that, and the love in her eyes as she said it, when later that evening I sat on the bathroom floor staring at a pregnancy test.

A positive pregnancy test.

FORTY-ONE
LOUIS

Three weeks after we took over London, things were finally starting to run smoothly. Or as smoothly as it can when you're dealing with criminals and thugs.

Thankfully, the brutality of our takeover seemed to have brought the other Families to heel. What took the longest was weeding out those of our own men we could still trust from the ones who'd been loyal to our father.

Wesley was the biggest problem. Even our stepmother accepted the death of her husband meekly enough and got on the train to Scotland we put her on without a complaint, probably thanks to the several million we wired to her bank account. She might have been our father's wife, but none of us had any beef with her. She'd mostly been a quiet, shadowy background figure since the day she married into the family, obviously having no interest in her husband's kids but no ill will toward us either.

Wesley, however...

The list of his crimes committed on behalf of our father was long, and none of us felt particularly comfortable knowing he was still breathing London air. But he *had* killed him, in the end, and that counted for something.

When we presented him with a one-way ticket to the States and told him what would happen if he ever returned to British soil, he accepted it without a word. Liam and I made sure he got on the plane—and that was the last loose end from our father's reign tied up.

William Steel's presence had been cleansed from the city, his body buried in a cemetery across town from where our mother rested, and only his memory remained to haunt us. But as deep as the scars he'd inflicted upon us were, and as unrelenting a stain as he'd put on our name, it was still so much easier to breathe now.

Except it wasn't.

I could see it on Marcus' and Blaine's faces; the relief that they no longer had to look over their shoulder, that their families were safe. And on Isaac's, when ransacking our father's files brought up the evidence we needed to have a judge open his case again.

But for me, there was no relief. Not really. Despite our victory, despite all of us being as safe as you could be when ruling a major city's underworld, I felt nothing but emptiness. Emptiness, and a dull pain in my chest every time I looked at my twin.

I knew he felt it, too. He didn't say anything, neither of us did, but we both knew. Seeing Blaine and Marcus reuniting with their wives, congratulating Evelyn on the small baby bump clearly visible on her stomach when Marcus proudly announced her pregnancy... it hurt so fucking much I could hardly breathe.

I'd never have that. I'd never be whole—never be happy. How could I, when *she* was gone?

He felt it, too, Liam. My other half, and the reason I couldn't go to her and tell her she was mine, whether she thought so or not. Neither of us felt relief at our father's passing because there was no relief to be had without Audrey. For either of us.

"We can't keep doing this."

I glanced at Liam, who was still staring straight ahead at the road as he drove our Jeep through the busy London traffic back from Heathrow.

"We can't keep going on as if she was never there," he continued, confirming that his thoughts, too, had been of Audrey.

"I know," I said.

"What do we do, Louis?" It wasn't often that my twin sounded so lost. The last time I could remember was at our mother's funeral.

"What is there to do?" I clenched my fist and stared

out the passenger side window, not wanting to see the pain on his face. "She was right. There is no way this can end well—if she chooses one of us, the other will..." Wither and die. I couldn't quite make myself say those words out loud, but we both knew them to be true. If one of us were with her, the other would be alone. Forever. I didn't know much about love, but I did know a woman like Audrey only came around once in a lifetime.

This way, at least we still had each other. We might be in for a lifetime of bitter regret, but at least we'd still be alive.

"I know if she chose me, and you... I couldn't bear to watch that, Liam. No more than I could bear to be the one she didn't pick. Could you?"

"No."

The silence spread between us again, blanketing us in the same misery we'd so desperately tried to avoid by burying ourselves in everything that came after our takeover of London. But Wesley was the last thread. There were no more places to hide.

"Louis."

I glanced over at my twin again. Something in his voice, a note of... excitement, perhaps, piqued my interest enough to pull me out of my wallowing.

"What if... what if she didn't have to choose?" he said. He was clutching the steering wheel. Yeah, something had perked him right up.

I frowned at him, trying to work out what sort of devious plan was cooking in his brain. "What do you mean?"

"We could both be with her. Share her. That way she doesn't have to choose, and she'd never get between us. Well, at least not figuratively speaking."

"You mean..." It took my brain a couple of seconds longer to wrap around what he was suggesting, but my heart rate picked up as I tried to picture what that'd be like.

"It'd be like in the bothy. Except I wouldn't feel the urge to beat your stupid arse every time I see you."

A flash of Audrey, moaning between us like when we'd both fucked her in that bothy, made my cock stir. I glanced at Liam again, and knew he was having similar thoughts, judging by the smirk playing across his lips.

As many times as we'd fucked the same girl, we'd never been with one at the same time. Apart from Audrey. The idea had never even crossed my mind, before her. And after... it'd kinda been in the cards that it was a one-time deal, something that just happened in the heat of the moment.

I'd never considered making it a regular occurrence, never mind sharing her in more ways than just physically. And yet... It would solve everything, wouldn't it? We'd both get to be with her, without ever losing each other.

Perhaps *society* wouldn't approve, but when had I

ever given any fucks about what *society* thought anyway?

Could I share my wife with Liam?

I kept waiting for that twang of discomfort the thought of willingly sharing the love of my life with my brother should have brought, but it never came. I'd shared everything with him since the day I was born. Audrey was the first thing I hadn't, until that afternoon in the bothy. It'd seemed so natural then, and the more I thought about it, the more perfect the idea of the three of us as a permanent unit seemed. In hindsight, it was the obvious solution. It'd always been me and him against the world. And Audrey belonged with us. Both of us.

"D'you think she'll agree to it?" I asked, turning more fully toward my twin.

"Probably not," he said with a grin. "But as long as we're both on board, I'm sure we can find a way to, ah, *convince* her."

AUDREY'S PARENTS' house was exactly as stuffy upper-middle class as I'd expected. We'd gone to her flat first, but the angry old biddy across the hall had informed us that *Miss Waits* no longer lived there, and could we take our hooligan-selves off the property immediately, or she'd call the police.

So Liam had driven us to her parents' house in a typical suburban neighborhood with typical, suburban garden and typical, suburban neighbors who peered out their windows when we walked up the path to knock on the door.

A couple of moments later, the door opened and revealed a small, slim woman in her fifties. The neutral look of inquiry on her face changed the second her eyes fell on us, turning pinched with disapproval. "Yes?"

If voices could freeze, we'd have both been ginger icicles.

"We're looking for Audrey, Mrs. Waits," Liam said, sounding more polite than I'd ever heard before. I turned to glance at him, just to make sure he hadn't been replaced by a some body snatcher or something.

"I think it's best if you leave," the woman said. "Now."

I placed a hand on the door as she tried to close it on us. "We need to speak with Audrey."

"You've done enough damage to my daughter," she snapped, and for such a small woman who obviously spent most of her life wearing pastels and a polite smile, the fire in her eyes was mildly impressive. "Leave, or I'm calling the police!"

Well, damn. Guess Audrey had told her parents we were the reason she'd disappeared on them.

Before either of us could respond, an achingly

familiar voice called out from within the house, "Mum? Who's at the door?"

My stomach knotted with excitement and that aching, hollow feeling I'd carried around with me since the day Audrey left us. I'd recognize her voice anywhere.

"It's nothing, honey, just go rest," her mother called over her shoulder, but to no avail. The door was opened a little wider, and then she was there, standing next to her mother, a look of surprise—and pain—on her face.

"Oh."

"Audrey, we *need* to talk," Liam said, sounding every ounce as desperate as I felt at the sight of her pretty face.

"Please, just for a few minutes," I added, even though I had no intention of ever leaving her side again. "It's important."

Her mother—still looking like she was about to erupt like a damn volcano—opened her mouth, undoubtedly to turn us away. But Audrey placed her hand on her shoulder. "It's okay, Mum. They have a right to know."

Mrs. Waits hesitated, shooting daggers at us before she turned to her daughter. "Are you sure?"

Audrey gave her a small smile. "Yeah, it's fine. Could we have some tea in the conservatory, please?"

Despite what the woman obviously thought of us, manners won out in the end. She gave a clipped nod and stalked off to the kitchen.

"Sure she won't put rat poison in it?" Liam asked with a hesitant look after her mother.

Audrey huffed, an amused sound, and pushed the door all the way open. "Come in."

We followed her through the house decorated in cream and beige into a large conservatory overlooking the back garden. Audrey closed the french doors behind us and gestured for us to sit on the cushioned wicker sofa. She took a seat herself in the matching chair on the other side of the glass table.

For the longest while we simply sat and looked at each other in silence.

It wasn't until I let myself study her pretty face more carefully that I realized something was off. Her skin was paler than normal, and a little gray, and there were dark circles under her eyes. The hollows of her cheeks far more pronounced than they'd been even when she was living off fish and canned beans in Wales.

Sick, mind-numbing fear sunk into the pit of my gut when I recalled what she'd told her mum: *They have a right to know.*

"Are you sick?" It came out as a hoarse whisper, my vocal cords tightening with a kind of panic I hadn't felt before. I couldn't lose her. *We* couldn't lose her—not now, after everything we'd been through. It wasn't fucking fair, it—

"No." She straightened up and took a deep breath. "No, I'm not sick. I—"

The French doors banged open, and her mother stepped in balancing a tray with a tea pot, cups, sugar, and milk. She put it down on the coffee table with a huff and another glare at Liam and I before she exited the conservatory again, slamming the doors behind her.

"What on Earth did you tell that woman we did to you?" I asked as Audrey poured the tea for us.

She laughed, a small sound, but it was still beautiful. Soothing.

"And what's wrong, love? Something's obviously not right—you look..." Liam trailed off, and I shot him an amused look. He didn't want to tell her she looked like shit.

"I know." She rubbed her hands along her thighs, obviously nervous as she shot us both a glance. "I've had a hard time keeping food down lately."

"Been to the doctor?" I asked, a worried frown making its way back on my face as I watched her. She was clearly not happy about what she was about to tell us, but she'd said she wasn't sick. I clung to that as I stared at her, willing her to just fucking tell us what was wrong.

"Yeah."

"And?" Liam asked. I could tell by the agitated energy emanating from him by my side that he was doing everything he could to rein himself in and let her tell us at her own pace, too.

"Remember that last afternoon? In the shack?"

I blinked at the subject change—and at her flushed cheeks.

"When we fucked?" Liam asked bluntly.

Her blush deepened. "Yes."

"What about it?"

"God, how can you be so calm talking about that?" she asked. Clearly stalling.

"Love, are you going to tell us what's up or do we have to force it out of you?" I asked, too nervous to let her get to the point at her own pace.

"I'm pregnant." The words rushed out of her mouth, a mix of relief and anxiety on her taut face as she looked at us.

I stared blankly at her. Somewhere, a buzzing sound made its way into my conscience.

"I didn't exactly get to pack birth control before we left for Wales, and if I recall correctly, no one thought about condoms. I guess it's not the first thing one thinks of when fleeing for your life." Audrey's voice was higher pitched than normal, her hands rubbing up and down her knees as if she needed something to do with them to not fall apart.

"You're *pregnant?*" Liam asked, sounding about as dumbfounded as I felt. "From Wales?"

"Well, yeah. It's the only time we haven't... used protection." She refused to meet our eyes.

Pregnant. Our girl was pregnant. Flashes of Marcus' proud smile as he showed off Evelyn's baby bump made its way past the weird buzzing sound, drowning it out as my pulse picked up until it thundered in my ears. I could feel a slow smile of my own spread across my face, wide and tight as something that felt an awful lot like happiness bubbled in my gut.

Shit. I was going to be someone's father. Some poor fucking kid was going to grow up with me and Liam as role models.

I kept waiting for the panic to set in, but it didn't. Only this slow, creeping sense of complete and utter elation that slowly filled me up from the bottom of my toes up through my body until it finally reached my heart.

"Audrey—"

"I *know!*" she said, despair in her voice. "I know it's fucked up. That this makes things a hundred times worse for you."

"Audrey—"

"But I'm keeping it, so don't even ask. If you want nothing to do with it, that's your choice. I don't want anything from you. This is my choice, and my baby."

"Audrey!" Liam snapped, finally managing to force her eyes to lift to his. They flickered from him to me and back again, and I could see fear plain as day in those dark pools. But also grim determination.

"It's not your baby," I said as I got to my feet. By my side, Liam mirrored my movements. "It's *ours.*"

"That's the bloody problem, isn't it!" she said, her

voice definitely pitching toward hysterics. "I don't know who of you... and there's no way we'll *ever* find out! Did you know a paternity test can't distinguish between identical twins? There is literally no way of knowing which of you is the father to this child. So I absolve you of any responsibility toward it—you don't have to go through that pain. We'll be fine."

"Do you really think that little of us?" Liam murmured as he stepped around the right side of the coffee table to be by her side.

"That we would abandon a pregnant bird and our baby?" I continued, stepping around the left side. We both reached for her, but she flinched away.

"Don't," she said, trying to pull away, but neither of us were having it. We stepped in, trapping her between us, and simultaneously wrapped our arms around her.

The moment she felt our bodies press against her, whatever had been keeping her together crumbled to dust. She sagged between us, and this awful, broken sob tore out of her throat.

"Audrey," I murmured, tightening my hold on her so I could rest my head against hers.

"Don't cry, love," Liam said. "This is happy news."

"Happy?" she hiccuped. "I don't even know whose name I'll write on the birth certificate!"

"Doesn't matter," I said, giving her a small squeeze. "It's just a piece of paper. The three of us know the truth. And so will the kid."

"We'll both be the father," Liam said. He nudged her gently to get her to look at him, and smiled softly at her tear-stricken face. "We *are* both the father."

"How can you accept this so easily?" she sniffled. "It's..."

"It's exactly how it should have been from the start." I glanced at Liam and he gave me a short nod in return. Breathing deeply, we both stepped back from her.

The small box that'd been burning a hole in my pocket since we stopped by the jewelers on the way to Audrey's flat felt heavy as I fumbled to get it out. My heart pounded so hard in my chest I could hear my own pulse drumming in my ears, a heavy mix of excitement and just plain fear making me shake as I sunk to one knee next to my twin.

"Audrey—"

"What are you doing?" The look on her face was priceless—sheer shock.

"Audrey—"

"Get up!"

"Audrey!"

"For fuck's sake, *what are you doing?!*"

"God, woman, would you shut up for just one second and let us do this?" Liam laughed. He carded the hand he wasn't holding his box with through his hair, eyes dancing with mirth when they met mine. "You'd think being two about popping the question would make this easier."

I smirked at him and returned my attention to Audrey. She was shaking. Badly.

"It's going to be okay, love," I said, grabbing her hand with my box-free one. "We've worked everything out—it's going to be okay. Just take a deep breath and let us do this. Trust us."

She didn't say anything, but I could see her chest moving as she breathed in deeply.

"Good girl." I glanced at Liam, and he grabbed her free hand.

"First off, we want to apologize. Both of us."

"We've not made any of this easy on you, and we are truly and deeply sorry for all the pain we've caused you."

"We can't promise that we won't give you a few gray hairs over the years..."

"But we can promise you that we will never, ever, put you through the kind of bullshit we have while we got our heads out of our arses." I offered her a small smile.

"We should have known from day one," Liam continued. "It's always been Louis and me. We've always been a unit. And yet it never occurred to us that when we fell in love with the same woman, it was always meant to be that way."

"There is no other way, Audrey. You're not meant to be with me, you're not meant to be with him. You're meant to be with *us*. Both of us."

"W-what?" Her eyes widened as she struggled to accept what we were offering her.

"We're saying, love, that we want to share you. It's the only thing that makes sense."

"And before you get any ideas—we're not taking no for an answer." Liam flicked the lid of his box open, revealing the ring inside. I followed suit.

"You know this is how it's meant to be, love," I said, gently, when I noticed how she was still shaking. "Deep down, you know."

"You're insane," she whispered. "We can't do this. You can't... you can't *share* me, I'm not a... a... sandwich."

"A sandwich?" Liam grinned at her lame ending. "You're not a sandwich, so we can't marry you?"

"Shut up, you know what I mean!" she hissed, cheeks reddening. "For one thing, it's not legal. And who's to say you wouldn't end up resenting the hell out of me down the line? That you wouldn't regret it?"

"You're telling two mafia sons you can't marry us because '*it's not legal*,'" I said, shaking my head at her. "Do you think we give a flying fuck, as long as you say yes? It doesn't matter whose name goes on the bloody paperwork, it doesn't matter what the *law* says. All that matters is how we feel about you. And how you feel about us."

"We've got no hesitation, Audrey. We want this, and

we'll always want this. If you worry we might change our minds, don't. We won't."

"Do you love us?"

"You know I do," she whispered. A single tear slid down her cheek.

"Equally?" Liam asked.

She pressed her lips together and nodded. More tears trickled down her pretty face.

"Then say yes, Audrey. Let us make you happy— today, tomorrow and every day after that."

"And ideally sometime soon," I mumbled, cringing at the strain on my shoulder from keeping the damn box outstretched for so long. "Some of us are still healing from broken bones here."

She made a barking noise, a mix between a laugh and a sob and shook her head. "You'll be the death of me."

"Nah, love. We'll be the reason you wake up laughing every day for the rest of your life."

"Or moaning," I interjected with a sly smile.

"That too," Liam agreed.

"You're *sure*?" she asked, the worry clear in her teary eyes. "You're sure I will never come between you?"

"Well, I mean, we were hoping you'd come between us pretty damn often, to be honest..." My playful tone died at the scathing look I got from Liam. Right. Not the time.

"We're sure, Audrey. Or we wouldn't be here."

"Then... yes." She sniffed, straightened her back and gave us both a small smile. "Yes, I will marry you. Both."

Elation so intense it nearly made my heart skip several beats rushed through me at her acceptance. I'd been prepared for the worst, even as I'd hoped for this very outcome, but to actually hear her say the words... I pressed a kiss to her knuckles and slid my ring on her right hand. To the casual observer it looked identical to the ring Liam placed on her left hand—a solitaire diamond flanked by two small rubies set in a white gold band. You'd have to study them both closely to find the small difference in them—like she had with us to notice the scar on Liam's hand that set us apart.

Grimacing, I got to my feet and rolled my shoulder, which gave Liam enough time to swoop in and steal the first kiss from her lips.

"We'll make you so, so happy," he murmured against her ear when I gently turned her head to kiss her, too. Her lips were sweet and soft and exactly as perfect as I remembered against my own.

This was it. This was everything I'd wanted out of life, even if I hadn't realized it before she came into my life. Not moving my mouth from hers, I slid my hand down to her still-soft belly. Everything and so much more.

Liam's hand bumped gently against mine as he rounded it on the lower part of her belly and pushed his forehead in against the side of her head. "Your parents are gonna love this."

Audrey snorted and pulled away from our kiss, a little breathless but with mirth dancing in her eyes. "I don't know, maybe it'll actually be an improvement. Sure, it'll be hard to explain to their friends why there are two grooms at the wedding, but at least you'll make an honest woman out of me. *Ish.* At the very least it can't get much worse than their reaction when I told them I didn't know which of you were the father of my baby."

Liam arched both eyebrows at her. "You told them? Shit, no wonder your mother looked like she wanted to bash our heads in with the teapot."

Audrey smiled happily, apparently not too worried with her parents' obvious wish to see us dead. "Yeah, I wasn't about to lie. Not about something as important as my baby."

"*Our* baby," I growled, pressing my hand firmer against her stomach. A flush of possessive emotions toward her and the still-invisible baby bump came rushing up from the deepest part of my core. The part that'd known she was going to be my wife from the first time I got between her thighs. It felt like a lifetime ago. "It's *our* baby, love."

"Or bab*ies*," Liam said with a smirk. "You never know, might be twins. Pretty sure it runs in the family. On our mother's side."

Audrey's smile paled significantly. "Don't even joke about that."

"What? What's not to love about that idea?" I gave her my best shit-eating grin. "Two adorable ginger babies to keep you on your toes."

"Mum did always say she would've stopped after just two if we'd been her firstborn," Liam said, a wicked smirk on his face. "I'm sure she meant because we were the most perfect children you could imagine."

"Of course there *was* that time we set fire to the kitchen while playing tag," I mused. "Pretty sure she mentioned something about wishing we'd come with return labels then."

"Purely accidental, of course," Liam interjected.

"Or the time we swapped her hair gel with glue."

"You two need to shut up, or I'm giving you your rings back," Audrey growled, though the glint of amusement in the corner of her eye sparkled with suppressed laughter.

"No take-backsies," I said, giving her a gentle squeeze.

"You're stuck with us now," Liam agreed. "For life."

"Well, let's see how long that'll be, exactly. Come on, let's go tell my parents the happy news. I sure hope your sweet-talking abilities improve right quick, or I'll likely be a widow before we even get married."

I laughed, and caught Liam's eye over the top of her

head. The smile on his so familiar face echoed through me, and I knew I looked as happy as he did then.

No matter what shit came our way—today, tomorrow, or the day after that—it didn't matter. We'd thought we'd been a unit before, him and I, but we'd been wrong. We'd been missing *her*.

She was the glue tying us together tighter than we'd ever thought possible; the sun we both orbited around.

With Audrey between us, there was nothing we couldn't overcome.

I looked from my twin to the woman who'd given me more than I could ever put into words, and I knew the rest of my life would be filled with laughter.

EPILOGUE

AUDREY

1 Year Later

"You *just* ate not half an hour ago. How are you still hungry?" I frowned down at the ginger baby latched on my left breast. "I swear you know when we're in a rush."

As if on cue, an angry wail erupted from the other side of the room. My shoulders slumped in defeat as my very pregnant, soon-to-be sister-in-law laughed and carried my other daughter over to me, deftly placing her in my right arm. "We are definitely not making it on time."

"Probably not," Mira said as she patted the now remarkably quiet baby's head. "But I do think being a new mother of twin girls *and* the bride gives you some leeway when it comes to punctuality."

"Not to mention the bride of Louis *and* Liam,"

Evelyn, my other sister-in-law, said dryly from her seat by the door. She was holding her own, sleeping baby boy in her arms. Jeremy was only a couple of months older than my girls, and I was intensely envious of how calm he always seemed. He never fussed, hardly ever cried, and generally had a reputation of being the most chilled-out baby in history.

At just over three months old, it might be too early to say, but I was convinced Lily and Rose had inherited their fathers' distinct taste for causing mayhem. Hence why I was currently nursing two satisfied-looking babies with my wedding dress pooled around my waist—only half an hour after their last meal.

"Yup. Saints get to be as late as they want," Mira agreed with a teasing smile.

I sighed and sank further back in the chair as I looked down at my daughters happily taking their sweet time. It was still hard to believe that they were mine, even three months after giving birth to them, with Liam and Louis anxiously clutching at my hands from each their side of my hospital bed. There'd been a couple of raised eyebrows when the nurse had asked for everyone but the father to leave and the twins had made a point out of closing the door, both remaining inside, but I'd been in too much pain to care. And frankly... the further along I'd gotten in my pregnancy, the less I'd been worried about what other people thought—in general, and about my relationship with the two men I loved, more specifically.

They told me I'd wake up laughing every day if I said yes to their proposal, and they'd kept that promise. Happiness had been a concept I thought I knew before they asked for my hand in marriage. It turned out I'd only ever seen a pale shadow of what it truly could be. I did wake up laughing every day, and at night, I fell asleep between them, safe in their arms and satisfied all the way into the marrow of my bones.

Yes, not everything was sunshine and rainbows, and it never would be. They were mafia. They would always be mafia. And now, so would I. But I had entered into this world of darkness and corruption with my eyes wide open. I knew what was waiting for me, despite the new leadership the Steel brothers implemented the day after they took over London. Death was only a last resort instead of the first choice when punishment had to be doled out, but that didn't mean my new world wasn't violent. Or dark.

I looked up from Lily's sparse, ginger locks and caught my mother's eye. She was sitting in the corner of my dressing room, her mouth drawn into a worried line as she watched me nurse my babies.

My parents didn't know what exactly my new family was engaged in, but I was pretty sure they'd put at least part of the puzzle together when big, burly guys showed up outside their house, standing vigil day and night. It was the twins' insistence that my parents get 'round-the-clock protection, and I hadn't argued. Neither had they. The only mention they'd ever made was when my father asked me if I knew the guy currently standing next to their privet bush. When I said yes, his lips flattened, but he didn't ask me any further questions.

They'd taken my engagement to the twins better than could have been expected. There'd been a few moments' stunned silence. Then my mother had asked me if I was sure this is what I wanted. I'd said yes, and they'd both congratulated us, albeit perhaps a tad stiffly. I didn't mind—I knew it was a lot for them to take in, and honestly, I was just thankful they didn't kick me out the door for ruining their perfect image. Turned out my parents—though thoroughly entrenched in their golf-weekends and suburban bliss —truly just wanted me to be happy. Even if I found that happiness in ways they didn't necessarily approve of.

And once Rose and Lily arrived, my mum had pretty much melted. I'd even caught her giving the twins extra servings of cake when we visited, presumably as a thank-you for finally giving her the grandkids she'd been not-so-subtly sighing for since I rounded thirty.

I gave my mother a smile across the room just as Rose finally popped her tiny mouth off my boob and, with the cutest little yawn, closed her eyes and went straight to sleep. "Would you hold her, please, Mum?"

The worried frown between her eyebrows smoothed a little as she got to her feet to pick up her granddaughter. A gentleness I only vaguely remembered from when I was a kid eased over her face as she cooed at the sleeping baby in her arms, rocking her gently. Rose, probably exhausted from eating like the piglet she was, didn't so much as flutter an eyelid. But then again, she was used to being transferred from arm to arm. She and Lily had a very large family of adoring aunts and uncles, and as the only girls born to the Steel empire thus far, they were already getting spoiled rotten.

I looked around the small room, and something warm fluttered in my belly as I looked at the three women there. My own sister had opted not to be a part of my pre-wedding session, making her views of my *"heathen lifestyle"* known as passive-aggressively as only Mel could.

The women here—my mother and my two almost-sisters-in-law—were all the support I needed.

I'd bonded with Evelyn and Mira pretty much instantly. Something about marrying into a mafia Family definitely created some fast and deep bonds, and both they and their husbands had welcomed me with open arms.

A rap of knuckles against the door pulled me from my mushy thoughts—and Lily from her nursing. She gave an irritated little huff at being disturbed mid-snack, but then closed her eyes and fell into the same instantaneous food coma as her sister.

"Come in," I called as I covered up my leaking breasts with a soft towel. Breastfeeding was all well and good, but I wasn't about to get milk all over my expensive wedding dress.

Isaac popped his head in the door. "The twins were wondering if you've changed your mind? Can't say I blame ya if you have, but I did promise them I'd make sure you don't leg it."

I grinned. "Just feeding their unruly offspring. In fact, would you take them down with you so I can get ready without being interrupted by these two gaping maws again?"

"Sure." Despite Isaac's confident tone, the look of unease as he stepped into the room to take his nieces from me and my mother was pretty priceless. Marcus and Blaine, who both had kids of their own, didn't blink when asked to hold my two tiny bundles of terror, but Isaac always looked like he'd rather be anywhere else than stuck with two babies in his arms.

"We should probably get down to the ceremony as well," Mira said, taking pity on her brother-in-law. She deftly snatched a sleeping baby from his grip, leaving him with just the one. "Come, Evelyn. Let's go make sure Audrey's grooms haven't set fire to anything."

"I thought Marcus was on fire extinguisher duty?"

Evelyn teased as she followed the two other Steels out the room, blowing me a finger kiss before shutting the door behind them.

"I don't know what's up with all the fire cracks," I said as I got up and, making sure my nipples were done leaking, shrugged back into my bra and pulled my dress up. "It's been more than a decade since the twins last set any fires, as far as I know."

My mum smiled thinly, but didn't respond as she walked up behind me to help me close my dress. The worried frown was back on her face, now she didn't have an armful of grandbabies to distract her.

I sighed as I watched her in the mirror. "You're not happy."

"I am," she protested. "I'm happy that you're happy."

"But?"

She shook her head and looked down, but not before I saw the single tear trailing down her cheek.

I turned around and put my hand on her cheek, wiping the tear away with my thumb. "If you're so happy, why are you crying? You know the twins will take good care of me, Mum. And I thought you and dad kind of liked them, despite how they're leading me into a lifetime of sin?"

"It's not that," she said, waving my hand away so she could dap at her eyes. This time, the smile she gave me was a bit more genuine, even if her lower lip still quivered a little. "They're good men. I would have preferred you just marry *one* of them, of course... it would make explaining your wedding photos on our mantel a heck of a lot easier. But I... When I look at you these days, sometimes I can hardly recognize you. You're such a smart and strong and beautiful woman. So confident. And I... I can't help but think of everything I did wrong that I can look at my own daughter on her happiest day and not recognize her, because she's brimming with strength and confidence. And happiness. This is how you should have always looked."

"Oh, Mum." I didn't pause to consider my dress this time, before I pulled her into a tight hug. "Don't think like that."

"How can I not?" she sniffled against my shoulder. "We raised you how we thought you'd be happiest—to be just like all the other kids we knew, so you could grow up and be... just like everyone else. But that isn't you. It never was you, and we didn't see it. You were never meant for the same kind of life as we were. Or as Melissa. And when I see you now... I can't believe I nearly stopped my daughter from evolving into this amazing young woman."

I wiped my own stray tears and pulled back, keeping my hands on her shoulders. "You and Dad gave me everything I needed to get to where I had to go before I was ready for this next step. It was up to me to make it that final bit of distance, and thanks to everything you have done, I had the tools I needed to make it. So what if you thought a safe career was the best thing for me? If I hadn't been in that career, I would never have met Liam, or Louis. You've stood by me when I told you I was homeless, jobless, didn't know who the father of my child was. And when I decided to marry two men, knowing what everyone will say about you for having such an outrageous daughter."

"We'll always stand by you, Audrey." Mum placed a hand gently against my cheek and gave me a soft smile. "Now let's finish getting you ready. You've got two good men waiting for you downstairs, and a life filled with happiness to live."

My mother was right. I did have a happily ever after waiting for me.

CONNECT WITH NORA

Want to chat ruthlessly sexy book-boyfriends?

Join Nora's Reader's Group:

EMAIL:
www.nora-ash.com/newsletter

FACEBOOK:
https://www.facebook.com/groups/Yayromance/

ALSO BY NORA ASH

MADE & BROKEN SERIES

Dangerous

Monster

Trouble

DEMON'S MARK SERIES

Branded

Demon's Mark

Prince of Demons

ALPHA TIES

Alpha

Feral

THE OMEGA PROPHECY

Ragnarök Rising

Weaving Fate

Betraying Destiny

ANCIENT BLOOD SERIES

Origin

Wicked Soul

Debt of Bones*

DARKNESS SERIES

Into the Darkness

Hidden in Darkness

Shades of Darkness

Fires in the Darkness

———————————

WWW.NORA-ASH.COM

Made in the USA
Middletown, DE
19 January 2024

48174312R00272